Swift to Chase

A Collection of Stories

By
Laird Barron

JournalStone

JOURNALSTONE
YOUR LINK TO ARTISTIC TALENT

JournalStone books may be ordered through booksellers or by contacting:
JournalStone
www.journalstone.com

The views expressed in this work are solely those of the authors and do not necessarily reflect the views of the publisher, and the publisher hereby disclaims any responsibility for them.

ISBN: 978-1-945373-05-3   (sc)
ISBN: 978-1-945373-07-7   (ebook)
ISBN: 978-1-945373-06-0   (hc)

JournalStone rev. date: October 7, 2016

Library of Congress Control Number: 2016949884

Printed in the United States of America

Cover Art & Design: Chuck Killorin

Edited by: Vincenzo Bilof

Acknowledgements

Thank you to my friends, family, and colleagues:

Publisher Christopher Payne at *JournalStone*; Paul Tremblay (for a fine introduction); John, Fiona, and David Langan; Ron Wier (technical advice on "LD50"); and Chuck Killorin (for the excellent cover art); Mark Tallen; the marvelous Deborah Gordon Brown; Yves Tourigny; Jason and Darci Duelge; Jason and Harmony Barron and the kids; and Timbi Porter.

Special thanks to Vincenzo Bilof for his edits.

My gratitude to the editors who originally acquired these stories: John Joseph Adams; Steve Berman; Ellen Datlow; Mike Davis; Aaron French; Paula Guran; Gerry Huntman; Ross Lockhart; and Robert S. Wilson.

Extra Special thanks to my agents, Janet Reid and Pouya Shahbazian, and their wonderful support staff, Penny Moore and Chris McEwen.

As always, thank you to my readers.

For Jessica M

Table of Contents

Introduction

By

Paul Tremblay

"People call it this or that but our club doesn't have a name."

If you're not already a member of our club (I find it hard to believe that you're not a member. Honestly, how could you not be a member?), you will be soon enough.

Laird's brilliant first collection, *The Imago Sequence*, was published in 2007, and you have his fourth in your hands, all of which seems temporally incongruous to me. It's hard to imagine a time when I wasn't either reading his fiction or eagerly anticipating it. In such a relatively short period of time, that Laird's work looms so large within the horror community speaks to his talent, his singular vision, his uniqueness in his uncanny ability to move us, to make us see, and to his maniacal/stubborn (you choose the adjective; likely both) levels of hard work.

Many argue that we are in the middle of a renaissance or golden age of horror fiction. I'm inclined to agree, and Laird's success is both reason for and reflection of the rising cultural relevance of horror. Whether Laird has simply mainlined into the zeitgeist and our post-millennial nightmares *feel* like a Laird Barron story, or his literate mix of the horror, noir, and pulp adventure has already left its fingerprints (oh they're there if you look hard enough) on more than one pop cultural moment, doesn't matter. In a community often desperate to proclaim literary/artistic/popular agency and legitimacy (and given to promote saviors, the-next-Stephen-King, and historical all-timers *way* too prematurely), Laird is one of our proven champions.

Welcome back to the club, friends.

* * *

"In my dreams, I always die."

Roughly ten years ago, Laird trekked to the east coast to attend Readercon. I hosted a small, impromptu cookout at my place the night before the convention started. Before Laird and a few other guests arrived, I prepped my two kids (at the time, ages four and eight) to not ask Laird about the why of his eye patch, knowing that my youngest, Emma, wouldn't be able to help herself. I tend to over-worry about things, so I was nervous about my unrelenting four-year-old making Laird feel uncomfortable in any way. I'd only known Laird for a year or two at this point. We were friends, but new friends, and he'd previously expressed to me that he was hesitant to talk (or write) about his experiences growing up in Alaska.

Sure enough, the moment I went inside and foolishly left Laird sitting at the rickety patio table in the backyard with the kids, Emma pounced and asked Laird why he had an eye patch. Cole, ever the responsible, twitchy first-born, was embarrassed and horrified, but not so much that he interceded or went to get me in a desperate attempt to stop his renegade sister. Emma asked what he wanted to ask, and he leaned in close to hear Laird's answer.

Laird said (and I imagine he said it dryly and straight-faced): "Has your dad ever told you not to run with a sharp pencil?"

His answer was a playful, mischievous joke, one I'm sure my kids (hopefully they're less gullible than I am) were in on, but at the same time, it left them asking *what if it was true*? They didn't know and couldn't know for sure. They could visualize a terrible accident happening to Laird, but because of how he phrased it, how he didn't come right out and explicitly say he'd stabbed out his own eye with a pencil, he let them extrapolate, and create their own conclusion, and maybe they could see it (viewed through metaphorical fingers covering their eyes, or brazenly wide-eyed) happening to them as well. His answer was a ten second horror story, one that was totally Laird.

I didn't find out about the secret Clarice/Lector-style *quid pro quo* until later that evening. Laird was laughing as he told me about it, and so was I. I'm convinced that Emma still frequently asks when Laird is coming over to the house again due in part to his answer to her question.

* * *

"It didn't originate in Alaska. It was around before Alaska."

Swift to Chase is Laird's Alaska book. The landscape is as integral, active, and unknowable as any character and as a result these stories are dangerous, raw, primal, and desperate. They are also intricate and complex, and wonderfully varied thematically. One can certainly find Laird peering into his past as revenants abound. Jessica Mace, Laird's recurrent ultimate survivor, runs like a vein through this collection. She is forever fending off the Eagle Talon ripper (a killer as large and mysterious and perhaps as ancient as Alaska) while she continues to recklessly drive ever forward into a most uncertain future. That Laird opens the collection with two Jessica Mace tales and saves her mesmerizing origin story "Termination Dust" for the third spot is genius, and you'll understand why when you read it.

Like the calling of names in the first paragraph of "Slave Arm," you'll find all manner of friends, enemies, dogs, loves, lives, heroes, failures, hopes, dreams, nightmares, and inspirations within the stories. There's Clive Barker and an unforgettably human Raw Head Rex in "the worms crawl in,"; Robert E Howard and Roger Zelazny in the bloody, bold, and soulful high fantasy/adventure/science fiction/horror hybrid "Ears Prick Up"; Flannery O'Connor in the personal, touching, and dread-filled "Black Dog."

Swift to Chase is a not a simple case of what is old is new again. His universe expands even as his focus contracts. He is most definitely not playing it safe and rehashing old favorites. These stories are a thrilling and daring step forward into Laird's literary future. The experimentation with plot structure, narrative form, and point of view in the aforementioned "Termination Dust" and "Slave Arm," and in the wickedly entertaining and almost unimaginably brutal "Andy Kaufmann Creeping through the Trees" adds to the feeling of danger and unpredictability. In "Frontier Death Song," a manic and doomed chase across the country, Laird is totally messing with us; he knows you *think* you know who all the players are and how everything connects, but you don't. And it's exhilarating.

*   *   *

"We're waiting for you pal. We know where you live."

Lines are blurred and Laird's past, present, and future are all in these pages. The stories in *Swift to Chase* are confessionals and artistically crafted lies, and they ooze confidence and bravura, and sadness and vulnerability. As an admirer and friend, I recognize the bits of flesh Laird tore off himself and stuffed into these pages, but the best part is that we're all there too. That's the magic of Laird's fiction: despite the scope and exotic Alaskan landscapes and locales we recognize ourselves within his stories. We see who we are, who we could be, and what will happen to us all eventually. We see ourselves running with that sharpened pencil when we shouldn't be, even though we might not have a choice because we're the ones being chased. Or are we the ones doing the chasing?

Swift to Chase drops us within the wide vista of a brave new world in Laird Barron's fiction. It's thrilling, and of course, terrifying. He has managed to somehow expand and personalize his cosmic horror universe. This collection is the cosmic horror of *me*, the cosmic horror of *us*, and the horror is boundless.

"We don't suckle at the breast of a god, it suckles at ours."

Paul Tremblay

1/5/2016

Swift to Chase

I: Golden Age of Slashing

Screaming Elk, MT

Near dusk a trucker dropped me at a tavern in Screaming Elk, MT, population 333. A bunch of locals had gathered to shoot pool and drown their sorrows in tap beer. CNN aired an hour-long feature on survivors of violent crime. The *Where is Jessica Mace?* segment popped around halfway through and I told the bartender to switch it pronto. A sodbuster on the next stool started to bark his offense, then he took a closer look at the file photo of me larger than life onscreen and things went from bad to ugly.

"You're that broad! Yeah, yeah, you're her!" Shitkicker had crossed over to the dark side of drunk. "Nice rack," he went on in a confidential tone. "I wouldn't pay a nickel for anything above the tits, though."

I threw a glass of whiskey in his face, as a lady does when her appearance is insulted by an oaf. No biggie—I'd been nursing the cheap stuff. Besides, the move was only a cover to get my knife unsheathed and pressed flat against my inner thigh, all ready to do its work. A couple of his comrades at the bar laughed. He recovered fast —animals are like that — made a fist and cocked it behind his left ear. I puckered my lips. Don't suppose that I enjoy getting punched. It's simply that I can make pain work for me if it comes to that.

Despite my gravelly voice and rough edges, I know how to play the femme fatale. I can also hold my booze. It's a devastating combo. During our youth, my brothers Elwood and Bronson were the brawlers, the steamrollers. Elwood has gone to his reward and Bronson crashes cars for a living when he isn't playing a hockey goon. Me? Let's say I *prefer* to rely upon a combination of native cunning and feminine wiles to accomplish my goals. Flames and explosions are strictly measures of last resort.

I'll put my life in mortal danger for a pile of cash. No shock there, anybody would. Goes deeper, though. I'll also venture into hazard to satisfy my curiosity, and that's more problematic. The compulsion seems to be growing stronger. Violence, at least the threat of violence, is a rush. I'm addicted to the ramifications and the complications.

As the CNN story so luridly explained, I put paid to a serial killer up in Alaska, the Eagle Talon Ripper, and nothing has been the same. It's as if the stars and the sky don't align correctly, as if the universe is off its axis by a degree or two. Since pulling that trigger I haven't figured out exactly what to do with myself. I wander the earth. It would be romantic to say I'm righting wrongs or seeking my destiny. Feels more like I'm putting my shoe into one fresh pile after another.

A good friend who worked in the people-removing business for the Mafia once told me there aren't coincidences or accidents, reality doesn't work that way. Since the first inert, super-dense particle detonated and spewed forth gas and dust and radiation, everything has been on an unerring collision vector with its ultimate mate, and every bit of the flotsam and jetsam is cascading toward the galactic Niagara Falls into oblivion.

The dude possessed a more inquisitive nature than one might expect from an enforcer by trade. He said, *Jessica, you're a dancing star being dragged toward the black hole at the ragged edges of all we know. Drawn with irresistible force, you'll level anything in your path, or drag it to hell in your wake.*

Load of horseshit, am I right? Sloppy, I-love-you-man drivel. Yet, his words come back to me as I travel east, ever east. I'm starting to believe him. I'm a dancing star and my self-determination is a facade.

Cut to the drunken asshole in the bar rearing back to knock me into next Tuesday. Not so fast, Tex, said the universe.

A rugged, burly fellow in a safari shirt and work pants stepped in and introduced himself with a left hook to the sodbuster's jaw. Put the cowboy to sleep with one blow. I hadn't needed a white knight. I had my knife and knew where to stick it. But, I must admit, the crunch of the cowpoke's jawbone and the fast-spreading blood on the scuffed floorboards thrilled me a little. A lot.

Mr. White Knight rubbed his hand. All those nicks and notches on his knuckles, like rocks that had been smacked together a thousand times.

"I'm Beasley. What are you drinking?"

"Ah, the beginning of another beautiful friendship."

* * *

Mist flooded across the marsh and erased the country road. Rounding a bend, we were transported from present day Montana to Scottish moors circa 1840s, or a Universal Studios sound lot with Bela Lugosi poised to sweep aside his cape along with our feeble protestations.

"Can't-find-your-own-ass-with-both-hands-and-a-flashlight-weather," I said to cut the tension. I twisted my rings until they bit in. That night, I wore five in honor of the dead samurai lord—bands of iron, silver, and titanium on the left hand. A mood ring and a biker-large death's head on the right. The latter pair were gifts from Mom who'd used them plenty in her skating days. Jawbreakers.

Beasley stepped on the pedal. His face by dashboard light put me in mind of Race Bannon and Doc Savage. The unbuttoned safari shirt contributed nicely. Ten, maybe fifteen years my senior, but some juice left in him; I loved that too. A crucifix dangled from the rearview mirror; also sprigs of dried flowers. More dried flowers peeked from the ashtray. I wondered if these details meant anything; made a note.

We were rocking and rolling like a motherfucker now. The rickety farm truck's tires cried mercy. But when the moon hove nine-tenths full and full of blood over the black rim of night and screamed white-hot silver through the boiling clouds, everything stood still.

"The Gallows Brothers Carnival, huh?" I said after I caught my breath. I would have said anything to break the spell. "I heard that name somewhere. Want to say a news story. Which means somebody got maimed or murdered. Wouldn't be news otherwise."

He grunted and hit me with a sidelong glance.

"So, uh, you know how to shoot?" Maybe he meant the rifle rattling in the window rack behind our heads. A light gauge shotgun; nothing fabulous. "Also, would you say you're fast on your feet? On a scale of, oh, let's say a chick in high heels to Carl Lewis sprinting from a lion."

"I hate it when dudes ask me that. The line of inquiry seldom leads anywhere pleasant."

"You dames have all had bad experiences."

I laughed, low and nasty.

"Yeah, it's weird. Can't figure what the common denominator might be."

He shut his mouth for a while, smarting. Guy like him, pain didn't last long. A whack upside the head with a two-by-four was positive attention.

My thoughts went to a previous fling with another brutish loner type; a coyote hunter in Eastern Washington. I hoped my luck was better this go-around. I hoped Beasley's luck was better too.

"You're not really a carnival roadie," I said a few miles later. "You lack a particular something or other."

"Well, I wouldn't get on any of the rides."

The Gallows Brothers Carnival had set up shop in a pasture a few miles outside of town. Unfortunately, I had missed the last show. The great machinery lay cold and silent and would soon be dismantled. Beasley lived in a modular at the end of a concourse of shuttered stalls, tilt-a-whirls, and tents. All very Beaver Cleaver 1950s. The night breeze swirled sawdust and the burned powder of exploded firecrackers.

A wolf howled from the north where the forest began.

Then we were inside Beasley's shack, barring the door behind us. Down, down into the darkness we dove, to the bottom of a blue hole at the bottom of the earth. The wolf howled again. Its pack answered and the Ponderosa pines closed ranks, as Beasley's mighty arms closed me in.

* * *

A hazy nightlight fumed at the foot of the bunk. Beasley, with a physique straight from a picture book of Norse gods, could've wrestled bears, looked as if he'd done so on occasion. Once Beasley and I got going he held back for fear of breaking me, the fool. I wanted to tell him it was only really good once it started to hurt, but I'd gone past the vanishing point and dissolved into another, primal self, the one that doesn't speak English.

He performed as his swagger advertised, or close enough. Afterward, he lay slick and aglow, perfectly scarred. I asked him if he did any acting, because he radiated mucho charisma. He only smiled boyishly and took a swig from the bottle, took it in like water. I suspected his fate would be to die horribly of cirrhosis, or under the claws of a beast, and young, or to turn fifty and appear as if he'd gone face-first into a wall, haggard as a kerosene-swilling bum. Probably the dying young deal, which meant he'd better get started soon. I kept seeing a bleached skull when I caught him in my peripheral vision.

"Gimme some sweet, sweet nothings," I said to keep him from nodding off and leaving me alone with my 2 A.M. thoughts, and alone with the howls in the wood.

"Look, doll, I'm a man of action. Sweet talk ain't my bailiwick."

"Your wick isn't going into my bailey again if you don't humor me."

"As you say." He cleared his throat. "How can you be sure you're here?"

"What, think you were humping your pillow?"

"Sorry, Jess, you started this. Maybe all of it is a projection. Or a computer program. You're a sexy algorithm looping for eternity."

We shared a cigarette. Not my brand.

"Kinda smart for a dumb guy," I said. What I knew of Beasley's past derived from a few hours over pints—ex Army, ex-footballer, a hunter, a bodyguard, expert driver. Man-at-arms slash valet and satisfied with the role. College had served as a central hub for womanizing, boozing, and playing ball.

"No offense taken, or anything." He even made petulance sound manly.

"Don't get riled, handsome. Playing dumb is your protective coloration. It's how you fool the predators. *Most* of us are fooled."

"My protective coloration is a surly disposition and a buffalo gun that'd blast a hole through a concrete bunker."

"Neither of those require smarts." I squinted at a movie poster of Robby the Robot carrying unconscious Anne Francis against a backdrop of shooting stars, and another of Lon Chaney Jr. bursting the buttons of his natty white shirt as a devil moon blared through evergreen branches.

"Wait a second. Is that wolfsbane in the pot?"

"Jessica…you're not a hologram, you're a dream." He kneaded my breast. "It had to be the right woman, but I hoped it would be a flake, a bumpkin. I was afraid you'd come here. Ever since I dreamt of you there's been a dark spot floating in my mind. A mote."

"Make sense, man!"

"Yeah, it's wolfsbane." He rolled away from me, the oldest trick in the book.

* * *

I woke to a little girl screaming her heart out, out in the darkness. Beasley gently clamped his hand over my mouth, his other arm wrapped around my waist. I wasn't going anywhere unless I took extreme measures. Not so much of a turn-on in this context.

"It's all right." He spoke softly and I almost didn't catch it. "They say an elk screams like a child. Go back to sleep."

A long time and a lot of silence passed before he let me go.

* * *

Oatmeal and kiwis for breakfast in the commissary. Beasley introduced me around to the early-risers. *Hey, everybody, this is Jessica Mace. She's wandering the earth. Make her feel at home.* Damned if I didn't despite their clannishness. Free food is free food.

Strongman (actually a *strongwoman*, after a double take), Bearded Lady, Wolf Girl, Poindexter the Geek, the Knife Thrower, Ephandra the Contortionist, and Perkins and Luther— head carpenter and electrician respectively. The Gallows Brothers, Benson and Robert, weren't on hand. The proprietors had departed on a hush-hush mission, or so Beasley intimated when I asked to meet the gents.

Beasley's request notwithstanding, I received the hairy eyeball from the company. Nobody said two words to me except for Earl, the Illustrated Man. Earl repeatedly inquired where oh where on my delectable body I might be inked. Answer: nowhere, jerk. I kind of hoped Beasley would bust his jaw too, but it didn't happen. Several children lurked on the periphery. The oldest, an adolescent girl; the youngest, a grubby boy maybe a year or two out of diapers. They gawped at me from a safe distance, until their minder, a matronly lass named Rocky, swept them away with brisk efficiency.

After breakfast, Beasley escorted me on a tour of the environs. I tasted snow. A lot of the stuff covered the mountain peaks.

"This doesn't jibe," I said. "Are you hiding from the law, or what?"

We'd moseyed a distance from the encampment. He wore a battered Australian drover's hat, light jacket, workpants, and lace-up boots. He also carried a big-ass hunting rifle slung over his shoulder. Double-barrels, very serious.

"Whatever happens, don't get scared."

"Scared of what? And, too late."

"Of nothing. I'm not on the lam, by the way. Vacation." He knelt and traced flattened grass with his entire hand. We were surrounded by an ocean of it, tall and white, dying.

"How everybody spoke to you, you've been here a while."

"Ten months next week."

"Ten months! Sounds more and more like you're on work release."

He laughed. Nice white teeth. Considering the battered condition of his face, it was a small miracle he'd kept most of them.

"I live back east. My regular employers are having a disagreement."

"Dare I ask what they do?"

"Big brains. Quantum physics, exobiology, anthropology. They're famous, infamous, one of those things. A pair of mad scientist types. They'd love to build a time machine or a doomsday device for the kicks."

"Sounds like wacky fun. I could use a spin in a time machine, for sure."

"Backward or forward?"

I shrugged, bored.

"Sorry your bosses are trying to kill each other. Family feuds are the worst."

"It's all the shooting that made me nervous." He turned away and scanned the ground again.

"What's the argument about?"

"The ethics of temporal collocation of sapient organisms."

"No shit?"

"I shit you not. Mainly, they're at each other's throat about a dog."

"Oh, I get that. *I'd* kill over a good dog."

"Hmm. This one sure as hell is. Or it will be, after they build it."

"Build it? Are we talking about a robot?"

"A cyborg. It—he—is a war machine. Weapons contractor is financing the project. My bosses are making history. Rex has a positronic brain. First of its kind, and Toshi and Howard are fighting over the ethics. Look, stick around a few days, we'll fly to the compound, I'll show you. Easier that way."

"Okay," I said.

"Man, I wish Rex was online. We'd make short work of…" He cleared his throat and stood. "Be seven or eight years before the prototype is even in alpha phase. Gonna have to do this the old-fashioned way."

"Do what the old-fashioned way? Aren't you on vacation?"

"So to speak. Personal business. I traveled with this carnival as a kid. Ran away from a bad scene at home. The Gallows took me in, gave me a job, made sure I got an education. They're my uncles and they're in trouble."

"A debt of honor. How sweet." Sweet like rat poison. Daddy the Marine had taught us kids a whole lot about honor. Honor had put him and my eldest brother into early graves. Can't say I have much use for the sentiment.

"I didn't pick you out of that bar simply because you're a looker," Beasley said. "You're something special."

"Huh, that's some heavy duty charm you're laying down."

"Yeah, it's exhausting. I'll stop."

"Since you've already had your way, I'm steeling myself for the worst."

"The Gallows Carnival is cursed. I've come to put things in order."

"Wait, what? A curse?"

"Right."

"Like voodoo, desecrated Indian burial grounds kind of curse?"

He pointed to a splotch of maroon on the grass.

"Stay tuned."

I decided to give Twenty Questions a break. I stuffed my hands into my pockets and tagged along as he inspected a rusty overgrown fence. Soon, he found a break in the wire. A black funnel bored through a copse of pine trees, juniper, and nettles. The hole had obviously formed by the crush of a massive body wallowing its way through the tangle.

Then the breeze shifted and the reek of putrefying flesh almost knocked me down. Beasley handed me his hat and unlimbered his rifle. He carried a flashlight in his left hand. Its beam didn't cut very far into the darkness.

Motioning for me to stay put, he crouched and moved into the burrow.

"Bad idea, Beasley. Bad, very bad." Over the stench of death, I whiffed something else, something born of musk, dank fur, sweat, and piss. This was the lair of a ravenous beast, a creature of fang and lust. The combination of scents, the crimson aura of the den, made me dizzy, made my nipples hard and my thighs weak. I slapped myself across the mouth and the sting shocked me out of my little swoon.

Maybe slightly too effective. Every birdcall, every snapped twig caused me to twitch. The shadows in the trees became sinister. I gave serious thought to leaving Beasley there, of strolling back to camp. I'd have coffee with a nip of bourbon and wait to see if he ever returned.

"Jess." His voice floated from the tunnel, muffled and strange. "Dial 911. Ask for Sheriff Holcomb. Tell him to come right away."

I made the call. The dispatcher asked the usual questions and said a squad car would be on site shortly. Beasley crawled from the den, shirt torn and stems in his hair. He tossed a man's severed head on the ground. Dead two or three days at most. The left eye was still intact. Blue as milk. Hours later, I still saw my shadow reflected in it, the beetles and the flies crawling around, unsure where to start.

"Five or six bodies in there," Beasley said in a hoarse voice. He lighted a cigarette. Reached for his hip flask of whiskey, glanced at the sun, and reconsidered. Then reconsidered again and down the goddamned hatch. "Gonna have to reassemble the pieces to know for sure. Lotta pieces."

"Cops are on the way."

I'm not sure if I said it to reassure myself or to warn him there'd be no more axe-murdering on my watch. I ninety-nine percent dismissed the possibility of his involvement in a massacre. My instincts are hellishly sharp when it comes to detecting the evil that lurks in the hearts of men. Beasley had issues. Cold-blooded murder wasn't one.

The sun inched across the sky. Beasley checked his watch every couple of minutes.

"Did the carnival lose a tiger?" I said. "Or a lion? The neck wound is…chunky. That's how a big cat might savage its prey." As if I knew jack shit about big cats or mauled corpses. My mouth pops into gear when I'm nervous.

"The Gallows own three panthers. All accounted for. This ain't a wild animal attack. This is a whole other thing."

I couldn't stop staring at the head, its mouth agape, teeth and tongue clotted in gore. I ran my thumb along the scar on my throat, felt a sympathetic pang, and relived the searing slash of the blade as it sawed on through.

"Here's the sheriff," Beasley said. He looked me in the eye, hard. "Be careful."

"We're hunting rabbits?" I always try to be brave.

"Don't get cute with him. He's not your friend. Take my word."

I decided to heed his warning. A bad black vibe pushed forward thick as the dust from the cop cars tearing along the road.

* * *

Two Lewis and Clark County police cruisers nosed into the field. Several cops in midnight blue suits and white Stetson hats trudged the rest of the way to us. They patted the guns on their hips. One had a German shepherd on a leash. Poor dog wanted fuck-all to do with the murder scene. He pissed himself and cowered between the legs of his mortified handler, a lantern-jawed gal in mirrored shades.

Beasley shook hands with the sheriff. Two dogs deciding whether to sniff asses or get to tearing each other apart.

Blond-bearded and heavy through shoulders and hips, Sheriff Von Holcomb seemed at least a decade under-seasoned for the post. On the other hand, one glance at the austere panorama and I concluded that finding a taker for the position might mean the electorate couldn't afford to be too picky.

"Huh, well fuck a duck." Sheriff Holcomb toed the severed head. He dabbed his mouth with a bright red handkerchief. His deputies took tape measurements and snapped photographs of the crime scene. The unluckiest of them all, a goober with a painfully-large Adam's apple, got sent into the burrow with a Maglite and a camera.

"Any idea who we're lookin' at here?"

"Alfred Fenwood." Beasley passed the sheriff a bloodied driver's license. "Don't know him. Drag the bars, you'll find Al likes cheap beer and long walks along the highway after dark."

"We got missing person reports galore over the past three weeks. Hikers, ranch hands, some folks snatched out of parking lots. Lots of wild animal calls, too. Ripped to hell pets, the usual sort of crap." The sheriff glanced at me slyly, propped his boot on the head like a kid resting on a soccer ball, and slipped off his wedding band and made it disappear.

"Oh, man, are you kidding?" I stepped back and gripped the Ka-Bar under my coat. Come to it, I'd stab a hillbilly psycho, badge or not. My shiny new policy.

"You snuffed the Eagle Talon Ripper," he said.

"No surprise you're the lead detective in Timbuktu," I said. A mistake because his smirk suggested he mistook contempt for flirtation.

"See my girl Friday with the dog?"

"Hard to miss."

"Know why she wears them mirror shades? My mama was a gorgon. Deputy Cooper thinks some of the evil runs in my blood. She's afraid to look me in the eye." He grinned when I didn't answer. Ogled my scars. "Wow. It's true, you Alaska broads are tough as leather. Bastard really did slice your throat from ear to ear. Then you rose from the dead and sent him to hell. Amazing. Marcy at dispatch ran your name. It's flagged, big time. I suppose we're gonna have to keep tabs on you while you're visiting our fair state. Mm-mm-mm.

"How you survive something like that, eh? Don't seem possible. Don't seem possible, 'tall. That freak cut you anywhere else?" He actually reached for my collar and I tensed, ready to shorten his fingers by a knuckle or two.

"Von," Beasley said, saving the day. "We've got a situation. Best to focus."

"Plainly." Sheriff Holcomb grudgingly lowered his hand. "The Gallows think Injun-ground gonna do the trick when nothing else ever has?"

"This ground represents a full circle. Fifty years, Von."

"Ain't sacred. Ain't holy. It's elk shit and dirt."

"Red moon last night."

"I ain't blind."

"We proceed with the plan. Gallows' orders."

"Ha! Oh, as if I jump when they yell froggy."

"Today you do."

Sheriff Holcomb watched the Shepherd twist himself into a pretzel and snap at his deputy K-9 partner. The cop in mirror shades swore and danced to avoid losing a hunk of her flesh.

"Things fallin' to pieces around here," the sheriff said.

"And you gotta keep a lid on this mess," Beasley said. "Unless you want the feds on it like flies."

"Be serious, amigo. The feds won't figure into this."

"Fifty year is a high water mark. I assume nothing. Hell could be waiting in the wings."

"And her?" The sheriff jerked his thumb at me. "Where she fit into your plan?"

"She's our secret weapon."

"You mean bait."

"Same thing."

"Bait?" I said.

"Secret weapon," Beasley said.

* * *

"The sight of blood doesn't faze you," Beasley said after he got me back to the camp. We sat at a bench while two bearded guys in coveralls loaded boxes onto a trailer.

"Are you kidding? It fazes the shit outta me. Just that I see more than my fair share. I'm building a tolerance, one snake-bite at a time." I took a slug from Beasley's flask. Too early in the day, even by my Bohemian standards, but I'd earned it. "Let us recap. There's a pile of human bodies in yonder animal den. You knew they'd be there. Or, like me, you're super-duper unflappable."

"Ain't a den. It's a trophy room. We're not dealing with an animal. Not in the strictest sense of the term. I'm not very cool, either. Scared spitless, honestly."

"Uh-huh. These murders are revenge-oriented, sex fantasies, rituals, what? Your sheriff pal said something about fifty years…"

"Revenge ritual. The Gallows Curse. Goes back to the fall of 1965. There was an…incident, I suppose you'd say. I'll have Conway fill you in. He's our knife thrower. Been with the carnival since the '60s."

I raised an eyebrow.

"A curse?"

"What they call it," he said.

"Going to stop you right there, big fella. I don't live in a hut in the Dark Ages."

"Well, my uncles swallow the whole bit. Power of suggestion cannot be denied."

"Fine. Go on."

"They say it clouds the minds of outsiders. The carnival settles into an area, some gruesome murders occur, the carnival pulls stakes and moves on. The cycle repeats. Reports get filed, news stories are written. Locals squawk. Nothing comes of it, though. The outside world forgets, as if the incident is erased from memory. It becomes an urban legend, a wooly tall tale to scare the kids, and everybody accepts it as myth.

"Only family remembers the details. Blood kin and those who are so tangled up with the carnival they may as well be kin. Company members who flee? They disappear or wind up in pieces. Doesn't matter where they run. Our last sword-swallower made it to Malaysia. Authorities found his arm in a hedge.

"The Gallows travel far and wide and the cycle continues. Sometimes it goes weeks, sometimes months, maybe even a year or two. The company members aren't the ones who suffer the worst. Those victims in the woods? Locals. The curse cuts down innocent bystanders like a lawnmower through grass. I was around for the last occurrence. Ohio. Seventeen citizens in three weeks. Horrible, horrible shit. Not a peep in the national news."

I gave this a few seconds to percolate in my imagination.

"Some freak has a hard-on for your uncles, okay. Obviously it's an inside job."

"Could be. Might be something stranger."

"Either way, you gotta have a theory."

"Sure, I've got suspicions. About all I got, though."

"How many people work this joint?"

"A couple dozen."

"Kind a narrows down the suspect list."

"Jess, you don't understand. This isn't simple."

"Doesn't seem complicated either. Can't the cops catch this murderer? Must be a trail of corpses strewn across the country. Clueless as law enforcement tends to be, brute force will out eventually. For the love of God, all those bodies, dude. Where's Nancy Grace and Geraldo? This is national news. A CNN spectacular."

"You'd think so," he said.

"My instincts are razorblades, else I'd figure you were running a con, Bease. Is this reality TV? Got a camera crew stashed nearby?"

"Trust your instincts."

"Dude, I'm open-minded, as you are intimately aware. What I saw in the field, how the cops reacted…None of it adds up. Sheriff Blondie seems to be in it to win it, though. What's his story?"

"His great-grandfather was sheriff in '65 when the, ah, inciting incident, occurred. Vinette, a woman who worked at the carnival, got butchered by a jealous suitor. That suitor went on to terrorize the countryside until Grandpa Holcomb helped bring him down with a load of double-aught buckshot. He didn't get re-elected. Von's the first Holcomb to be appointed sheriff since the curse took hold."

"You keep using that word as if it's not superstitious bullshit."

Beasley dragged a cardboard box from under a table. He emptied its contents on the bed — a meticulously dissected series of clipped newspaper articles and photographs. The oldest were blurry, preserved from the decade of Flower Power and Vietnam, the newest had been shot recently. Articles about wild animal attacks, mysterious slayings, missing persons, all connected by some elusive thread. The connection seemed patently obvious — every article covering these incidents was juxtaposed with another featuring the Gallows Brothers Carnival.

He watched me thumb through the clippings.

"Curses might be country bumpkin nonsense, sure. I try to see it from the rustic perspective. Forget curses. Imagine…Imagine there's a conspiracy. Nasty, violent, spans generations, and we're going to put an end to it. You and me."

"*Conspiracies* I can sink my teeth into."

"Now we're speaking the same language."

"The authorities can't make a dent in this case, what makes you think I can help?"

"Because we only need you to play a role—you get to stand in for the woman who got murdered back then. The Gallows, Victor, our resident guru, they all believe a reenactment of that original crime will allow them to interrupt it and break the curse. None of the ladies with the carnival has the guts to act as a decoy. I'm good at taking a person's measure. My hunch is, you've got a gift for survival."

I had another sip.

"Bait doesn't sound fun."

"Bait hides the hook."

"This is about Alaska. Oh boy, you're barking up the wrong tree if you think Eagle Talon qualifies me for what the fuck ever Freak-Olympics you got going on here."

"Damned right it's about Alaska. Alaska was the crucible that made you. Your life ended when that man slashed your throat. The old you went up in smoke. You're a dancing star."

"What did you say?" Fear stirred in my heart. Fear and an incongruous trickle of exultance. A sense of deeper purpose.

Beasley retrieved his flask.

"I recognized your face the second I walked into that tavern. What's more, I recognized the light in your eyes. I wasn't there looking for Ms. Goodbar or a heroine to pull our fat from the fire. I went there to get drunk because we'd failed to find a leading lady for the big night. Meeting you is fate. Can't be anything less than the machinery of the universe clicking into place."

"Flattering, except I still don't understand what you want. Eagle Talon doesn't mean anything. I went head to head with a creep and lived to tell. The media tried to spin the hero angle. It ain't me. I'm a survivor, not a savior."

"Remains to be seen, Jess. Come on, you need to speak with Conway. He's the only one left alive from the bad days."

"Ask the dismembered people in the den, they'd probably say *these* days are pretty lousy," I said.

"The other bad days."

* * *

On the way to the Knife Thrower's tent, we crossed paths with Victor the Magician, the carnival's resident fortune teller/mentalist. Youngish guy, seven or eight years my senior. He dressed in a white shirt and jeans. Lacking the glamour and glitz of a stage, his salt and pepper goatee belonged on a ski bum rather than a fortune teller or magician.

Victor did a double take at the sight of me. He clutched my hand and kissed it with unctuous ardor.

"Oh, you magnificent man," he said to Beasley. "You have done the impossible. She is perfection."

"Yeah?" Beasley said. His cheeks seemed ruddier than usual.

"No question. Ephandra must be wild with jealousy." Victor finally released my hand. "My dear, it is a pleasure. You must visit Conway. Go, go! Time is short."

The interior of the tent lay in gloom, although it didn't matter — Conway the Knife Thrower blindfolded himself and continued to chuck the knives with eerie accuracy.

"Oh, Beasley, what have you done?" he said. He spoke in a deep, trained voice that made me marvel why he wasn't an actor instead of a knife thrower. Tall, and muscular. Wouldn't have guessed him for his mid-seventies. Raw-boned with the hands of a pianist. The Ace of Spades tattooed his left forearm.

He threw a brace of specially balanced knives at a slowly rotating wheel with a busty silhouette for a non-bull's eye. A scantily-clad assistant would occupy the blank heart of the wheel whenever the curtain lifted again. I'd seen the chick, Gacy, stumble from the animal wrangler's shack, hung-over and falling out of her sun and moon robe. Every fifth or sixth cast of a knife *thunked* solidly in the center of the silhouette. Obviously, Conway knew where she'd slept too. I'd caught a gander of Niko, the Lord of Beasts, and he was easy on the eyes. Conway had run afoul of an immutable law of physics—chicks dig a guy who knows his way around cats.

"I'm not sure if I should go into family matters with young Jessica," Victor said. "For her own protection...It is unethical to inveigle her into our wretched troubles."

"I agree," I said. "This whole deal seems extremely personal."

Beasley smoked a cigarette. His hair stuck every which way from crawling into the bushes. He smelled rank. Still sexy.

"There's a bus station half an hour down the road, Jess. Say the word."

I didn't give the word. Could be my heart in my throat blocked the way. My ever-intensifying death wish might've compelled silent complicity, or whatever wish it was that had followed me since the debacle in Alaska. There was also the distinct possibility I desired round two in the sack with Beasley. What can I say? I'm a complicated woman.

"Okay, tell it," Beasley said to his pal the Knife Thrower.

Conway shrugged and orated a real potboiler. Back in 1963, when the Gallows Carnival was purchased from a central European mountebank who shall remain nameless, some of the original players immigrated to the US and continued under new management. Chief among them, a pair of star-crossed lovers: Artemis, the Animal Trainer, and Vinette, lovely assistant to the Magician from the Black Sea. The Magician was a handsome and acerbic mature gentleman named Milo. Milo, a long-time widower, coveted the sexy, young Vinette and schemed to win her affection from his rival Artemis.

Predictably, nothing good came of this situation. Milo failed to woo the object of his affection through honest means. He turned to skullduggery, black magic, and plain dirty tricks. It failed. Then Artemis and Vinette announced their engagement and Milo lost the remainder of his wormy, rotten mind.

Upon the couple's engagement night, while everyone else attended the celebratory feast, Milo slinked into the tent where the dancing bears, big cats, and wolves slept in their cages. Some beasts he poisoned and they died, foaming at the muzzle. Others he slew with a carbine. The aftermath proved so disturbing, even hardened veterans of World War II (and there'd been several on staff) wept at the carnage.

Ah, the worst remained. Innocent Vinette, who had no conception of the magician's sickness, considering him a dear and trusted friend, slipped away from the supper to collect him. After searching high and low for the magician, she came upon the scene and screamed in horror to witness Milo skinning Artemis's prize animal, a black wolf. A massive and terrifying beast, originally captured along the Mackenzie River, the wolf hadn't gone down without a struggle—a savage slash of its fangs took a swathe of the magician's face to naked bone.

Legend insisted Vinette had fled blindly, Milo on her heels. She in her dinner gown, he wrapped in the dripping pelt of the wolf, his face flayed. He brought her down in the field and tore her flesh with nails and teeth. When he had finished her off, the magician fled into the hills. His wounds festered, as did his madness. Over the course of a fortnight, he roamed the land, murdering farmers, truck stop waitresses, untended children, and other hapless folk.

Eventually, he took shelter in an abandoned wolf den on a desolate mountainside. The men of the carnival, led by an enraged and grieving Artemis, came with lanterns and rifles. Milo charged the hunters and they cut him down in a blaze of gunfire. He cursed them with his dying breath. And lo, a few years later, the carnival troupe became aware of a dark presence haunting the show. Mysterious and brutal killings began. Beasley had filled me in on the rest.

"Tonight is the fiftieth anniversary of Milo's murder of Vinette," Conway said.

"Of course it is." I considered a void, then a crack of white light, all the fire pouring forth, and a sweet young thing's face contorted in screams at the heart of the inferno.

Beasley leaned over and whispered into my ear.

"Please help. The Gallows will make it worth your while."

We'd see, wouldn't we?

* * *

Benson and Robert Gallows returned from wherever in an antiquated flatbed truck. Paternal twins, middle-aged, dressed in fleece and plaid and denim. It appeared Benson was the drinker of the pair. His hair had gone white. Gin blossoms patterned his squashed nose. Robert's hair was dark, his features somewhat delicate. No burst blood vessels nor cauliflower ears. Both wore revolvers under their coats and wolfsbane garlands around their necks.

Beasley explained that I knew the history of the alleged curse and that I hadn't entirely decided to play the role of doomed Vinette.

"What do you think?" Benson Gallows said.

"She doesn't resemble Vinette," Robert Gallows said. "However, the proper spirit counts for everything. There's also the factor that we have little choice."

"Agreed."

"Hello, boys," I said. "You two could try talking to *me* since I'm standing right here."

"You were with Beasley when he discovered the remains," Benson Gallows said. "You haven't high-tailed it for the hills. An intriguing sign."

"Technically we're in the hills. Also, I think you're a bunch of kooks, or you're having me on."

"Come now, you saw the corpses," Robert Gallows said. "No chicanery there."

"I've some experience with murderers and none with mumbo-jumbo curses. Primarily because murderers are real while curses are not."

"The belief some hold in them is real enough to draw blood. Leaving that aside, what would it take for you to indulge us our roleplaying exercise tonight?"

"Roleplaying?"

Robert Gallows nodded.

"Easy as pie, my dear. You dress to the nines, enjoy a world-class supper with the company, and then retrace Vinette's path from the night she died."

"From the night she was horribly murdered, you mean."

"Yes. While you're wandering in the field, the rest of us will enact—"

"We'll perform our mumbo-jumbo," Benson Gallows said.

"Your hoodoo is going to do what? Trap the ghost, or werewolf? My bad, I don't know what you boys are calling your fairy nemesis."

"It's a revenant, a spirit of vengeance. We want to trap it in a circuit. Then open that circuit. Not your concern. Your concern is to look pretty and follow a scripted sequence of movements."

"So, how much?" Robert Gallows said.

I thought fast.

"Uh, ten grand. Cash." The ol' Mace piggy bank rattled emptily of late. My heart sank when the brothers smiled as one.

"Done," Robert Gallows said. "Let's make you presentable, shall we?"

"Keep your creepy sheriff away from me. He's a deal-breaker."

"As you say. Sheriff Holcomb will not come within a country mile of your person. Right, Beasley?"

"A country mile," Beasley said without enthusiasm.

"Then we have a deal," Benson Gallows said. "I must warn you, however. A deal is a deal. Sealed in blood as far as we're concerned."

"Indeed," Robert Gallows said. "Should you renege on our arrangement, there will be consequences. The Sheriff sounds as if he's taken a shine to you, Ms. Mace. I am sure he'd be amenable to drumming up any number of phony charges to lock you in his jail for a while. Vagrancy and trespassing on private land among others." At least the bastard had the decency to seem embarrassed. He shuffled his feet and glanced away. "Apologies for this element of threat. The warning is necessary."

"Beasley," I said.

"Hey, you shook hands." Beasley too averted his gaze.

Benson Gallows sighed in exasperation.

"Please, please, everyone. Dispense with the melodrama. No one is going to jail. Keep your word and all will be well. Simple as that."

"I'll alert the girls," Robert Gallows said. "They'll prepare you for the festivities."

"Blow it out your ass," I said. But, I went along.

Mary the Magnificent and Lila the Bearded Lady took me into their trailer to get ready for the "dinner and a séance" portion of my upcoming date with Beasley. I had doubts about Mary — her spine was so twisted with muscle she hunched; her hands were enormous and rough as cobs. Even so, she could've had a chair in a Beverly Hills salon if the magic she worked on my snarled mane with a jug of warm water and a washtub was any indicator. After bathing and styling came the glamour detailing. I'm okay with makeup, though I don't usually apply much, if any. The ladies laid it on thick. Lila took charge, and she too exhibited a deft touch. After the detailing, they put me into a dress that would've done well for a night on the town visiting swanky 1960s hotspots. White and flowing, open in back and slit up to here on the side. Entirely too seductive for supper in a carnival tent in the Middle of Nowhere, Montana.

When they finally handed me a mirror I gasped.

The ladies' reflections smiled at one another. I turned my head and dark clouds descended.

"Lila and I ran away from the circus," Mary said. "This is where we landed."

"A grave mistake," Lila said. "Carnivals are even worse."

"Because of the psycho-killers?" I admired my cleavage. "Or because this one killed the clowns? Seriously, what gives? I've hunted high and low and seen nary a trace. Isn't that carnival sacrilege?"

Mary smiled venomously.

"It is easy to scoff. We thought the curse was a joke too. Bitterly, bitterly we've learned otherwise. We are trapped."

"Someone should do something," I said, dry as toast.

"We've tried," Lila said. "This is beyond our reckoning."

"It's not beyond mine. People's heads are getting severed. Kinda physical for a ghost."

"Perhaps you are an expert in this area," Lila said.

"I straighten horseshoes with my bare hands. I can lift a grand piano on my back." Mary flexed her massive biceps. "Even I could not hope to confront the terror in the hills and survive."

"Run," Lila said. "And don't look back. You aren't a part of this yet."

"She won't run. Ever seen a more stubborn jaw? Our friend is a warrior. She will fight."

"Who's out there?" I said. "Really, no bullshit."

"Some sort of Jungian manifestation," Lila said. "The shadow personified."

"Baby, that's the best description I've ever heard." Mary kissed the Bearded Lady's cheek. "Whatever the truth, don't mess with it, it'll turn you to mincemeat."

"A shadow? Here I thought we were dealing with the wolf man. Silver bullets, belladonna, etcetera." I sighed. "Come on. I've seen the horrible shit man does to man. No need for werewolves or shadow monsters."

They exchanged unhappy glances.

"A shadow personified," Lila said, emphasizing each word. "Whether it's man or beast is irrelevant for it is most certainly a distilled and concentrated horror that exists on the edge of human experience. Tread lightly."

Mary lifted my dress and strapped a stiletto in its sheath to my thigh. Snugged it against the stocking. All right, this improved my mood.

"Your Ka-Bar is a good blade. Won't help. Mine is cold iron and it has been blessed. Doubt it'll help either. Still, you're okay. I like you."

"See you two at the event, I guess."

"No," Lila said. "We've decided to skip this one. Good luck, Ms. Jessica."

"Remember to take off those heels if you need to start running," Mary said.

"Don't try to teach your grandma to suck eggs," I said.

I thanked them and tottered out the door.

* * *

Benson Gallows handed me a bag with scads of rolled hundred dollar bills stuffed inside. I stashed the bag under Beasley's bunk and we gathered to head for the big top and supper. The boys could spin whatever fantasy they liked. Made no difference to me. Besides, I trusted Beasley, insomuch as I trust anyone. More importantly, I trusted myself and the belly gun, a .25 caliber derringer I'd swiped from his footlocker and slipped into my sweet little handbag.

Beasley and the Gallows Brothers carefully explained my duties, which were negligible, considering the amount of dough they parted with to secure my participation. They assured me all aspects of the ritual had been assiduously researched and rehearsed. As long as I followed my cues, events would unfold smoothly. In some respects, this felt akin to the slavish preparations of hardcore Civil War re-enactors. Except for the actual pile of human heads and assorted parts in the back forty.

"I'll be out in the field tonight, in case." Beasley had squeezed into a cream-colored number, slicked his hair down, the whole bit.

"In case of what?"

"Uh, in case you run into a rabid coyote."

"Or a rabid elk," I said. "Mary and Lila seem to think—"

"Those broads are eccentric," Beasley said.

"This is a carnival. What else would they be?"

"Yeah, well, even for a carnival." He offered his arm.

The séance cum last supper, or whatever you'd care to name the ritual, occurred in the big top. The roadies had broken out a massive mahogany table inlaid with granite and matching chairs. They left a flap open in the ceiling. No moon yet, but plenty of stars sprinkled against the black. Jazz piped in soft and slow.

Our fateful supper included a honey-braised roast, wild rice, pineapple and grapes, sorbet, and plenty of red wine. I may have proved slightly unladylike in my enthusiasm for the various dishes. Free meals this swanky were rare.

I had nothing better to do than stuff my face, anyhow.

The girls wore dresses, although none as nice as mine, and the boys were in suits.

"Yowch!" I said as Beasley pulled out my chair. "Did I tell you how hot you look?"

His melancholy expression merely flickered.

"Do me a favor and don't argue," he whispered. He slipped the crucifix from his truck around my neck.

I would've given him grief except for the fact that bit of adornment drew the attention of every man at the table who hadn't already surreptitiously ogled my bosom since I'd strolled in.

Though I was supposed to be the centerpiece of the evening, it seemed as if the entire company had secretly agreed to exclude me from the conversation. Fine, the silly bastards could stare at my tits and leave me out of it.

Ephandra, a lovely, long-in-the-tooth contortionist and apparent paramour of Benson Gallows, eyed my vampy dress, silver choker, purple eyeshade, and hair piled high. She smirked with voluptuous malice, pulled on a pair of ermine gloves, and lit a cigarette. She smoked it in a holder, Greta Garbo-style, or some other Golden Age actress.

"Tell me more about the séance," she said to Benson Gallows.

"You're a little séance virgin?" His white eyebrows lifted.

"Oh, I did a séance in spectacular fashion. And *you*?" She stared at him now, like a cat at a bird.

"There was this one time...Me and a couple of my cousins spooked each other on an overnight camping trip. I was in middle school."

"Did you make contact with the beyond?" Ephandra said.

"I made contact with my cousin's boob for a second or two," Benson Gallows said.

Victor the Fortune Teller frowned at this exchange.

"Perhaps this is not the occasion for jocularity." He'd gone the extra mile and decked himself out in a fabulously extravagant black silk cape and a red turban studded with gemstones.

"*Nice*, Ben," Ephandra said, dismissing Victor with an eye-roll. "Weren't we supposed to hit a séance gig together once?"

"No. Wait, yes — we were on a break. You called, but I had a date with, what's her name? Crazy blonde who dragged me to the pool hall every other night."

"Ginny the psych student? Her dad had a place in Coeur d' Alene. Slut. Whore. Bitch."

"Yes, you met, apparently. I never got past first base, then you snatched me off the market."

"Sorry, honey." She stretched to stroke his arm, digging with her shiny white nails.

"What was the deal, anyhow?" he said.

Ephandra shrugged.

"The medium slaughtered a cat. Slit its throat."

"Ahem! Now that we're all in the proper mood — thank you, Ephandra — I propose a toast," Robert Gallows said.

I reached for the wine and Poindexter deftly snatched the bottle.

"Vinette did not touch a drop the evening of her, er… demise. Here, try the cider."

"Sorry, dear." Benson Gallows poured a glass of cider from a ceramic jug and set it near my left hand. "Absolutely no blood of the vine for you. We must not risk spoiling the ritual, hey?"

I gritted my teeth. Ten thousand dollars bought this cuckoo crowd a tiny bit of forbearance. I tasted the cider and nailed Beasley with my most reproachful glare. He wilted, then raised a glass of cider in a gesture of solidarity.

"Did you folks know that Sheriff Holcomb's mom is a gorgon?" I said.

Victor sighed.

"*The* Gorgon. There's only one. Von's a liar."

"Most definitely a liar," Ephandra said. "The only creature that let his bloated sack of lard father touch them was a hick sheep-herder maid from Butte. Probably not twice, either."

Perkins the Carpenter killed the electric lamps and the music. The chamber fell into shadow, illuminated by a candelabrum and the edge of the moon now shining through the screen in the roof of the tent. The moon burned with a ruddy light.

Robert Gallows tapped his glass with a spoon.

"I propose a toast — to the memory of those poor souls taken before their time, and to a reversal of our own prolonged misfortune. Thank you, Jessica Mace, for making this restoration possible."

Everyone drank. Beasley rose, gave a courtly bow, and exited the tent. My mouth dried and I instinctively touched the crucifix before I realized what I'd done. Stupid, inane, social programming at its worst.

"Shall we begin?" Robert Gallows said. "Jessica, be so good as to stand over there—perfect. Victor, I cede the floor."

Victor waited for complete silence.

"Join hands." He inhaled deeply and blew out the candles.

Took a few moments for the moonlight to kick in.

"Milo," Victor intoned. "Milo are you with us, you scurrilous fuck? We've brought you an offering. Come among us and claim your prize, if you've the balls."

Well. I am not too proud to admit this spiel caught me flat-footed.

Chairs creaked. A staccato thumping emanated from the table; it and the chair-creaking grew louder, becoming violent. Knuckles, rings, and bracelets clacked against wood as the shadowy company trembled and twitched, caught in a mass seizure. Their spasms ceased and the enclosure fell silent.

Was this a con job? Or had they taken a psychotropic drug and were frying together? Damned weirdos. The lovely vision of ten grand in a bag steadied me, although I was tempted to step forward and shake Ephandra, see if she was playing possum.

"Girl, that's your cue," Perkins said, inches from my elbow. He didn't seem quite himself in the near darkness.

"Gah!" I thought about having a heart attack.

A dozen chairs squeaked as the company unfolded to their feet in a unified motion. All of them stood stock still and regarded me in eerie silence. Their eyes blazed white with captured fire from the moon.

Hell of a cue. I got going.

* * *

Outside, a cold breeze sliced through my barely-there ensemble. I called upon my reserves of hardcore Alaska-ness and merely shivered.

Stars flared and died. The moon burned a hole through the black and into my mind. I decided to heist a truck and haul ass for town, or anywhere directly away from the remnants of the carnival. Keys were in everything around here. I didn't heist a truck. I decided to fetch my loot from under Beasley's bed and ride shank's mare in a straight line until I hit something like civilization. But, no. I didn't do the smart, obvious thing. Sensible action slipped my grip.

I walked toward a massive rectangular tent, domain of Hondo the Panther Lord, as I'd been instructed. My flesh tingled the way it does when I've gone over my limit of booze. Strange, since I hadn't had a snort since early in the day. I wiggled my fingers and clucked my tongue to test the theory. All systems go.

An offering, Victor had said. A human sacrifice, he'd said. Okay, he hadn't said as much, merely implied it. How much danger was I in? My hair-trigger alarm system kept sending garbled messages filtered through static. Meanwhile, there went my sun-darkened hand on the mesh screen, and there went my feet, bearing me into a den of beasts, and there awaiting my arrival, crouched Satan, golden-black in the glare of a kerosene lantern suspended from a hook.

I name her Satan because she smoldered with an inner radiance I'd intuited from a thousand glimpses of the Devil's likeness in stained glass windows and illuminated manuscripts of the holy and the occult. Her shadow spread across the floor and up the wall, massive and primeval and bestial.

Satan, AKA Deputy Cooper who served as Sheriff Holcomb's K-9 expert, wore blue and white uniform pants streaked in dirt, and nothing else. Broad-shouldered, narrow-hipped, sinewy, her feet sank into a puddle of gory mud. Before her, lay the carcass of her K-9 partner, its jaws caked in red. She'd skinned it with a flint knife from the Neanderthal King exhibit.

Deputy Cooper slowly pivoted and revealed that the dog had eaten some of her face before it died. I swallowed bile.

"Damndest thing," she said. "I was chilling in the cruiser. Baxter tore through his kennel and went right for me."

I almost didn't recognize the deputy, for obvious reasons. She'd also ditched the mirrored shades. Her shape twisted and thickened into steroid-fueled contortions. Her hands were bigger than Mary the Magnificent's, and those long, sharp nails weren't press-ons. Incongruously, she lacked much in the way of body hair. Folklore and Hollywood have conditioned us to expect pointed ears and a fur coat.

We were alone in the tent. Earlier in the day, a crew had loaded the animals into traveling enclosures and cruised toward Idaho. Victor had said that the phantom of Milo wouldn't require the meat of a panther or wolf. The only force acting upon the Black Magician was his lust for Vinette. All else was pantomime. The dog's corpse and Deputy Cooper's wrecked face suggested Victor might not have possessed total command of the facts.

None of this was following the script. Dead dog, mutilated cop, me armed and dangerous.

"Good fucking God, Deputy." I pulled the derringer from my purse, aimed at her head, and cocked the hammer. The pistol felt like a toy in my fist, in the presence of evil.

She drove the flint blade into the ground and straightened. Blood oozed over her breasts and painted her belly and slicked her pants. The blood flow showed no sign of slowing. Black-gold blood.

"You smell…great," she said through impressive canines.

"Thanks," I said. "Get on the ground."

She tilted her partial death's head. Her eyes were bloodshot and yellow.

"I'm going to eat your whoring heart, Nettie."

"Okay, lady." I pulled the trigger, saw a tiny hole bore into the exposed bone of her skull. A wisp of smoke curled from the wound.

Deputy Cooper blinked.

"There's mud in your eye," she said.

Her arm looped around fast and smacked me across the chest. Oof, let me tell you. Back in junior high Julie Vellum drop-kicked me in the head. Another time a kid walloped me full force with an aluminum bat. This felt kind of similar, except somebody had filled the bat with rebar and Babe Ruth slugged me with it. A flash of insight suggested that in a parallel reality, the blow had struck claws-first and my insides had splashed all over the place.

I flew backward through the tent opening and landed on my ass. Here came the skull-faced wolfwoman, striding toward me. Mary, dressed in her carnival tights that showed off a lot of grotesquely-bulging muscles, stepped out of the shadows and clobbered her across the back of the neck with a steel wrecking bar. The steel clanged meatily. Deputy Cooper dropped to a knee and Mary hit her again like she was chopping into a log.

Deputy Cooper caught the bar on the third swing, ripped it from Mary's grasp and slung it away. She covered her ruined face with her hands and wailed. Neither woman nor animal should be able to produce such a cry. The kind of sound you experience once and hope to never hear again. The deputy shuddered and collapsed into a fetal position and remained still. She appeared to diminish slightly, to sag and recede, as if death had taken from her a lot more than twenty-one grams. Made me seriously reevaluate my contempt for the Catholic Church and its hang-up with demonic possession. Sir Arthur C. Clarke once said that any sufficiently advanced technology would be indistinguishable from magic. In my humble opinion, that goes double for sufficiently advanced lunacy being indistinguishable from supernatural phenomena.

"I suppose that's one way of solving the problem," Mary said.

"Is it solved?" I said.

"The Gallows will have to send a postcard with the news. I'm taking Lila away from here."

Beasley's mention of the sword swallower who got chopped to bits in Malaysia occurred to me. I kept it to myself.

"Thanks, Mary. Adios."

She nodded curtly and walked away. Deputy Cooper lay there, one eye glistening as wisps of steam rose from her corpse.

I gained my feet and stumbled along the concourse. Dim lights peeped here and there from the recesses of shuttered stalls. The moon swallowed all else. I swear the moon resembled Deputy Cooper's flayed skull, and it wouldn't stay put, it rolled across the heavens to glare at me. I staggered to an empty squad car parked on the grass between the shooting gallery and a temporary-tattoo stall.

My lucky night, keys in the ignition, shotgun missing from the console rack. The interior reeked of wet fur. I jumped in, got her revving, and then floored it, barefoot on the cold pedal. I raced along the dirt road that curved away from the carnival. A veil of dust covered the sky and the damnable moon in my wake.

Crippling pain set in as the bouquet of survival chemicals polluting my veins diminished. Cracked ribs for sure, deep tissue bruises in my back, everywhere. I'd bitten my tongue and jammed my neck. My feet hurt. It began to settle into my frenzied brain that I'd commandeered a patrol car, was mostly naked, had helped murder a sworn officer of the law, and worst of all, left ten grand behind. Perhaps I should turn around and retrieve the money, at any rate. Hard to split for parts unknown without a few dollars in one's pocket.

That's when the wheel wrenched in my hands. Front tire blown. The cruiser slewed violently and I couldn't work the pedals fast enough to avert disaster. It left the road at forty-five, flipped over and skidded upside down until it came to a halt in the bushes.

The crash tossed me around inside the cab. Ruined my hair and tore my gorgeous dress all to shit. Might've loosened a tooth or two as well. I was still partly stunned when Sheriff Holcomb got the driver side door open and pulled me out and dumped me onto the soft ground without ceremony. He looked pissed. The pistol in his hand accentuated my impression of his mood.

"Nice shooting, Tex," I said with groggy reproach.

"Jumping Jesus lizards," he said. "That rig is totaled. Biggest clusterfuck I ever did see."

"I bet you've seen a bunch too."

He holstered his pistol with an expression of regret.

"What the hell are you doing in Coop's car? Where is she? I heard a shot. What the fuck happened?"

"Easy, easy. Give her a second." Beasley emerged from the gloom, rifle in hand. He knelt at my side and checked for broken bones. Contusions, mainly, but I didn't mind the attention. While he worked, I closed my eyes and related the appalling tale of the past few minutes. I considered editing out the part where I put a slug into Deputy Cooper's brain — admittedly, it might not have killed her, the wrecking bar swung by a carnival performer who could bench a grand piano was the most likely candidate. Once I started spilling, I couldn't stop, though.

"Real sorry about your deputy," I said at the end and wiped my eyes to emphasize the point. "Sorry about the dog, too. He was probably a good dog."

Beasley stood and faced Sheriff Holcomb.

"Shut up, Von."

"Screw you, Beasley. I didn't say anything. She's admitted—"

"To putting down a murderous psychopath. Damned good at it, isn't she? All those bodies? I'm sure lab work is going to connect your girl to the crime scene."

"Shit, man. We were all there. That scene is a mess."

"Montana's finest," I said.

"Put things in order," Beasley said. "Be the hero who solved the case."

"Huh. Think the curse is broken?"

Beasley shrugged.

"Can't see how it matters for you. If it is, you're sheriff for life. If the situation remains unchanged, nobody outside of our circle is gonna remember anything in a week or two. Besides, there's Jessica's not insubstantial fee. Check under my bed."

"Yeah? How much."

"Ten grand."

"Beasley!" I said, too weak to jump up and slap him.

That did it. The clouds cleared from Sheriff Holcomb's demeanor. He grinned.

"Okay, then. Okay." He clapped Beasley's shoulder. "Yeah, okay. Reckon I'll mosey on back to camp and straighten everything out."

Watching the predatory smirk and swagger of the sheriff, his easy acceptance of such a dramatic turn of events, was chilling. How many two-bit criminals had he left in the woods? How many hookers had he strangled and dumped along the highway?

I only exhaled when he tipped his hat and ambled toward town.

"Lean on me," Beasley said. "I parked not far from here." He half carried me to his truck and put me inside. He gunned the engine and got us moving.

"I can't believe you gave that pumpkin-headed sonofabitch my cash."

He smiled.

"Von's gonna be hot. It's behind the seat."

I relaxed. A hundred aches and pains faded into the background and I almost smiled. Didn't last long — the dead cop's face would haunt my dreams, or worse.

"Where to?"

"Home. Ride with me as far as you want."

"Oh, is it that easy? We're done? Weren't you planning to trap the...spirit in that den? Sure Mary and I didn't totally blow the whole deal?"

"I'm done is all I know. Gave it the college try. You look sort of spectacular in what's left of that dress, in case nobody mentioned it yet."

We continued in silence until we hit the interstate and turned east.

Beasley reached over and patted my scraped knee.

"Yep, it's over. The moon feels different."

I didn't have the heart to tell him the last thing I'd seen before I booked out of there in Sheriff Holcomb's cruiser was Deputy Cooper's grin, her eyelid sliding down in a ghastly wink. Could have been my imagination. What else?

Besides, Beasley was right. The moon did feel different. Surely it did.

I gave him a cheery smile and rested my head against the window. We drove deep into the night, cleaving through a vault of stars. The air thinned until the stars burned through the windshield. Beasley pulled over at a motel and got us a room with a radio and a box television. After showering off the blood, grime, and stink, I stared at my reflection in the bathroom mirror. My eyes were ringed from exhaustion and wide with the exultant aftermath of terror I'd come to recognize. Question was, were these the eyes of a doomed woman? I blinked, no closer to an answer.

Beasley had fallen onto the narrow bed, fully dressed. He snored counter-time to golden country oldies. I lay next to him, my hand on his arm, and regarded the ceiling. Those water-stained tiles were the bottom of an inverted tea cup, promising me, warning me of my fate. I waited for a coyote to yip or a wolf to howl. Waited some more as Hank Williams Sr.'s lost highway carried me into dreams.

LD50

Despite the pervasiveness of instant communication, smart phones, video-capable eyeglasses, and twenty-four-hour cable media, I generally slip under the radar. While I'm not homely, I've got one of those faces you can't help but forget even though the name Jessica Mace trips off the tongue, the answer to a crossword puzzle, no doubt. In this age of daily horrors going at ten cents a bushel, what happened to me in Alaska three years ago is ancient enough news to be catalogued alongside floor plans for the Pyramids.

The first thing people ask if they catch me without a turtleneck or a scarf is, Oh my God, what happened to your neck? Then I tell them to go piss up a rope, with a rasp because the blade went deep, and that is inevitably that. We aren't going to discuss it now, either.

Moving on.

I won't give you the entire picture. You can have snapshots. Order them any way you please. Make of them what you will. This is your mystery to solve.

* * *

Late one summer I was hitching through Eastern Washington.

Joseph on a camel, *there's* a whole lot of nothing for you. Chatted up a few locals and got the lay of the land. Twigged to the fact that

that part of the world rivaled Alaska for incident rates of theft, murder, rape, and diabolism — amateur and professional.

A long-haul trucker who gave me a lift bragged that the meth labs were so prevalent they formed a Crystal Triangle. He worried that the Mexicans were taking over; first wave was migrants working the apple orchards and now the cartels had their hooks sunk, like in Arizona and Texas. Tourist attractions included the Hanford Nuclear Reservation, Walla Walla State Prison, and the J.W. Trevan Memorial Testing Facility. The first and the last concocted the poison and the middle supplied the control population. Kidding, everybody knew big animal shelters in Seattle and Spokane provided the subjects, forever homes his foot. He offered me a twenty-spot to blow him and I bailed at the weigh station before the wheels stopped rolling.

A farmer and his grandson chided me for thumbing, it wasn't safe for a young lady, insert lecture here. The farmer was aggrieved because somebody poisoned his German shepherd and hacked off its paws. Stole the paws, left the dog. I mean, damn. That bad news was making the rounds. The waitress at the diner where I got dropped by Farmer Brown said it was a shame, the Devil Hisownself at work through the instrument of some godless sicko. *Thirty dogs since Easter,* said the fry cook as he watched me push my cheeseburger aside. *Nuh-uh, eighty or ninety,* chimed in a barfly who was sipping from a brown paper bag at nine in the A.M. *A serial killer of mutts,* said the cook, shaking his head. Pooches snatched from yards and kennels, later found stabbed, decapitated, pierced with arrows, ritually dismembered. *You know what mutilating animals leads to,* said the waitress. *People!* said the barfly and grinned. The sheriff's department was on the case, which meant there'd be three hundred dogs slaughtered before that nimrod Sheriff Danker Brunner caught a clue. Then cookie got going on a rape trial concerning a high school football team the next county over and I tuned my brain to another frequency.

Did some loon think a dog's foot might be a lucky charm? Did he string them from his rearview? Did he mount the heads on the wall of his shack? Did he have a Fido to call his own? Those interstate hookers might want to watch themselves, being a lateral link in the food chain, except nobody cares about hookers the way they get out pitchforks and torches for the plight of mutts.

Rednecks flying Dixie colors from the antenna of their monster truck chucked a bottle at me as I waited for the next hitch at the pull in. Who says you can't go home again. Who says you ever get away.

* * *

I danced with a cowboy named Stefano Hoyle at a tavern near the freeway off-ramp. His shirt smelled of Old Spice and tobacco. He possessed an aura reminiscent of the Yukon fishermen and hunters I'd known in the Forty-ninth state. A radioactive strangeness that drew me like a magnet, made me all tingly. Said he'd never been to Alaska, had always lived here in purgatory. Hated the cold and Eastern WA got plenty. He didn't have much more to give, measured his words as if they were pearls. I am a reader between lines kind of gal so we got along dandy.

One Cuervo led to a shitload more Cuervo and we fucked away half the weekend back at his trailer. Basking in the afterglow, I decided to hang around and see where the ride went.

Hoyle didn't ask about the bitchin' scar in his haste to get my clothes off, although he was also pretty goddamned drunk and it was dark, so I figured for sure by the cold light of morning, etcetera, and still not a peep. Tall, dark, and handsome fixed us bacon and toast and I finally became exasperated lounging there in a bra and Hello Kitty panties and told him the score, how I got my throat cut and how I got back my own, or maybe got back *some* of my own, at the end of that spooky fairytale in the frozen north. Real deal fairytales are all about nasty sex, blood, and cannibalism, same as real life. I tend to babble after a righteous fuck, but I possessed the presence of mind to leave out a few details of the incident, such as me busting caps into a dyed-in-the-wool mass murderer. Girl has gotta hold something in reserve for the second date.

He shrugged and tipped his Stetson back and said how'd I like my eggs and then served them to me overdone as steel-belted tires anyway. That Stetson, incidentally, was the only thing he ever wore until five minutes before exiting the trailer to perform his cowboy routine.

Nice enough body, could have made the grade for a young nekkid Marlboro Man calendar in a pinch. It was also obvious that between chain smoking Pall Malls, chugging booze, and taking a beating from the elements, he'd be a woofer in a few more years. Weathered, is the polite term and it's why my policy is to snag them while they're young.

He pulled on a long sleeve shirt and blue jeans and grabbed a rifle from where it rested against a pile of laundry. Flicked me a Gila monster glance as he limped into the yard. Real deal cowboys, not assholes who wear ten gallon hats and dinner plate belt buckles to the office or while sipping wine coolers, are bowlegged, and *all* of them limp, speak Spanish like it's the mother tongue, and hail from the State of Coahuila. I gave Hoyle a pass on the last item.

When you call out to a real deal cowboy, he turns his body, not his neck. Busted ribs, busted vertebrae, and yeah getting kicked in the face by a bucking bronco smarts. They all chew, or smoke, or both, and they drink. Every mother loving one of them.

His trailer was an Airstream from the '50s. One door. Windows so tiny you'd have to be a rattler to shimmy through. It teetered on cinderblocks, verging that big ass nothing I mentioned earlier. Two acres of empty chicken coops, junk cars, and a pair of corrals taken over by ant mounds. A fire ant colony, the advance guard of a South American invasion force. The barn had collapsed. Country & Western version of the projects. He'd inherited the whole shebang from his folks. Dead for ten years, Mom and Dad; a brother, or sister, in Canada soaking up that sweet, sweet, socialized everything. No pets, pets were a tie down. I looked around at the desolation when he said that, kept my mouth shut for once.

Hoyle proudly showed off his motorcycle, a Kawasaki he'd gotten on the cheap from his pal Lonnie. Did I know anything about motor bikes? Told him my late uncle was a motocross fanatic, took me riding on the Knik Flats when I was a kid, showed me how to tune a carburetor and change a spark plug; the basics. Hoyle seemed impressed with my tomboy ingenuity. His bike had some problems, it stalled and stuttered, and he wasn't exactly a mechanic, although he tinkered with it every chance he got. His cousin died in a motorcycle crackup, rear-ended a semi at highway speed and after divulging that info he changed the subject by not speaking again for half an hour.

Way off through the haze and the hayricks and rough hills were mountains, the ancient worn down kind. The landscape was arrested mid evolution; all the worst qualities of salt plain and high desert and not a tree for miles, frozen like that forever. Could have been tar pits from the look of things, mammoth tusks scattered. Even in hot weather -- and Jesus it was hot that year -- the dry wind had an edge. The grit between my teeth tasted of alkali and it was always there, always made me yearn to rinse my mouth. Made me wonder if it was the same phenomena here as on the tundra, if the emptiness treated your mind like a kid deforming a slinky.

I asked where to as he climbed into his old Ford flatbed. Gods, I hated my voice. Sounded like a rusty hinge. Another detail that raised brows, but not his. Unflappable he, I bet a scorpion could scuttle over him and not get a rise. He laid the rifle on the rear window rack and cranked up his rig. Of course the radio was dialed to a station that spun the ghosts of Hank Williams, Roger Miller, and Ernest Tubb.

The roads were either cracked blacktop, dirt, or wagon trails, depending. You traveled in a cloud of dust. I lighted another cigarette and squinted through a pair of sunglasses I'd swiped at a liquor store in Vancouver.

"Last book I read was *Stallion Gate,*" Hoyle drawled. A recitation. "Favorite movie is *The Food of the Gods.* You agreed to come home with me because there's something about my eyes." This was in response to a survey question I'd asked at the bar thirty-six hours prior. So it went with him. Drop in a quarter and the music would play sooner or later if you stuck in there.

"Smith's least appreciated book, that movie is terrible, and yeah. You're right on. You've got angel eyes, like Lee Van Cleef." I shifted on the bench seat because the Ka-Bar strapped to my hip was digging in. I'd ditched the .38 since I didn't qualify for a concealed carry permit and none of the cops I'd met had any sense of humor, so a pistol was too risky for my taste. The knife had already earned its keep when a sketchy dude hassled me at a campsite along the AlCan Highway. Scared him off, no slicing necessary. I didn't think Hoyle harbored ill intentions, hoped not. Time would tell. Mr. Ka-Bar gave me a little security anyhow.

"You like to shoot?" he said out of the blue.

The road reeled us further and further into North American badlands variety of veldt. I almost laughed, caught myself, lowered my shades, and gave him a bug-eyed glance that passed for innocence.

"What are we shooting?" I said.

"Sunday's my day of rest," he said. "So, coyotes."

"One thing leads to another."

"What?"

"It's not a country song," I said.

* * *

Hoyle parked in the middle of nowhere and we walked to a blind of grass and brush built on the lip of a gully. Perfect three hundred and sixty-degree view of the great empty. Patches of cattle tried to stay in the shade of cloud dapples. Fences between them and us. Corroded barbed wire, petrified posts, rocks, tumbleweeds, lightning-struck charred bones.

He brought a jug of water and a pair of binoculars; decided against the Varmint Suit, as he called it: an olive gray camo set of matching pants and coat; a sniper outfit webbed with netting and faux vegetation. Gave me the chills to see it bundled there by the spare tire like some discarded rubber monster suit from a Universal sound stage. I felt relief that he didn't climb inside, didn't strip away his humanity through the addition. The VS was hot and bulky and he saved it for tricky hunts, the kill of kills. Today wasn't tricky, it was straightforward as she got.

We nestled onto a mat in near darkness of the shelter and peeked through cunning slits in the blind at the bright old world. The blind was one of a dozen he'd erected across the prairie. His custom was to tour them over the course of a season, catch as catch could. Mainly, he strung wire and drove tractors for the neighborhood farmers. This was how he earned tequila and cigarette money. Picking up bitches money, is what he mumbled, or what I heard.

"I don't think I like this," I said, quiet as if we were in church.

He told me how it was, laconic, nothing wasted.

Government paid fifty bucks a pelt with a waterproof form to fill in — time, date, sex, method, latitude and longitude, a tiny print wall of other bureaucratic bullshit. The state predator culling program guide claimed winter and spring to be superior to late summer for purposes of controlling the population. Hunters didn't give a damn. Fifty bucks was fifty bucks and a dead coyote was one less coyote, which was good.

"Predators-schmedators. Everything's got a right to live," I said, believing it.

"They eat kittens," he said.

"Coyotes do not eat kittens. Where the hell do they find kittens?"

"Kittens. Puppies. Lambs and calves. Foals if they can get 'em. You name it. Scarf 'em bloody and bawlin' out a mama's womb. Wile E. is a merciless fucker." He smiled at me and his eyes had a bit of merciless fucker in them too. Made me a teeny bit hot.

"Kittens? Really?"

"A pack went for a baby at a picnic a few years back. A human baby."

"Ah. This is a noble enterprise. You're an exterminator. That it?"

"Sure. I guess."

"You enjoy it so much, I'm kind of surprised you don't do something about all these fire ant condos."

He cracked a smile. "Now, that's not neighborly. They're getting a foothold this far north. Besides, I don't get paid to blow up anthills, Jess."

Normally, Hoyle used electronic decoys and artificial scents and other kinds of high tech bait. Culling was an art and he'd learned everything that he knew from a true master, wouldn't say who, though. That afternoon he kept it simple with a pocket call. A piece of plastic that created a spectrum of horrendous screeches, squeals, and yowls. Distressed and dying rabbit was his specialty. A scrawny female coyote slunk from the tall grass and froze, nose lifted to get a fix on lunch. He shot her dead at two hundred yards.

We went to the carcass and he dressed it on the spot with a buck knife while the sun hammered and cooked. The slices went A B C. Done it before a thousand times, easy, you could tell. Blood, guts, the works went into a plastic bag and he made his notations of record on the waterproof form. Then back to the truck and a hop, skip, and a jump to another vast quadrant of prairie and a fresh killing blind.

"Next one's yours," he said and handed over the rifle.

"No way, Jose," I said. "I'm not bushwhacking some hapless critter."

"Oh, yeah you will."

"Get bent," I said.

"This is sacred. You'll offend the gods."

I worked the bolt to test the action, and maybe to back him off his he-man perch a tad. An ex taught me plenty about shooting, it simply wasn't my pastime of choice. That said, the rifle, a Ruger .223, was sleek and ultra-phallic. I tasted the linseed and Three-In-One oils on it, whiffed the powder tang from the barrel. The stock fit my shoulder, snug. Deer gun, a woman's gun.

I shot two males, but made him do the skinning.

* * *

It got dark and we knocked off for dinner at that seedy tavern of our initial fateful rendezvous. I compounded my daily quota of moral transgressions by chomping a steak and powering a couple of beers on his tab. Although, much as it pained me to acknowledge, blasting coyotes hadn't been bad.

In fact, I'd rather enjoyed it, tried to convince myself coyote murder was therapy, if not law of the jungle justice. Doing unto predators who surely did unto the weak and the wounded, and kittens. I am human, thus a justifier of irreconcilable behavior. Therapy, right.

Therapy shouldn't get the pulse pumping, no. Lining up the trotting coyote in the scope, waiting for the precise instant, then half an exhale, squeezing the trigger, and watching the animal kick over, its slyness no bulletproof shield. Goddess of death, that's me. We aren't so far removed from the primitive iterations of our species that slurped blood from the jugular. Like dirty, sleazy sex with a complete stranger, I'd probably hate myself later. As long as my pet cowboy plied me with drinks and physical comfort, that eventuality could be held at bay. I could drown myself in his bad influence and not worry about the bill that was surely coming due.

The waitress, a double dee bimbo, hung on him as floozies will do, called him Steffy and batted her fake lashes to put out a fire. I wondered if he'd fucked her, thought probably, definitely. He went to the men's room and I caught her in passing, asked how they knew each other, sizing up the competition, I told myself. Flexing the claws, that was it. She gave me a dead cow stare and said she didn't know my boyfriend, slung him drinks and that didn't mean shit from Shinola, and kept trucking. Busy woman. Bumpkins at every table and bellied to the bar, even on a Sunday night. Her whore purse would be stuffed with folding green by last call and the long walk in the dark to her Pinto at the employee end of the lot.

Hoyle returned with more beer. Sauntered back to the table with more beer, to be accurate. Bar lights backlighted him Travolta style. Best looking dude in the joint that night, maybe every night. His totem animal was something savage and furtive, it watched me from beneath heavy lids.

Expansive with alcohol, I said, "It occurs to me that this dog mutilation spree could be the work of a coyote hunter. Or any kind of hunter."

"What spree?" Hoyle sipped Pabst. His lips were thin and secretive. His lips and his teeth also belonged to the animal.

"The thing. The thing. Ninety dogs, minus heads and paws. A satanic cult or a thrill kill club, according to the yokels. The sensation sweeping the nation."

"Yeah, that. I don't really like dogs very much. Haven't paid attention to the gossip. On your mind, huh?"

"*I* like dogs. A lot."

"Coyotes get no love?"

"Humans have a pact with dogs. You don't break a pact."

"Not particular to them. Not really."

"Humans or dogs?"

"Dogs. Animals. They're filthy."

"It's an unattractive quality in a man."

He smiled, slow and easy. Occurred to me that I wasn't expansive, I was drunk.

"You think I'm stupid. The way you speak to me." He didn't sound mad.

"Shallow. I think you're shallow." The double dee bimbo with her Daisy Dukes and red pumps, the fact he'd had her every which way, provoked my mean streak.

He studied his fingernails. Took a long pull on his brew, wiped his mouth. When he looked at me I saw myself, a pale blur, Casper the Friendly Ghost's sarcastic little sister. "Did you hear they're building a telescope in Hawaii that's more powerful than anything ever invented?"

"Why, no, Steff. I did not." *Steffy* is what nearly escaped.

"Know what they're going to look at with that super-duper telescope?"

"The mother of all telescopes? Let me guess…The stars?"

"The beginning."

"The beginning of what?"

"Of everything."

* * *

He poured cheaper than Cuervo tequila all over my skin and lapped it up. No lights, no radio serenade, his breath hot in the hollow of my throat, kissed bruises on my arms, my inner thighs. After, the trailer became cold as a grave and an inkling of the consequences began to sink into my thick skull. Stars blinked through the window slot. Coyotes sang of death and vengeance on the prairie.

Hoyle rolled onto his side. His breathing steadied. I thought he'd fallen asleep when he said in a slurred voice, "It doesn't follow that a coyote hunter is going after dogs. Not a real coyote hunter, I mean." His lighter *snicked* and soon came a slow roll of smoke. That cigarette was almost gone before he finished his thought. "The coyotes are business. This other thing. It's pleasure."

My nakedness became quite acute.

He laid his rough hand on my belly and said, "Considering what you've seen, what you've been through. Maybe you should leave this alone."

The trailer settled. Out there, a breeze moaned and wind chimes clinked to accompany the coyote chorus. All those dead stars shone on.

"This has been waiting for me," I said to him while he snored.

* * *

Monday was riding-a-tractor-in-the-back-forty-of-some-hayseed's-ranch-day and Hoyle departed before sunrise. I slept in until the heat made an oven of the Airstream. Glass of warm water from the tap in hand, I explored the property, ducking under withered gray clotheslines, and forging through stunted shrubs, stumps, and earth mounds that disgorged ant convoys that streamed black in the sand. Little biting fuckers were everywhere underfoot. Tried to avoid crushing too many, but you know. That ubiquitous breeze whispered in the grass, fluted through soda bottles arranged as dingy candelabrums made of sticks, rattled the chimes and mussed my hair. The wind chimes were clumped in the petrified grasp of bushes and scrub trees, dozens of them. Metal tinged and pinged and it was almost there for me. Almost. The puzzle squirmed and refused to crystallize.

I got that sense of unfriendly scrutiny, of being the object of a malevolent desire, how the coyote must feel as crosshairs zero in right before its brains are blasted out the other side, yet different, this was all around me, and I ditched the glass and beat it for the trailer, ran no different than the panicked heroine in a horror flick with a chainsaw gunning maniac on her heels. Locked the door and had a breather, fists clenched, heart in spasms, gulping for air. No safer inside, though, I knew that.

Nothing happened and I calmed down, tried the television, got no picture, tried the radio, a scratchy gospel station only, and for a long stretch I sat in a lawn chair, knife balanced on my knee, while dust motes swirled and sweat poured into my socks. I put the knife away and eyed the clutter. Laundry, boxes upon boxes of magazines and Christmas lights and photograph albums, yellow receipts, camping gear, miscellanea.

Better believe I took the opportunity to ransack the place. It didn't amount to anything.

* * *

There wasn't a discussion regarding how long I'd stay or what it meant. Hoyle drove into the dark heart of each dawn. I'd smoke my first cigarette while his taillights dwindled. Evenings he'd straggle in from the red haze, caked in range dirt, pockets full of hay and gravel, shower and wolf his supper, down a six pack, collapse, roll onto me to fuck me somewhere along the line. My contribution was to shovel the long neglected barbeque pit and throw on hamburgers to chase all that beer, and to get fucked. Could have been worse duty and it got me where I wanted to go, or at least it got me closer and closer.

Other nights we hit the tavern.

Weeknights it was just us chickens in a suddenly cavernous hall. *Everybody off hunting Grendel*, I said, curious if he'd get it. With him it was impossible to tell. He was a cold one, my Steffy Hoyle, sharper than he appeared, possibly. No stray emotions. He didn't raise his voice or get overly excited, not even during sex, except I woke from a nightmare of strangulation to hollering and war whooping, the strident whine of an engine, stared out the window and he had that Kawasaki hell bent for leather, headlight drilling a hole into the perfect darkness. Dead drunk, naked but for hat and boots, he shrieked in atavistic joy as he slalomed through the minefield of stumps and gopher holes in the field, revving that bike for crazy as a motherfucker jumps over fallen logs and grassy berms. Crashed it in the yard while cutting donuts. Laid the machine over and it flew fifty or sixty feet, smoked and died. Took some skin off his shins and palms, the bloody mess not quite as bad as it looked. I cleaned him up, picked gravel and bits of grass from the wounds. He didn't flinch, sat stinking of alcohol, legs akimbo, eyes wild, then dull and duller, sank into a stupor, then fell asleep and in the morning it hadn't happened. But it did happen, and several other times, although he managed not to wreck the bike so badly that he needed medical attention. Matter of time. Man with a death wish usually gets what he wants.

Once, we cruised over to his friend Lonnie's house, a shotgun shack not far from the county landfill. Lonnie was a biker, or a biker wannabe, kept a massive Harley in a makeshift carport under a canvas tarp because he didn't have a garage. Guy was brawny and hairy, wore tinted aviator glasses indoors and out. Smelled of hair gel and musk. His fingernails were blacked from getting mashed. Tats and a death metal T shirt. *Death to Tyrants, Death to Infidels, Death to Everybody.* Chained a pair of scarred and muscular pit bulls to the bumper of a truck on blocks. Grizzled brutes with jaws wide enough to crush my head. Sweet as puppies, not a mean bone in them. He didn't appear overly fond of the dogs and they were indifferent to him. Dogs were real friendly toward me, though. Slobbery kisses and paws to the jaw rough housing and such. I played with them while the boys chatted about riding choppers and hunting and guns. Lonnie also moonlighted as a coyote culler. Birds of a feather, right?

On the ride home I asked if Lonnie fought the dogs, tried to make it sound casual. Hoyle didn't answer. He pressed on the accelerator and drifted into the oncoming lane as we rounded a bend. Needle pegged at eighty. Almost went head to head with a good old boy on a road grader with the blade up. Got to give it to Hoyle — he tapped the brakes and swung us past with inches to spare and his free hand never stopped stroking my leg.

During the second week I dragged a ten-speed from under the trailer where it rusted among abandoned tire rims and sheets of tin siding. A bit of chain oil and wrench work, I got the bicycle fixed right up and I pedaled my ass into town. Hadn't ridden a bike since high school and the six-mile slog nearly precipitated a coronary conclusion. Instant blisters, instant sunburn, steam rose from me in a trailing shadow. I staggered inside the mom and pop on Main Street and drank two quarts of lime Gatorade while Methuselah the Clerk observed my antics with gap-toothed bemusement. Goddamned Gatorade made a snowball in my gut that wanted to ricochet right back out, but I held on, held it down. I hung tough and paid the clerk, smiled sweetly as if my lobster sunburn and chattering teeth weren't nothing but a thing.

I composed myself and moseyed around town for the rest of the afternoon. Youngish female and not terribly unattractive, nobody mistook me for a pervert or a weirdo as they would've if I'd been some bearded, sunbaked dude lurching in off the prairie. People skills, I had them, and most folks were willing to shoot the shit with me as they watered lawns, or washed cars, or slumped in the shade of their porches. I wore my shades and gave everybody a different story, all of them pure baloney. Nobody knew Hoyle, although stoner skateboard kids loitering in the mom and pop parking lot had seen him around, and I'm confident the pancake makeup tarts at the realtor and plumbing supply offices would've gotten misty-eyed at his mention.

A wasted Vietnam vet parked in a wheelchair at the entrance to the Diamond Dee Gentleman's Club panhandling for change knew Lonnie; of course he fought his dogs, Leroy and Gunther, tons of locals did. Pit fighting was real popular. The veteran owned a collie mix with the softest, saddest brown eyes I ever did see and he covered the dog's ears when he leaned close to confide that the hardcore crowd used house pets and strays as bait for the killer breeds. The bait thing notwithstanding, fighting dogs in gladiatorial exhibitions was innocent, really! Death was rare, usually an ear or an eye got removed at the worst, a lot of yip and yelp signifying nothing, so to speak. The other stuff going down? The dogs piled into sacrificial mounds off route 80, or buried alive in burlap bags down to Stabinham Creek? Now, *that* was insane. Whoever was scragging dogs wholesale was a psycho sonofabitch from the darkest pit of hell and woe unto the sap he eventually turned his knife and arrows against, because sure as horses made little green apples it would come to human butchery. See if it didn't. That assessment seemed to be the consensus and a page three story in the paper confirmed law enforcement, including the FBI, agreed. Whether the feds planned to make it a priority was another matter.

Damned if I knew what I hoped to learn from this shotgun approach to detective work. Definitely I was bored out of my skull, lurking at Hoyle's trailer. Definitely recent life events had activated a recessive sleuthing gene.

I pedaled home. Redness pooled on the horizon.

* * *

In a disappointing development, Hoyle and I didn't screw for four nights running. He poured liquor down his throat and fell into a slumber that was as unto death itself. Did not even snore, did not so much as twitch. I began to wonder what was in it for me because my days in that backwater town weren't proving out in any way, shape, or form. I dreamed of old loves lost to shipwreck and mayhem, and I dreamed of dogs I'd known, all of them gone back into the dirt. Dad waved to me from a distance where he stood amid knee-high grass, a warning in his grim smile, the white skull of a cow he raised in his left hand. He'd seldom tried to tell me anything requiring words when I was a hellion child and he didn't now. A golden darkness radiated from him and pushed me into the territory that lies a breath or two on the other side of waking. Erotic nightmares followed. These involved Hoyle, although his face was obscured by the shadow of his hat. After he'd gotten his rocks off he'd shove me from the moving truck, or leap from it himself, leave me to tumble down a cliff, be consumed in fire. Or I'd emerge unscathed and a piece of the underbrush would detach and come after me, a bear covered in leaves, bits of a shredded net, reared on its hind legs and full of Satan's own desire to fuck me or devour me, one then the other.

I'd emerge into consciousness, aroused and afraid.

With the frustration of one type of lust, the wandering kind crept into my thoughts, had me eyeing the straight shot to the distant highway, phantom engines rumbling, phantom exhaust on my lips, headlights branding an SOS into my frontal lobes. Except, Sunday came around before I got resolved and it was coyote sniping time again.

Hoyle pushed coffee at me, said he hadn't toured this particular zone in several months, then we were in the rig and moving toward a seam of light above the mountains. We didn't talk, not that there was ever much chatter, but this was two-cactuses-on-a-date quiet. The drive was longer than I expected. The road went on and on, degraded from blacktop to gravel, to dirt, to scabbed tracts of bare earth in a sea of bleached grass. Plains spread around us, larger and deeper than the sky. Spectral and wan, gradually acquiring substance like film in an acid bath. Landmarks I'd learned recently were absent or in the wrong direction.

He stopped the truck and shut it off. Reached into a duffel bag and presented me with a rabbit facsimile. Plush and brown, wired to emote vulnerability at various decibels. My task was to pace one hundred steps upwind and set the decoy in play. Once I trotted back we'd find a likely spot with a clear line of fire and settle ourselves to wait. He pecked my forehead by way of dismissal and began to scribble in his culling book. I was tempted to argue, to sneer and inform him he wasn't the bwana of me. Wasn't worth the hassle. I had a hunch I'd get on the highway east any day now, leave this shit-kicker paradise in the rearview. Thus and so.

I trudged into the prairie, sullenly counting paces, each step precisely, more or less, one yard as my Dad the Marine had taught his kiddies. Made the football field-long hike and set the robot rabbit on a log in a patch of sand and weeds. I turned and saw the truck, grill blazing with reflected sunlight, and no sign of Hoyle.

As I approached, I fully expected him to step from behind the opposite side of the cab, shaking the morning dew off his pecker, but he didn't. It became apparent he wasn't crouched in hiding and I came over and tried the doors. Locked tight, no keys in the ignition, no duffle bag with food and water. His rifle was missing from the rack. I shaded my eyes and turned a full circle, scanning for his outline against the blankness. I shouted his name, and in the middle of all this I glanced at the bed of the truck and realized the Varmint Suit wasn't there either. The spit in my mouth dried.

Oh, what goes through a woman's mind at a moment like that.

Instinct kicked in and I went from a standstill to a sprint, six maybe seven strides in a random direction, and did a Supergirl dive. Scratched, bruised, winded, I didn't feel a thing except my heart trying to climb out of my mouth. Those newsreels about trench fighting in World War I, G.I.'s belly-down kissing the dirt as they wriggled under barbed wire? That was me navigating a shallow depression away from the track.

I wormed along until my arms failed. I rolled over and lay still, half covered in swaying grass. Clouds inched past my face. Horses, a hound, Dumbo's lopsided head. A pair of hawks drifted along crosscurrents, wheeling and wheeling. Gnats bit me and I didn't care, my being was consumed with listening for the crunch of footsteps, although I imagined if he spotted me I would hear exactly what the doomed coyote did in its last split second on earth.

A wail rose and fell somewhere to the left. A trilling *eee-ee-eeee* that made my flesh prickle, made me bite my tongue lest I cry a response.

The robot rabbit's sobs described an arc that moved closer, then farther from my hiding place. I considered crawling some more once my arms revived. Too afraid to move, I pissed myself instead, counted down the seconds until the end came brutal as a tomahawk blow to my noggin. Had time to think back on a wasted youth, a life of misdeeds. I contemplated my possibly fatal morbid fascination with things better left alone. Sure, I was furious with myself. Two weeks playing chicken with dark forces, yet never truly admitting I was in over my head. I'd known, always known. The colossal scope of my pride and selfishness bore down to smother me as I bit hard on the flesh of my arm and tried to keep it together, tried not to whine like prey.

The sky grew dim, then dark. Lightning tore the blackness and thunder cracked a beat or two afterward. The cavewoman running the show in my brain, the primordial bitch dispensing adrenaline and endorphins, knew what I'd listened to throughout the day hadn't been any mechanical rabbit and that almost undid me, almost got the waterworks going.

I sucked it up and stood. Every muscle in me complained and for a few seconds I couldn't bring myself to actually breathe. What Dad and his hunting buddies told me back in the Alaska days was if I felt the bullet, it'd be like a heavy punch. A few seconds of that and it became apparent I wasn't going to be smote from afar.

The truck was gone, probably had been for hours. It began to rain.

* * *

Sonofabitch had my purse and knapsack with the spare clothes, the handful of knick-knacks and keepsakes I brought with me when I split from AK. All that shit was in a burn barrel by then, and no, I didn't equivocate or second guess myself, didn't say, *Jess maybe this is a misunderstanding, maybe life has made you a wee bit paranoid. Maybe there's a logical explanation.* I was indeed a wee bit paranoid. Thank the gods.

Saving grace was I'd dressed sensibly for the trip. I had my wallet, a pack of Camel No. Nines, and a lighter. I veered due east, walked until lights from a farmhouse appeared, kept going and the clouds rolled back and stars shined upon me. Dawn came and I crossed a rancid stream. Dunked my head underwater, drank until I was fit to puke and rambled on, came to a two lane road I hadn't seen before and followed it back to the highway. Getting dark again. Cleaned up in a gas station john, then walked into a no tell motel one block down and rented a single. Room service pizza and two scalding showers, no booze, but that was fine. Cigarette burns in the carpet, broken box springs, and an ammonia reek was all fine too.

Comatose for eighteen hours with the TV and air-conditioner humming white noise, a chair propped under the doorknob, Mr. Ka-Bar cool against my cheek. Dreamless sleep, except in those moments before I came fully online again and a misshapen shadow lunged, made a hissing, shushing sound as it trampled the grass. I stabbed it with my knife and poof. The fact I'd doubtless be haunted by that goddamned Varmint Suit until my dying day filled me with the white hot rage men are always being warned about. Could be that's what changed my plans from flight to payback. An old high school enemy called me VH1. Vindictive Hoochie Number One, and she wasn't wrong.

Hopped a ride to the next town with a salesman going to Seattle for a conference. He politely declined to mention the gouges on my face and arms, left me at the off ramp and went his way. Thinking to hell with hitching, I haggled with a kid over the hatchback gathering rust in front of his house. The engine had a million miles on it and sounded iffy and the tires were screwed to hell. Good thing that jalopy only had to get me down the road a state or two. Better would come along. I paid three hundred cash and put a lie on the receipt. Kid was so stoned I doubt he even knew I was a woman, much less be able to ID me if it came to such a pass.

As for where I got the dough, listen. Just because I enjoyed pilfering stores for sundries didn't mean I was destitute. *People Magazine* once gave me sixty grand for an interview they pared to three and half sentences and a muddy headshot. I socked that shit away.

I bought basic camping gear at a sporting goods store and spent four nights on the grounds of a state park, four more along a big river where it didn't feel as if anybody would notice. On the ninth day I parked in a gravel pit a half mile from Hoyle's trailer, sneaked closer for recon. He wasn't around. I proceeded with caution, stealthy as any woodland critter, and let myself in. Forty-five minutes on the property was forty more than necessary. Did what needed doing and got the hell out and drove to another motel, a nicer setup, and treated myself to an evening on a soft bed and half a bottle of red wine.

Swung back to check on him late the next afternoon. Hoyle's truck sat in the yard. I glassed the property with a pair of binoculars, gave it an hour before moving in. My ex-lover lay behind the trailer, sprawled face down, stark staring naked except for his boots. Nearby, his bike was a crumpled mess of spokes and leaking fluids. The results were certainly more spectacular than I'd hoped for while sawing through the brake lines.

I poked him with a stick, unsure whether he was dead or playing possum. Neither, as it developed. Rolled him over and he smiled at me, teeth stained with grass and dirt. His arms worked, but that was it. I didn't see any marks beyond some bumps and abrasions. Whatever was wrong with him, I bet he'd be fine with proper medical attention.

"Hi, darling," he said. "You had me worried, runnin' off like that."

I squatted and hooked under his armpits and lifted, began to shuffle backward. His legs bumped along lifelessly. Went a few steps, rested, and repeated. I dragged him into the nearer of the two corrals and propped him in a seated position, his spine braced by a post. He didn't say anything the whole time except to ask for his Stetson because the sun was powerful warm on his neck. I fetched the hat and gave it to him. An ant climbed atop the toe of my boot, another clung to my pants cuff. I bent and brushed them aside, moved my feet to discourage the rest. Hoyle stared at the looming mound, its teeming inhabitants. The breeze stirred.

"Why?" he said, as if genuinely curious.

I strode to a dead dogwood and tore free the chimes strung in its branches, flung the mess at Hoyle. He snatched it midflight, glanced at the handful of dog tags —rabies vaccinations and ID platelets — and nodded. Dozens upon dozens more clinked in their constellations on bushes, posts, clothes lines, woven into the trailer vents, every fucking where. I let him think about it while I used a branch to cover my tracks, the grooves where I'd towed him.

"Don't you think the cops will put it together? They'll catch you, Jess."

"I hear Sheriff Brunner is a dumbass," I said.

"Yeah. It's true enough."

Daylight was burning and restlessness overcame me. I gave the old boy a sip from my water bottle and tried to think of the proper words, settled for a goodbye kiss, quick and dry. We didn't say anything for the longest time and eventually I turned and walked away.

I looked over my shoulder as I crested a rise that led to the road. Hoyle reached forward and passed the Stetson over his legs, back and forth.

* * *

On the way through town to wherever, I stopped bold as brass at Lonnie's house. There was a bad moment where I worried Gunther and Leroy might've forgotten, had visions of getting rent limb from limb as I knelt to unleash them from the bumper of the truck. Not a chance. And when I popped the hatch, those bruisers piled into the back like they'd always belonged there.

We hit the highway eastbound, ascended into the hills and then the mountains. Kept right on going, flying.

The car eventually crapped out in Idaho. I spent a time with a reverend and his family on what had been a potato farm until the latter '70s. God works in mysterious ways, so said the right reverend. He'd lost a pair of mastiffs to old age and cancer respectively. His kids fell in love with Leroy and Gunther. I left the dogs in their care when I slipped away one night by the dark of the moon. Headed east across the fallow fields with a knife, backpack, and a pocket Bible I lifted from the reverend's shelf. I'd hollowed out that good book. It's where I stashed my possibles.

Camped in the lee of an abandoned barn, I rolled over onto a black widow. Little bitch stabbed the living shit out of me. Sorry, so very sorry that I crushed her in my thrashing. Spent two days curled tight, my guts clenched into a slimy ball. In my delirium I chewed dirt and fantasized about being skinned alive. Laid my bottom dollar on dying out there in that lonely field.

I didn't die. Nah, I did what I always do. I got over it.

Termination Dust

Let be be finale of seem.
                    --Wallace Stevens

Hunting in Alaska, especially as one who enjoys the intimacy of knives, bludgeons, and cords, is fraught with peril. Politically speaking, the difference between a conservative and a liberal in the forty-ninth state is the caliber of handgun one carries. Despite a couple of close calls, you've not been shot. Never been shot, never been caught, knock on wood.

That's what you used to say, in any event.

People look at you every day. People look at you every day, but they don't see you. People will ask why and you will reply, Why not?

*   *   *

Tyson Langtree's last words: "I tell you, man. Andy Kaufman is alive, man. He's alive, bigger than shit, and cuttin' throats. He's Elvis, man. He's the king of death." This was overheard at the packed Caribou Creek Tavern on a Friday night about thirty seconds before bartender Lonnie DeForrest tossed his sorry ass out onto a snowbank. Eighteen below zero Fahrenheit and a two and a half mile walk home. Dead drunk, wearing coveralls and a Miners Do It Deeper ball cap.

Nobody's seen the old boy since. Deputy Newcastle found a lot of blood in Langtree's bed, though. Splattered on the walls and ceiling of his shack on

Midnight Road. Hell of a lot of blood. That much blood and no corpse, well, you got to wonder, right? Got to wonder why Langtree didn't keep his mouth shut. Everybody knows Andy Kaufman is crazy as a motherfucker. He been whacking motormouth fools since '84.

You were in the bar that night and you followed Langtree back to his humble abode. Man, he was surprised to see you step from the shadows.

For the record, his last words were actually, "Please don't kill me, E!"

* * *

Jessica Mace lies in darkness, slightly drunk, wholly frustrated. Heavy bass thuds through the ceiling from Snodgrass' party. She'd left early and in a huff after locking horns with Julie Vellum, her honorable enemy since the hazy days of high school. Is hate too strong an emotion to describe how she feels about Julie? Nope, hatred seems quite perfect, although she's long since forgotten initial *casus belli* of their eternal war. Vellum — what kind of name is that, anyhow? It describes either ancient paper or a sheepskin condom. The bitch is ridiculous. Mobile home trash, bottom drawer sorority sister, tits sliding toward earth with a vengeful quickness. Easiest lay of the Last Frontier. A whore in name and deed.

JV called *her* a whore and splashed a glass of beer on her dress. Cliché, bitch, so very cliché. Obviously JV hadn't gotten the memo that Jessica and Nate were through as of an hour prior to the party. The evil slut had carried a torch for him since he cruised into town with his James Dean too-cool-for school shtick and set all the girlies' hearts aflutter a few weeks before Katrina leveled New Orleans a continent away.

Snodgrass, Wannamaker, and Ophelia, the beehive-hairdo lady from 510, jumped between them before the fur could fly. Snodgrass was an old hand at breaking up fistfights. Lucky for Julie, too. Jessica made up her mind to fix that girl's wagon once and for all, had broken a champagne glass for an impromptu weapon when Snodgrass locked her in a bear hug. Meanwhile, Deputy Newcastle stood near the wet bar, grimly shaking his huge blond head. Or it might've been the deputy's evil twin, Elam. Hard to tell through the crush of the crowd, the smoke, and the din. If she'd seen him with his pants down, she'd have known with certainty.

Here she is after the fracas, sulking while the rest of town let down its hair and would continue to do so deep into the night. Gusts from the blizzard shake the building. Power comes from an emergency generator in the basement. However, cable is on the fritz. She would have another go at Nate, but Nate isn't around, he is gone-Johnson after she'd told him to hit the bricks and never come back no more, no more. Hasty words uttered in fury, a carbon copy of her own sweet ma who (before her ultimate vanishing act) ran through half the contractors and fishermen in the southeast during a thirty-year career of bar fights and flights from the law. Elizabeth Taylor of the Tundra, was Ma, though everybody called her Lucius. Nate, an even poorer man's Richard Burton. Her father, Esteban Montgomery Mace, the man who put up with his wife's humiliating exploits? Dad (like poor Jack and many Alaskan fishermen) died at sea and Jessica thought of him nevermore.

Why hadn't Nate been at the party? He *always* made an appearance. Could it be she's really and truly broken his icy heart? Good!

She fumbles in the bedside drawer, pushing aside the cell charger, Jack's photograph, the revolver her brother Elwood gave her before he got shredded by a claymore mine in Afghanistan, and locates the "personal massager" she ordered from Fredericks of Hollywood and has a go with that instead. Stalwart comrade, loyal stand-in when she's between boyfriends and lovers, Buzz hasn't let her down yet.

Jessica opens her eyes as the mattress sags. A shadow enters her blurry vision. She smells cologne or perfume or hairspray, very subtle and totally androgynous. Almost familiar. Breathless from the climax, it takes her a moment to collect her wits.

She says, "Jack, is that you?" Which was a strange conclusion, since Jack presumably drifts along deep sea currents, his rugged redneck frame reduced to bones and sweet melancholy memories. All hands of the *Prince Valiant* lost to Davey Jones's Locker, wasn't it? That makes three out of the four main men of her life dead. Only Nate is still kicking. Does he count now that she's banished him to a purgatory absent her affection?

Fingers clamp her mouth and ram her head into the pillow hard enough that stars shoot everywhere. Her mind flashes to a vivid image: Gothic oil paintings of demons perched atop the bosoms of swooning women. So morbidly beautiful, those antique pictures. She thinks of the pistol in the dresser that she might've grabbed instead of the vibrator. Too late baby, too late now.

A knife glints as it arcs downward. Her attacker is dressed in black so the weapon appears to levitate under its own motive force. The figure slashes her throat with vicious inelegance. An untutored butcher. It is cold and she tastes the metal. But it doesn't hurt.

* * *

Problem is, constant reader, you can't believe a damned word of this story. The killer could be anyone. Cops recovered some bodies reduced to charcoal briquettes. Two of those charred corpses were never properly identified, and what with all the folks who went missing prior to the Christmas party…

My life flashed before my eyes as I died of a slashed throat and a dozen other terrible injuries. My life, the life of countless others who were in proximity. Wasn't pretty, wasn't neat or orderly, or linear. I experienced the fugue as an exploding kaleidoscope of imagery. Those images replay at different velocities, over and over in a film spliced together out of sequence. My hell is to watch a bad horror movie until the stars burn out.

I get the gist of the plot, but the nuances escape into the vacuum. The upshot being that I know hella lot about my friends and neighbors; although, not everything. Many of the juiciest details elude me as I wander purgatory, reliving a life of sin. Semi-omniscience is a drag.

In recent years, some pundits have theorized *I* was the Eagle Talon Ripper. Others have raised the possibility it was Jackson Bane, that he'd been spotted in San Francisco months after the *Prince Valiant* went down, that he'd been overheard plotting bloody revenge against me, Jessica, a dozen others. Laughable, isn't it? The majority of retired FBI profilers agree.

No matter, I'm the hot pick these days. Experts say the trauma I underwent in Moose Valley twisted my mind. Getting shot in the head did something to my brain. Gave me a lobotomy of sorts. Except instead of going passive, I turned into a monster, waited twenty-plus years, and went on a killing spree.

It's a sexy theory what with the destroyed and missing bodies, mine included. The killer could've been a man or woman, but the authorities bet on a man. Simple probability and the fact some of the murders required a great deal of physical strength and a working knowledge of knots and knives. I fit the bill on all counts. There's also the matter of my journal. Fragments of it were pieced together by a forensics team and the shit in there could be misconstrued. What nobody knows is that after the earlier event in Moose Valley, I read a few psychology textbooks. The journal was therapy, not some veiled admission of guilt. Unfortunately, I was also self-medicating with booze and that muddied the waters even more.

Oh, well. What the hell am I going to do about it now?

If you ask me, Final Girl herownself massacred all those people. What's my proof? Nothing except instinct. Call me a cynic — it doesn't seem plausible a person can survive a gashed throat and still possess the presence to retrieve a pistol, in the dark, no less, and plug the alleged killer to save the day. How convenient that she couldn't testify to the killer's identity on account of the poor lighting. Even more convenient how that fire erased all the evidence. In the end, it's her word, her version of events.

Yeah, it's a regular cluster. Take the wrong peg from this creaky narrative and the whole log pile falls on you. Anyway you know. You know.

What if…What if they were in it together?

* * *

Nights grow long in the tooth. A light veil of snow descends the peaks. Termination dust, the sourdoughs call it. You wait and watch for signs. Geese fly backwards in honking droves, south. Sunsets flare crimson, then fade to black as fog rolls over the beach. People leave the village and do not return. A few others never left but are gone all the same. They won't be returning either.

The last of the cruise ships migrated from Eagle Talon on Saturday. The Princess Wing blared klaxons and horns and sloshed up the channel in a shower of streamers and confetti, its running lights blazing holes through the mist. A few hardy passengers in red and yellow slickers braved the drizzle to perch along the rails. Some waved to the dockworkers. Others cheered over the rumble of the diesels. Seagulls bobbed aloft, dark scraps and tatters against the low clouds that always curtain this place.

You mingled with the people on the dock and smiled at the birds, enjoying their faint screams. Only animals seem to recognize what you are. You hate them too. That's why you smile, really. Hate keeps you warm come the freeze.

Ice will soon clog the harbor. Jagged mountains encircle the village on three sides in a slack-jawed Ouroboros. The other route out of town is a two-mile tunnel that opens onto the Seward Highway. This tunnel is known as the Throat. Anchorage lies eighty miles north, as the gull flies. Might as well be the moon when winter storms come crashing in on you. Long-range forecasts call for heavy snow and lots of wind. There will come a day when all roads and ways shall be impassable.

You've watched. You've waited. Salivated.

You'll retreat into the Estate with the sheep. It's a dirty white concrete superstructure plonked down in the shadow of a glacier. Bailey Frazier & Sons built the Frazier Estate Apartments in 1952 along with the Frazier Tower that same year. History books claim these were the largest buildings in Alaska for nearly three decades, and outside of the post office, cop shop, library, little red schoolhouse, the Caribou Tavern, and a few warehouses, that's it for the village proper. Both were heavily damaged by the '64 quake and subsequent tsunami. Thirteen villagers were swept away on the wave. Four more got crushed in falling debris. The Tower stands empty and ruined to this day, but the Estate is mostly functional; a secure, if decrepit, bulwark against the wilderness.

You are an earthquake, a tidal wave, a mountain of collapsing stone, waiting to happen. You are the implacable wilderness personified. What is in you is ancient as the black tar between stars. A void that howls in hunger and mindless antipathy against the heat of the living.

Meanwhile, this winter will be business as usual. Snowbirds flee south to California and Florida while the hardcore few hunker in dim apartments like animals in burrows and play cribbage or video games, or gnaw yourselves bloody with regret. You'll read, and drink, and fuck. Emmitt Snodgrass will throw his annual winter gala. More drinking and even more fucking, but with the sanction of costume and that soul-warping hash Bobby Aickman passes around. By spring, the survivors will emerge, pale as moles, voracious for light as you are for the dark.

With the official close of tourist season, Eagle Talon population stands at one hundred and eighty-nine full-time residents. Three may be subtracted from that number, subtracted from the face of the earth, in fact, although nobody besides the unlucky trio and you know anything about that.

Dolly Sammerdyke. Regis and Thora Lugar. And the Lugars' cat, Frenchy. The cat died hardest of them all. Nearly took out your eye. Maybe that will come back to haunt you. The devil's in the...

* * *

Elam Newcastle is interviewed by the FBI at Providence Hospital. He has survived the Frazier Estate inferno with second degree burns and frostbite of his left hand. Two fingers may have to be amputated and the flesh of his neck and back possess the texture of melted wax. In total, a small price to pay considering the hell-on-Earth-scenario he's escaped. His New Year's vow is to find a better trade than digging ditches.

He tells the suit what he knows as the King of Pop hovers in the background, partially hidden by curtains and shadows. This phantom, or figment, has shown up regularly since the evening of the massacre at the Estate. Elam is not a fan and doesn't understand why he's having this hallucination of the singer grinning and gesticulating with that infamous rhinestone-studded glove. It is rather disturbing. Doubly disturbing since it's impossible to attribute it to the codeine.

The investigator blandly reveals how the local authorities have recently found Elam's twin brother deceased in the Frazier Tower. It was, according to the account, a gruesome spectacle, even by police standards. The investigator describes the scene in brief, albeit vivid, detail.

Elam takes in this information, one eye on the moonwalking apparition behind the FBI agent. Finally, he says, "Whaddaya mean they stole his hat?"

* * *

Scenes from an apocalypse:

Viewed from the harbor, Eagle Talon is an inkblot with a steadily brightening dot of flame at its heart. The Frazier Estate Apartments have been set ablaze. Meanwhile, the worst blizzard to hit Alaska since 1947 rages on. Flames leap from the upper stories, whipped by the wind. Window glass shatters. Fire, smoke, and driving snow boil off into outer darkness. That faint keening is either the shrieks of the damned as they roast in the penthouse, or metal dissolving like Styrofoam as the inferno licks it to ash. Or both.

Men and women in capes and masks, gossamer wings and top hats, mill in the icy courtyard. Their shadows caper in the bloody glare. They are the congregants of a frigid circle of Hell, summoned to the Wendigo's altar. They join hands and begin to waltz. Flakes of snow and ash cover them, bury them.

The angry fire is snapping yellow. Pull farther out into the cold and the dark and fire becomes red through the filter of the blizzard, then shivers to black. Keep pulling back until there are no stars, no fire, no light of any kind. Only the snow sifting upward from the void to fill the world with silence and sleep.

* * *

We make love with the lights off. The last time, I figure. She calls me Jack when she comes and probably has no idea. Jackson Bane died on the Bering Sea two winters gone. His ghost makes itself known. He knocks stuff over to demonstrate he's unhappy, like when I'm fucking his former girlfriend. Not hard to imagine him raving impotently behind the wall of sleep, working himself toward a splendorous vengeance. Perhaps that makes him more of a revenant.

My name is Nathan Custer. I fear the sea. Summertime sees me guiding tours on the glacier for Emmitt Snodgrass. Winter, I lie low and collect unemployment. Cash most of those checks down at the Caribou. Laphroaig is my scotch of choice and it's a choice I make every livelong day, and twice a day once snow flies. Hell of an existence. I fought with Jack at Emmitt Snodgrass' annual winter party in '07. Blacked his eye and demolished a coffee table. Don't even recall what precipitated the brawl. I only recall Jessica in a white tee and cotton shorts standing there with a bottle of Lowenbrau in her hand. Snodgrass forgave me the mess. We never patched it up, Jack and I.

Too late, now. Baby, it's too late.

While Jessica showers, I prowl naked through her apartment, peering into cupboards and out the window at snowflakes reflected in a shaft of illumination pitched by the twin lamps over the lobby foyer. Ten feet beyond the Estate wall lies a slate of nothingness.

Depending on the direction, it's either sea ice and, eventually, open black water, or mountains. This is five-oh-something in the P.M., December. Sun has been down for half an hour.

"What are you doing?" Jessica, head wrapped in a towel, strikes a Venus pose in the bathroom doorway. The back-lighting lends her a halo. She's probably concerned about the butcher knife I pulled from the cutlery block. Wasn't quick enough to hide it behind my leg. Naked guy with a knife presents an environmental hazard even if you don't suspect him of being a homicidal maniac, which she might.

"Getting ready for the party," I say, disingenuous as ever.

"Yeah, you look ready." She folds her arms. She thinks I've been using again; it's in her posture. "What the hell, Nate?"

Unfortunately for everyone, I'm not an outwardly articulate man. I'm my father's son. Mom didn't hate his guts because he slapped her at the '88 Alaska State Fair; she hated him because he refused to argue. When the going got shouty, Dad was a walker-awayer. I realize, here in my incipient middle age, that his tendency to clam up under stress wasn't from disrespect. He simply lost his ability to address the women in his life coherently.

"Uh," is what I come up with. Instead of, *Baby, I heard a noise. Somebody was trying the door. Swear to God, I saw the knob jiggle.* I don't have the facility to ask her, *If I was jacked up, wouldn't you have noticed it while we were in bed?* More than anything, I want to tell her of my suspicions. Something is terribly wrong in our enclave. People are missing. Strange shadows are on the move and I have a feeling the end is near for some of us.

"Jesus. Cal's right. He's right. The bastard is right. My god."

"Cal's right? He's not right. What did he say?" Add Building Superintendent Calvin Wannamaker to my little black book of hate. I grip the knife harder, am conscious of my oversized knuckles and their immediate ache. Arthritis, that harbinger of old age and death, nips at me.

"Hit the road, Jack." She points the Finger of Doom, illustrating where I should go. Presumably Hell lies in that general direction.

Maybe I can bulldoze through this scene. "That makes twice you called me Jack today. We have to get ready for the party. Where the hell are my pants?" I look everywhere but directly into the sun that is her gaze.

"You've lost your damned mind," she says in a tone of wonderment, as if waking from a long, violent dream and seeing everything for how it really is. "You need to leave."

"The party. My pants."

"Find another pair. Goodbye. And put that back. It was a present. From Jack!" She's hollering now.

"Wait a second…Are you and Cal—"

"Shut your mouth and go."

I put the cleaver in the block, mightily struggling to conjure the magic words to reverse the course of this shipwreck. This isn't love, but it's the best thing I've had in recent memory. No dice. Naked guy hurled from the nest by his naked girlfriend. This is trailer park drama. Julie Vellum will cream over the details once the gossip train gets chugging. Maybe I'll throw a fuck into her. Ah, sweet revenge, hey? The prospect doesn't thrill me, for some reason. I walk into the hall and lurk there a while, completely at a loss. I press the buzzer twice. Give up when there's no answer, and start the long, shameful trudge to my apartment.

The corridors of the Estate are gloomy. Tan paneled walls and muddy recessed lights spaced far enough apart it feels like you're walking along the bottom of a lake. The effect is heightened due to the tears in my eyes. By the time I get to the elevator, I'm freezing. The super keeps this joint about three degrees above an ice-locker.

"Nate!" The whisper is muted and sexless. A shadow materializes from behind the wooden statue of McKinley Frazier that haunts this end of the fifth floor. It's particularly murky here because the overhead has been busted. A splinter of glass stabs my bare foot. I'm hopping around, trying to cover my balls and act naturally.

"Nate, hold still, pal." Still whispering. Whoever it is, they're wearing all black and they've got a hammer.

Oh, wait, I recognize this person. I'm convinced it's impossible that this could be happening to me for the second time in twenty years. This isn't even connected to the infamous Moose Valley slaughter. It's like winning top prize in a sweepstakes twice in one's lifetime. Why me, oh gods above and below? I'm such a likeable guy. Kurt Russell wishes he was as handsome as I am. So much to live for. Living looks to be all done for me.

The hammer catches the faint light. It gleams and levitates.

"What are you going to do with that?" I say. It's a rhetorical question.

* * *

Jessica Mace can't actually speak when the feds interview her. She's still eating through tubes. The knife missed severing her carotid by a millimeter. She scribbles responses to their interrogation on a portable whiteboard. Her rage is palpable, scarcely blunted by exhaustion and painkillers.

Ma'am, after this individual assaulted you in bed, what happened?

Came to. Choking on blood. Alive. Grabbed gun. Heard noises from living room. The killer had someone in a chair and was torturing them.

Who was in the chair?

Nate Custer.

Nathan Custer?

Yes.

Did you see the suspect's face?

No.

Approximately how tall was the suspect?

I don't know. Was dark. Was bleeding out. Confused.

Right. But you saw something. And you discharged your firearm.

Yes.

You're sure it was a him?

Him, her. The killer. My vision was blurry. A big, fuzzy shadow.

Are you admitting that you fired your weapon multiple times at…at a shadow?

NO! I shot a goddamned psycho five times. You're welcome.

How can you be certain, Ms. Mace?

Maybe I can't. Killer could've been anyone. Could *be* anyone. The doctor. The nurse. Maybe it was you. YOU look fucking suspicious.

* * *

Calvin Wannamaker and his major domo Hendricks are bellied up to the bar at the Caribou Tavern for their weekly confab. They've already downed several rounds.

DeForrest is polishing glasses and watching the new waitress's skirt cling in exactly the right places as she leans over table No. 9 to flirt with big Luke Tucker. Tucker is a longshoreman married to a cute young stay-at-home mom named Gladys. Morphine is playing "Thursday" on the jukebox while the village's resident Hell's Angel, Vince Diamond, shoots pool against himself. VD got paroled from Goose Bay Correctional Facility last month. He has spent nineteen of his forty-eight years in various prisons. His is the face of an axe murderer. His left cheek is marred by a savage gash, freshly scabbed. Claims he got the wound in a fight with his newest old lady. Deputy Newcastle has been over to their apartment three times to make peace.

The bar is otherwise unoccupied.

"Found a dead cat in the bin." Wannamaker lights a cigarette. A Winston. It's the brand he thinks best suits his Alaskan image. He prefers Kools, alas. "Neck was broke, eyes buggin' out. Gruesome." The super loves cats. He keeps three Persians in his suite on the first floor. He's short and thin and wears a round bushy beard and plaid sweaters, or if it's a special occasion, black turtlenecks. Hendricks started calling him "Cat Piss Man" behind his back and the name kind of stuck. Neither man was born in Alaska. Wannamaker comes from New York, Hendricks from Illinois. They've never adjusted to life on the frontier. They behave like uneasy foreigners in their own land.

"Oh, yeah?" Hendricks says with a patent couldn't-give-a-shit-less tone. No cat lover, Hendricks. *Don't like cats, love pussy,* he's been quoted time and again. He's taller than Wannamaker, and broad-shouldered. Legend says he worked for the Chicago Outfit before he got exiled to Alaska. Everyone considers him a goon and that's a fairly accurate assessment.

"Floyd found it, I guess is what I mean," Wannamaker says.

Floyd is the chief custodian and handyman for the Estate. He was also a train-hopping hobo for three decades prior to landing the Estate gig.

"The hell was Floyd doing in the bin?"

"Makin' a nest. Divin' for pearls. I dunno. He found a dead cat is all I know. Thinks it belonged to the Lugars. They split ten days ago. Must a been in a rush, cause they locked their doors and dropped the keys in my box without so much as a by your leave. Earlier and earlier every year, you know that? I don't get why they even make the trip anymore. I get three or four calls a day, people looking for an apartment. At least."

Hendricks sips his beer. He doesn't say anything. He too is checking out the posterior of Tammy, the new girl.

"Yeah, exactly." Wannamaker nods wisely in response to some ghost of a comment. "I hate snowbirds. Hate. Too cheap to pack their old cat and ship him to Florida. What's Lugar do? Snaps the poor critter's neck and dumps him in the garbage. Bah. Tell you what I'm gonna do, I'm gonna file a report with Newcastle. Sic the ever lovin' law on that sick jerk. Shouldn't have a cat. If he didn't own his apartment I'd yank his lease faster than you can spit."

Hendricks pushes his bottle aside. "That's a weird story."

"Lugar's a weird dude. He sells inflatable dolls and whatcha call 'em, body pillows."

"Is that what he does?"

"Oh, yeah, man. He flies to Japan every so often and wines and dines a bunch of CEOs in Tokyo. They're nuts for that stuff over there."

"Huh. I figured he'd be retired. Guy's gotta be pushing seventy."

"I guess when you love what you do it ain't work."

Words to live by.

* * *

Last words of Mark Ferro, aged thirty-three as he is executed by lethal injection for a homicide unrelated to the Frazier Estate Massacre: "It was meeeeeee!"

* * *

You've exercised a certain amount of restraint prior to the blizzard. That's over. Now, matters will escalate. While everybody else has gathered upstairs for Snodgrass' annual bash, you sneak away to share a special moment with Nathan Custer.

Does it hurt when I do this? *It's a rhetorical question.*

You don't expect Custer can hear you after you popped his eardrums with a slot screwdriver. Can't see you either. Blood pumps from the crack in his skull. Smack from a ball peen hammer took the starch right out of our hero. He coughs bubbles. Don't need tongue or teeth to blow bubbles, though it helps.

It may not even be Custer under that mask of gore. Could be Deputy Newcastle or Hendricks. Shit, could be that arrogant little prick Wannamaker at this rate. True story, you've fantasized about killing each of them so often that the lines might well be erased.

Except, haven't you wanted to end your existence? Sure you have. You'd love nothing more than to take your own miserable head off with a cleaver, string your own guts over the tree the way those cheap Victorian saps strung popcorn before Christmas went electric.

This is where it gets very, very confusing.

For a lunatic moment you're convinced it's you, slumped there, mewling like a kitten, soul floating free and formless while an angel of vengeance goes to work on your body with hammer and tongs. Yeah, maybe it's you in the chair and Custer, or Newcastle, or Wannamaker, has been the killer all along. It ain't pretty, having one's mind blown like this.

You were certain it was Custer when you put him in the chair, but that was a long time ago. So much has changed since then. The continents have drifted closer together, the geography of his features has altered for the worse. It's gotten dark. There's the storm and your sabotage of the reserve generator to thank. You've gathered wool and lost the plot. Can't even remember why you'd reserve special tortures for this one.

Why are your hands so fascinating all of the sudden?

Oh, Jesus, what if Snodgrass spiked the punch? He'd once threatened to dose his party-goers with LSD. Nobody took him seriously. But, what if? That would explain why the darkness itself has begun to shine, why your nipples are hard as nail-heads, why you've suddenly developed spidey-sense. Oh, Emmitt Snodgrass, that silly bastard; his guts are going to get extracted through his nose, and soon.

You detect the creak of a loose board and turn in time to see a snub-nosed revolver extending from a crouched silhouette. A lady's gun, so sleek and petite. Here's a flash of fire from the barrel that reveals the bruised face of the final girl. Don't she know you're invulnerable to lead? Didn't she read the rules inside the box top? Problem is, it's another sign that your version of reality is shaky, because you are sure as hell that you killed her already.

Sliced her throat, ear to lovely ear. Yet, here she is, blasting you into Kingdom Come with her itty bitty toy pistol. What the fuck is up with that?

Double tap. Triple, dipple, quadruple tap. Bitch ain't taking any chances, is she? You're down, sprawled next to your beloved victim, whoever he is. Your last. The final girl done seen to that, hasn't she?

Custer, is that you? you ask the body in the chair. He don't give anything away, only grins at you through the blood. Luckily you're made of sterner stuff. Four bullets isn't the end. You manage to get your knees and elbows underneath you for a lethal spring in the penultimate frame of the flick of your life, the lunge where you take the girl into your arms and squeeze until her bones crack and her tongue protrudes. When you're done, you'll crawl away to lick your wounds and plot the sequel. Four shots ain't enough to kill the very beating heart of evil.

Turns out, funny thing, the final girl has one more bullet. She hobbles over and puts it in your head.

Well, shit—

* * *

"Christ on a pony, what are you *dooo-ing*?" This plaintive utterance issues from Eliza Overstreet's ripe mouth. She's dressed as a cabaret dancer or Liza Minnelli, or some such bullshit. White, white makeup and sequins and tights. A tight, tight wig cropped as a Coptic monk's skullcap. All *sparkly.*

Emmitt Snodgrass cackles and pops another tab of acid. The rest of the batch he crushes into the rich red clot of punch in a crystal bowl shaped as a furious eagle. The furious eagle punch bowl is courtesy of Luke Tucker, collector of guns, motorcycles, and fine crystal. The suite is prepared — big Christmas tree, wall-to-wall tinsel, stockings and disco balls hung with care. Yeah, Snodgrass is ready for action, Jackson.

Eliza gives him a look. "Everybody is going to drink that!"

He grabs her ass and gives it a comforting squeeze. "Hey, hey, baby. Don't worry. This shit is perfectly safe to fry."

"But it's all we've got, you crazy sonofabitch!"

The doorbell goes ding-dong and the first guests come piling in from the hallway. It will be Bob Aickman, bare-assed and goggle-eyed on acid, who will eventually trip over the wires that cause the electrical short that starts the tragic fire that consumes the top three floors of the Estate.

* * *

Deputy Newcastle operates two official vehicles: an eleven-year-old police cruiser with spider web cracks in the windshield and a bashed-in passenger-side door, and an Alpine snowmobile that, by his best estimate, was likely manufactured during the 1980s. Currently, he's parked in the cruiser on Main Street across from the condemned hulk that is the Frazier Tower. The sun won't set for another forty-five minutes, give or take, but already the shadows are thick as his wife's blueberry cobbler. It's snowing and blowing. Gusts rock the car. He listens to the weather forecast. Going to be cold as hell, as usual. Twenty-seven degrees Fahrenheit and sinking fast. He unscrews the thermos and has a sip of cocoa Hannah packed in his lunchbox. Cocoa, macaroni salad, and a tuna sandwich on white bread. He loathes macaroni and tuna, loves cocoa, and adores dear Hannah, so it's a wash.

His beat is usually quiet. The geographic jurisdiction extends from the village of Eagle Talon to a fourteen-mile stretch north and south along the Seward Highway. Normally, he deals with drunks and domestic arguments, tourists with flat tires and the occasional car accident.

Then along came this business with Langtree and the slaughterhouse scene at his shack on Midnight Road. A forensics team flew in from Anchorage and did their thing, and left again. Deputy Newcastle still hasn't heard anything from headquarters. Nobody's taking it seriously. Langtree was a nut. Loons like him are a dime a dozen in Alaska. Violence is part of the warp and woof of everyday existence here. Takes a hell of a lot to raise eyebrows among the locals. The deputy is worried, and with good reason.

The angel on his shoulder keeps whispering in his ear. The angel warns him a blood moon is on the rise.

Despite the fact his shift ended at two o'clock, Deputy Newcastle has spent the better part of an hour staring at the entrance of the abandoned Frazier Tower. Should have gotten leveled long ago, replaced by a hotel or a community center, or any old thing. Lord knows the village could use some recreational facilities. Instead, the building festers like a rotten tooth. It's a nest for vermin — animals and otherwise — and a magnet for thrill-seeking kids and ne'er-do-wells on the lam.

Custodian Floyd is supposed to keep the front door covered in plywood. The plywood is torn loose and lying in the bushes. A hole leads into gloom. This actually happens frequently. The aforementioned kids and ne'er-do-wells habitually break into the tower to seek their fun. Deputy Newcastle's cop intuition tells him the usual suspects aren't to blame.

"I'm going in," he says.

"You better not," says MJ. The King of Pop inhabits the back seat, his scrawny form crosshatched by the grilled partition between them. His pale features are obscured in the shade of a slouch hat. He is the metaphorical shoulder-sitting angel.

"Got to. It's my job."

"You're a swell guy, deputy. Don't do it."

"Who then?"

"You're gonna die if you go in there alone."

"I can call someone. Hendricks will back my play."

"Can't trust him."

"Elam."

"Your brother is a psychopath."

"Hmm. Fair enough. I could ring Custer or Pearson. Heck, I could deputize both of them for the day."

"Look, you can't trust anyone."

"I don't." Newcastle stows the thermos and slides on his wool gloves. He unclips the twelve-gauge pump action from its rack and shoulders his way out of the cruiser. The road is slick beneath the tread of his boots, the breeze searing cold against his cheek. Snowflakes stick to his eyelashes. He takes a deep breath and trudges toward the entrance of the Frazier Tower. The dark gap recedes and blurs like a mirage.

True Romance isn't Deputy Newcastle's favorite movie. Too much blood and thunder for his taste. Oddly, he identifies with the protagonist, Clarence. In times of doubt Elvis Presley manifests and advises Clarence as a ghostly mentor.

The deputy adores the incomparable E, so he's doubly disconcerted regarding his own hallucinations. Why in the heck does he receive visions of MJ, a pop icon who fills him with dread and loathing?

MJ visited him for the first time the previous spring and has appeared with increasing frequency. The deputy wonders if he's gestating a brain tumor or if he's slowly going mad like his grandfather allegedly did after Korea. He wonders if he's got extra sensory powers or powers from God, although he hasn't been exposed to toxic waste or radiation, nor is he particularly devout. Church for Christmas and Easter potluck basically does it for him. Normally a brave man, he's too chicken to take himself into Anchorage for a CAT scan to settle the issue. He's also afraid to mention his invisible friend to anyone for fear of enforced medical leave and/or reassignment to a desk in the city.

In the beginning, Deputy Newcastle protested to his phantom partner: "You aren't real!" and "Leave me alone! You're a figment!" and so on. MJ had smiled ghoulishly and said, "I wanna be your friend, Deputy. I've come to lend you a hand. Hee-hee!"

Deputy Newcastle steps through the doorway into a decrepit foyer. Icicle stalactites descend in glistening clusters. The carpet has eroded to bare concrete. Cracks run through the concrete to the subflooring. A wasteland of fallen ceiling tiles, squirrel nests, and collapsed wiring. He creeps through the debris, shotgun clutched to his waist.

What does he find? An escaped convict, dirty and hypothermic, like in the fall of 2006? Kids smoking dope and spraying slogans of rebellion on the walls? A salmon-fattened black bear hibernating beneath a berm of dirt and leaves? No, he does not find a derelict, or children, or a snoozing ursine.

The Killer awaits him, as the King of Pop predicted.

Deputy Newcastle sees shadow bloom within shadow, yet barely feels the blade that opens him from stem to stern. It is happening to someone else. The razor-sharp tip punches through layers of insulating fabric, enters his navel, and rips upward. The sound of his undoing resonates in the small bones of his ears. He experiences an inexplicable rush of euphoria that is frightening in its intensity, then he is on his knees, bowed as if in prayer. His mind has become so disoriented he is beyond awareness of confusion. His parka is heavy, dragged low by the sheer volume of blood pouring from him. He laughs and groans as steam fills his throat.

The Killer takes the trooper hat from where it has rolled across the ground, dusts away snow and dirt, and puts it on as a souvenir. The Killer smiles in the fuzzy gloom, watching the deputy bleed and bleed.

Deputy Newcastle has dropped the shotgun somewhere along the way. Not that it matters — he has no recollection of the service pistol in his belt, much less the knowledge of how to work such a complicated mechanism. The most he can manage at this point is a dumb, meaningless smile that doesn't even reflect upon the presence of his murderer.

His final thought isn't of Hannah, or of the King of Pop standing at his side and mouthing the words to "Smooth Criminal," eyes shining golden. No, the deputy's final thought isn't a thought, it is inchoate awe at the leading edge of darkness rushing toward him like the crown of a tidal wave.

* * *

A storm rolls in off the sea on the morning of the big Estate Christmas party. Nobody stirs anywhere outdoors except for Duke Pearson's two-ton snow plow with its twinkling amber beacon, and a police cruiser as the deputy makes his rounds. Both vehicles have been swallowed by swirls of white.

Tammy Ferro's fourteen-year-old son Mark is perched at the table like a raven. Clad in a black trenchcoat and exceptionally tall for his tender age, he's picking at a bowl of cereal and doing homework he shirked the previous evening. His mother is reading a back issue of the *Journal of the American Medical Association*. The cover illustration is of a mechanical heart cross-sectioned by a scalpel.

Tammy divorced her husband and moved into the village in September, having inherited apartment 202 from her Aunt Millicent. Tammy is thirty-three but can pass for twenty-five. Lonnie DeForrest's appreciation of her ass aided her in snagging a job at the Caribou Tavern waiting tables. She earned a degree in psychology from the University of Washington, fat lot of good that's done her. Pole dancing in her youth continues to pay infinitely greater dividends than the college education it financed.

She and Mark haven't spoken much since they came to Eagle Talon. She tells herself it's a natural byproduct of teenage reticence, adapting to a radically new environment, and less to do with resentment over the big blowup of his parents' marriage. They are not exactly in hiding. It is also safe to say her former husband, Matt, doesn't know anything about Aunt Millicent or the apartment in Alaska.

Out of the blue, Mark says, "I found out something really cool about Nate Custer."

Tammy has seen Custer around. Impossible not to when everyone occupies the village's only residence. Nice looking guy in his late forties. Devilish smile, carefree. Heavy drinker, not that that is so unusual in the Land of the Midnight Sun, but he wears it well. Definitely a Trouble with a capital T sort. He goes with that marine biologist Jessica Mace who lives on the fifth. Mace is kind of a cold fish, which seems apropos, considering her profession.

She says, "The glacier tour guide. Sure." She affects casualness by not glancing up from her magazine. She dislikes the fascination in her son's tone. Dislikes it on an instinctual level. It's the kind of tone a kid uses when he's going to show you a nasty wound, or some gross thing he's discovered in the woods.

"He survived the Moose Valley Slaughter. Got shot in the head, but he made it. Isn't that crazy? Man, I never met anybody that got shot before."

"That sounds dire." Guns and gun violence frighten Tammy. She doesn't know if she'll ever acclimate to Alaska gun culture. However, she is quite certain that she prefers grown men leave her impressionable teen son out of such morbid conversations, much less parade their scars for his delectation. Barbarians aren't at the gate; they are running the village.

"It happened twenty years ago. Moose Valley's a small town, even smaller than Eagle Talon. Only thirty people live there. It's in the interior...You got to fly supplies in or take a river barge." Mark isn't looking at her directly, either. He studies his black nails, idly flicking the chipped polish.

"Gee, that's definitely remote. What do people do there?" Besides shoot each other, obviously.

"Yeah, lame. They had *Pong*, maybe, and that's it. Nate says everybody was into gold mining and junk."

"Nate says?"

Mark blushes. "He was a little older than me when it all went down. This ex-Army guy moved in from the Lower Forty-Eight to look for gold, or whatever. Everybody thought he was okay. Turns out he was a psycho. He snapped and went around shooting everybody in town one night. Him and Nate were playing dominoes and the dude pulled a gun out of his pocket. Shot Nate right in the head and left him on the floor of his cabin. Nate didn't die. Heh. The psycho murdered eleven people before the state troopers bagged him as he was floating downriver on a raft."

"Honey!"

"Sorry, sorry. The cops *apprehended* him. With a sniper rifle."

"Did Nate tell you this?"

"I heard it around. It's common knowledge, Mom. I was helping Tucker and Hendricks get an acetylene bottle into the back of his rig."

She hasn't heard this tale of massacre. Of course, she hasn't made many friends in town. At least Mark is coming out of his shell. Despite the black duds and surly demeanor, he enjoys company, especially that of adults. Good thing since there are only half a dozen kids his age in the area. She's noticed him mooning after a girl named Lilly. It seems pretty certain the pair are carrying on a rich, extracurricular social life via Skype and text…

"Working on English?" She sets aside her magazine and nods at his pile of textbooks and papers. "Need any help?"

He shrugs.

"C'mon. Watch ya got?"

"An essay," he says. "Mrs. Chandler asked us to write five hundred words on what historical figure we'd invite to dinner."

"Who'd you pick? Me, I'd go with Cervantes, or Freud. Or Vivien Leigh. She was dreamy."

"Jack the Ripper."

"Oh…That's nice."

* * *

A young, famous journalist drives to a rural home in Upstate New York. The house rests alone near the end of a lane. A simple rambler painted red with white trim. Hills and woods begin at the backyard. This is late autumn and the sun is red and gold as it comes through the trees. Cool enough that folks have begun to put the occasional log into the fireplace, so the crisp air smells of applewood and maple.

He and the woman who is the subject of his latest literary endeavor sip lemonade and regard the sky and exchange pleasantries. An enormous pit bull suns itself on the porch a few feet from where the interview occurs. Allegedly, the dog is attack-trained. It yawns and farts.

The journalist finds it difficult not to stare at the old lady's throat where a scar cuts, so vivid and white, through the dewlapped flesh. He is aware that in days gone by his subject used to camouflage the wound with gypsy scarves and collared shirts. Hundreds of photographs and she's always covered up.

Mrs. Jessica Mace Goldwood knows the score. She drags on her Camel No. 9 and winks at him, says once her tits started hitting her in the knees she gave up vanity as a bad business. Her voice is harsh, only partially restored after a series of operations. According to the data, she recently retired from training security dogs. Her husband, Gerry Goldwood, passed away the previous year. There are no children or surviving relatives on record.

"Been a while since anybody bothered to track me down," she says. "Why the sudden interest? You writing a book?"

"Yeah," the journalist says. "I'm writing a book."

"Huh. I kinda thought there might be a movie about what happened at the Estate. A producer called me every now and again, kept saying the studio was 'this close' to green-lighting the project. I was gonna make a boatload of cash, and blah, blah, blah. That was, Jesus, twenty years ago." She exhales a stream of smoke and studies him with a shrewd glint in her eyes. "Maybe I shoulda written a book."

"Maybe so," says the journalist. He notices, at last, a pistol nestled under a pillow on the porch swing. It is within easy reach of her left hand. His research indicates she is a competent shot. The presence of the gun doesn't make him nervous — he has, in his decade of international correspondence, sat among war chiefs in Northern Pakistan and ridden alongside Taliban fighters in ancient half-tracks seized from Russian armored cavalry divisions. He has visited Palestine and Georgia and seen the streets burn. He thinks this woman would be right at home with the hardest of the hard-bitten warriors he's interviewed.

"Life is one freaky coincidence, ain't it though?" She stares into the woods. Her expression is mysterious. "Julie Vellum died last week. Ticker finally crapped out."

"Julie Vellum…" He scans his notes. "Right. She cashed in big time. Author of how many bestselling New Age tracts? Friend of yours?"

"Nah, I despised the bitch. She's the last, that's all. Well, there's that guy who did psychedelic music for a while. He's in prison for aggravated homicide. Got involved with a cult and did in some college kids over in Greece. Can't really count him, huh? I'm getting sentimental in my dotage. Lonely."

"Lavender McGee. He's not in prison. They transferred him to an institution for the criminally insane. He gets day passes if you can believe it."

"The fuck is this world coming to? What is it you wanna ask me?"

"I have one question for you."

"Just one?" Her smile is amused, but sharp-honed by a grief that has persisted for more than the latter half of her long life.

"Just one." He takes a recorder from his shirt pocket, clicks a button, and sets it on the table between them. "More than one, of course. But this one is the biggie. Are you ready?"

"Sure, yeah. I'm ready."

"Mrs. Goldwood, why are you alive?"

Wind moves the trees behind the house. A flurry of red and brown leaves funnel across the yard, smack against the cute skirting. A black cloud covers the sun and hangs there. The temperature plummets. Gravel crunches in the lane.

The dog growls, and is on its feet, head low, mouth open to bare many, many teeth. The fur on its back is standing in a ridge. It is Cerberus's very own pup.

"Oh, motherfucker," says Jessica Mace Goldwood. She's got the revolver in her hand, hammer cocked. Her eyes blaze with a gunfighter's fire as she half crouches, elbows in tight, knees wide. "It's never over with these sonsofbitches."

"What's happening?" The journalist has ducked for cover, hands upraised in the universal sign of surrender. "Jesus H., lady! Don't shoot me!" He glances over his shoulder and sees a man in the uniform of a popular parcel delivery service slamming the door of a van and roaring away in a cloud of smoking rubber.

"Aw, don't fret," she says. "Me and Atticus just don't appreciate those delivery guys comin' around." The pit bull snarls and throws himself down at her feet. She uncocks the revolver and tucks it into the waistband of her track pants. "So, young man. Where were we?"

He wipes his face and composes himself. In a hoarse voice he says, "I guess what happened in Alaska doesn't let go."

"Huh? Don't be silly — I smoked that psycho. I hate visitors. You're kinda cute, so I made an exception. Besides, you're gonna pay me for this story, kiddo."

He tries for a sip of lemonade and ice rattles in the empty glass. His hand trembles. She pats his arm and takes the glass inside for a refill. Atticus follows on her heel. The journalist draws a breath to steady himself. He switches off the recorder. A ray of sun burns through the clouds and spotlights him while the rest of the world blurs into an impressionistic watercolor. A snowflake drifts down from outer space and freezes to his cheek.

She returns with a fresh glass of lemonade to find the journalist slumped in the lawn chair. Someone has placed an ancient state trooper's hat on his head and tilted it so that the man's face is partially covered. The crown of the hat is matted with dried gore that has, with the passing decades, indelibly stained the fabric. A smooth, vertical slice begins at the hollow of his throat and continues to belt level. His intestines are piled beneath his trendy hiking shoes. His ears lie upon the table. Steam rises from the corpse.

Atticus growls at the odors of shit and blood.

Jessica gazes at him in amazement. "Goddamnit, dog. *Now* you growl. Thanks a heap." She notices a wet crimson thumbprint on the recorder. She sighs and lights another cigarette and presses PLAY. Comes the static-inflected sound of wind rushing across ice, of snow shushing against tin, of arctic darkness and slow, sliding fog. Fire crackles in the background. These sounds have crept across the span of forty years.

A voice, garbled and muted by interference, whispers, "Jessica, we need to know. Why are you alive?" Snow and wind fill a long gap. Then, "Did you cut your own throat? Did you? Are you dead, Jessica? Are you dead, or are you playing? How much longer do you think you have?" Nothing but static after that, and the tape ends.

Intuition tells her that the journalist didn't file a plan with his network, that he rolled into the boondocks alone, that when he doesn't arrive at the office on Monday morning it will be a fulfillment of the same pattern he's followed countless times previously. The universe won't skip a beat. A man such as he has enemies waiting in the woodwork, ready to wrap him in a carpet and take him far away. It will be a minor unsolved mystery that his colleagues have awaited since his first jaunt into a war torn region in the Middle East.

She can't decide whether to call the cops or hide the body, roll the rental car into a ditch somewhere and torch it. *Why, yes, Officer, the young fellow was here for a while the other day. Missing? Oh, dear, that's terrible…*

"Jack?" she says to the hissing leaves. Her hand is at her neck, caressing the scar that defines her existence. "Nate? Are you out there?"

The sun sets and night is with her again.

* * *

Three years, six months, and fifteen days before Dolly Sammerdyke is eviscerated and dropped down a mineshaft, where her bones rest to this very day, she tells her brother Tom she's moving from Fairbanks to Eagle Talon. She's got an in with a woman who keeps the books at a shipping company and there's an opening for an onsite clerk. Tom doesn't like it. He lived in the village during a stretch in the 1980s when his luck was running bad.

"Listen, kid. It's a bum deal."

"Not as if I have a better option," she says.

"Bad place, sis."

"Yeah? What's bad about it? The people?"

"Bad people, sure. Bad neighborhood, bad history. Only one place to live in Eagle Talon. Six-floor apartment building. Ginormus old tenement. Dark, drafty, creepy as shit. It's a culture thing. People there are oddballs and clannish. You'll hate it."

"I'll call you every week."

Dolly calls Tom every week until her death. He doesn't miss her calls at first because he's landed a gig as a luthier in Nashville and his new girlfriend, an aspiring country and western musician, commands all of his attention these days.

* * *

Did the Final Girl do it? Was it this person here or that one over there?
You can only laugh at the preposterousness of such conceits. You can only
weep. As the omniscient narrator of some antique fairy tale once declaimed:
Fool! Rub your eyes and look again!
You will never die — nothing does.

* * *

From the journal of Nathan E. Custer as transcribed from the original
text by the Federal Bureau of Investigation, Anchorage:

I've never told anyone the whole truth about Moose Valley, or
this recurring dream I've suffered in the following years. Probably
not a dream; more of a vision. For clarity's sake, we'll go with it being
a dream. The dream has two parts. The first part is true to life, a
memory of events with the tedious details edited from the narrative.

In the true to life part of the dream, Michael Allen and I are
playing dominoes in the dim kitchen of my old place in Moose
Valley. I'd seen him standing in the yard, a ghostly shape in the
darkness, and had invited him to come out of the weather without
thinking to ask why he was lurking.

It is fall of '93, around four in the morning. He's winning, he
always wins at these games — pool, checkers, cards, dominoes —
although everybody likes him anyway.

Allen has only been in town a few months. A few years older
than me, from back east, also like me. An ex-Army guy, so he's
capable, with an easy smile and a sharp wit. Long hair, but kempt.
Keeps to himself for the most part in a one room cottage by the river.
He's passionate about Golden Age comic books and the poetry of
James Dickey. I was in the cottage for maybe five minutes once. Dude
kept it to a minimum and neat as you please. Gun oil scent, although
no guns in view. Yeah.

He pockets my last eleven dollars with a shrug and an apologetic
grin. Says, Thanks for the game, and pulls on his orange sock cap and
stands. I turn away to grab a beer from the icebox, hair of the dog
that bit me, and the bullet passes through my skull above my ear and
I'm on the floor, facedown. He squeezes the trigger again and I hear

the hammer snap, a dud in the chamber. Or he hadn't reloaded from slaughtering the Haden family across the street. We'll never know. Anyway, I'm unblinking, unresponsive, paralyzed, so he leaves me for dead. The front door slams and sunlight creeps across the tiles and makes the spreading blood shiny.

The second part of the dream is a fantasy cobbled and spliced from real events. I have a disembodied view of everything that happens next.

Allen slips down to the launch and steals a rubber raft. He lets the flow carry him downstream. He's packed sandwiches and beer, and has a small picnic. God, it's a beautiful day. The mountain peaks are white with fresh snow, but the lower elevations are yet green and gold. The air is brisk, only hinting at the bitter chill to come. A beaver circles the raft, occasionally slapping the water with its tail. The crack is like a gunshot. Allen scans the eggshell-blue sky from behind a pair of tinted aviator glasses.

The current gradually picks up as it approaches a stretch of falls and rapids. A black dot detaches from the sun and drops toward the earth. Allen unlimbers the 30.06 bolt action rifle he's stowed under a blanket. His balance is uncertain and the first round pings harmlessly through the fuselage of the police chopper. He ejects the empty and sights again, cool as the ice on the mountains, and this will be a kill shot. The SWAT sniper is a hair quicker and Allen is knocked from the raft. He plunges into the water and sinks instantly. The raft zips over the falls and is demolished.

A sad, tragic case closes.

The fact is, Allen survives for a few minutes. He is a tough, passionless piece of work, a few cells short of Homo sapiens status, and that helps him experience a brutal and agonizing last few moments on the mortal plane. He is sucked into a vortex and wedged under and between some rocks where he eventually drowns. This is a remote and dangerous area. The cops never recover the body.

Small fish nibble away his fingers, then his face, then the rest of it.

Andy Kaufman Creeping through the Trees

Autumn, 1998

Senior year of high school isn't the best of times. It is totally the other way. And how shall I count the ways? Cancer is eating my father alive. He's got six months, a year, it's anybody's guess. How many of those days will be worth a damn? He's sort of a tough-as-shoe-leather guy and I bet he'll make it hard on himself, on us all. Both our dogs, Little Egypt and Odysseus, bit the dust from old age during summer vacation. Not enough drama? The last week of August I almost kill myself on the new trampoline. Okay, technically, I fly off the trampoline and do a half-gainer into the side of our house. Instant KO.

Why does this even happen (and why me)? Solution: The Universe is a real bitch. Sometimes she smirks and gives you what you want. My heart's desire is a full-sized trampoline to practice cheer moves on. Well done, cosmos, you perverse whoremaster. A neighbor lost his job way up north in the Prudhoe Bay oil fields and put basically everything he owned out on the lawn at fire-sale prices. The neighbor kids cried when we loaded the trampoline into the bed of our truck. Flash forward twenty-four hours and it's me singing the blues.

I get cocky and bounce hard near the edge and *Kaboing!* Thank Satan the rhododendron bush cushions the impact. Also, thank you, dearly departed Anton LaVey, our Lord and Savior, I am alone for this debacle. None of the other girls bear witness to my humiliation. Dad has passed out drunk earlier than usual and doesn't hear the thud or the shattering china. Also kinda bad, though. I lie stunned for a few seconds, then angry yellow jackets swarm from their nest in the bushes and sting the ever-loving hell out of me.

Neck brace, knee brace, swollen face. The knee is the worst, although sharing Renee Zellweger's squinty pout for a week is not to be envied. The sorry result of my misery? One of my rivals (probably trailer park queen Reyline Showalter) will lead the cheer squad when our boys pillage their way to state again. Grr! Is it too petty of me to hope the team suffers a rash of injuries and misses the playoffs?

Damn our soon-to-be ex-neighbor and his stupid discount trampoline he bought for his stupid brats. Damn the universe and all its devices, such as gravity, colorectal cancer, and children.

* * *

The mound of get-well cards is impressive. So many, many flowers and gift baskets, it becomes tedious to sort them for the contraband. Chocolate! Stuffed toys! Poppers (bless you Benny Three-Trees)! Porno disguised as *Cosmopolitan, Girls' Life,* and *Seventeen!* Rob Zombie and Weezer CDs!

I'm blonde, taut, and hot. Everybody loves me and everybody else hates me. I know who's who — pals write, *Hey Julie Vellum, Yo, Julie V, get well, babe;* meanwhile, fools call me Julie Five, or Stuck-Up Bitch, and say, *Too bad you only sprained your neck.* It's vital to know the sides. High school is a cold war no more or less a game than East versus West. Most of the girls, pro or con Julie Vellum, are super smooth and you can't go by kind words or a friendly smile. If you don't keep the factions and the alliances straight, you'll get a knife between the shoulder blades. Been there (middle school), no thanks.

Human nature; what are you going to do? After my tragic accident and the initial flood of sympathy, even my tightest friends avoid me like I'm Typhoid Mary. A knee brace or an arm cast can be sexy if you work it right. *Neck* braces, visible swelling, and contusions are totally uncool. Emotionally, I'm not well-equipped to cope, even if my upbringing suggests otherwise.

Being an only child kinda sucks when it doesn't totally rock. My shrink (Mom's idea), an ex-pill dispenser to the stars, says ugly sibling rivalries are transferred to my peers and blown up on the stage and that I should watch my step. She's right despite her ignominious status as a Beverly Hills refugee — I sharpen these claws on classmates and it's earned me a bit of a reputation for being a super-bitch. Meanwhile, Grandpa says acting snotty is a cover for weakness and it's too bad I don't have a brother to keep me in check. He seldom wears shirt or pants and handily out-drinks Dad, believe it or don't.

I take this wise counsel in stride.

Haters can talk shit all they like, I am *not* an entitled high school slut cheerleader. I am a regal and voraciously *sexual* high school cheerleader. Besides, I didn't actually do the deed until Rocky Eklund, then the backup quarterback, popped my cherry after the team took state last fall. Junior freaking year. Yeesh. Ask Robin Sloan or Indra Norse when they first gave it up. Ask those skanks, Jessica Mace and her cousin Liz Lochinvar. *I* was practically a cloistered virgin before the dam broke. Unless we're counting hand jobs and BJs. In that case, it would be fifth grade and creepy, so let's not.

* * *

A week of school convinces me that I'm in political exile. Woman without a Country. The second tier girls and hangers-on occupy my table in the cafeteria; talk about a come-down. Greetings range from nervous to frosty. Nobody looks me in the eye. Smiling the hard smile Jackie taught, I seriously worry my face will get stress fractures. I read the history of the Borgias during lunch and fantasize about a mass poisoning.

Rocky has football practice (I'm giving my beau his space; got to provide him political cover until I shed the scaggy collar) and then beers and pool at Mike Zant's house after Thursday class. Doc won't let me drive until I can turn my head again.

I catch a lift with Steely J. We have business anyhow. His ride is a Toyota wagon with Visqueen taped over the rear side windows. Two hundred and thirty thousand miles on the odometer. He keeps the wagon spiffy as a military bunk, oddly enough, and daisy-sweet with a cluster of air fresheners rubber-banded to the rearview. Be that as it may, I spread a handful of cafeteria napkins on the passenger seat. My hunch says a blacklight would paint a very different picture of the environment.

Steely J resides in the friend camp. He's in the friend camp for *most* of us, not to be confused with a buddy or a pal or a member of the crew. Dude is like Australia or Switzerland; up for hijinks and not the teeniest bit judgy. He's a fixer and you don't have to like a fixer to love one. Tall, really quiet, although not broody, he-man quiet; closer to a great white shark cruising through the shallows. And white is right — he's Whitey McWhite cream cheese complexioned. He walks soft, sorta hunched in his lumpy sweaters, buzz cut, black frame glasses, and sneakers for sneaking.

A man of unexpected facets, he's obsessed with ancient aliens (Greys built the Pyramids!) and a hundred and one doomsday scenarios. The universe is a hologram and the only real gods are likely horrifically evolved humanoids or giant blobs of sentient protoplasm. His father worked for a pharmaceutical company and had taken his whole weirdo family on months-long business vacations to Borneo and the Amazon Basin when the kids were little.

We've shared bizarre conversations. Craziest exchange happened after I paid him to get the test key to Math finals. Apropos of absolutely nothing (although I had the sniffles), he said, *Wonder why I never get sick?*

Not really. Fair question though. Granted, the pasty bastard isn't an exemplar of health, yet I don't recall him ever missing school from the seasonal crud.

I bleed myself.

Like Dark Ages bleeding? Smoke enemas? Barf me out, dude.

Dark Ages is recent history. Bleeding goes back to the Hellenic. In the 1920s missionaries brought it here from South American death cults. Got to propitiate them old black gods with rivers of blood, y'know.

I'm quite sure I don't.

Bad blood out, fresh blood in. Ever want to give it a whirl, I've got the kit. Make a superwoman out of you for real.

Fresh blood in? What did that even mean? I decided I didn't give a shit. I'd let it return to haunt me at some future 3 A.M.

He doesn't do sports despite his "perfect" health and even though he'd wallop most of the boys with his bizarro, predatory grace. Elmer D. (the only dude I know who *might* take Steely J mano a mano) said there was an incident at wrestling tryouts and Coach Grinky eighty-sixed Steely J hardcore.

Side note: I fooled around with Elmer the summer of our junior year, but have since nixed our romance. His dad wrecked their truck this past winter. Mr. D. burned and Elmer survived with some wicked scars. I pretend he doesn't exist because now I'm rolling with Mr. Future-All-State-full-ride-to-some-powerhouse-football-town. JV be trading up, haters.

Steely J is solid with the rich kids (especially Fat Boy Tooms). Rumor is, he gophers for them since he can pass for legal, has a boss fake ID, knows no fear, and, most importantly, is scruple-free. You want weed, booze, or heavier stuff, you call Hostettler or Benny Three Trees. You need somebody to hold for you, alibi for you, or step-'n-fetch-it,

Steely J is your prole. He makes book on sports events and makes unwanted pets vanish. He's the source for cheap designer clothes, "borrowed" power tools, scalped tickets, and VIP invites to password-at-the-door-parties. It's this last detail that interests me at the moment.

I hit him with the lowdown. "Okay, dude, look. My dad. He has cancer." This confession has the opposite effect from what I expected. Instead of relief, my stomach tightens. The bile in my throat must be remorse.

"Sorry to hear it." Steely J speaks in a monotone drawl that pitches slightly to indicate his mood. In this case, it descends toward baritone. He gives a shit, although not much of one. "What kind?"

"The way he guzzles Maker's Mark, you'd think cirrhosis, but nope. Rectal cancer."

"Huh."

"This is eyes-only need to know, so keep your lips zipped."

"Not planning to do a press release. Damn."

"Good, or it's your balls."

"Sure your purse has got room for 'em?"

"It's a coin purse. Plenty of room for your junk. I need a favor."

"Heck of a way of asking."

"My dad's birthday is October ninth. He loved Andy Kaufman, see. Absolutely adored him, is more to the point. Dee Dee Andersen says her brother knows a guy at the Gold Digger who saw the booking sheet for Halloween. That lounge singer character Kaufman did in the '70s is on the schedule—"

"Tony Clifton."

"Yes, Tony Clifton. Live and in person. What I need—"

"*The* Tony Clifton…Here, in Anchorage?" Steely J's monotone pitches higher.

"Uh, yeah, sure."

"Fucking A! Who's playing him? Zmuda, I bet. Has to be Zmuda."

"*One* of Kaufman's buddies, obviously. That's not the important—"

"You'd assume one of his compatriots. On the other hand, maybe Clifton actually exists. True story, Kaufman and Zmuda planned to work on a film biography of Clifton and how Kaufman originally discovered him at a hotel in Vegas and they got to be friends, and so on. Fell through because *Heartbeeps* didn't sell enough tickets. Bummer." He drives like turtles screw so we've apparently got all the time in the world.

"You should write a book."

He doesn't react to my sarcasm. "Comedians tap into the infinite. Black Kryptonite."

"Fascinating, not really, but—"

"Kaufman faked his own death. Something hinky about these random gigs Clifton does. Think about that — fourteen years and he's still dropping in to do his old routine, and for what? Nobody except fogies like your dad even remember him. The *whole* setup is hinky. Kaufman might've been sick of the limelight. Fame gets some people down. *Heartbeeps* was pretty bad. Okay, it reeked. That's why he faked his death and retired to a South Pacific island and he comes around to yank our chains every once in a while. It's possible, right?"

"For the love of…No, J. Neither of those are possible. I don't even." My lips hurt, we're way off in the weeds, and I'm about to blow a fuse. The pressure of being Julie Vellum can be crushing.

He licks his cheek. "Yeah, yeah. I know. It would be cool."

"Please pay attention. Dee Dee says the show is a hush-hush exclusive. One night only. There's a secret list. I want Daddy on that list."

He smiles. His incisor is silver. The smile doesn't change his expression much more than a lone cloud moving across the sky. "Clifton rules. Best character Kaufman ever did, easy. I'll make some calls, see if it's legit."

"Super. What's it gonna set me back?"

He flicks a glance my way. His tongue protrudes again, tasting the possibilities. "I dunno. BJ?"

I tap the brace that ratchets my neck and chin so severely it might as well be one of those Elizabethan collars the vet puts on a dog. My eyes and nose are still swollen and my lips are fat enough I'm taking vital nutrients through a straw. "You probably play the lottery too. C'mon, dude. I'm in no condition. *You're* in no condition. Blowing you is against the Geneva Convention."

"Well, you look like a walking glory hole. Fifty bucks. Plus whatever the tickets go for, if this is legit." Fifty bucks is his asking price for everything from shoplifting eyeliner, to scoring tickets, to committing grand larceny or felonious assault.

"Deal!" I almost shake his pallid, sweaty paw before I come to my senses. His parents own a place on the hillside. Didn't mom and dad J relocate to the Midwest in '95 and basically abandon the property? Rings a bell. He's got a litter of younger siblings. Pale, snot-nosed ankle-biters who look like they should be floating in jars of formaldehyde. Did his family abandon him? You can attend public school until the age of twenty-one. I think he's close. Does he sleep in his car? In the trunk (a coffin?)? Is he communicable? He wears the same sweater several days in a row. Dirt under his nails is a given. Drops of blood crust the toes of his sneakers. His favorite all-weather ensemble is a Seahawks track suit, plus a goose down parka when the mercury dips. He smells ripe and his cheap aftershave is insufficient to the challenge. He habitually sips I-don't-have-a-clue-what from a mason jar jammed inside a grody Starbucks cup holder. His breath is raw as fuck. He appears pudgy unless you've been around ball players and weightlifters and recognize there's earth-moving brawn under the panda-bear-softness. Why do his eyes make me think of fish? I consider these mysteries for half a second and we're home sweet home.

Steely J says as I open the car door, "Ever have an imaginary friend? When you were a kid?"

"Jesus," I say.

* * *

Mom insists I call her Jackie. It's a Unitarian thing, maybe? She and Dad lived in California right out of high school. Jackie got knocked up, then she got religion. She was too busy giving birth to me to finish college. By the time I entered Kindergarten, she'd ditched the whole stay-at-home-mom routine (bailed on the church, too), took a few night classes in business, and embarked on a career as a hotshot saleswoman of water purification systems.

Dad couldn't hack UCLA no matter how he tried. He slunk home to Girdwood, Alaska, in defeat. Grandpa gave him a superintendent job at the chemical plant in Anchorage. Dad's name is Jeff. He doesn't let me call him Jeff; he's not a Unitarian and the Valley didn't rub off on him. Mom, I mean, Jackie, got the full dose and passed it along to me.

Jackie travels the globe. She stays on the road two weeks out of every month. She's an absentee parent, which makes her pretty damned rad. Sure, it blew chunks (and to whom it may concern, I don't suffer from bulimia; my athletic figure is purely genetic) during pre-adolescence not having a mom to teach me how to navigate middle school and getting my period and so forth. Past is the past (Grandpa says it's prologue). I've come to appreciate the combined-arms-power of neglect and guilt. Besides, when she is around, she displays the demeanor of an indulgent queen dishing boons willy-nilly. Boys? *Do be careful, dear. Here's a variety pack of condoms.* Money? *Let's tack another twenty onto your allowance.* Out late? *Be home by dawn.* Can I have a car for my sweet sixteen? *Tell your father to take you to the dealership. Nothing too fast, okay?* Best part is, once I grew tits I magically became eligible for her Machiavellian advice, which she dispenses freely.

Fun and games notwithstanding, there is a single ironclad rule. On my first morning as a freshman at Onager High, Jackie drove me to the front entrance and we sat in the car bopping to "Black Hole Sun" and verifying our makeup. A dark-haired girl in a leather jacket, jeans, and combat boots got out of a stone age Ford truck.

Jackie grabbed my arm real hard and said in a witchy, hateful voice that surely belonged to someone else's mom, *See that little twat dressed like a Jet? That's Jessica Mace. Her bitch mother is Lucius. Redneck losers. Stay away from them or you'll be sorry.*

I didn't have the slightest clue as to her damage (and the fact a lot of people consider *us* to be barely one step out of the trailer park made me wonder if dear old Ma was projecting). My arm hurt with those talons squeezing tight. Why the drama? Yeah, the Mace chick was trouble from the way she stood, all badass nonchalant with her mouth crimped like a real bad ass, somebody who carried a switchblade. Still, I could handle it. *Jeez, Jackie. Get real. I'm not scared of redneck trash.*

Fear me, then.

What? I'm not scared of you either.

Pow! Jackie backhanded me and smashed my lip. Prior to that shocking moment, she'd never lifted a finger to check my antics. Dad did the discipline in our house. I sat there in shock while she dabbed the blood with a hanky and straightened my hair.

We're copacetic? She smiled, gangster-hard. Nobody ever really knew her, or this is why Dad drinks.

I swallowed my tears and bailed. Had to slink past Mace loitering on the sidewalk. The girl appraised me with narrowed eyes and a smirk.

You've got something on your face.

Jackie needn't have worried. I hated Mace already.

Three years on and we haven't revisited the topic. Everything seems rosy between mother-dearest and me. Jackie may be less creepy than Steely J, however that doesn't make it easier to read her. She is, after all, the one who assigned *The Prince* as bedside reading. *Smile, then stick it to them, honey. Instead of wrist-wrist, elbow-elbow, it's smile-smile, stab-stab. It is totally better to be feared than loved.*

She recently returned from a trip to the Midwest, hell-bent as ever on expanding her empire conference by grueling conference. I haven't told her of my plan to surprise Dad with Tony Clifton tickets. Maybe I will, when I get some more courage. Since Dad got diagnosed with the big C, she acts as if she almost loves him again. Freaks me the hell out.

Dad's on a permanent vacation from the plant. He drinks more than ever. Surrounds himself with cartons of Natty Light and Maker's Mark and slouches in the den in the dark watching horror flicks with the sound low on his pride and joy RCA box — he doesn't need the volume; he knows the script by heart and mutters his lines with the embittered diligence of a failed actor. He surfaces for dinner that Jackie or I cook (defrost). Sits at the head of the table (at least two beer cans or a whiskey next to his plate) with a drowning man's grin and asks how our day went. Doesn't slur, although he speaks slowly and his eyes are bloodshot.

Today, he's absorbed in the *Montel Williams Show* and oblivious to me limping past on the way to my bedroom. Bunko, the grizzled tomcat, follows at my heel, same as he always does. Jackie feeds Bunko, Dad kicks him, and *I* pet him and give him love. He's as close to a brother as it's going to get around here.

By the way, the reason I'm an only child is Jackie had two miscarriages and an abortion before she gave birth to breech-baby me. According to her, she'd argued with Dad about whether to keep me at all. I'm not sure which of them was pro or con Julie. My foes say she conceived me in the backseat of Dad's jalopy and that she needed a baby to keep him leashed. For the record, she doesn't deny it.

Reflecting on grade school, I realize how lonely our home was due to Mom's relentless travel schedule. Dad let me stay up late and watch *Taxi* reruns with him when she was away. Sloppy Joes, Tang, and an ice cream sandwich for dinner on a TV tray on the couch in my Cabbage Patch Kids PJs. Movie of the week or a western or some standup comedy from his stack of VHS tapes. I'm not exaggerating — he loved Kaufman, and Robin Williams, and Bill Hicks (grooved on horror by Lewton, Carpenter, and Romero, but decided I was too young to go that heavy). The rough stuff did it for him — brutal satire and white man madness fumed from those comedians. Except for the profanity, most of it went over my head. No worries; those were the rare occasions that I got to be Daddy's little girl instead of a piece of furniture.

He cried his eyes out the day after Kaufman passed away. Drank himself into a stupor in honor of Hicks a decade later. Dad didn't shed tears over Hicks, though. I'm not sure he had any left after 1984.

Whatever our problems, he's my dad and he's dying and I have to believe it's a signal from the universe that Dee Dee Andersen told me about Clifton's forthcoming surprise appearance. I'm infamous for deviousness not imagination. Until this opportunity, I haven't thought of a single meaningful gesture to show Dad I care the way a daughter is supposed to care (even though my heart feels kind of numb). I'm selfish and big enough to admit the failing.

* * *

I lie in bed and crank the Matthew Good Band. I do a couple of poppers and hope they can help sort out some of this bullshit. My prayer is, *Save the day, Steely J, you weird, weird dude.* Bunko nuzzles under my jaw, where the brace seam is snuggest, and purrs. He loves the shit out of my cone of shame.

Rocky calls on my rhinestone-studded telephone in the wee hours after Dad has fallen asleep in front of the TV and Jackie disappears into her bedroom lair downstairs to consult spreadsheets. Rocky's favorite topics are football and his car in no particular order. Tonight is more of the same. Eventually he remembers to ask how I'm doing. Am I already an afterthought? Did he call so late because he took one of my many, many rivals on a cruise of the Eklutna Flats in his damned midnight-blue Iroc-Z? Time for another popper. Bingo-bongo, better.

Rocky says, "Babe, I ran into your pal, Steely J at the store. Freaky you should ask him to score Clifton tickets. You and him are Kaufman nuts?"

"Hey, now. I wouldn't exactly say I'm a nut—"

"Fucker gives me the willies."

"Steely J isn't for everyone. Still, where would you get your discount 'roids without him?"

"I meant Kaufman."

"Kaufman's definitely not for everyone either," I say. "You're in luck, considering the fact he's dead as a doornail, Jim. Supposedly, haha."

"He was evil."

"How evil was he?"

"Caveman in a cave raping all the cavewomen evil. Freeze frame his face next time you watch one of his old shows. Pure, violent malevolence." Rocky breathes heavily, the way he does after a hard practice or a screw-session in his car. "The others have other ones. These celebrity haunts. Jim Morrison. Jim Belushi. Freddy Mercury. Bette Davis. Charlie Chapman. Gilda Radner. Marilyn Monroe. Elvis."

"Uh, baby? Is this a joke?" I'm losing my pleasant buzz with a quickness. Rocky isn't the sharpest knife in the drawer. I would not have guessed "malevolence" is within a million miles of his vocabulary. His jokes concern bodily functions and referring to his rivals as faggots. If this isn't a joke, I'm not sure I want to know what it is.

"Stifle yourself and listen. There's an entry with a roster in the black almanac, but I haven't read it, and maybe it's a lie. I knew one unlucky kid who claimed visitations from Peter Lorre. Makes my blood run cold and mine is bad enough. Sometimes I see Andy Kaufman creeping through the trees outside our house. He shows himself when something awful is on the way."

"Uh, you see Andy Kaufman. Lurking. Am I hearing you right?"

"You're hearing me right. Months go by and nothing, then poof! He's every-damned-where. Follows me home from school and stands under my window and grins. Winks at me through the stacks at the library. I know he's real because I've seen his tracks and because it's happened to members of my family going back generations. How far? How deep? Deep as a cobra back-slipping into its hidey hole? Is it just entertainers? Maybe it's all sorts of dead famous people. Did the pale visage of George Washington vex my child grandfather as he huddled with his Boy Scout troop around the fire? Did Ben Franklin meet the Bard on some lonely deer path in Virginia? The way Franklin doped and drank and forswore a Christian deity, I bet it is so."

Visage? Vex? This is pod person talk. Has my boyfriend had a brain transplant? I let the silence stretch. "Rocky, have you been hitting the nitrous again? You sound totally fucked up."

"I'm high on plasma. Speaking of fucking. To be honest, babe, I *had* to get my rocks off. Today was a real stressor. I drove Reyline to the flats and banged her like a drum. Didn't mean anything. She's a skank. I double-wrapped my junk." He waits for me to respond; I don't because my heart is a lump of ice in my throat. He eventually goes on, "Don't be pissed. You are, aren't you? I get it. I was disgusted with what I'd done and I thought about capping her on the spot. Crack her open and dump the whole mess into the bay. I've done it before. Usually I stick to dogs because nobody misses them. Nobody makes a federal case over a dead animal. You still there?" Rocky laughs and it's not his laugh, it changes. Steely J says, "Sorry, JV. Just messing with you. I've got a natural talent for mimicry."

"Holy shit, you asshole. Be sure to put that in as your yearbook quote. *A natural talent for being a douche.*" I can't tell if I'm having a heart attack. Bunko wakes from whatever cats dream of and his fur puffs. He yowls, swipes a claw at my phone-hand, and leaps from the bed.

Steely J laughs again and says in a not-quite perfect imitation of Rocky, "For the record, your boyfriend is a schmuck. Two to one he *is* taking a cruise with Reyline as we speak. Probably imagines he's spiking a puppy instead of a football whenever he scores a TD. It's in those beady eyes. What I said about Kaufman is also true. He really started coming around my place one dark autumn. For my dad it was James Dean. I'll tell you the whole story later."

He hangs up before I can answer with a stream of profanity. Amazement overcomes my immediate anger. Got to hand it to the freak — it's an epic prank. I laugh it off like I'm supposed to. Not so deep down, I wish there was someone like a friend to call and unburden myself.

* * *

I ditch the neck brace and my lips finally deflate to regulation air pressure. Better than a poke in the eye with a sharp stick (one of Granddad's top five quotes, although the way my luck is running, the pointy end of a stick might have my name on it).

After a week with no contact, I track Steely J to the school stadium. It's lunch period. He's hanging with Jessica Mace on the football stadium bleachers. Surprising, given their history of mutual animosity. During seventh grade, he snapped her bra strap on a dare from Nolan Culpepper. Mace clobbered Steely J with a bicycle pump. Thirty stitches and no truce. Yet here they are, thick as thieves. Like I said: high school is global politics in microcosm. Factions are ever-shifting ice sheets, calving, drifting, merging.

Mace rises with languid insolence and blocks the path. She wears a faded jersey that reads ANCHORAGE WOLVERINES ROLLER DERBY SQUAD 1978. Her mom's blood is still spackled in the fiber. Lucius Lochinvar (her maiden name) had skated under the handle Scara Fawcett. A goon. Jackie knew her, even back then. Whatever happened with them led to a twenty-year feud. Violence is my bet. Thuggishness seems to be a Lochinvar-Mace trait.

Down on the field, my girls of Raven Squad are drilling — *Raven Power! Let's go, Ravens, Let's Go! Raaa-ven Power! Juke To The Left, Juke To The Right! Beat Em Up, Beat Em Off, Fight-Fight-Fight! Raven Power! Raven Power! Rat Shit, Bat Shit, Yay Team!* Something along those lines.

"Hey Julie Five. How's tricks?" Mace smiles, and like Steely J, it means less or more or worse than you'd think it does. She may as well have a storm cloud boiling overhead. Her eyes are fierce. Eyes of a drunk or a woman who just had angry sex. Her fighting rings glint — three on the left, two on the right. The death's head could crack a bone.

My inclination is to smack her with my crutch. I rein in the impulse.

She puts her hands on her hips. "Julie, you're a cooz and I'm calling you out."

"What's up your ass?"

"Elmer's a dear personal friend of mine. You kicked him to the curb. Broke his heart. I'm going to do unto you by breaking your face."

"Think so?"

"Know so."

"Isn't this is a teensy bit out of the blue?"

"Been on my honey-do-list for a while."

I flash a sneer to cover the fact my knees are knocking. "Real brave picking a fight with a girl halfway in traction."

"Don't worry, sweetie. I like cold dishes. This'll wait until that chicken leg is out of the brace. Be sure to keep your veterinarian on speed-dial. You're gonna require his services."

"Fuck you in the ear," is my witty rejoinder as I squeeze by.

Mace sticks a cigarette into the corner of her mouth. "Save the date, bitch."

Steely J sits on a bench, filming the cheer squad with a handheld movie camera. He doesn't glance at me as I collapse beside him. "Jessica M. is in a bad mood. Might want to avoid her." His lips barely move. He did a ventriloquist routine at the school talent show once. His dummy had lacked a lower jaw and its sundress costume was rotten with mold. He'd called her Veronica. Have I mentioned Steely J is an odd duck?

"Nice, thanks. What're you doing, perv?"

"Picking out victims."

"Hello?"

"Annual sacrifice to the death gods is nigh. If I'm gonna be the American Fulci, got to get my hands bloody."

"Sick. Start with Showalter. You could be right and the twat is gunning for my spot at the head of the squad."

"Only a virgin sacrifice will do."

"The death gods are going to starve around here, I guess."

"Sometimes terror is enough. Put on the mask of the dark of the moon and wander the earth."

"Damn, Steely, you say some loco bullshit. Ought to hang with the goth kids. They'd love your shtick."

"I'm too edgy. The goths don't feel me."

"Go figure. Anything on those tickets? You're supposed to be hooking me up. You gonna come through, or is your rep bullshit too?"

He sets the camera in his lap. "Meant to tell you, I checked with my sources. Clifton isn't on the schedule."

"Dee Dee swears he is."

"Dee Dee got suckered by secondhand info. It's smoke. Somebody probably thought it'd be a great joke to start the rumor. Classic Kaufman."

I close my eyes and concentrate on not shrieking my frustration. I imagine the last time I kissed Rocky. Two days before the trampoline debacle. We've fucked thirty or forty times and it's okay, although I never come. Is it me, or is my stud merely adequate? A busload of other girls would love to double-check my findings and that's why I don't complain. I imagine tripping Mace down the concrete staircase on the other side of the cafeteria. I've only seen her cry once after her younger brother was in a car accident. The memory of her ugly tears keeps me warm on long arctic nights. It helps now, too.

Steely J says, "There's another possibility. We could get creative. Do some community theater. My audition was convincing, right?"

"This a *creative* way to separate me from fifty bucks?"

"*One hundred* bucks."

"Where the hell am I going to get a hundred dollars?"

He mimes sucking a cock. "Seriously, though. I'll need a week or two to rehearse. Perfect the delivery."

"Rehearse? Rehearse what?"

"A command performance."

"How come you're so great at imitating voices?"

"Told you — it's natural talent. I meditate at night. Sit in the middle of my room and open my mind to the cosmos. All kinds of shit is floating around in the dark. Seeps into us every minute of the day. I just figured a way to make it happen faster."

"Anybody can meditate."

His expression slackens by one or two turns of a screw. His pupils expand. Funny how a millimeter or two can change someone's face so dramatically. "See, I'm really into it now. Used to take all night in full lotus. I can slip sideways at will." He wriggles his tongue and says in a Don Pardo voice: "Would you care to hear my idea?"

"I'm all ears." A glib pronouncement that belies serious misgivings regarding my deepening association with Steely J, Man of a Thousand Voices. I should have obeyed my instinct to tell him to piss up a rope.

* * *

Diehard leaves in the birch trees turn yellow and drop after a real cold snap toward the end of September. A few minutes past six and dark. I'm pacing in front of the window, nervous as a freshman awaiting her prom date. Hilariously, Jackie and Dad figure from the way I'm behaving Rocky is going to pop the question. Dad has spent a significant portion of the afternoon sharpening a Bowie Knife from the display case in the basement. He's only half drunk. There's an omen for you. Jackie warms him a TV dinner. The gusto with which he attacks his Salisbury steak confirms he'll adjust to his inevitable group home environment with aplomb.

Steely J's car parks with one tire on the curb. Even though he'd warned me, I'm jarred by his radical transformation from oafish, pervy teenager to the hulking schlub in the Vegas lounge singer suit who strolls up the walkway. Middle-aged, pale, bad toupee, worse skin, tinted glasses, ruffled shirt and bowtie, gut overhanging his belt, disco pants, and scuffed loafers. He carries a case sheathed in red velvet in his left hand. The change wouldn't be more complete if he'd transformed into a werewolf.

I open the front door and do a spit-take. It's really Tony Clifton, or at least someone who resembles Clifton. No way, no freaking way — Steely J has to be under there somewhere, right? Unless he's paid one of his pals to act as an accomplice and *really* sell the gag. He knows everybody and one of them could be an actor on the make.

"J, is it you?" I whisper as he grips my fingers near the tips and gives them a shake the way you do with a toddler.

"Tony C, baby. Tony C plays live." His accent is nasally and he smells like he took a bath in Aqua Velva. I still can't decide. "Course, you've invited me in, I can return anytime I wanna." He says it deadpan.

Jackie comes around the corner. Her stare wavers between bewilderment and horrified recognition. Mommy dearest is a control freak. She dislikes the unexpected. "Who is this, dear?" That stilted tone reminds me of the time she slapped my mouth. She's wearing a red blouse and a black skirt and the shoes she won't be caught dead in away from the house. I also know she knows Tony Clifton from her conversations with Dad over the years. I hate it when she plays coy. She truly does take Machiavelli to heart.

Steely J winks. "Hi, toots. Be a doll and fix me a drink, will ya."

Before she can yell at him, I tell her it's Dad's big surprise. Step aside and let the magic happen, Mom! She frowns and departs for the kitchen to mix a tray-load of cocktails. Monday is Caribou Lou night at the Vellum casa. Steely J, or whoever the fuck, ambles after me into the den and there's Dad slumped on his La-Z-Boy throne, a yellow Husqvarna ball cap tilted back. Blue light from the oversized TV screen glints in his eye as he regards the spectacle of Steely J unpacking a karaoke box and microphone. After a few minutes of strained silence, Dad gestures at me with his knife. His expression is similar to Mom's. Expectant with dread and willfully ignorant. "Honey, what the Sam Hill is going on?"

I take his free hand and say in a well-honed baby-girl voice, "Daddy, a friend of mine heard you're a major fan of Tony Clifton. Tony's in town for a couple of nights and—"

"Don't bore your old man to death, sweetheart," Steely J says and the accent slips. However, his patronizing contempt is one hundred percent authentic Clifton. "You're giving me an earache. Where's my highball?" He snags a glass from Jackie's tray as she edges by and swats her ass hard enough to make her bunny hop.

I'm astonished: A) the jerk has the nerve, and B) my mom blushes and keeps stepping as if she's a cocktail waitress pulling a shift in a 1960s club. What the fuck, over?

My heart flutters — Dad will blow sky-high; aggression and territorial pissing are hardwired into him. Instead, he smirks and a trapdoor opens in the collage of my memories of childhood. Sure, I'm used to their civil antipathy. Nonetheless, there's a rawness to Dad's smile; his hatred is laid bare. Things with them are more complicated and bitter than I'd dared to imagine.

Steely J leans over and his pants ride his crack. He switches on the sound. After a burst of feedback piano keys tinkle, building. "All right, all right, everybody park your caboose so's I can get this show on the road. I can't stay here all evening, I got a gig in Anchorage. My manager lined up this charity crap or else I'd be at the Gold Digger squeezing pole dancer titties and drinking real booze. You know it, cousin."

Dad guffaws. "Gimme some Pat Boone."

"Shuddup, wiseacre. I'll sing what I wanna sing." Steely J clears his throat. "As it happens, I wanna do a number by Pat B." He proceeds to sing, or kind of sing, "Speedy Gonzalez," including the cartoonish bridges by Speedy and his put-upon wife. Visualize, if you will, a flat affect teen mimicking a dead comedian imitating a middle-aged crooner who enunciates through his nose imitating a faux Spanish accent and fucking the lyrics over precisely enough to sprain your brain, and you get the picture.

"Sweet baby Jesus, what am I hearing?" Jackie mutters through her clenched teeth. She grips my elbow while smiling to shame a constipated beauty queen. "Who is this idiot?"

I return the grin with interest. "Tony Clifton, Ma. None other. Look how happy Daddy is."

"Speedy Gonzalez" wraps. The lull segues into an instrumental. Steely J huffs and puffs. Sweat makes tracks in his makeup. He sips the highball and nods at Dad. "Alaska, huh? Land of the Midnight Sun. Where men are men and so are the women. That wife of yours, buddy. Whadda ya do? Kidnap a mountain goat and slap a dress on it? Lady, another round and keep 'em coming." He hands Jackie (who looks like she's chewing tenpenny nails) his empty as the intro for "Green, Green Grass of Home" kicks in.

At this point, I'm naïve enough to hope it's going to be a success. Alas, during the instrumental, Steely J says to my dad, "Last time I did a charity set, it was at a children's ward. Cue-ball central. Really pathetic, I tell ya. Now, you look pretty good for a guy with the big C. Really good, really vibrant. Can't tell what's under your hat. Looks like a full head a hair. You got some meat on your bones. Got a nice gut goin', hey? Dunno, maybe beer has cancer-retarding qualities and that's why your hair hasn't all fallen out yet. Cancer of the ass, right?"

"Jeff isn't on chemotherapy," Jackie says coldly. She directs a withering glance at me. "Julie, I don't know who this...lout is, or if he's a friend, of yours, but I've had quite enough—"

Steely J snickers and waves dismissively. "'Quite enough'? Way you stomp around the house in your fuck-me pumps, you ain't had *any* in a while. Amirite, Jeff? Cancer of the asshole does take a man's zest for life out of the equation. How you supposed to concentrate on shtupping the missus when you're distracted by a burning ring of fire?"

"Oh my." I cover a horrified smile with my hand. I can smell the brimstone. The roof is sure to collapse and bury us alive any second. Such is my desperate plea to a non-existent God, at any rate. Dad and Jackie appear dumbfounded.

"Christ almighty, I'm thirsty." Steely J tosses the mike and does his penguin-strut out of the den.

"He has to leave. Immediately!" This from Jackie. She grips a shelf for support. Weakened and shocked, she'll recover to assume her ultimate form in a minute, I have no doubt.

"Mom—"

"Fine! I'm calling the police!" Strength returning. Rage will do the job.

"Overkill, Mom. Overkill."

"No, that's it. I'm calling 911."

"Mom, Jackie, what do you want the cops to do?"

"What do I want? What do I want! I *want* him to take his crappy karaoke box and get the hell away from us!"

"I'm gonna stab him," Dad says thoughtfully. He hasn't moved, and his expression is sort of dopey rather than furious, but he's white-knuckling the Bowie knife. "Jackie, I don't like how he's talking. I'm gonna slice his neck."

I tell them to cool their jets and stay put for the love of God. I go after Steely J. He's not in the upper living room or the kitchen. I'd run through the back door if I were in his shoes. Not the dude's style. His car remains parked on the street. He's the sort to hang his head and absorb whatever verbal or physical punishment is dished at him. At the moment, it's the physical punishment that Dad will inflict that has me worried.

The door to the half bath is wide and there's Steely J on all-fours, head dipped into the toilet. His foot twitches as he gurgles and laps with the rabid gusto of a hound attacking his favorite bowl. Gag me with a spoon. I kind of scream and he shudders and gazes over his shoulder, water dripping from his askew fake mustache.

"Yeah?" He says in a voice I haven't heard before this moment. It isn't Tony Clifton's and it isn't quite his own.

"My parents are straight tripping. Holy shit. Get your ass out before Dad stabs you or my mom calls in SWAT." I'm convinced he's got to go for several reasons. Imminent injury will suffice. "Are you...Are you drinking that?"

He paws his smeary lips and cracks his neck. "I'm due a commission." Almost in character, although his pancake makeup is ruined.

"Please, dude. I'll catch you with the dough later."

"Fine. Pay Steely J." He rises unsteadily. His bulk crowds the whole bathroom. The front of his suit is soaked.

"God! Beat it before I hurl." Well, too late on that count.

* * *

I expect a mushroom cloud and nuclear fallout. Instead, Jackie tiptoes through the house with a sheepish expression. We mumble weather-related factoids. Dad continues to marinate. I hobble around campus and grit my perfect teeth (thank you, retainer manufacturing company!) when I hand Steely J his hundred bucks. He's cool; counts his money and walks away like nothing.

I tell the adventure to Rocky Friday night after a hot and heavy session on the Eklutna Flats. The neck brace is history and I'm looking fly, so we're on again. It's cold and he lets the engine idle. Stars are embedded in the steamy glass. Every passing set of headlights on the highway illuminates the interior of the Iroc with a spangled glow.

"Toilet water?" Rocky says. "Sounds like a laugh riot. Bet your parents lost their shit. Eric Michaels told me Steely J's dad and Zane Tooms's parents are asshole buddies with a whole slew of Chinese investors. They fund illegal hunting expeditions in Africa and Siberia to snuff endangered animals and drive up the prices of sex drugs and diet pills. The Asians think powdered rhino horn will get their shit hard. Anyway, these guys are betting that once a bunch of animals go extinct, their market share is gonna pay big bucks. Pretty cold, huh?"

I agree it's pretty cold.

"I hope you didn't pay for the Steely J con."

"What else was I going to do?"

"Tell him to blow it out his ass. You owe him dick."

"Nobody crosses Steely J on a debt."

"Yeah, but the punk didn't come through as promised. No deal."

"I don't know, Rock. He came to the house and did his routine. Technically, we're the ones who pulled the plug—"

"Screw that noise." His hair is mussed and sweaty. His shirt is unbuttoned. He reeks of me. He sets his jaw with gung-ho stubbornness. "What's going to happen is, you're receiving a refund. Right now. We'll roll up to his pad and get him with the program."

I don't bother to argue. Rocky has the brains of the aforementioned blood-crazed rhino and there's no point. "It'll keep until tomorrow. How about we go another round, champ?"

"Another round." He glances at his crotch with a flicker of doubt.

"Ding-ding."

And that's how I start along a path that teaches me there are worse things than calamitous domestic scenes or getting accidentally knocked up.

* * *

Rocky cruises by my place the following afternoon. Mike Zant idles behind him on Mike's dad's Kawasaki motorcycle. Mike is varsity fullback, totally hot, and a lunkhead among lunkheads — exactly the type of goon you bring along when you're planning something stupid. Rocky dares not approach the front step (he is familiar with Dad and Dad's knife). He honks until I get it together and walk over to see what he wants. He tells me to hop in. After some back and forth, I do.

And we're off to see Steely J with intentions of malice. I spend the next twenty minutes half-heartedly trying to convince Rocky this is a bad idea. I stole the hundred dollars from Jackie's sock drawer, she doesn't miss it, and so on. Nothing doing. He clenches his jaw and presses harder on the gas. Eventually I hunker in my seat and get quiet. Lots of hairpin turns on the road up the mountain to the house of J.

Lunkhead Mike won't wear a helmet over his majestic afro. The way he's laying the bike over on curves trying to match Rocky's pace, I'm worried he'll miss one and crash among the spruce.

Much as I protest against this trip, the cruel bitch inside of me hopes Rocky and Mike have to slap Steely J around. He embarrassed me in front of my parents and I'd love to have the money I stole from Jackie back in my hot little hand; there's a shoe sale on at the Dimond Center Mall in Anchorage.

The house lurks at the end of a steep drive (rutted and broken pavement), eighty or ninety feet off the main road. It might have been tits a decade ago, but the place is going to hell fast. Funky shake roof and siding peel from the house. Mother Nature rules Alaska. Lower floor is a daylight basement wedged into the hillside. Cruddy brown-yellow curtains are drawn. Trees everywhere. Last mailbox I noticed is a mile back, at least.

Steely J's Toyota is angled next to a state trooper cruiser on blocks. The cruiser may have been in a fire. Smashed in windows and busted light bar. Nearby, a rotting doghouse, but no dog. Reminds me how much I miss mine. Spruce branches, shorn by the last few windstorms, lie tangled in the dead grass. A raven perches on a splintered, disconnected telephone pole and gives me a knowing eye.

I pretend the hood of the Iroc is a piano and lounge atop it (awkwardly) while Rocky and Mike move up the driveway, climb a flight of rickety stairs, and knock on the front door. The door opens and they step inside. The door closes and they're gone.

It's much cooler here. Sunlight slants through the canopy, feeble as a candle in a huge, wrecked mossy cathedral vault. Too chilly. I huddle in the car for a while. Problem is, Rocky took the keys and now my feet are totally freezing. Worse, no tunes.

This drags along for an unbearable while until Dee Dee's number beeps on my cell phone. Bored and vengeful, I answer. Just the twat I want to ream. She asks if my dad enjoyed the show at the Gold Digger and I tell her to cram it where the sun don't shine. She's genuinely taken aback — *Say what? Why you trippin'?* and like that. I thank her for the false info, and ruining my dad's birthday, fuck you very much.

"Whoa-whoa — I didn't feed you any bullshit."

"You said your pal was in the know about Clifton. Only the guy was never scheduled to appear. Nice, real nice."

"Julie, Julie, calm down. I told you, it was a private show. Clifton played — 10PM sharp. My parents went. Dude's an asshole. Everybody loved it. Dad got an autographed photo. You're really spun, girl."

I tell her to blow a goat and end the call. Oh, dear dog, my wrath toward Steely cocksucker J has reached a crescendo. Murder is a possibility. The conniving bastard failed to secure tickets and concocted the whole performance to cover himself and charge me double. Fuming and plotting, I glance toward the house and notice the door has swung open again.

Somebody yells my name. The muffled cry doesn't repeat. Leaves me guessing. My imagination runs wild — Steely J's fat face getting knocked in by Mike's fist; Steely J's nads getting kicked around like a hacky sack. This is a pleasing fantasy, except...What if the boys go too far? What if they beat him to a pulp and forget to collect the loot? This situation practically begs for a woman's touch.

My knee is better every day. Rage makes a beautiful painkiller. I ascend the grade and climb the steps with less difficulty than I'd feared. Gets my heartrate going is all. Gawd, the house, though. Steely J carved something, maybe a crescent moon, into the wooden door panel. Inside, Lemon Pledge partially masks an underlying dankness. I wander around a dim maze. None of the light switches work. Doors are nailed shut except to the kitchen and a half bathroom. Both rooms are Spartan and neat. Reminds me of his car.

Anger deserts me the way sweat evaporates, and leaves me clammy and flustered. Why would a person nail doors shut inside his home? Why haven't I heard any commotion? Why don't I call to Rocky and Mike? To this last, I can only say that the last thing a person does when exploring a semi-abandoned building is draw attention to one's self. It's a survival trait culled from inhaling enough slasher flicks. No fucking in an empty room and no calling out, *anybody there?* as you sneak around in your Nancy Drew shoes.

Thump-thump-thump goes my rubber-tipped crutch on floorboards in a long hall. I am a girl and instantly notice the lack of photos, paintings, or any form of decoration. Shit ain't right. At the end of the hall are stairs heading down into the basement. Of course, I hear Rocky's voice. He chuckles and so does someone else.

I get to the bottom of the steps and push through a heavy rubber sheet. Okay, creepy. The basement is a box and it's hot as a greenhouse. Afternoon light dribbles in at the edges of the curtains and there's a desk lamp glowing from a distant corner. TV monitor with the sound muted. Comedians are performing. A rich, earthy reek gets into my nose and gags me. Fertilizer, shit, dead leaves, wet copper, and green growing things. A squirmy smell. The J family used to summer in the Amazon. They brought some with, apparently.

Furniture is totally Steely J. An aquarium, or terrarium, not sure which, except it's economy sized. Two hundred gallons or more, pushed against the far wall. Racks of the sort you find in hospitals are positioned opposite one another and strung with IV tubes and baggies of what surely must be blood and other, clearer stuff. I've seen plasma; it's plasma. Wonderful.

Rocky squats in an inflatable pool near the terrarium. He doesn't acknowledge my appearance. He's in a zone. His jacket is unbuttoned. He's not wearing a shirt or pants. I linger on this image: Shirtless. Pantless. Unbuttoned jacket. Squatting in a kiddie pool of water. An object sticks to his breastbone. Fat as a big old rubbery turd from a novelty catalog. Grayish-brownish-black, and shiny-slick. Attached at his left nipple, it trails to his belly. Vaguely familiar, possibly a specimen I've seen in Mr. Navarro's biology class. My poor brain will catch up real soon. The lighting is bad, but the passing seconds improve my vision and I'm sorry. More reverse-C crescent moons are spray-painted in white on the curtains and the walls.

Steely J reclines upon a bench seat torn from a truck. He's naked as a Greek statue. His eyes roll back and forth, white to black. Leeches, that's what my brain was trying to say. Leeches of varying length hang from his neck and his man-tits. One, swollen to the heftiness of a kid's arm, gloms onto his groin, its bulk flopped across his thigh like a nightmarish wang. Makes sense — femoral artery runs through there. A prime tap. He slurps from a mostly deflated bag of blood, his expression dreamy and fucked up. In with the fresh, right? Those are Mike's boots poking from behind the bench seat-couch, for sure.

Another stark-naked man rises from behind the couch and moves around the side. He kneels and gently detaches the leech from Steely's groin. Cheeks gleaming sweat, the stranger glances at me and smirks the dopey, amiable peasant smirk that has enthralled nightclub audiences since 19-fucking-74. He tenderly lays the leech on a towel and sticks it with a horse-needle syringe. Pulls the plunger and draws creamy black blood into the barrel.

Steely J rouses himself. His marble gaze rolls to me. "Hi, JV. What can I do for you?"

"Never mind."

I turn and head for the stairs. No keys for the car. Mike's motorcycle is beyond my capabilities. Town is a major hike for a girl with a bum leg. Too afraid to look over my shoulder. Swear there's heavy movement behind me, though. The universe and its bullet-fast molecules slow to a crawl.

First things first. I have to make it out of the house and call for help (that should be an interesting conversation). What are the odds I'll make it? Everybody knows that when seconds count, the state troopers are minutes away.

The TV volume kicks in. A laugh track swells and booms and fills my ears.

II: Swift to Chase

Ardor

—*Yukon-Kuskokwim Delta*, February, 1975

What is it Pilot John says right before we drop from the sky?

Where is Molly's body? No, that's my own voice haunting me on account of someone else's ghost, someone else's guilt.

The pilot's head inclines to the left, slick as any disco floor pro. He gasps and takes the good Lord's name in vain. There's a quality of terror in the sharp inhalation that precedes this utterance. There's rapture in the utterance itself. His words are distorted by electronic interference through the headset. The snarl of a lynx wanting its fill of guts.

Obligingly, the world rolls over and shows its belly—

—I come to after the crash and call Conway's name the way I sometimes do upon surfacing from a nightmare. In this nightmare he is kissing me but his left eye is gone and I can see daylight shining all the way through his skull. He says hot into my mouth, *This wound won't close.*

Now I'm awake and alive. Hell of a surprise, the being alive part.

Snow trickles down through a hole in the fuselage and crystallizes in my lashes and beard. The last of the daylight trickles through the hole too and the world around me resolves into soft focus. Buckets of white light saturate everything until it's all ghostly and delicate. I'm strapped into the far back seat of the Beaver. I close my eyes again and recall low mountains rising on our left and the shadow of the plane descending toward an ice sheet that seemed to stretch unto the end of creation.

Our particular jag of beach lies south of Quinhagak, not that that helps. In the summer, this is a vast circulatory system of bogs and streams on the edge of the Bering Sea. Ptarmigan and wolves, bears and fish dwell here, feast upon one another here. In the winter, it's one of God's abandoned drawing slates. The temperature is around negative thirty Fahrenheit. That's cold, my babies. The mercury will only keep dropping.

"Conway's in Seattle," Parker says. "He's safe. You're safe. Who's your favorite football team?" His breath is minty. He thinks I'm slipping away when I'm actually slipping *back* into the world. Sweet kid. Handsome, too. Life is gonna wreck him. That's funny. He grips my shoulder. His mittens are blue and white to match the stripes on the plane. "C'mon Sam, stay with me. Who'd you root for in the Super Bowl? The Vikings? I bet you're a Vikings man. My cousin met Fran Tarkenton, says he's a gem. Can't throw a spiral, but a hell of a quarterback anyhow."

"Cowboy fan." I'm remarkably calm, despite this instinctive urge to smack the condescension from him. He means well. His eyes are so blue. Conway's are green and green is my favorite color, so I'm safe, as Parker keeps saying.

"The Cowboys! No kidding? Seattle doesn't have a club. One more year, right?"

"Dad is from Galveston." I haven't thought about my father in an age, much less acknowledged him aloud. Could be a concussion.

"Where's your accent? You don't have an accent."

"Dad does. Classic drawl." I hesitate. My tongue is dry. Goddamned climate. "How are the other guys?" The other guys being pilot John, regional historian Maddox, and our wilderness guide extraordinaire Moses.

"Don't worry about them. Everybody's A-okay. Let's see if we can get you outta here. Gonna be dark any minute now. Moses thinks we need to be somewhere else before then."

His voice is too cheerful. I'm convinced he's lying about everyone being all right. Then I catch a glimpse of Pilot John slumped at the controls, his anorak splashed red. His posture is awkward, inanimate—he's a goner for certain. The engine has to be sitting on his legs. Snapped matchsticks, most definitely. The windshield blasted inward to cover him in rhinestones. I lack the strength to utter recriminations. Abrupt stabs of pain in my lower back suggest my body is coming out of shock. It isn't happy.

Parker strips free of a mitten and there are pills in the palm of his hand. He feeds me the pills.

I clear my throat and say, "Somebody will be along. The posse can't be far." Lord, the aspirin is bitter. A slug of lukewarm coffee from Parker's thermos helps. "John got a Mayday out, didn't he?" But what I recall is John with both hands on the wheel while the rest of us yell and pray. Nobody touches the radio in the eight or so seconds before it all goes black. "Sonofabitch. Tell me it's working." I know it's not working, though. The radio was smashed on impact along with Pilot John's body. That's how this tragedy is unfolding, isn't it? After making a career of fucking over others, finally we are the ones getting the screw job. O. Henry or Hitchcock should be on the case.

Parker says, "I wonder if you can walk."

While he struggles to extricate me from the ruins of the plane, I'm thinking not only is it a damned shame Pilot John failed to transmit a Mayday, he didn't even file a flight plan that accounts for our detour to this wasteland of tundra and ice. We're at least two hours southwest of the original destination. That potentially lethal blunder is on me. I'd gotten greedy and tried to squeeze in an unscheduled stop. Thanks to me we are all the way up shit creek.

A storm is moving in off the sea. Blizzard conditions will sock in search and rescue craft at Bethel. That means three, possibly four days of roughing it for us. If we're lucky. How lucky we are remains to be seen.

I cough on the raw taste of smoke.

"Heck." Parker glances over his shoulder. "Guess she's on fire."

Yes, Virginia, we're in trouble—

—Professor Gander invited me to lunch at the Swan Club in Ballard and laid it all on the table. Entrusted me with a withered valise stuffed with documents and old-timey photos. He endeavored to explain their significance through suggestion and innuendo. Two things I dislike unless we're talking romance, which we weren't. I disguised my fascination with a yawn.

He lighted a cigarette and set it in the ashtray without taking a drag first. "The papers were written by RM Bluefield, allegedly a mysterious Victorian fellow whom Stoker based the Renfield character upon. Bluefield was an avowed mystic, a fascination he acquired abroad in Eastern Europe and Asia. He possessed medical training…was obsessed with the concept of immortality, but then, so were many others of that era. His particular interest lay in the notion that it might be obtained through certain blood rites or the consumption of animal organs. Stoker, it is thought, perused the fellow's papers and then mocked in print Mr. Bluefield's eccentricity.

"The journals changed hands, most recently belonging to an actor from the 1950s and '60s named Ralph Smyth. Where *he* acquired them is a matter of conjecture, although it's of scant consequence. For our purposes, we simply need to locate Smyth himself."

"Ah, the royal we. There's a booster, I presume. Got to love those guys. Richer than rich if he's going through you."

"Yes, Mr. Cope. I represent a patron. One with very deep pockets."

"God love 'em. And what does this patron want with Smyth?"

"You will locate him and ask a single question. Return with his answer, whatever that may be."

"A question?"

"One question. I'll even write it down for you." He produced a fancy pen and indeed did write it on a coaster. He also wrote his home address and a set of numbers that represented the payment on offer. A nice plump round figure, to be sure.

I lingered over the coaster and then put it in my pocket. "This is a little odd, professor. Not exactly my normal brief, so to speak. I take it this Smyth character is missing, or else you'd go ask him yourself."

"It is possible the fellow's dead, although we suspect he's very much alive. In hiding, we think. Took a powder into the Alaskan wilderness during the spring of 1967. There are more recent accounts, multiple sightings of a man matching Smyth's description."

"Seven years is a long time to be on the lam. The cops want him?"

"The authorities don't possess evidence to implicate him in any nefarious dealings, such as the disappearance of my patron's daughter. My patron suspects otherwise, naturally. That's where you come in."

"Maybe Smyth's got an aversion to overly aggressive film buffs." I smiled, but he didn't seem amused. "So, I'm going to put together a team and fly all over the ass end of Alaska, hunting for some guy basically nobody's ever heard of..."

"Ralph Smyth, Ralph Smyth, surely you recall..." Professor Gander buffed his signet ring and waited for the light to dawn in my presumably Neanderthal brain. Fucker wore a cardigan and rimless glasses. He'd gone prematurely white like Warhol.

"Surely I do not." I took a gulp of Redbreast. Glass number three. I'm not a heavy drinker, but suffering the good professor required extreme measures.

"A poor man's Lon Chaney, Sr. who eked a career from getting violently offed in a dozen Hammer films. What he's famous for, however—"

"Nothing, apparently," I said, a teensy bit drunk already.

Gander bared his mismatched and silver-capped teeth. He wanted a taste of my blood, it could be assumed. "Bravo, Cope. The man is famous for nothing. What he's *infamous* for is his final role in a French-Canadian art film. *Ardor.* An exceedingly liberal interpretation of *Dracula.* Ten years ago this spring *Ardor* premiered at a Quebec festival, then sank into obscurity. It is reviled by critics and forgotten by the public. Have you seen it? Amazing work."

"Oh, by art, you mean smut, eh? I dig."

"Yes, a pornographic movie. Rated X for sex and violence. A notorious piece of cinema, even by genre standards. Banned in many countries. Only a few copies rumored to survive, etcetera, etcetera."

"I'm sorry I missed this one. A porno retelling of *Dracula.* What will they think of next?"

"The forces at work in the world are endlessly inventive. Artistic autocoprophagy is here to stay."

I studied him through the haze of his untouched cigarette, preferring not to dignify his comment with a response. I made a mental note to look up *autocoprophagy.*

He said, "Why don't you come by my place tonight and I'll show you the film? I've got a bootleg reel. A few colleagues and some friends of the university will be in attendance. You can mingle, make new acquaintances. A fellow in your line can always use new connections, and a better class of them, too."

"You and your cronies going to gather around the campfire to watch a stag flick, huh?" I said. "A banned stag flick. That's a relief. I prefer the company of miscreants."

"There's another item we'll need to discuss," he said. "The client is a dear friend of mine. That's why he's come to me in the wake of the law's failure to rectify his concerns. Regardless, I've reason to believe Smyth went to Alaska on a specific mission. He's a bibliophile and an antiquarian. His home, which he abandoned, was stuffed with extraordinary...items, shall we say? By all means extract the information my patron requires, but if you can bring home any significant papers or relics, or lacking that, photographic evidence of said, you'll be generously compensated."

"Well, in that case, here's another coaster." –

—I drove over to the professor's house around nine. Late enough that people would've settled in, but before any craziness had gotten started, or so I hoped. Gander struck me as a buttoned-down freak. Perhaps a Wally.

The address he'd scribbled on a coaster led me to an old mansion in the U-District, set back from the street. Parking is hell in the U, so I left the car in a likely spot and walked three blocks. The windows were dark and I wondered if it was the right place until Gander's housemaid answered the bell and greeted me by name. More of a gasped epithet, really. Her face was pale. She held a candle in an ornamental bowl.

The maid led me to a study eerily illuminated by a silver screen on the far wall. She fled. I got the impression of antique furniture and lots of bookcases. A throng of silhouettes was back-lighted by the screen. I whiffed cherry pipe smoke and fancy cologne, a hint of marijuana.

A film played for this crowd of rustling shadows. Its frames jumped, were poorly spliced; the scenes were muddy and marred by frequent cigarette burns; the color flickered. Tiny subtitles and a strange, scratchy orchestral symphony accompanied the grunts and cries of the actors, all a half-beat offset from the action itself. Somebody was fucking somebody. Somebody was murdering somebody. Cocks everywhere, thrusting into every opening. A guillotine blade dropped through the neck of a devil clown. Gore splashed the thirteen dancing brides of Dracula and flecked the camera lens. Darkness flooded in. For an instant the gallery dissolved and I became dislocated, a bullet shot into the vacuum of deep space.

The lights came up while the film kept running. Someone said, "Jesus Christ!"

I beheld a congregation of the crème de la crème of UW faculty; fifteen or so middle-aged dudes in sweaters and slacks, drinks and smokes in hand, all of them sniffing in my direction like moles. The departments of anthropology, psychiatry, and literature were well-represented.

Horror stretched Gander's face in all kinds of unpleasant directions. "What are you doing here?" He gestured as if to ward away an evil spirit. "What are you doing here? You can't be here."

I wanted to tell him to piss off, he'd invited me, but I couldn't speak. There was too much blood in my mouth. I looked down and realized I was naked and covered in blood. I extended my arms like the Vitruvian Man and the room rotated. Centrifugal force pinned me in place. On the screen, washed out, yet immense and wicked, naked Dracula embraced naked Renfield and crushed the life from him. The camera zoomed in on Renfield's glazed eye, penetrated the iris into the secondary universe, the anti-reality. It was snowing there, in Hell. I was in there, in Hell, in the snow, waving to myself.

A white glow ignited on my left where the doorway to the long hall should've hung. Instead, an ice field bloomed through a porthole. So bright, so beautiful, filling up my brain with fog—

—The team assembled at the Bull Moose Diner in downtown Bethel, Alaska to plot a final sequence of site flyovers. Alaska is a big place. We were running out of places to search for our quarry, though. If I couldn't find Smyth in the next few days, that might be curtains for the expedition.

The frigid Alaskan winter wasn't doing my mood any favors. Relocating to western Washington for a vacation didn't sound half bad. I could take Conway to Lake Crescent for a romantic idyll, or hiking along Hurricane Ridge. Or maybe we'd hole up at my house and drink wine and watch the rain hit the windows.

Is retrieving the bones of a person treasure hunting? Or would you call it grave robbing? Conway posed this question with a smile — he could afford to smile because he didn't know the half of what I did for a living. That was the last time I'd seen him in the flesh. He'd spent the night at my place on Queen Anne Hill. The next morning would find me aboard a jet to Anchorage. He lived across town in North Gate; sold insurance to corporations. The job took him out of my life about as often as mine took me out of his. We'd been lovers for three years. I'm tallish and homely; he's shorter and handsome enough to model if he wanted. He's a man of his word and I'm shifty as they come. The arrangement worked, barely.

Grave robbing? Maybe Conway had it right. Over the past decade I'd flown thrice around the world in the service of numerous scholarly profiteers of the exact same mold as Professor Gander. Missions revolved around wresting artifacts of historical significance from the locals, or better yet, absconding with said relics before the locals even suspected chicanery. Sometimes, this job being an example, I was sent to retrieve a real live person, or extract information from said. You never knew. My chief talents? A willingness to follow orders and endure a not inconsiderable measure of privation and hardship along the way. I don't balk at getting my hands dirty. Runs in the family. Granddad shot people for the Irish mob back in the Roaring Twenties; made an art of it, or so the legends go. I'm not even close to being that kind of a hardcase, just sufficiently mean to get matters across when it's called for.

The future would take care of itself. Meanwhile, here I sat in Bethel with a string to play out: four sites within striking distance of the village. Gold Rush mining camps abandoned since World War II, except for infrequent visits by tourists, researchers, and ne'er-do-wells. That last was us. My comrades were more inclined to the business of looting and pillaging native artifacts under the guise of academic inquiry.

"A sentient being isn't an artifact separate from the universe," said Moses as he counted out bills for the waiter. None of us had the first clue who he was speaking to. "Sentient beings are the sensors of the universe, its nerve endings. A colony of ants, a gaggle of geese, a city-state, are the places where enough sensors amass and the universe becomes self-aware." He paused with a scowl. "Somebody needs to kick in another two bucks."

That was doubtless Maddox who'd skimped on the tip. I tossed a five-spot on the table to save time and frustration for all concerned. Prior to this assignment I'd not worked with any of them. I preferred the Southwest states. My Alaska network was weak, forcing me to rely on a subcontractor in Juneau who'd made the initial referrals.

Over the months I'd gotten to know this group, on a superficial level, at least. This line of work doesn't engender intimacy, it heightens eccentricities. A man becomes known by his foibles, his personality tics. Illusions of bonding or brotherhood are perfidious.

Pilot John was a boozy loser who'd washed out of life in Vermont. Maddox was a boozy loser who'd gotten dumped from the faculty at the University of Anchorage for a variety of sordid offenses; one too many coeds had dropped her panties for him, I gathered. Moses, our Yupik guide, was a boozy loser who'd blown his Western State degree and done five years in the pen for grand larceny. Nowadays he guided hunters and hikers and nefarious types such as me, even though his expertise lay somewhere in the area of philosophy and he didn't know an iota more about snow than anybody else schlepping around the Yukon Delta. Parker, I couldn't figure. Didn't smoke, didn't drink, so what did he do? Clean as a whistle except for some domestic bullshit with a younger brother. His specialty was photography and he knew his way around the Northern Territories. The mystery was why a smart, clean-living guy like him couldn't get a reputable gig. Punching his brother in the kisser wasn't a satisfactory explanation for why he'd become persona non grata.

I hate mysteries, but the solution to this one had already suggested itself to me. What to do with my conclusions was the problem—

—I kicked in a lot of doors and looked under a lot of rocks to discover five pertinent facts of the Ralph Smyth case.

Fact One: He'd received training as a playwright and dramatic actor and it hadn't helped. His oeuvre mainly consisted of crappy black-and-white monster flicks that would've mildly entertained my twelve-year-old self. His shtick was playing second banana to the main villain. He chewed scenery as Igor or Renfield in at least half the movies and as an enforcer, arm-breaker, or button man in most of the others.

Fact Two: Smyth had had the reputation as a real sonofabitch. Small-time actor, yet connected behind the scenes. His father had owned majority interest in a lighting and set-making company. Money opened all the right doors. Ralphie baby was chummy with Karloff, Lugosi, and Cushing, and every two-bit producer that came down the pike. He enjoyed conning young, naïve starlet wannabes.

He seduced them, screwed them, strung them out on dope and then turned them over to one of the slimeball directors for further abuse and exploitation. Molly Lindstrom, so keen to escape the tyranny of daddy dearest, was another fly in Smyth's web. She vanished six months after principal photography wrapped on *Ardor*. The authorities looked into it, Burt Lindstrom being important and such. Never came to anything.

Fact Three: The case went cold and Smyth dropped the acting gig and disappeared into the woodwork. His trail wound all over, from Juneau, to Anchorage, to Fairbanks, and west toward the bitter coast. He was a ghost with many aliases: George Renfro, Ogden Shoemaker, Bobby Stoker, and Gerald Bluefield were the popular ones. He had plenty of cash and Alaska isn't the kind of place where people ask a lot of prying questions. There was a long line of secretive white men seeking some grand destiny in the wild.

I grudgingly admitted Professor Gander was correct in his assessment that Smyth was on the trail of something big. He was a man of disconcerting depths. For example, our long-lost actor hadn't simply starred in the much reviled *Ardor*, he'd written the script and sold it to the studio. Uncredited to boot. He'd allegedly gotten wasted at a cast party and told a grip that the Dracula legends were rooted in fact. *Yeah, Vlad the Impaler*, said the grip. Smyth laughed and said, *Not the Tepes horseshit. Think the Devil's Triangle. Think the sailing stones of Death Valley.*

Fact Four: Nine people had gone missing in the various regions of Alaska coinciding with Smyth's travels. Drunks, lost hunters, adventurers. Folks nobody would miss unless, like me, one paid attention to patterns. My man Smyth was a pervert and a cad of the worst sort. Sorting the old papers he'd lovingly collected on ritual cannibalism and human sacrifice, I suspected he was also a murderer.

Fact Five: There are six quarts of blood in the body of a man and I'm low, very low. Now I know I should've stayed in Seattle with my true love—

—Sprung joints of the plane seethe smoke. Flames streak from the cowling that's half nosed into the ice. The smoke is black and thick. The column rises several feet, and then spills down over the ground, pressed hard by the frigid temperature. Visages of devils float in the tide and shoot forth hot red tongues. The wind whips it until it boils. Concupiscent curds of death. Where oh where is my shirtless and muscular roller of big cigars? Call that bastard in here on the double! I have my second chuckle of the day in celebration of wit undimmed by the impingement of certain doom.

We've trudged a good distance inland. The plane is a toy. My glove blocks sight of it easily. We are even farther from the brightening stars. The blue-black horizon has enfolded the ocean like a curtain dropping onto a stage. Moses leads. Parker and Maddox drag me and our pitiable remnants of gear on a canvas tarp salvaged from the wreckage. My knee is sprained; my back is in spasms. I can but hope that's the worst of my injuries. We'll know tonight when the universe freezes and the aspirin supply disappears.

Pilot John screams way back there where we left him in his pyre. I can barely hear him over the rising wind and the crunch of boots in the snow. The men stop in their tracks and gaze back across the flats. Vapor wisps from their mouths. For a moment they resemble a lonely trio of caribou, separated from the main herd and bewildered at a sound foreign to their existence.

"Hey, he's not dead," Maddox says to Moses. His tone is reproachful.

Moses pulls down his hood. His face is broad and dark. His mustache is silver with frost. He frowns. No, he definitely doesn't look like a man who wants to believe what he's hearing. He stares wordlessly into the gathering darkness, into the coal at its heart.

"Oh, no. Moses, you said he was dead."

"That's the wind."

"No, it's him. God help us." Maddox crosses himself.

Parker glances from man to man. "What's happening?" He really doesn't get it. His hat has fur-lined earflaps; maybe that's why.

"Pilot John is frying," I say through gritted teeth. Nobody says anything for a minute or so. The screams have stopped. My hunch is the unlucky bastard woke up to his flesh popping like bacon, then promptly succumbed to smoke inhalation. Here's hoping. I can't help myself; I quote from the poetry of that long dead Yukon sage, Robert Service: *The Northern Lights have seen queer sights, but the queerest they ever did see was the night on the marge of Lake Le Barge I cremated Sam McGee!*

Moses raises his hood again. His coat is a really nice homemade one with a wolf ruff and more fur trim at the wrist and ankle openings. It'll take him a lot longer to freeze to death than it will for everybody else. He starts walking again, toward the foothills of the Kilbuck mountains. I can't help but imagine them as tombstones.

"Shouldn't we stay with the plane?" Parker says this for the third or fourth time. He managed to save his best camera and carries it on a lanyard around his neck.

"We'll die in the open." Moses doesn't glance backward. Shoulders squared, head lowered, he plods on.

"Gonna buy it either way," Maddox says, low and grumbly. Not a protest, it is an utterance of fact.

"Somebody might see the smoke," Parker says. His is the faint and fading voice of reason swallowed by the wilderness and the indifference of his comrades.

"C'mon," Maddox says. A bear of a man, red-eyed from lack of drink. He and Parker grasp the edges of the tarp and begin dragging me again.

According to the maps, long ago there was a village around here. I'd hoped to find Smyth or some clue regarding Smyth's whereabouts. The village has crumbled, or the ice has buried it. No trace of the fish camps or the mining camps either. A cruel wind blows, scouring the ice to dirt in spots and making brick ramps of the snow in others. The wind doesn't ever really stop in this place. It has, like Sandburg's grass, work to do erasing all signs of human habitation. The wind is the tongue of a ravening beast. It licks at our warmth, the feeble light of our miserly souls.

Our company founders and staggers and scrambles onward. It is dark when we tuck into the shelter of a rocky crevice. Nearby, the face of the mountain is glaciated. Water oozes and steams over ice stalactites and we lap at it. My lips are already cracking and it's only been a few hours. This kind of weather leaches a man, withers him to a husk.

By the beam of a heavy-duty flashlight, the men stretch the tarp as a windbreak. They shore and buffer the enclosure with hastily gathered alder branches and rocks. In the end, we cuddle into a hole and pull the lid over ourselves. I'm wedged between Parker and Moses. A rock digs into my spine. It is cold, concentrated cold, and numbs me with dreadful immediacy. The canvas molds over my face in a death mask, tightening, then slackening with the gusts. The wind roars in the absolute blackness. Farther off, a fluting note as ice shears free of its mooring and is dashed upon the rocks.

Tomorrow we'll find a better shelter, build a fire if we can, if we survive the night. I shiver uncontrollably. I am a particle adrift in a gulf. The horizontal fall is endless—

—"What's going on with you?" Conway says. He's got my cock in his hand, but not much is happening. "You're different these days." A not good kind of different, apparently, because his voice is too flat to mean anything else.

I'm on my back on the bed, staring at the wall, at the Wawal tapestry of a stigmatic Christ that I appropriated from the estate of a wealthy geezer in Maryland. The image doesn't thrill me, nothing does. I am bereft and confused. I am still falling; have been since the night I went to Gander's house. When was that anyway? Before or after the year in Alaska? Before or after the crash?

"Sam?"

I turn my head and look him in the eye. He's whole, handsome. I understand what he wants and choose to play dumb, which is a mistake. Despite his Ivy League degree Conway's not the sharpest knife in the drawer, but he's far from dull. He's intuitive as the devil. Sometimes we're so synched it's as if he's in my head. Cue the persistent whisper in the back of my mind: *I came here to the coldest place I could find because it slows everything. The cold.* There is no way to explain my experience in Alaska to Conway any more than I could to the investigators or the shrink. Not in a truthful fashion. To the cops and officials, I gave lies. With my beloved, I let my smile be the lie. Only, he isn't having it.

"Sam. Where are the others?"

I wish I knew. Except, I do know—

—The storm lasts thirty-nine hours, then there's a lull. Maddox crawls forth, reborn from the stone womb into a new Ice Age. The sun is a crimson blob low on the horizon, Polyphemus glaring through a hole in the clouds. The other two men follow him, creaking and cracking as they move. They are stick men, dry as tinder. It is so cold spit freezes on my lips. It is so cold my tongue is a clammy lump, separate from the rest of my flesh. Thirst gouges my throat. The others stand over me, black silhouettes seething. Maddox and Parker yank me from the hole like I'm a sack of feathers. Parker hands me a snowshoe to use as a crutch. I'm wobbly and in a lot of pain. On my feet and under my own power, however.

Moses says, "There's gonna be another blow." He's covered in a glittery coat of hoarfrost. He resembles a ghost. We all do. I'm thinking we're very close to it now. The abyss that men tumble into when they shuffle off the mortal coil is right here, always present in places such as this one. The bones of the earth are all around us.

We need a shelter, a fire, and water. Moses chops ice with a hatchet and stows it in a bag. We move against the flank of the mountains, searching for a cave or an abandoned cabin, any kind of habitation. The wind picks up again–

–There's a scene in *Ardor* that transcends the smut and the schlock. It is the scene wherein dutiful Renfield and the Count repose after a murderous orgy. The count reveals that his body is an illusion, a projection of pure darkness given fleshly form. He isn't a sentient creature, merely the imitation of one, the echo of one. The consumption of blood is a metaphor, larger than sex, more terrible than repression. *There's a hole no man can fill,* says the count. *No amount of love or hate or heat poured into the pit. No amount of light. I am the voice of the abyss.*

The idea of Dracula as genius loci is, well, genius. Vampires as black holes, the dull and ravenous points of a behemoth's fangs. Out of place for a smut flick, I admit, yet brilliant. Too bad it didn't clue me in to my imminent peril. By a trick of the camera, *Dracula* implodes in slow motion, a star collapsing into itself, and for a moment the bed is rent with a slash of radioactive blackness and bits of ash.

Then the film skips and it's back to fucking and sucking–

–I emerge from the bathroom and find Conway naked atop the covers. He's peering through a magnifying glass at the papers from the antique valise Professor Gander gave me.

Valise and contents are dated at approximately ninety years old. The leather is wrinkled, the documents crinkled and yellow as the piss I just took. These items, the curious circumstances of its last owner's flight from civilization, are supposed to convince me. Silly, wicked Gander. The only thing that convinces me is money.

Conway frowns. "Who wrote this? The fellow's penmanship was atrocious. From this passage all I can make out is, "*My wound won't close.*"

I don't get a chance to answer because the next slide clicks into place and I'm shot forward in time and back to Alaska. Nobody knows the trouble I see, except my comrades and none of them can do shit about it either.

Smyth emerges from the storm to deliver us from our predicament. His skull is stove in, as if by a hammer blow, so I can make out the ossified coils of his forebrain and I'm trying to remember if Dr. Seward trepanned Renfield in an attempt to save his life. Smyth's appearance is more monstrous than any master makeup artist could hope to devise. He is an upright cadaver manipulated by strings of icy vapor.

His song is irresistible, although he explains it's not his, that he's merely a vessel. He speaks of cabbages and kings and how a combination of saline and cold will send a death spike into the depths of the sea, killing everything it touches. He describes a crack that runs through the dark of space and how it bends the light, how it wears faces and how it wails. How it drinks heat. He is a madman. I've never seen a tongue so long or black.

Eventually, he lights a wooden pipe and passes it around the circle. Claims the hash is from a batch made by monks in 1756, so it's the good stuff. Calls it crypt dust, or something like that. Insists we fortify ourselves for the walk, and nobody argues. I don't taste much of anything, don't feel much of anything, and decide it's probably leaves and twigs. I change my tune a few minutes later when the sun begins to contract and expand like an iris.

He leads us to a palace he's carved from ice and rock. Nothing lives anywhere around his home. The desiccated carcasses of bats lie strewn everywhere. Hundreds of them. A carpet of shrunken heads and brittle matchstick bones. Rocks for furniture, icicle stalactites for chandeliers, an irregular pit in the tilted floor. The pit is approximately four feet in diameter. It wheezes a foul, volcanic draft.

Smyth says coming down from the experience of starring in *Ardor* was nearly the death of him. In a fit of despair, he went to his dressing room and drank a fifth of bourbon and shot himself in the head. He wore hats everywhere after that incident.

I came here to the coldest place I could find because it slows everything. The cold. It keeps me. While he's talking, we're in a state of exultant exhaustion. We've taken a hit of the dragon and the world has the substance of a dream.

Parker asks about the hole.

"That's the crack that runs through everything," Smyth says. "I dug it myself." The sonofabitch doesn't even need to move fast, we're all dumb and stuck in our tracks as cows lowing on the ramp to the killing floor. He uses the hatchet that Moses brought along, two or three licks apiece. I'm lucky, it's only my thigh, and Parker's kind of lucky too.

The bodies of the unfortunate slough into the pit that's awaited us a million years—

—My parents are old as the dust that blows across Texas where they've retreated to for those golden years. I haven't spoken to them since Vietnam got cooking. Dad didn't take to his son turning out gay, honorable combat service or not, and Mom, well, as her husband went, so did she.

It's been a few months and I've slowed down on the pills and the booze and am sufficiently restored to humanity to report my true findings, the findings I haven't told anyone, not Professor Gander, not the cops, not Conway.

Molly Lindstrom's parents remind me of mine, except a bunch richer. Their house is in a gated neighborhood amid carefully manicured forestland outside of Seattle. Burt Lindstrom made his dough in the engineering division of a certain well-known aerospace company. His is a precise and austere mind. Wouldn't know it from the décor. Antique hunting rifles, swords, and moose-heads on the walls and nothing to do with aviation or aviators. He favors red and black checked plaids, denim pants, and logging boots. Makes Lee Marvin seem soft and cuddly in comparison. His wife, Margaret, a former bathing beauty, has gone thick in the middle. She's in a dress, a blue one. Her eyes are cruel as a bird's.

Their guard, a goon named Larry, stands at the window. He's peering through binoculars back the way I drove in. "Brown sedan, last year's model. Just pulled a U-turn outside the gate. Two guys." He keeps on scanning with the binoculars. His lips move silently. He's got a gun slung under his ugly tweed jacket.

I'd seen the car on the highway, trying to blend with traffic and not quite making it.

"That'll be the feds," Mr. Lindstrom says to the goon while he stares at the brand-spanking new scars on my cheeks where the frostbite laid its brand. "Got you on a short leash, huh? They reckon you kilt that man of theirs. Left him on the ice. I gotta buck says you did. Kind of hombre you are."

Parker's white smile flickers in my mind. "I didn't kill him," I say with real weariness. It's the hundredth-and first time I've said the words.

"And I don't give a shit," says Mr. Lindstrom.

"A drink?" Mrs. Lindstrom is already gliding toward the liquor cabinet. She's got the grace of a magician's assistant. Lickety-split, hubby and I are each clutching a scotch and soda in front of the hearth. There's a fire in there. I'm sweating in the nice suit Conway made me wear, but frozen at the core. After Alaska, nothing will ever warm me up again.

She says to him, sweet as pie, "Civility, Burt. We agreed how you'd be." Those eyes again. I wouldn't want to be trapped on a lee shore with her and no supplies.

He smiles like you do when you get punched in the balls. "Sure, hon. How's the booze, Cope? Fix you another?"

"No, sir. I'm fine." I'm not fine. I'm minus a leg and I use a cane and I've gone from recreational drinker to hardened drunk.

"Gander says you have something for us. You met Smyth." Mr. Lindstrom's mouth twists and he visibly restrains himself, turns away and says to the goon, "Get some air, Larry." The goon makes himself scarce.

Mrs. Lindstrom moves close to me. I doubt there's much contact between her and the husband, and she's starved. She smells bitter, like winter flowers. "He told you about my daughter?"

I nod and sip scotch.

"You anglin' for more cash?" He gives a snort of contempt. "I'll write you a damned check on the spot. Out with it, man!"

"Easy, dear, easy," she says to her husband. Then to me, "We saw the film, Mr. Cope. There isn't anything you can say that will shock us. All we want is a little peace. Her marker is over an empty plot. I can't bear it anymore."

He drains his glass, seems poised to chuck it at the fire. "She had a bit part. Basically an extra, for Chrissake. Bride of Dracula Number Three. So what? Those rat bastard producers seduced her. Smyth sold her a bill of goods how he was gonna make her the next Monroe. Molly was a good girl. She mixed with bad people." He runs out of steam and stares dumbly into the distance.

"No argument here," I say. Bride of Dracula Number Three took it in the ass on screen, and did some other naughty stuff too. Not mine to judge. I steel myself. "Molly's dead, ma'am. She died ten years ago in Los Angeles. Remember when Mr. Lindstrom flew to LA to help the private dick he'd hired to search? Well, he and this lowlife named Brent Williams found her all right, shacked up with a hood from the projects, strung out on heroin and hooking for rent money. *Ardor* ruined her. Ruined her in every way you can imagine. There was an argument. Your husband killed her and the pimp in a twenty-dollar-a-night motel room. It was an accident, everything simply got out of hand. The dick got rid of the bodies himself." I stare at her, try to project compassion at her blank, shocked face. "It was you who hired me, isn't that right, ma'am? Your husband signed the check, but it was you, because you couldn't have known, and he went along, played the part of the grieving dad. And I guess maybe you *are* grieving, Mr. Lindstrom. Maybe you're sorry for what you've done."

Nobody says anything for a bit. Then Mrs. Lindstrom bursts into tears and flees the room, face buried in her hands.

"You bastard," Mr. Lindstrom says and shakes his head the way a confused bear might. "You come in here and make my wife cry? Bad mistake, son." He takes a knife from his pocket. A big one with a fixed blade that would've done nicely as a bayonet.

The guard confiscated my piece when I came onto the property. That's why I'm standing next to a pair of crossed cavalry sabers. I hope against hope they're sharp—

—Smyth wrote this in one of his abandoned journals: *As a boy I started with bugs and small animals. I accidentally clipped the end of my index finger off at age sixteen while stacking chairs in the school gymnasium. It completely repaired itself within two and half years. Spontaneous regeneration. This was long before I discovered the Bluefield papers. Bluefield was a crank living in the wrong century. Still, his instincts were true. After my last film with Lewton I visited Borneo on holiday and trekked into the brush, learning the old ways. I ate a fresh human heart. The hetman of a friendly tribe told me I'd inherit the strength and the vigor of the fallen warrior. It tasted sweet. There's no returning from that. Sadly, it's only part of the secret. The keyhole you peer through. The dark mystery itself is unapproachable. —*

—Parker is still ticking, still got some fight in him. He's missing some pieces, so not *that* much fight. He says to me in a tired voice, "I suppose the fact your grandfather was a gangster makes us meeting like this sort of poetic."

"You say poetic, I say pathetic. Wait a second. You're a cop?" I mug at him, best as I am able. He smiles weakly. I'm groggy. Haven't had a sip of water in hours. Two days since I last ate. The tips of my fingers and toes are numb and my heart knocks too fast. I'm bruised, possibly concussed. My back is sprained, and worst of all, my left thigh has suffered a severe laceration. None of this bodes well.

Beyond this litany of woes looms a bigger problem.

The others have bled out on the ice floor of the crystal cave. All that life coagulated into a crimson slick. The enormous cascade of blood is too hot to completely freeze. It oozes toward the hole in the floor. The pit that has awaited us for a million years.

Parker and I cling to a rough section a few feet upslope. We've linked arms and combined our waning strength. The ice is damp and slippery. Inch by inch our purchase loosens and we slide toward doom.

The man who once played Renfield on the silver screen throws back the hood of his bearskin parka and laughs. His hands are bare to the elements, fingernails blackened or gone. I try not to consider what he's done, what he's going to do.

He says, "The tragedy is that the Renfield figure wants what the master already has. Immortality. After all my searching, all my supplication, all my obeisance, I have found only a slower way of dying."

The walls of ice molt crimson. They seep and drip.

My grip fails. Parker groans and slides past me, down the bloody ice chute into the shaft that probably goes straight past Hell to China. The groan is merely a sound he's making. It doesn't touch his eyes. I'll never get to ask him if he'd gone undercover to bust me or to get a line on Smyth, that alleged murderer of starlets.

A moment later I'm gone too and Smyth whistles to mock my departure—

—And then I die—

—Maybe an eon passed in the void. How would I know? Mostly I spent the time falling like a stone into an abyss. There were interludes when I segued from falling into walking through a vast maze, a hedgerow of obsidian. The sky was also obsidian splintered by jags of white light. The light was so dim and so far away it might've been the inverse of itself. Figures moved in the distance. Moses and Maddox. I couldn't quite catch them to see for certain. Parker paced me by trudging backwards. A bit green around the gills and sickly pale. Breathing, though. I cried out to him and he smiled and drifted away.

Sometimes Smyth's disembodied voice echoed along the twists and turns. "I didn't travel into the wilderness to find the dark. I brought the dark with me. The seed is inside everybody, waiting for a chance."

Another occasion he said, "I went out there to be alone. You got what you wanted, you stupid twit?"

I realized I was probably talking to myself and in those moments of clarity the maze disintegrated and I'd be lying in that grave on the ice between my comrades, or plummeting from the sky in the plane, or kissing Conway at the Phoenix Theatre, or transfixed in a study while *Ardor* squelched and squealed on the wall and stodgy guests gawked at my apparition.

In every case the snow returns, and covers me—

—I wake in the summer to a good morning blowjob, but the ruined nerves in my remaining leg kill me and the vertigo unmans me and I scream and Conway has to hold me down until I stop. I lie there in a sweat and tell him the fog has lifted. I remember everything in Technicolor.

He cautions that I can't trust my recollections, claims I returned to Seattle a night before I ever left and then blinks and says he didn't say anything that crazy. He leaves red marker messages on the mirror: *Where's her body, Sam?* I confront him and he kisses my ear and says I didn't get eaten by the Ouroboros and shit out into an alternate universe. Take your meds and do your physical therapy, Sam. Where's her body, Sam? Where's Parker's body? Where are they, Sam?

If I didn't die, if this isn't Hell, then what has actually transpired is worse. Always something worse. That first night in the storm does for Moses, his fabulous parka notwithstanding. Maddox may or may not have had life in him. Parker is only strong enough to tow one of us and despite my length, I don't weigh much. The good cop drags me back to the seashore and we await rescue near the plane's wreckage. Along the way a diamond-hard sliver of ice or a jagged rock has torn through my overalls and sliced my thigh to the bone. I don't feel it happen and the blood covers my legs like I've a lap full of rubies. We hunker for two days. Parker's face turns black and his eyes go milky blue. He stays with me a while, and then between buffets from the north wind he's gone.

The troopers are able to dig Pilot John's remains from the barbeque pit. They are mystified at the bullet hole in his skull. Bits of glass in there, so the bullet was fired from the ground as he banked the plane for a pass is what they conclude. Helicopter rides, hospital wards, a long white veil over the universe come next. Ice covers the Earth, then recedes and reveals the green. I'll never walk quite right again. I lose an ear, a leg, all my fingernails, my belief in the rational, my sanity.

Night after night I dream of *Ardor* and Renfield in his cell with worms, lice, and flies for sustenance. He gibbers and hoots until the Count slips into his cell and maims him, leaves him paralyzed in the shitty rags of his bedding. I follow the camera into his glazed eyeball and come out on the other side inside a cheap motel room in Van Nuys. I'm a fly on the wall during the encounter between Papa Lindstrom and his private dick and Molly Lindstrom. The shouts and the tears are flowing freely when the pimp walks in. Bullets don't have names on them. The girl and the pimp get bundled into the dick's Caddy for a long, lonely ride to the landfill.

I don't have a shred of proof, but the fucking imagery is so vivid, eventually it eats away at me, plagues my waking hours. Lately, I'm convinced that nothing is real, so the unreality of this scenario assumes the same weight as anything else. Conway helps me into the suit I usually wear to funerals and drives me to the Lindstrom estate. I leave him in the car, tell him it won't be fifteen minutes and then I hobble inside to say the awful things I've got say.

Here's the test. Here's where I receive validation or comeuppance. Maybe it'll be both. For a moment I hesitate on the steps while a goon named Larry approaches. It is lush and green and sweetly humid. Not a glacier in sight—

—Lindstrom charges me with the knife brandished. I'm a step ahead of the game. I drop my cane and snatch the cavalry saber from its ornamental wall hooks. Coming in I'd expected mockery, perhaps indignant outrage, the threat of arrest, and certainly the risk of getting roughed up by one of the old man's goons. Hell, if they'd simply laughed and phoned the funny farm, it wouldn't have surprised me. What I didn't account for was how fast the situation escalates into a killing. In retrospect, I can't blame myself for not entirely buying that the dreams were bona fide. Crazy people believe their own bullshit and so forth.

The snarl, the savage glint in his eyes, this is the murder in L.A. reprised. Man, it's not as if I'm a fencer, or anything. I make a haphazard swing when he gets close and there goes the knife and two of his fingers under a table. Unfortunately for both of us he doesn't take a hint. He leans down and retrieves the knife with his left hand and I hobble forward two steps and swipe at him again, both hands wrapped around the hilt. The sword cleaves through his neck without any trouble and his head plops onto the Persian rug and rolls onto its side so those devil-dog eyes are blinking at me.

"Oh, shit," I say.

The wife doesn't return and there's a hell of a mess in the parlor, so I leave. The goon doesn't intercept me on my way out the door. I do a spot check of my reflection at the car and don't see any blood on my suit. My hair is mussed and I'm sweating, but that's me these days. I smile at Conway and tell him to take us home. He doesn't suspect anything and I retreat into myself with alacrity. My brain wants to shutter the doors and call it a day. I roll down the window and breathe in the smells of grass and leaves.

A cloud swoops in and paces the car. The breeze gains an edge and snow begins to fall. My heart stops. But it's not snow, it is hail and Conway hits the wipers and in a minute or two we're through it and gliding beneath glorious blue skies. I place my hand over Conway's and close my eyes and try not to make that transcendental journey to Alaska, or visualize Lindstrom's mouth working up a voiceless curse.

I figure if this isn't a dream, the cops will be waiting at the house. And they are.

the worms crawl in,

the worms crawl out. *The worms play Pinochle on your snout.*

We chanted that at mock funerals when I was a kid. Shoot your sister playing cowboys and Indians and she fell dead, that's your dirge. The playground bully challenges you to a duel after class, that's the ditty your friends hummed as the hour of doom approached.

Hadn't heard the worm song since I was twelve, but it's coming back into style, thanks to my wrath. I've been done a great wrong, you see. Done a great injustice by a man named Monroe. However, I've come to think of him as Fortunato. It makes me smile to do so.

He "tricks" me into going on the hiking trip. I've always had a hate-hate relationship with the great outdoors. Bad enough I'm stuck working nine to five in the weather; camping is a deal breaker. My feelings don't matter. He's as smooth as a magician or a shrink: talks about one thing, shows you one thing, but there's always another something up his sleeve. He knows his con, short or long. Can't dazzle 'em with brilliance, baffle 'em with bullshit, is his motto. Much as the hand is quicker than the eye, Monroe's bullshit usually defies my perception of it until after the fact when it's time to cry.

Phase one of the scam, he invites Ferris and me over to the house for a barbeque. Optimistically, I assume that's merely a cover to regale us with his latest sexual exploits, and yes, Monroe does chortle over a couple of girlfriends he has squirming on the hook, each completely ignorant of the other. But it turns out that this gloating is actually a pretext to maneuver me into a conversation about Moosehead Park and its fabulous game trails.

So, Elmer, you hunt, right? You lived in the woods when you were a kid. The only way he could know that, since I've never mentioned it, is from Ferris. And of course, I correct him. My dad had been the big white hunter in the family; the rest of us were simply dragged along for the ride. Monroe believes in education via osmosis. It isn't hunting that intrigues him. He is far too much of a wilting flower to lay hands on a rifle, much less put a bullet into the brainpan of some hapless animal. He needs street cred, as it were, wants to butch up his résumé with the ladies, and a brief foray into the swamps of south central Alaska is the cure for what ails him. First rule of disappearing into the wilderness is, always bring a buddy.

We chew some ribs, toss back a few brews, and thus plied with meat and drink I agree to tag along this very next Saturday for an overnight campout. It has to be me. Not a chance any of his colleagues will blow a perfectly good weekend with the shifty motherfucker. Plenty of them will gather for a free feed and trade shop gossip, but that is the extent of it. Dude probably thinks he's really clever, manipulating his lummox of a pal, albeit pal might be too strong a word.

Joke's on him. I'm not as dim as I pretend. The trip is exactly what I want. It's my big chance to settle the score.

Ferris doesn't say anything. She *looks* plenty worried. I pretend not to notice. Can't have her suspecting that I suspect she suspects I *know* there is something going on between her and Monroe. In that unguarded moment, her expression says she thinks her boyfriend is out of his gourd, putting himself at the mercy of a paranoid husband who can load a six-hundred-pound engine block barehanded. Alas, Monroe's downfall is his unremitting narcissism. He doesn't want to get away with snaking my wife, he wants to rub my nose in it.

If Ferris were to get a whiff of my true mood she'd forbid Monroe's excursion under no uncertain terms and spoil everything. Although, even in her most febrile visions, it's doubtful she could imagine I plan to off him in some devious manner and drop the body into a deep, dark pit. One of my flaws is jealousy. Not the biggest of them, either, not that she has the first inkling. We've been together since our late twenties. Going on fifteen years, and parts of me remain Terra Incognita to my lovely wife. See, there are some things you should know about me, things I should get out in the open. I won't, though.

Not until later.

*   *   *

Ferris worked as an administrative assistant at the high school where Monroe taught English. Fancied himself a poet, did our man Monroe. A skinny, weepy fella who preened as if his scraggly beard made him kin to Redford's Liver-Eating-Johnson and that his sonnets were worthy of Neruda.

Sonnets, for the love of God.

Ferris started bringing the shit home in a special folder, wanted my "professional" opinion. I'm no expert, I drill wells for a living. But sure, I published a few pieces in lit journals over the years, had one chapbook about blood and vengeance picked up by Pudding House when I was younger and angrier. I read Monroe's poems, told her what I thought of them, which wasn't much. Classic poseur artiste. The kind of asshole who upon learning he can't strum a guitar to any effect minors in poetry or fiction to impress the doe-eyed girls who hang around coffee houses and the bored ones at faculty parties. One of those, *I'm writing a book* shitheads who isn't really doing any such thing.

Everybody hates those guys.

Guys who kiss married women on the mouth aren't too popular either. Even though I was likely the last to know, I'd finally gotten wise at Monroe's Fourth of July house party. A fateful glimpse of him and Ferris in a window reflection was a splash of cold water for sure. Shielded by an open refrigerator door, both of them leaning in for a beer, and by God, Monroe laid it on her. The door swung closed and they acted casual. Cheeks a bit rosier, laughter a notch too sharp, and that was all. I played the oblivious fool. Wasn't tough; waves of numbness filled me, that big old local anesthetic of the gods. It was as if the enemy had dropped depth charges. Those bombs sink real deep before detonating. First time I'd ever thought of Ferris as an enemy.

I didn't fly into a rage or fall into despair. Nah, my reaction was to get chummy with Monroe. I fucked Ferris more often and a lot more vigorously than was my habit. Also, I took some dough from a rainy day account and paid my pal Benny Three-Trees, a dope dealer who moonlighted as a private eye, to tail those lovebirds for two weeks. The results were inconclusive. No motel rendezvous, no illicit humping in their cars, but they did frequently meet for drinks at the tavern on 89 when she told me she was shopping for office supplies or groceries. Practically mugging each other in the photos. The detective offered me a cut-rate package to tap their phones and intercept email communications. I declined, paid him, and sent him on his way. He'd shown me enough. My imagination would do the rest.

Then I took that thumb drive of photos and locked myself in a room and brooded. As my dad would've said, I went into the garden and ate worms.

* * *

Moose have learned to steer wide of Moosehead Park. Hunters and redneck locals blast the poor critters the second one pokes its muzzle out of the woodwork. The park isn't all that park-like; it's an expanse of marsh and spruce copses in the shadow of the Chugach Mountains that got designated public use. Basically, the feds looked around for the armpit of the great outdoors and said, Fine, peasants. Enjoy! Thanks a lot, Jimmy Carter.

The government hacked a path through it, east to west. Take a step left or right and you're ass deep in devil's club or bog water. You would not believe the mosquitoes that rise in black and humming clouds. Spray on the chemicals, layer your clothes, throw netting over that and spray it too for good measure, and you're still fucked. Those tiny stabbing bastards will find a way to your tender flesh.

I stop by Monroe's house at dawn, load him and his gear, and then drive us to the trailhead. My truck is the only vehicle in the lot. Camping season is kaput and blood-sucking bug season has begun. This is early fall before the first hard freeze or fresh termination dust on the mountains. Any second now for one or both, however.

Monroe is a willowy fellow of Irish descent, so he slathers his pale skin with sunblock, dons a fancy vest he probably snagged off the rack the night before, and squeezes himself into a high tech pack with a slick neon yellow shell and enough elastic webbing to truss a moose, if we see one. It looks heavy and probably is since he's stuffed all of the camping gear in there. I carry my meager supplies, including a sixer of suds, in a rucksack. In my offhand I heft a fishing rod. Trout run in the streams yonder and I've a mind to hook a couple for dinner if the opportunity arises.

Ominous clouds sludge in from the east as we begin our trek. The plan is to hike a few hours, pitch the tent, and maybe recon the surrounding area. In the morning we'll head home. Nothing fancy, nor prolonged or grueling. We rest periodically. I slug water from my dented canteen and lover boy pops the top on a wine cooler. The trail winds through barren hills and stands of black spruce. Gloom spreads its wings over the land. The air tastes damp, and yes sir, the mosquitoes and the gnats taste us.

No point in making this an epic: At last we reach a patch of dry ground on a hill and set camp. Tent, fire pit, the works. Monroe asks about bears, and he asks about them a lot. I'm not too worried as they tend to be fat and complacent this close to winter. Spring, when the beasts emerge lean and starved, is the dangerous time.

I tell Monroe that dearie-me, we'd best be on guard against those man-eaters. I instruct him to keep trash and scraps in a sealed container to minimize ursine temptation, which is a sound idea, but fun to watch him perform as he casts worried glances into the underbrush. I scan the horizon and judge that indeed a storm is approaching, although the weather forecast has made no such mention.

I grab my fishing rod and tell him to fall in.

"Fishing? In this weather?" He cups his hand to catch the first raindrops.

"Morning is better. But it's okay. A little rain won't keep them from biting."

His expression is glum as he zips his fancy yellow pastel slicker that matches the glaring yellow backpack shell. The idea of hooking a fish doubtless hurts his tender feelings. I try not to sneer while thinking that Ferris had certainly gone the whole nine yards to find my opposite.

The map indicates a creek within a mile or so and I wade into the bushes, hapless Monroe on my heel. The possibility of a fresh trout fillet appeals. It amuses me to let branches whip back at his face and hear his muffled exclamations. I chuckle and think of the skinning knife strapped to my hip. It's the journey, not the destination, right?

I almost trip headlong into the hole. Monroe saves me. He snatches my belt as I teeter on the crumbling brink, and yanks me back. Faster reflexes than I'd have guessed. He has to use his entire bodyweight, and thus counterbalanced, we fall awkwardly among the alder and devil's club.

"What the hell is that?" he says.

"A hole in the ground," I say. Thorns in my shin, rain trickling down my neck, mosquitoes drilling every available surface, all conspire to provoke my ire. I'm wrong. This is more than a sinkhole, or an animal burrow, or anything of nature. Upturned clay rings the pit. Water seeps gray and orange from its rude walls.

"You know, it looks like a grave." He gains his feet and peers into the hole. "Oh, man. Somebody dug this thing not too long ago."

"It's not a grave. The shape is fubar."

"Yeah? That a rule? Gotta be six by six on the nose? Maybe they were in a hurry. Digging around big rocks. I'm telling you."

"Maybe a retarded hillbilly dug it."

Sarcastic as I might be, he has it right. This is a grave, albeit an oblong, off-kilter grave, six or seven feet deep and freshly dug. It doesn't matter that the shape is wrong; the hole radiates unmistakable purpose the way an empty slaughterhouse or jail cell radiates unmistakable purpose. I don't see a shovel or tracks. The latter bothers me. Should be tracks in the wet dirt. Should be more dirt. Should be broken branches. Something; anything. I'm not a tracker. Yet, the consistency of the clay, the wisps of steam, convince me that the mysterious digger did the deed and left within the past hour or two.

"Man, what do you think?" Monroe says with less worry and more eagerness than I like.

"I think we should mind our own business and get back to camp. Call it a day."

"Hold on." He swats away a cloud of mosquitoes. "I'm curious. Aren't you?"

"No, Monroe, not really. Either it's a grave, or it's not. If not, then who gives a shit? If it is, then presumably someone will be along presently to dump a corpse. I'd prefer to be elsewhere." I don't wait around to hold a debate. Hell with fishing. Nightfall looms and I want to put distance between us and that site. The need to get away is overpowering.

We make it back to base without incident. I feel Monroe's sulky gaze the whole way. I consider pulling stakes. The idea of folding the tent is unappetizing and impractical. Blundering through the forest in darkness is how tinhorns and Cheechakos wind up with busted legs or lost for a week. No thanks. I light a fire and boil water for the MREs I brought. Keep my trusty .9mm pistol handy, too. Rain starts pissing down for real. We huddle under a makeshift canopy of spruce boughs and a tarp. Blind and deaf, and choking on campfire smoke.

Isn't until after supper and a third brew that I realize I've forgotten about my half-assed plan to kill my little buddy.

* * *

Late that night I wake to the drum of rain on tarp. Pitch black.

"Elmer." Monroe sounds tense.

"Yeah?"

"Why'd you bring me here?"

"I didn't. You wanted to."

"Uh-uh. *You* wanted this."

"Monroe, shut the fuck up and let me sleep."

"Something occurred to me when I saw that grave. You made it. You made it and then brought me to it."

I lie very still. I smell the fear on his breath.

"Elmer?"

"Yeah?"

"Great minds think alike. This is for Ferris."

He sighs heavily in the dark before smashing the rock down on my head.

* * *

You are stripped utterly naked when confronted by your own mortality. You are stripped utterly naked when you are dropped to the bottom of a hole and buried in the mud, handful by handful, and left to rot. The worms crawl in.

* * *

Two items from the grim days of my youth.

Dad and his brothers were into cockfighting. Many a blue-collar paycheck was won and lost on his prize Lubaang and Asil warrior birds. My people spent generations in El Paso and they'd picked up the sport from the Mexicans. Gorgeous destroyers, our fighting roosters. These weren't simple chickens like you see on a farm. A damn sight bigger and meaner than their domestic kin. Orange and black and sheened emerald, tall as a man's knee, and eager for violence. One glimpse and you could see the devil in them, you could trace the line of descent back to dinosaur raptors.

Dad taped razorblades and jags of glass to their spurs and turned them loose in a killing pit. Hell of a lot of blood and feathers, afterward. I liked the blood and the smell of the blood. The black feathers were my favorite. I gathered a bunch and made a war bonnet. A boy at school offended me and I pursued him in my war bonnet of orange and black feathers and threw him down and rubbed his face in the playground dirt.

In retrospect, Mom and little sister flying the coop — so to speak— when I was four, the cockfighting, boozy gambling, and a procession of whores that followed my dad around might've had an effect on me. Also, we relocated from Texas to Alaska. The main difference between the two states is the distinct lack of an electric chair in the Land of the Midnight Sun.

The other thing is, I could do a weird trick with my mind. Got hooked on the idea of telekinesis after reading an old science fiction novel called *The Power* about some dude with superhuman abilities. God alone can say how many hours I spent squinting in concentration. And it worked, sometimes. I tipped water glasses and caused electronic devices to go haywire without touching them. I could stop a clock by beaming death-thoughts at it. Once I concentrated hard enough to levitate a cinderblock about six inches above the garage floor. Dad stumbled upon me; I was out cold, bleeding from my nose and ears. A three-day coma followed; doctors diagnosed it as epilepsy. Dear lord, the apocalyptic nightmares I suffered: Oceans of blood, rivers of maggots, the damned leading the damned across plains of fire and ash. The damned pointing their crisped, skeletal fingers at me and wailing in unison.

Shot a silver streak through my hair. At least the girls thought it cute. I was too scared to screw around with ESP and telekinesis after that. Set it aside with other childish things.

* * *

There's nothing dramatic about the transmogrification of lowly Elmer D. from dead meat into a walking and talking abomination unleashed upon the hapless people of the Earth. It occurs between one drip of rain from a spruce bough and the next. An owl glides in and snatches a squirrel. A cloud smokes across the face of the moon. The night takes a long breath, and then I am among all that is.

I have no memory of clawing up out of the muck, although it would be keen if my cadaverous hand had thrust free of the soil like in all those old movies. One moment I lie interred in smothering blackness, the next I find myself striding through a twilight forest where mist hangs from evergreen branches. Gray upon gray. In this instant, I question nothing, I ponder nothing. My only goal is to plow forward into the infinite grayness.

A strange sensation to be plugged into every birdcall, every snapped twig, every stir of grass in the breeze, the scents of dead leaves, loam, and moose droppings; yet disconnected, numb. My body is a lead float, adrift. It oscillates between here and there, and fat and thin. Hideously immense, yet helium light. I lurch, dragging my left foot. My power is enormous. I brush tree trunks and they crackle and uproot and crash.

Flames leap from a pile of logs. This clues me in to the fact it isn't sunset or dawn, but rather the dark of night. My sight penetrates spectrums beyond the human norm. Constellations flare, white against gray. I *hear* the stars as a celestial chorus, molten atoms colliding and chiming.

Three hunters squat around the fire as men have done since saber-tooth tigers prowled the land. A motor home is parked nearby. Electric light streams from the windows. I've crossed many miles in a blink to arrive in the parking lot. Sweat, beer, gun oil, I smell it all. Seven hundred yards to my left, an owl regurgitates the pellet of the squirrel it gobbled for dinner. I smell that too.

None of the hunters notice my apparition at the edge of the cheery circle of their fire. Unlike me, they can't see in the dark. Soap bubbles form above the head of the nearest man. The bubbles shimmer and expand. They contain images of a blue-collar truck commercial: happy children, barking dogs, muddy Fords; him sighting down on a bighorn ram and blasting it off a ledge; him plowing his stolid wife, blowing out the candles on a cake; that sort of deal. One glance tells me the life story of Hunter Numero Uno.

A phantom approximation of his face swells the last unburst bubble. It whispers to me in the language of electron particles, "Master!"

I nearly swoon in an ecstasy of desire and my tongue lolls to my grimy navel. I am starved.

One by one, I seize them and crack their skulls and scoop out the brain matter and gulp it whole. Sparks sizzle and drip down my chin, light me up from the inside. For a few moments, before the incredible rush fades, I, as Whitman said, contain multitudes.

* * *

This transformation started long before the inciting incident in the hole. Maybe it had been occurring my entire life. Ten bucks says Dad's sperm was already mutating when it t-boned Mom's egg. He'd gotten spritzed with Agent Orange during his tour in Vietnam and suffered all kinds of health problems afterward. He drank, and so did Mom. There was also a sense of cursedness haunting the family line. Dad went in a wreck. Dad's cousin was an ace Alaskan bush pilot who death spiraled his Cessna into Lake Illiamna. An uncle was eaten up by cancer despite living a clean, Presbyterian life, no smokes, no booze. An aunt did ten years in the pen and got hit by a motorcyclist three days after her parole. Somebody else got shanked in a brawl at the Gold Digger, back when it *really* was a saloon with sawdust and a mechanical bull and full of motorcycle club thugs and crank heads looking to stab you in the kidney. My sister, she joined the FBI. Her name was Jeanie and last I saw her she was eighteen months and counting. Rumor is she went down in a corruption sting and sliced her wrists.

Dumb luck I didn't pop out of the womb with two heads.

I like the idea that death is a transitory state; my passage from pupa to final instar. I'm a whole new insect. While the notion I've become posthuman sends my nerves a-twanging, I'm not exactly afraid, or even concerned. Oh, a tiny fragment of the old me mewls and screeches in its cage, but to no greater effect than the whine of a fly under glass.

The Usurper deigns to answer my imprecations at one point.

We are the next big thing. This whisper issues from inside me; it oozes forth. The whisper is blood welling from a puncture. Sexless, dispassionate. *We are Omega, we are Kingdom Come. We have always been; we will always be.* I receive a picture, muddy and flickering, of warm seas and green light, of trilobites and worms and moss. Dinosaurs have not been invented, but the devil is everywhere.

We are the apparatus. We are the apex. We are first.

I cannot reply. I'm trying to decide if apex means precisely what it intimates and if it's something I want to be (*of course you do, you ninny!*). Again, images coalesce from the ether, like bursts of speech through shortwave static. The future unravels in an arc of projectile vomit from the jaws of Saturn: an approaching tsunami of blood and peeled flesh and more blood. A thousand feet tall, rolling at a thousand miles per hour. The first of many such waves. Wave after wave of carnage, and me in gigantic repose atop a heap of bones. My friends and foes, beneath me at last!

Ferris is fucking Monroe. We don't have to take that kind of bullshit. We should fix their wagons. We are the apparatus. We are the way.

That sounds reasonable. A man should attend his priorities. Family comes first.

* * *

I loved monster movies as a kid. Don't all boys love monster movies?

Dawn of the Dead. Evil Dead. Re-Animator. From Beyond. The Fly. The Thing. Right on. I dug it, especially zombie flicks. The shambling undead did it for me.

Had my first hot and heavy teen make out session with Julie Vellum during a screening of *Night of the Living Dead* at her dad's split level house. I'd seen the movie plenty of times, but this was super-fucking hot cheerleader Julie Vellum; shag rugs, a leather couch, and her pop's brand new RCA television. That's why Mr. V tolerated me sniffing around his princess that lost summer of my junior year in high school — like me, he was a devout fan of classic fright features. Val Lewton and George Romero were unto gods in Mr. V's estimation. Death gods, I thought, but kept such smart-ass observations to myself by concentrating upon the sky-high hemline of his daughter's skirt. I didn't even find out until much later that Mr. V was dying of cancer. The Vellums kept it hush-hush until he finally got sick enough for hospice care.

The three of us camped on that giant couch. Me on one end, Julie on the other, her dad, larger than life, occupying the middle. We kids sipped bottles of Coke while Mr. V blasted his way through a fifth of Maker's Mark and talked over all the good parts. Soon, he slurred and blessedly lengthy gaps interrupted his monologue. He rose and staggered toward the kitchen in quest of more booze. There followed a series of thuds and then a crash that shook the living room.

I jumped a little and then froze, unsure about the etiquette of rushing to the aid of collapsed drunk who happens to be the father of the chick you're trying to score with. Do you say something or do you pretend you didn't hear a damned thing?

She came to my rescue.

"Oh, don't worry. That's him passing out. He does it all the time." Julie gave me a cat-eyed look. Two seconds later we met in the middle. She kissed me as my hands went roaming places they had no business, and then she jacked me off like she'd done it before.

I made it with Julie a half dozen times before school started again. Once the frost set in, she dropped me like a bad habit. Despite my momentary anguish, it was for the best. White trash, both of us. She had a little money, and that made all the difference. She also carried a torch for the quarterback on our football team. Beating his ass wouldn't have been a problem; I was really good at inflicting pain by then. Size and meanness were on my side, although I made certain to keep the latter under wraps. My gambit was to smile and keep my mouth shut whenever possible. Didn't matter. Most everyone was piss-scared of me for reasons they couldn't express. The assholes voted me most likely to wind up in prison or in an early grave.

That's why I suppressed my rage, and why I let JV saunter into the sunset with her trophy jock. The things I envisioned doing in the name of love would've landed me in Goose Bay Penitentiary or a nuthouse. Instead, I slunk into the garden and ate worms and went quietly mad exactly as the moldy poets from parchment and quill days had done.

Nightmares afflicted me with a ferocity I hadn't experienced since childhood. Who knows what caused them. Stress? Hormones? Whatever the case, these were the stuff of legends. Imagine being trapped inside a waxworks dedicated to atrocities, and all the doors sealed. Horrors from pre-adolescence reinvented themselves into subtler, more sophisticated iterations freighted with guilt and shame. My nightmares had *matured* and they took a cat o' nine tails to my psyche. I was visited every night for several months.

The phenomenon leaked into waking life. I became gaunt, pallid, and terser than ever. I forced myself to wear a shit-eating grin while secretly worrying that I'd gone around the bend. I began to hallucinate. At school I caught glimpses of my classmates and teachers wearing death masks. Some were pale and serene, others contorted and agonized, and still others dripping blood, or caved in, or sheared away entirely to expose the cavern of the mind.

The unexpected result of this being that I got better with my own mask, more scrupulous about tightening the bolts. Even so, it's a miracle I kept a straight face while gazing at exposed brains or punctured eyeballs. I got good at nodding and smiling.

A particular incident almost undid me anyhow. One morning during passing period Julie's locker door was open and for some reason – don't know what the hell I was thinking – I eased on over to chat her up. Second week of school, me being lonely and horny, not in my right mind— which covers any teenage boy — but me moreso. The door swung shut and there she stood, enfolded in the jock's arms, playing tonsil hockey. The bell broke up their tryst and they sauntered away, not acknowledging my presence as I stared after them.

I didn't feel anything, the exact same way I didn't feel anything the time Dad got drunk and slugged me in the jaw and laid me on my ass. The same lights flickered in the dark regions of my mind, the same roar of distant wind rose in my ears. The locker and a section of the concrete floor dissolved as if by acid. A hole bored into the earth and I had an erection that nearly split my pants. No nose bleed this time around. I was afraid, though. Terrified enough that I got away and got drunk on Dad's stock of Old Crow, damn the consequences were he to discover the theft, and I made myself forget. But the nightmares. Jesus. Jesus.

Dogged, simple-minded stubbornness got me though the autumn more or less intact, and largely unscarred.

What *scarred* me was getting ejected face-first through the windshield of Dad's '82 Chevy that winter. He hit a patch of ice and left the road doing around sixty-five and smacked a berm of snow packed tight as concrete by the state road graders. Never a compulsive buckler of seatbelts, I flew over the berm and burrowed into the virgin snow beyond. Dad burned up with the Chevy. Odd, how of all the folks that were rendered a horror show in my visions, I hadn't seen his death mask until I glimpsed him through the flames and melting glass.

No more nightmares for a long, long time after that incident. No dreams of any kind. Sleep became a chrysalis.

* * *

Apparently, a side effect of apex prowess is peckishness. The Glenn Highway spreads before me, a glistening buffet table strung with cozy sodium lights for mood.

Whatever manipulates me is not traveling of its own volition so much as being pulled as a steel filing by the mother of all magnets. The delays and digressions are but zigzag deviations of a neutron star as it's dragged into a black hole.

In any event, I zig through a rest stop near Eagle River and am compelled to annihilate the dozen or so inhabitants. Well, I *say* compelled — it's not as if I require much arm-twisting.

I wrench doors from semi-trucks and peel the roofs off compact cars. I am a beast cracking oyster shells. My need is overwhelming; my appetite is profound. I lick eyes from sockets, then the brains, the guts, the cracked-from-the-bone marrow, and even swallow a few bones whole. I expand and contract, I divide and reform. I squirm and slash. I am a pit that is everywhere. Light bends around me, or it is consumed.

A handful of survivors flee into the dour Plexiglas and cement octagon with a stylized eagle blazoned on the sloped roof. My reflection warps against the glass, or perhaps warps the glass itself. A cockscomb of jagged flint erupts from the sundered dome of my cranium. Spurs of razor-tipped basalt extrude from my wrists, elbows, and knees. Even as I take it in, its ghastly splendor, my physiognomy alters and is transfigured into something far worse, something that overwhelms my capacity to articulate its awfulness.

I am resplendently dire. I am a figure of awe. I am a horror.

They barricade the entrance with soda machines and that delays me for a few seconds once I finish outside. I find them cowering and gibbering prayers under Formica tables and in bathroom stalls. Somebody stabs me with a hunting knife, somebody else plugs me with a small caliber handgun. Six or seven teeny popgun flashes in the dark among the roaring and screaming. It hardly matters.

Toward the end, I flop, maw agape, on the concrete floor at the end of the demolished gallery and let that sweet hot stream of blood and viscera roll down my gullet. Overhead, the lights flicker crazily and shadows rip themselves apart. When it's finished, I shamble forth from the despoiled building. Pasted in gore and excrement, crowned by a garland of intestines, I strike a Jesus Christ pose in the center of the highway.

Traffic routes around me, makes me consider the legend of the stampeding buffalo herd breaking around a man if he remains motionless and tall in his boots. The sun arcs across the sky four times, and so swiftly it sheds tracers of flame. A green-gold ball of bubbling gas, a bacterium in division. The amoeba sun segments in rhythm with my own squamous brain cells. The sun strobes and vanishes. The sliver of moon swings down and sinks into my breast, cold as a fang of ice. That which nests within my DNA blooms and reticulates as it rewrites parameters of operation.

The city awaits. I project myself forward along a corridor of alternating light and darkness, contract through a crimson doorway, and flow into a dance hall. My need to gorge is satiated and replaced by an urge I don't recognize. A wormhole opens behind my left eye. The void shivers and yearns; it lusts for sensation. Music dies as the DJ apprehends me with his bemused gaze. Then the dancing. All heads turn toward my dreadful countenance.

What happens at the Gold Digger Saloon. I cannot speak of it. The ecstasy is the sun going nova in my brain. Nova, then collapsing inward, a snow crystal flaking, disintegrating, and then nothing left except a point of darkness, the wormy head of a black strand that bores its way to the core of everything.

* * *

We aren't rich. The pool house is our compromise — as long as Ferris didn't push for a mother-in-law cottage, I'd see she had herself a full length heated pool to do laps. Ferris was on the swim team in high school and college and she's tried valiantly to maintain her form. The YMCA is a no go. Too many sluggish old people in the lane, too many screaming kids, too many creepy dudes in the bleachers. Thus, the pool house. A gesture of defiance in the face of brutal Alaska winters.

I enter through the skylight. A long dead star field turns and burns over my shoulder.

Ferris lies naked and icy pale against the dappled green water. Her eyes are closed. Occasionally her arms and legs scissor languidly. Beneath her is her seal shadow and the white tile that slopes away into haziness. Vapors shift across her body and carry its scent to me, sharp and clean amid the faint tang of chlorine. She daydreams on the cusp of sleep and I taste the procession of phantoms that illuminate her inner landscape. Mine is not among them.

I descend like a great spider on its wire, then stop and hang in place. This thing that has hijacked and reconstituted my body, reduced my consciousness and placed it in a bell jar, is drawn to her. More specifically, that which I have become is drawn to something *within* her. I don't comprehend the intricacies. I can only bear mute witness to the spectacle as it unfolds.

A black spot stains the bottom of the pool. The spot spreads across the white bed, a ring of darkness widening as pieces of tile crumble into the depths. It is a pit, slackening directly below my lovely, frigid wife. My betrayer wife, my arm extending, my claw, hollow as a siphon, its shadow upon her betrayer's face, and the abyssal trench an iris beneath. Wife, come along to Kingdom Come, come to the underworld.

Her eyes snap open.

"I didn't fuck him," she says. "I fantasized about it, plenty."

Monroe is absent from the scene, and that's a shame. Every pore in me longs to drink his blood, to liquefy him, fry him, to have his heart in my fist. To ram his heart down her throat.

"I didn't fuck him. Elmer, I didn't. I should've."

Her blood. His blood. Their atoms.

I open my mouth (maw) to accuse, to excoriate, and the dead song of the dead stars worms out. She doesn't blink, she repeats that she hasn't fucked him, hasn't fucked him. She projects her innocence in an electromagnetic cone meant to kill. She is entirely too composed, this fragile sack of skin and water.

She says, "Are you here to hurt me, Elmer?" Her smile is pitiless, it cuts. "The time you came home drunk and forced me? There's a word for you, hon. Don't you remember what you've done?"

I don't remember. I seethe.

Difficult to concentrate through the interference of her thoughts that explain via pointillism how Monroe opportunistically slaughtered me and then so much like the narrator of the "Tell-Tale Heart" had succumbed to guilt and paranoia and eventually fled the country. The FBI hunts him in connection with my disappearance. He could be anywhere. She suspects Mexico. Monroe always had a romanticized notion about Mexico and what he could do there, a super gringo lover man.

The little shit swallowed her teary stories of my cruelty and violence. He'd done me in as an act of vengeance. An act that only earned Ferris's contempt. She is utterly my creature and let no man cast asunder what all the powers above and below had seen fit to forge.

I convulse with a complicated longing and snatch for her. She's too quick. She rolls, sleek and white, and flashes downward amid a cloud of bubbles into the pit. Fool that I am, I follow.

* * *

We meet in darkness, each illuminated by a weak spotlight that dims and brightens with our breathing. I sense immense coldness and space pressing against the bubble where we reside. I am whole. My cloven skull and rotting flesh are restored. My mind is papered over with gold star stickers and crepe.

She points an automatic pistol at me. I understand that it's a present from her would-be lover. The barrel aligns with my eye. I have traveled through the barrel and been deposited in this limbo.

"I warned him. Told him he'd never succeed. If I couldn't kill you, then there was no hope for him." She laughs and shakes the wet hair from her eyes. "Arsenic in your coffee every day for three months. Nothing. For God's sake, I frosted your birthday cake with rat poison."

Now that she mentions it, now that her thoughts bleed into mine, I recall the bitter coffee, the odd aftertaste of the icing on my last cake. A skull and crossbones has hung over our marriage for years. Yet, I remain. What does it mean?

"I hurt you, but I couldn't kill you. Monroe couldn't. Nobody can. You died in childhood. Maybe you were never born. Maybe the parasite that fruits your corpse is the only true part of you that existed."

Am I merely a figment? If so, I am the most rapacious, carnivorous, and vengeful figment she will have the misfortune to encounter. I strike aside the gun and reach for her. A black halo of light manifests around Ferris. Her arms spread wide and she becomes the very figure of a dread and terrible insect queen. The enormity of her eclipses my own.

She clutches me and the sting slides in. "It was always here, love. In all of us, always."

It's apparent that I've miscalculated again.

* * *

Reality has bent and bent. I look past the nimbus of black flame into her cold eyes. Reality goes right ahead and comes apart.

Darkness rolls back to daylight. It's spring and balmy. The breeze is redolent with sweet green sap and the bloom of roses. Guests and children of the guests clutter a lawn that's too bright and too green to be real. "Death to Everyone" by good old Will Oldham crackles over the speakers. I'm stuffed into a poorly fitted tux. At my side, Ferris shines as radiantly white as the Queen of Winter.

I have seen this, relived this, in a thousand-thousand nightmares.

My hand overlaps hers as we saw the blade into that multi-tiered cake. She opens her mouth and bites through the icing, the bunting, and my brittle soul. I shudder and kiss her. It feels no different than kissing ice bobbed up from the bottom of an arctic lake. She inhales my heat and my vitality before I can inhale hers. She's always been stronger, in the only way that counts. She always will be stronger.

Oldham's voice fades and the guests stare at us in hushed expectation.

Nearby, a little girl in a black funeral dress begins to sing the "Hearse Song" to the boy she's tormenting with malice or affection, take your pick:

> *They put you in a big black box*
> *And cover you up with dirt and rocks.*
> *All goes well for about a week,*
> *Then your coffin begins to leak.*
> *The worms crawl in, the worms crawl out,*
> *The worms play pinochle in your snout,*
> *They eat your eyes, they eat your nose,*
> *They eat the jelly between your toes.*

This time around, I do what I should've in the first place all those lost years ago. Instead of cutting a piece for the first guest in line, I grip the knife and slice my throat. Blood fans the cake and Ferris's white dress. She throws back her head and laughs. I sink to my knees in the thirsty grass. The sun pales and contracts to a black ring. Red shadows pour through the trees, drench the lawn, and reduce the paralyzed spectators to negatives. I try to speak. Worms crawl out.

* * *

Ferris's parents *loved* me. I first met them during Thanksgiving when she and I stayed over at the family casa — Ferris slept in her old room with the Prince poster and a mountain of heart-shaped pillows and teddy bears while I bunked in the basement on a leather sofa between her old man's pool table and a gun safe.

There was a tense moment when she removed her shades and revealed the Lichtenburg flower of a purple knot under her eye. Ferris was so very smooth. She spun a story about getting kicked in the face during swim practice, and her family bought it. She wasn't speaking to *me* except as required, probably hadn't even decided whether to stay with me or toss her engagement ring into the trash.

Hell of it was, at that early stage in our romance I didn't care much either way.

Turkey, gravy, pumpkin pie, and afterward, a quart of Jim Beam passed around a circle of a half-dozen of Ferris's menfolk. Salt of the earth bumpkins who raised coon dogs and revved the engines on four-wheelers at the gravel pit and picked through piles at the dump for fun.

You like John Wayne? one truck-driving uncle wanted to know. *Shore as hail, I love the Duke!* And with that, I was in like Flynn. My lumberjack beard, plaid coat, and knowledge of professional football didn't go amiss, either.

Her dad welcomed me to the family with teary eyes and a bear hug. I wasn't "nothin' like them pussies she usually brings home from college." How right my future in-law hillbillies were! Not three days before that Clampett-style feast I'd beaten a UAA fraternity brother within an inch of his life for giving me the stink eye as I staggered home from the Gold Digger Saloon. I made the letter-sweater-wearing jock try to eat a parking meter. The whole time Ferris's family exchanged jocular crudities at the supper table, my hand was in my pocket, caressing the frat boy's braces, with a few teeth still stuck in them, like a God-fearing Catholic fondling his rosary. It was the only thing that kept me from stabbing one of those bozos with a steak knife.

I gave the lot of those silly, inbred bastards my best aw-shucks grin, and daydreamed about how lovely and charred their slack-jawed skulls would shine from the cinders of a three A.M. house fire.

Aided by booze and a vivid imagination, I survived dinner and into the following day. Driving home, the stars were blacked. Snow fell like a sonofabitch. Every now and again the tires slipped against ice and the truck shook. Dad's ghost muttered in my ear. My heart knocked and I forgot to blink for at least forty miles. The high-beams carved a tunnel into the blizzard. Patsy Cline came on the radio out of Anchorage. Patsy sang "Crazy" and that was our song, all right.

Ferris reached across the gulf from the passenger side and held my hand. Her fingers pressed cold and tight over mine. In the rearview there was nothing but darkness, snowflakes endlessly collapsing in our wake, and a black slick of road painted red in the taillights' glow.

(Little Miss) Queen of Darkness

I: Initiation

I write this: *The cops don't know what really happened in Eagle Talon. Lies, all lies. Ask Jessica, if I ever see her again.* This isn't about Eagle Talon, however. I've never even been. No sir, Bob, if it's about anything, it's about that debutant ball Zane throws in his basement at the tail end of high school, 1998. The unfinished basement with the raw earth and a tunnel that smells of mildew and dankness. The tunnel is maybe three by three and is actually a cleft in the rock of the hill upon which this house rests.

I can't forget that tunnel. It drills through my mind.

Yeah, Shit Creek describes an imperfect circle right back to the bad old days. Oh, the party is rad, though: heavy metal, booze, drugs, psychedelic lights. The kids slam-dancing. Me with my hand on Stu Whitlock's hip the whole time and nobody the wiser. Then that damned hick brat Dave Teague racing overhead, naked and covered in blood (so the legend goes), screaming his head off. Ruins everything...

I also write: *People call it this or that, but our club doesn't have a name. It didn't originate in Alaska. It was around before Alaska. We don't suckle at the breast of a god, it suckles at ours.* Unfortunately, devoid of context, that stuff reads like the Unabomber's doodles.

Next, I make a list. Were I to title it, the title would be "People Who Died," like the song. Such an everyman tune because everybody can relate, right? The partial list is scribbled in a black moleskin notebook. I've left bloody fingerprints on the pages. Many of the names are illegible from the smears, or redaction with a magic marker. Names changed to protect the guilty. Four remain intact in truth and form. Hell if I know whether that's significant or not.

Zane Tooms & Julie Vellum: They could've been the power couple from the lowest circle of Hell. Alas, Zane already had a loyalist and Julie's not the kind to need any. These are your villains. Nuff said.

Steely J: Tall enough to play pro basketball. He's Zane's major domo. The Renfield to Zane's Dracula. Loyal through thick and thin — and I'm not kidding, I literally mean that. We called Zane "Fat Boy Tooms" until his folks croaked and he started in with the horse de-wormer and got slenderized. Steely J stuck with him down the line. Steely is what you might call inscrutable. Looks nice, dresses nice, and plays nice, if a teensy bit of a cold fish. His features lag behind whatever message his brain is sending. Somebody behind the curtain throws a switch and he smiles. Or, he smiles and picks up a claw hammer and comes for you. The Sandburg poem about fog creeping on little cat feet? That's Steely J. Except six-six with a hammer.

Vadim: My buddy Vadim often brags that he's an expert in Savate. He paid two hundred dollars for a six-week course at a strip mall. I let him drag me in once to meet the instructor (mainly I wanted to ogle some studly hotties kicking and stretching, but whatev) and the dude had a bunch of diplomas, certificates, and autographed photos of macho celebrities I didn't care to recognize. The French version of hi-ya for an hour. Bo-oring.

The strip mall closed shop when the economy cratered in '09. Not before Vadim got what he needed, however. He asserts that Savate is the elite of the elite fighting arts, natch. I don't know my foot from my elbow when it comes to violence. I'm a lover, always have been. That's why I keep the numbers of a few bigger, tougher friends in my mental rolodex.

Vadim talks lots of shit every time we go clubbing and the fraternity bros start hitting on me, which they totally do. I clutch his sleeve and say, "Whoa, there stud. They're just being friendly. Get mama another margarita, kay?" Vadim shoots the bros a venomous parting glare and then toddles off to fetch my drink. His thighs bulge his cargo pants so that he really does toddle. I think of it as having my own Siberian tiger on a leash, except with pouty, pouty lips, and six-pack abs! Nice while it lasted. He's dead too.

End of list.

* * *

Go back, not the whole way, not to high school. Three and a half years is far enough. We have gathered, dearly beloved. Gathered to sign on the dotted line and change the course of our stars forever. What a load of crap. *I'm* motivated by fascination, boredom, skepticism. Some of the others are buggy-eyed true believers. Have at it, morons.

The sun is bleeding out all over the Chugach Mountains. An inlet, ice-toothed and serpentine, lies below us somewhere, wrapped by mist that's freezing into black pearl. I'm not captivated by the austere beauty of the far north as seen through frosty picture windows. My feet are cold and I'm bored. I'm an L.A. girl trapped inside an L.A. boy. This arctic weather is for the birds.

Julie Five says to me, "Oh, Ed, quit sulking. You detest it so much, why'd you come? Nut up or shut up." She finishes me off with a sweet as pie smile. I beam one right back. Anybody more than arms-length away might get the impression we're peaches and cream. Big sister, little brother at worst. Then again, it's an intimate gathering of former classmates. Most of the others know how it is with us because it's been this way with us since junior high. Her nickname is JV, but I call her Julie Five. Our mutual acquaintance, the lamentably absent Jessica M, coined that bit of mockery. Sure, we're supposed to pity Julie Five for cowering in a closet while her lover got noisily disemboweled by the Eagle Talon Ripper in the winter of 2012, but her sob story doesn't move me — "victim-of-unspeakable-tragedy" is scraping the bottom of the barrel on a white trash reality show. Her sneaky path to fifteen minutes of fame and she didn't even *try* to stop the murdering bastard. Oh, dear heavens, no — she left that chore to her archrival, Jessica M, the girl who got the cover of *Black Belt Magazine* and interviews with every cable news show in existence. Good for Jess. Screw Julie Five. She's cowardly, treacherous, and mean. She like totally vacillates between vocal fry and ending every sentence on a rising note. Basically the darkest valley girl in the history of valley girls. I'd feed her a cup of lye if I had some.

Our host, Zane Tooms, stares at the sunset the way a man with an appointment compulsively checks his watch. He's dressed in a white shirt and black pants. No shoes. He never wears shoes at home. His shirt is unbuttoned two notches. A metallic chain gleams from the opening. I've seen the pendant when Zane had his shirt off — a smallish lump of vaguely horrid metal, or bone. Its color shifts, the film of a lizard's eye rolling aside. He folds his napkin, rises from his seat (throne) at the head of the table, and walks further into the decrepit mansion.

The house juts from a knoll with an impressive view of tidal flats and occasionally the water. The knoll was a bear den until hunters exterminated the bears and poured concrete back in when-the-hell-ever. Exactly the kind of place natives would say, "Don't build here! Bad medicine!" White Man doesn't give a shit about any of that and here we are. Even so, the Tooms residence lacks the sinister gravitas of a classic, gothic haunted castle. Made over once too often, the latest reconstructive surgery has rendered it a queasy amalgam of art deco and '60s kitsch. His home might have been cozy in its heyday. He let it go to seed after the senior Toomses shuffled into the next life. He travels and can't be bothered with upkeep. I've told him he needs a decorator because the ambiance sucks. Frontier chic it is not. Swear to God he doesn't even live here, it's so borderline derelict. If Zane confessed he only showed up to unlock the joint and turn on the lights half an hour before his guests arrived, I wouldn't be shocked.

The basement is carved into the den itself and mostly unfinished. Lots of exposed beams, pipes, and dirt. I shudder to think. Tunnels bore past the glow of any lamp. Can't say I'm impressed with the remote location or the bear catacombs. Way too rustic for this girl. What does impress me is Zane himself. These days, after slimming his chubby cheeks and beer gut, he's drop dead gorgeous. A walking, talking Ken Doll; brunette model. He oozes primal charisma. Night and day from the acne-riddled, blimpo Zane that we knew and abhorred as kids. I'd kill to learn his secret and that's part of why I RSVP'd yes on the invitation last month; why I ditched everything I had cooking in Cali and came like a dog to her master's whistle.

Steely J gives us a significant nod. We guests push away from half-empty plates and migrate into the parlor, wine coolers and rum and cokes in hand. I loathe the parlor. It's cold and dank, the books are moldy, and the stuffed moose head that presides here has gone blind with rot. The notion of accidently brushing against something icky gives me the shivers.

Zane unlocks a cabinet and sets a jewelry box upon the big circular granite table we're seated around. The table is slightly concave. Several parallel grooves radiate from the edge to a depression in the center. As for the jewelry case, it is an unpleasant box with the lacquer stripped. The wood is scored and blanched by patterns of fungal decay. An eighteenth-century caravel's lost antique dredged from the muck at the bottom of Cook Inlet in 1979, or so my peeps testify. Inside the box, a ring nests in crushed velvet. An indelicate description for those playing at home — its color is similar to a blood clot glistening against tissue paper. He plucks the ring and casually passes it to Morton, bing, bang, bong. No formalities whatsoever.

"Damn, it's heavy," Morton says. Morton always sounds bemused or surprised.

"Don't drop it," Julie Five says. She's cool and eager. She gave Morton a hummer last August while we were all on a tour bus at Denali State Park. They speak to each other with barely restrained antipathy. "Drop it, and it's ten demerits." Gawd, I hate her smug, bitchy tone. I hate that Morton accepted her blowjob and turned me down flat. Heel.

"By the way, the table isn't granite," Zane says as if he's peeked into my brain. His gaze is cruel. "Another rock entirely. There are chains of sea caves in the Aleutians. This table is carved from the bedrock of those caves. Men died acquiring this on my behalf." He looks at Morton. "Okay, Mort. Time to get bitten." He is indulgent, yet commanding. Two decades in Europe, and farther abroad, will do that to a guy, I suppose. Julie Five says Zane spent months lost in a desert and went barking mad. Eating-his-own-shoelaces fucked in the head. Wouldn't guess it to feast your eyes upon him, or maybe you would. The corners of his eyes twitch if you catch it at the right moment.

Morton makes a show of examining the ring, as if a middle manager role at an office supply store qualifies him to appraise jewelry. He's enjoying the spotlight. "Is this the Ouroboros?"

"Don't be ridiculous." Zane's sneer almost spoils the plastic charm of his perma-smile. I've long assumed his genial urbanity is a façade for darker impulses. Doesn't bother me. Everybody has got another side. It's exciting.

"If there were a *real* Dracula Ring, this would be the one," Julie Five says. "Lugosi's was pretty. Fake. Fake. Fake." She rocks, barely suppressed. Her face is so very animated. I've seen that expression. It's the wide-eyed, lips slightly parted expression women at boxing matches wear. I'm sure the rich hoes in Rome did it the same when they attended the gladiatorial games.

The ring is formed of thick, intertwined strands of corroded iron. There's a jagged gap opposite the shank. Whether from damage or by design, I haven't a clue. The shank is set with the aforementioned gory gemstone that also, if you squint, resembles a death's head in the way a thundercloud might resemble the skull of an angry god. The stone fitfully glints with the light from the table lamp. Almost a twin to the pendant hanging from Zane's neck.

"I thought it'd be a thumb prick." Morton slips the ring onto his finger.

"Ha ha, you said prick." I laugh, but not really. No, not really.

"Dude," Vadim says with ample foreboding. "This shit is how you get sepsis or peritonitis or something."

"Quiet, punk, you're next." Julie Five grins at him. I think of a northern pike opening its needle-fanged jaws to slurp down a hook.

Zane raises his eyebrow. "A dribble of claret for the cause seems reasonable. The price for betrayal is a blood eagle. JV's idea. Be warned."

"What's a blood eagle?" I say.

"You don't want one," Vadim says.

Steely J excuses himself. He steps through a panel near a bookcase and that's the last I see of him. I think it's the very last time *anybody* sees him for a few years. Candice, his latest girlfriend, remains at the table with an expression of abandonment. She's had too many wine coolers.

Neither Clint nor Leo speak. They're nervous, I can tell. Leo is a bit green around the gills. Real hard cases. Both of them agitated and wheedled to be included, and now their knees are knocking. And why are they spooked? The ceremony is bullshit. High school melodrama. This is supposed to be mock serious, like fucking about with Ouija boards and séances or homoerotic fraternity paddling rituals.

"Seven is a good number," Zane says. He's not counting himself, obviously. He's playing Satan. "Seven were the apprentices in the Devil's Grotto."

"Power number, baby," Julie Five says, Ed McMahon to his Johnny Carson.

We all stare at one another. Similar to gazing into a mirror — after a while, everybody is as plastic as Zane. I poke Morton in the ribs. Somebody has to be the first to leap and he's it. He makes a fist. Blood begins to flow. The blind moose watches as we each take our turn.

* * *

God, do You remember my third year in college when I saved that little old lady who fell on the ice in front of a moose that had wandered into town? I threw snowballs and shrieked until it ambled away into the trees. Surely, if You're the real deal You were there. God, please be real. Please help me now. Because I can't see anything. I'm flopped on my belly atop a heap of corpses. That can't be right. The dark is sticky. Warm, inanimate flesh yields beneath me. My pinky slips into someone's dead-staring eyeball. Eyelashes bat against my knuckle.

Zane kisses my cheek. I'd recognize his Rico Suave cologne anywhere, even here. He says, "Welcome and congratulations. You're part of it. You'll always be part of it. I'll see you at the party. Guest of honor, Ed."

The rest of the night is a blank. Or a hole. So, thanks for that, God. If you exist, which I figure you don't. The cut in my finger doesn't close for weeks. The hole in my soul remains the equivalent of a sucking chest wound.

II: Culling

Zane Tooms makes the CNN ticker three and a half years later.

Kind of a funny story. A terrific day until that point. I spend it shopping for vintage LPs at this fat cat record producer's annual garage sale. Vinyl is my true addiction. Stronger and purer than my fondness for baby dykes, or even my love of a self-effacing bear with real taste in the arts. I spend weekends with my boyfriend Tony at his Malibu beach house. This summer my theme resounds courtesy of

The Kinks: "Little Miss Queen of Darkness." I don't really identify. Drag isn't my thing and any sadness in my eyes is liable to be incidental tearing from my extra lush lashes. Nope, I love the song because its lyrics are true poetry. Poetry is distinctly lacking in this modern world. Barbarians have sacked the music industry, despoiled Hollywood. Publishing is a joke with celebrity tell-alls and Dan Brown as the punchline.

I'm lamenting these facts while sprawled on the sofa in Tony's giant game room. The news hits as I'm raising a mojito to my lips. Hard to believe my eyes. I didn't believe them either, though, when the accusations of seventy counts of Rohypnol-facilitated rape first came down to the clack of a magistrate's gavel. Apparently that dark side of Zane's was worse than I thought. Theory goes that seventy is a conservative estimate — who knows how many victims he's left scattered across Europe.

Now Zane is dead. The DEA and Mexican police shot him a bajillion times in some fleabag hotel in Mexico City. I don't know how to feel. There's a tiny white scar on the underside of my middle finger. I look at it and wonder if he ever raped *me*. Doubtful. Despite all indications, evidence is he didn't swing for dudes. Like I said, I don't know how to feel.

"Ha! Hell yes! I told you they'd get that rat bastard!" Tony wanders in from the shower and does a sack dance in celebration. He played ball for the Forty-Niners. His gut is enormous. The old me, lily-fresh college grad, would've cared. The worn and worried me is more concerned with Tony's heart. He's a kindly soul, his celebration of Zane's demise notwithstanding. Tony heard the stories and paid for my therapy. He's earned the right to cry, "Ding-dong!" et cetera.

Oops.

The doorbell rings and it's Julie Five on the step. I almost swoon at the shock.

"So, we meet again." She's wearing sunglasses and a white sundress. Her skin is softer and pinker than I recall. Time has rejuvenated her or she's gotten on the E. Bathory program. A midnight-blue Mustang is parked in the drive with the top down. The hood symbol looks more like a particular malformed death's head than any mustang. Three and a half years might as well be three and a half days. She moues in preparation for a kiss. I don't offer my cheek for the courtesy peck, no way. I'd rather let a tarantula sit on my face.

She crowds me backward. Her shadow crosses mine and my legs go weak and I collapse upon the rug where sunlight pools on nice days. This is California, so yes, the sunlight is doing that right now. She steps over my supine form and I get a peek at her goods, like it or not. Red panties to match her scary-long fingernails. The sun filtering through the fabric of the dress turns everything to crimson. She reaches into a demure handbag and produces the iron ring. Slides it onto the third finger of her left hand. She looms above me, smiling in a way I don't recognize from her repertoire. If evil and cruelty can mature the way wine does, then here you go. This goddamned cask of Amontillado's got cobwebs all over it.

"What's going on?" Tony arrives, half-naked and thundering. He quickly takes in the situation and gets right in her personal space. "Who the hell are you?"

I'm afraid he'll hit her, shatter her smirk with his mallet fist. I'm terrified he won't. Either way, it doesn't matter. I can't move, can't speak. My body is cold from the inside out.

"You're Anthony. Hello." She extends her hand.

He brushes her gesture aside. "And you're Julie. Yeah, I recognize you. Step, lady. You aren't welcome."

"C'mon, stud. Put her there." She smirks mischievously and reaches for him again. The light in the room dims because she's sucking it into her eyes. She snags his hand and clasps it tight with both of hers the way politicians do, the way a black widow fastens to her prey. Squeezes so hard that blood drips from their joined fingers. That's the end. Tony sways in place and she stands on tiptoes to whisper into his ear. It goes on for maybe ten seconds until she releases him and steps back.

"Oh, wow," he says. Tony usually talks loud enough to break your eardrums. This is a mousy little whisper. "I'm sorry. I didn't know." His face changes as he turns away. His skin tightens and his mouth and eyes stretch at the corners, but I only catch a glimpse. He shambles toward the living room, gone forever.

"Not with a bang but a whimper," Julie Five says, quoting the only Eliot she's likely memorized. Julie didn't use her own brain to get through college. She relied upon cunning and nascent savagery. The light in the room drains away and she floats above me, a pale gemstone revolving against the void. She draws the dwindling heat from my bones and into her huge, luminous eyes.

I belatedly notice the feathered dart protruding from my breast. Steely J drifts from the unknowable depths, pistol in hand. He salutes me and drapes his arm around Julie Five's waist.

I am very, very tired.

They wink, synchronized, and I wink out.

* * *

Vadim talks while he carries me in his arms, the Bride of Frankenstein.

"There are these worm things, or leech things, neither, but you get the picture, and they detach or get expelled from a central mass. These worms, or leeches, crawl inside you through whatever opening is available. The urethra and the anus are likely access ways. That's what happened to the dinosaurs. It's one theory. I think it works."

"Put me down, man." My voice is hoarse and my skull aches. My breast muscle hurts too. Whatever Steely J hit me with packs a nasty hangover.

We stand there, wherever there is. An abandoned hotel lobby? Lots of dust, boarded windows, and the light fixtures are fubar. Bright though, because sunlight streams through cracks and crevices. I ask the obvious and he shrugs. He too received a visit from Julie Five and a follow-up dart from Steely J. Like me, he came to in this place.

"Uh-oh."

I follow Vadim's gaze and see a thick man all in black standing on the mezzanine steps. His face is pale and freaky as shit. The flesh is so tight, his eyes stretch to slits, their corners near his temples. A machete dangles from his fist. Blood drips from the blade.

"Tony?" Right size, wrong face; except maybe it was the right face, I'd seen it changing at the casa...

"Tony isn't Tony no more. That's Mr. Flat Affect." Vadim grips my arm. "Let's book."

We book. I try the obvious things — exterior door handles are locked and chained from the outside; the windows are barred. I glimpse a dry pool in the courtyard. The yard has gone Planet of the Apes. Grass run riot. The palm trees are dull yellow. Mort is spiked halfway up the bole of the biggest tree. He's covered in dried blood, but I recognize his voice when he calls for help, for god, for death. There are several more people nailed to trees. Harder to identify. I don't want to know.

Before long, I stop to catch my breath.

"This is about the ritual."

"Duh," Vadim says. "The goon is one of Zane's pets, or something like that."

"But why are they after us? We're part of the inner circle, right? Ground floor of the new order and all that jazz?" I hadn't taken it seriously, had only gone along because of the pressure. I hadn't swallowed ZT's apocalypse fantasies. Now, here I am trying to lawyer my way out of getting murdered.

"He lied. We're the blood in the blood pact."

"Pact with whom?"

He gives me a sad look for not paying attention during class.

Another Mr. Flat Affect saunters through a door and confronts us. He too wields a machete. However, he's clad in a white paper suit. The suit is streaked and grimy. It's a bad moment, but Savate! I expect great things from Vadim's size 11 Doc Martens. Vadim yells, "Oh fuck!" and elaborately gathers himself like he's tossing a kaber and snaps this kind of slow-mo roundhouse kick that misses by a mile. Maybe a mile and a half. He lands on his ass. And it would be hilarious except I'm shitting my capris. Mr. Flat Affect doesn't hurry; I doubt he ever hurries. He raises the machete and splits my best friend's skull. Does him like the islanders do with coconuts, with a lazy overhand chop. The killer pauses to savor the gurgling and spurting.

Doc Martens are peachy. *I* swear by Nikes. Canary yellow with Velcro, nobody's got time for laces. I put mine to their best use — slapping tile at a high rate.

III: The Bear Catacombs

I run through an archway and am back in Alaska in the Tooms family basement. The bear catacombs. It has to be a nightmare because I instantly recognize the late 90s. Sister, those were bad times for yours truly — nobody told me "it gets better," they told me to sit down and keep my mouth shut.

A party is in progress — music on full blast, lights ablaze, half the kids from our high school graduating class doing the bump and grind. Zane lurks on the fringes, a loud, fat, glittery-eyed kid. His smile is sly. He's exactly as I remember, only more so.

There my high school self is, on the edge, crushed against a skinny senior track star. I look dreadful: spiked hair and a lime mesh tank top. Stu Whitlock flaunts a mullet. Merciful Jesus, I had no idea I had so much to apologize for.

The band grinds to a halt and the lead singer chugs from a bottle of whiskey. My youthful double disappears up the stairs. A few seconds later, the shrieks begin. That would be Dave Teague, naked and insane, busting a move for the front door. I remember the rest with unpleasant clarity — there's a hot blonde Ukrainian transfer student lying mangled and murdered in a bed on the top floor. Some lowlife snuffed her and tried for the daily double with Dave. The killer is in fact shambling after Dave into the night. In a few minutes, state troopers scrag the psycho killer on the access road. I also recall that someone mentions the psycho's face is white with greasepaint, or he wears a mask, and shit, it hits me — Mr. Flat Affect has been with us since when.

Mind. Blown.

"La!" Julie Five steps from the crowd. Modern day Julie Five, fully envenomed, egg sac probably full to bursting. She was sort of a cute kid. Not anymore. She grins and tweaks my nose. Her fingers are icy. "You're bleeding, sweetie."

The blood is Vadim's — I've come through so far without a scratch, and that's ironic, because I'd bruise if somebody stuck a pea under my mattress. I'm speechless, unable to twitch; Julie Five seems to have that effect on my nervous system. Behind her, kids begin milling around the exposed section of wall where the pipes and tree roots form a maw. There's some scuffling and I see my erstwhile date Stu Whitlock crawl inside. He's followed by that beefy guy who played linebacker the year we went to state. Then another, and another, wriggling like sperm to fit through the crack in the earth, burrowing their way to God knows where. Doesn't take long for the last pair of legs to disappear into the darkness and it's us chickens left behind in an empty basement.

Mr. Flat Affect emerges from the corner where the coats are piled. Sways in place, devilish gaze locked on me. He's a meat suit and whatever powers him came from the deep earth. I whimper.

"Don't be afraid," Julie Five says. "You made the cut. We wouldn't dream of harming a hair on your frosty little head. You're our final girl. I always hoped you would be." She takes my hand, leads me upstairs, and seats me in the parlor at a plain wooden table. The moon glows hard in the upper corner of a bay window. Its light seems to recede, shrinking to a dot as I watch. She removes a black moleskin notebook from her purse, opens it before me, and clicks the action on a ballpoint pen, places it beside the notebook. "Your memoir. It will be important someday, after everyone has forgotten how all this started. There's a fire safe in the den."

Two more Mr. Flat Affects have noiselessly appeared at her flanks. One in white, the other black. Their expressions are identically monstrous. She links arms with them and they glide into the shadows. "Good luck," she says from somewhere. Her voice echoes as if bouncing around a canyon. "Enjoy yourself."

I do as she says and write down what I know. I stash the notebook in the fire safe. Sun devours moon and the second decade of the twenty-first century absorbs the 1990s. The Tooms mansion decays around me. The table becomes stone and the stuffed moose head wilts unto a living death. I'm once again thirty-something and utterly fabulous despite the bags under my eyes, the tremor in my hand, and the caked-on gore.

Steely J, Julie Five, and Zane Tooms are long gone. The others remain as remains — Vadim, Morton, Candice, Clint, and Leo. Bloated, purple-black, in a pile near the hearth. Candice's shoe has fallen off.

Had the poison been in the ring or the liquor? The ring is how I bet. My crazy-person epistle isn't going to do me any favors in a court of law. Story like mine is a one-way trip to the booby hatch. What will happen to me when the authorities make the scene? The question gets an answer when the pair of troopers roll up to investigate after the anonymous call. They are none too reassured by my appearance and wild story. Two seconds after they nearly trip over the pile of corpses, I'm staring down the barrels of automatic pistols.

My finger bleeds from a wound that will never close. I make a fist without a thought as I mumble apologies for being here in this house of horrors, wrong place, wrong time — oh, so most def the wrong time. I needn't bother. The tearing pain in my hand lends an edge to my voice. My breath steams, a dark cone, and both troopers shudder in unison. Their guns clatter on the floor. Color drains from those well-fed faces, skin snaps tight and their eyes, their mouths, shiver and stretch. The transformation requires mere seconds. Their peculiar, *click-clicking* thoughts scratch and buzz inside my own psychic killing jar. They are mine, like it or not.

I *do* like it, though. A bunch.

Mist covers the world below this lonely hilltop. It's bitter cold and I'm barely dressed, yet it doesn't touch me. Nothing can. I am Bela Lugosi's most famous character reborn and reinterpreted. The Tooms estate is my mansion on the moor, my gothic castle. Time has slipped and I wonder if Tony is still out there in Malibu, waiting to meet me and fall in love. Do I care? Must I?

Who originally said some men want to watch the world burn? Whomever, he meant assholes like Zane and Julie. They chose me, corrupted me, and invested in me some profane force. Its trickle charge impresses my brain with visions of debauched revelry, of global massacre, fire, and slavery. Do my minor part to spread mayhem and terror and a few years down the road I can be on the ground floor of a magnificent dystopian clique. I can be a lord of darkness with minions and everything.

What shall I do with such incalculable power?

"Fix me a cosmopolitan," I say to the ex-trooper, ex-human, on my right. He does and it's passable.

There are numerous doors inside the Tooms mansion, to say nothing of the crack that splinters through bedrock and who knows where from there. I could wreak havoc in the name of diabolical progress. Or I could flap my arms and fly to Hollywood, whisper in the right ears and watch a sea change transform the industry. Or I could return to my senior year and seize Stu Whitaker by more than the hip, tell Father dearest to get bent with a martini in one hand and a smoldering joint in the other.

Decisions, decisions, you know?

Ears Prick Up

1.

My kind is swift to chase, swift to battle. My imperfect memory is long with longing for the fight. Gray and arthritic in the twilight of retirement from valorous service to the Empire, my hackles still bunch at the clink of metal on metal. My yawn is an expression of doom sublimated. I dream of chasing elk across the plains of my ancient ancestors. I dream of blizzards and ice fields that merge with the bitter stars. In my dreams, I always die.

2.

I traveled far from home in my youth. Dad and I slugged it out with a whole platoon of black hats one night as we strolled across the tundra of the Utter North. Military commandos hired to assassinate us; every man and dog marked with the mark of a secret gang, scents masked in case of failure. Poor, stupid fools. Probably sent by General Aniochles who figured Dad was gunning for his job. Bet my bottom chew toy the sonofabitch made the call. He gave Dad dagger eyes whenever they chatted at court. Bastard smelled guilty to me and that's what I knew. Well, I knew right.

I wasn't a pup then. I wasn't approaching my warranty date, either. My eyes glowed red with atomic radiation. My fangs gleamed in a grin that would have made a T. Rex flinch, appropriately enough, because they named me, my whole series, after the terrible king extinct these many eons, but unforgotten. Dad papered the walls of my kennel with color photos of dinos and wolves and exploding missiles to give me the right idea about how I should behave when he cried, "Sic 'em, Rex!"

Dad let slip the leash and I sicced, oh boy. Happiest of growls is the snarl of a locked jaw.

Bullets cracked all around us, and fire flashed all around us, while I lunged to and fro, hip deep in blood and mud the way dearly departed Kennel Master Callys and his best dog, Shotsum-Loathsum, taught me at the war academy. Shotsum-Loathsum was one of a kind, the failed Cerberus series, and they never again made his equal. He had two heads (a third just wasn't feasible), one more vicious than the other! Might've been the meanest mutt to ever prowl the yard. Gave me this beauty scar on my muzzle, and I thank him.

I belched hellfire and howled sonic death. With each snap I sheared an armored arm here, a leg there. Those days were my destroying angel days. I could tear the tread from a tank and whip you with it. Fear pumped acid through my blood and accelerated my reactions. Fear tasted like raw meat, made me drool. Fear made me greater than my design which had attempted to render me fearless. That's why they canceled my line too. Hard to control a thinking dog.

I leaped in front of Dad as somebody opened up on him with an antipersonnel gun and got shot a whole bunch for my troubles. The impact knocked me flat and splintered a stand of trees into kindling.

They shouldn't have done. Dad cursed his worst. He powered the prototype off-market rockets on his exoskeleton and gave back an eye for an eye, lighted a mushroom cloud where we struggled. Could have spotted us from orbit. In the end we killed the bastards and collapsed upon that slagged hunk of arctic plain, half done in ourselves. I groaned, fur shredded, titanium plates pierced and leaking the good stuff almost too fast for my personal cloud of nanobots to plug the works. Go little nanobots! My tongue lolled and I whimpered.

Dad patted my head. "Live it up, Rex. Once all the bad guys are dead, they'll retire us to the Happy Hunting Grounds."

Vexes me to this day that I don't know about the Happy Grounds. The pertinent entry seems to have been purged from my data banks.

3.

Revisit this twenty or so years down the line. I'm a grizzled veteran. The powers that be have phased out the Rex Series. Dad must truly be sentimental because he keeps me around despite an abundance of options. My joints ache, my servos grind louder. I hope nobody notices.

The train sprawls in the long grass, a ravel of silver below this bare hill. A stutter of pops and flashes and the tyrant is dead. I should be down there, jaws agape, eyes flashing fire, my howl obliterating the courage of the enemy. Instead I crouch at my master's heel and growl in malice. Younger men and younger dogs do the dirty work.

Dad has killed the Emperor with a word. Long live the Emperor.

Dad's men approach, green mud on their faces, and report that this is so. They are good soldiers. He picked them carefully as a farmer picks the best fruit from his orchard. They present him with a basket containing the tyrant's head — a basket of white birch in the ancient samurai custom. There are no longer samurai, but we do not forget.

Dad's men report that the tyrant's wife is also dead, the young, beautiful one who refused to part from him when the palace fell and his people lighted great fires and shouted for his blood. Dad's men report how they have killed the tyrant's children, even the one who hid cleverly below the floorboards. They are good men, thorough men. He is pleased. I see it in the relaxing of his shoulders, smell it in his scent. I smell sadness too — he and the Emperor were pack, once.

Our new Emperor Trajan is jubilant. He commends our valor when Dad calls on the red phone to explain the garden has been weeded. The new Emperor asks Dad to fetch the tyrant's banner to Prime. Trajan will spread it before the door of his toilet. There will be celebrations; we are invited. I will receive a medal of valor and a juicy ox bone. I have a cabinet of medals. I am the most decorated canine soldier in the history of the Empire.

Even as they speak on the red phone it rains, and through the rain I watch the tyrant's banner curl with flames. No matter. Dad knows of a three-fingered tailor in New Naples who will make us another.

4.

Mom is happy when we finally return to our home by the white cliffs. She feeds Dad grapes from the vineyard and cheese from the goat. She bathes him from a ceremonial basin. They retire behind a bamboo screen to mate.

In the morning I water the big tree near the main gate and rest there for a while. The ocean is off to my left, dull beneath the cliffs and patterned with hungry birds. The tree is to my right, like me, a piece of old metal — scarred and stained, white-puckered grooves radiating from the axis of its foundation. Such low, dark trees dot the ragged coast, but I am informed they do not spring native from this dirt. I wonder if they remember their birth-grounds by some impulse caught in the plexus of heartwood and cambial glue. When the winds rush off the water my tree seems to nod at the sky. It murmurs.

Marcello arrives in his glider when the sun grows fat. My tail wags with a crazy mind of its own. Marcello is black as pitch and always smells of violence, which I adore. His eyes are rivets in a cold bulk. Of all loyal hounds in Dad's stable, he is dominant. Oh, I could rend him, if growl came to snap, for I am Rex, greatest of my kind. What a battle that would be!

My brains are superior to most canines. Nonetheless, the primitive beast within me isn't much for long-term planning. *His* stratagems are Dad's long knives. Marcy (Dad calls him that when it's just the boys) is a ruthless man. This is his chief virtue, in my humble opinion — current events call for ruthlessness. It is the time of dog-eat-dog.

They recline near the scarred tree and discuss the situation in Prime. The ocean is smooth today and Prime is an invisible place where people from books compete for favors. These folk caper at court — clowns, buffoons, trained seals in bright clothes.

Dad too competed once. Oh yes.

The old Emperor loved him well. The previous ministers were less charmed by Dad's heroics in the war against the barbarians. General Aniochles, Dad's bitterest rival, had openly warned the old Emperor about the dangers of war heroes with the keys to the Legion. Aniochles was a foreigner—some speculate that barbarian water tainted his veins, and so the old Emperor chose to turn a deaf ear. Later, Aniochles got torn apart by the mob which stormed the palace during the glorious revolution. I wish we had found his body so I could have pissed upon it.

Marcello says that Prime is a safer place now. The partisans of the old Emperor have been rooted out and shriven. More importantly, the partisans of the old General have been dealt their rewards. During the plans for the Grand Transition, Dad had feared a Legion divided. To be sure, isolated centurions chafe in their barracks, yet this is nothing to dread. They need a head as a coin needs its head. Dad will more than suffice.

Marcello is confident all wounds will heal in short order, all petty complaints will be placed aside. He and Dad drink wine and congratulate themselves on a job well done. I lie at their feet and scheme to the best of my doggy ability. Unlike them, I am nervous of complacency. The new regime requires *something* to cement its unity. War dogs are not welcome in the parlor when the clamor of battle has subsided. Perhaps the conquered barbarians will test their chains and give us cause to rebuke them. If not the rebellious woodfolk, there is always a tribe rattling its shields. I think then of the pallid dwellers of Europa II, their vacuous demeanors and squirming mouths. We have not fired our rockets at the moon for too long. Dad should spread this message to those who command the Emperor's ear. Nothing serves to bury present troubles so well as fresh blood.

Marcello asks when Dad means to return to the Capital. Dad says that he shall return when the Emperor summons him. Until then he will enjoy the restful ministrations of his lovely wife, and pray red-handed Mars permits a soldier's ease. Marcello laughs and glides away on a trade wind.

Dad and I watch him go. A crow regards us from the branches.

5.

Twenty-two months since we discrowned the tyrant and installed his noble cousin Trajan. Dad is anxious that none of the new Emperor's promises have come to fruition. My master is a soldier's soldier and he plays the role. Part of that role is keeping one's mouth shut in public while complaining to one's dog in private.

Dad's duties as Consulate General carry him abroad. He has observed firsthand a growing discontent among the Legion ranks and the populace we protect.

We visit Prime at the wane of each moon and find her streets equally restless. Dad reports the news from fortresses along the rim of the empire. The Emperor's day to day security is overseen by Artificer Lyth and Commander Marcello. It is Lyth who frequently greets us in the Emperor's name. He is spindly and terrible. I do not enjoy the Grand Artificer's horrifying aspect, or the stench of malignance that seeps from the joints of his armor. Much occurs beyond the view of our esteemed leaders. The denizens of Europa II test our borders with increasing temerity. The jungles of Pash rustle with the activity of barbarian scouts. There are bombings. The Legion awaits word from Prime. No word is given. Dad hearkens whispers of discontent and his lips thin into a grim line I've seen too often of late.

Emperor Trajan is a wise ruler; he vows to restore Prime to her former majesty. He vows to repeal the heaviest taxes, to rekindle our aggression toward the barbarians and their allies. He vows to return the teeth of our empire. Yet his days are full of courtly doings unrelated to these pledges. His tastes are…curious. He craves exotic entertainment at court. The silken charms of Far Western nymphs consume his attention. He is enthralled by the ecstatic powders of the southern realms. Captive barbarian princes twist in wicker cages above slow steam, and their misery quirks his lips with amusement.

When Dad is finally granted a personal audience, he speaks to his eminence of concerns regarding the Legion and of our far-flung provinces. The Emperor nods his blond head and promises to address the Senate. His glassy eye does not shift from the pale forms wilting in their prisons. Our time is always short — Artificer Lyth hovers near, a monstrous cleg in red and black. He swoops to bleed the Emperor — *the woodland savages carry many plagues, many plagues, indeed!* — and for this, privacy is essential.

Dad takes leave, questions unresolved. I give the Artificer a baleful glare in passing.

Dad customarily sups with Marcello and dour Iade and commends them to protect our Emperor from harm. His lieutenants assure Dad that the Capital is proof versus the machinations of evildoers. In the end we fly from Prime, Dad smelling of uneasy thoughts. He should be pleased, except that he is too much like me in that regard. His instincts are powerful and they whisper to him of danger. He groans in his sleep, reliving battles, or anticipating new ones.

Consulate General is an exalted post. A wealthy post. With Trajan upon the throne, it proves fantastically more so. Trajan lives in dread of assassins. The Legion wants for nothing. Our home is splendorous. Our servants are many. Dad's lands stretch from deep into fertile plains and shaded hills down the coast. The trees are heavy with fruit; cattle mill in green tracts. Horses stream across wide grasses. He no longer rides them; his back hurts too much for the saddle. It pleases him to watch them gallop beneath puffed clouds as I nip at their heels.

Adjoining our home is a massive structure, low-beamed and windowless. A storehouse for Dad's greatest prizes. He owns several vehicles — skimmers, racers, bi-spindle gliders, and a light war chariot. This last trifle is prohibited for non-military use. I too am government property. General Aniochles had often raised this point to the Emperor — when not rending the enemies of the Empire, my place was a barracks kennel, not serving as a lap dog to a commander. Yes, well fuck him too. Rank hath its privileges. I'm a bit long in the tooth. Snoozing on the plantation appeals to me more than I would've guessed back in the days I chewed iron and pissed fire.

In the concrete floor is a concealed trap that leads to a vault where Dad stores much more interesting things. Here are his favorite toys — the blades and guns and armor of warfare. He keeps them in fine repair, each instrument polished and whetted in anticipation of grim eventualities. We do not enter the vault this day, although he glances at it with a far-eyed expression I know well. His scent causes me to sniff for hidden danger, yet I sense no enemies lurking. The odor I whiff from his pores is tinted with the same metal as his thrashing nightmares.

Today he does not wish to slaughter a barbarian regiment. He only wishes to drive a pleasure chariot. Before the barbarian troubles he amassed a fortune driving similar vehicles in races at the Hippodrome. Dangerous business, that. Perhaps more dangerous than being a war hero and a politician. He still likes to drive. So we go. I get stuffed into the copilot slot, webbed in and protected by a canine helm Artificer Trang devised before he took the long stroll into Night. Artificer Trang had looked and smelled so much better than Lyth. I mourn the dead man as the helm snicks into place.

It is a warm, listless day. From the state-sponsored radiocast — last week's news. An opera by Laconte. String music. Long static-filled pauses. Nothing about the garrison bombing in New Portugal. Nothing about the Coliseum riot. Marcello sends him a terse message: *General, your presence is not required. The dissidents are quelled.* Dad does not enjoy this news. His jaw bunches, his hands clench. The people are increasingly restless. The stability of the Empire is paramount. More and more, she is anything but stable. Even a dog can see this.

A narrow road cuts through the white cliffs. It is neglected; the pavement is cracked. There are craters and switchbacks, and hairpin turns. Sometimes the road drops to sea level where rocks lie scattered like ready teeth. We flit past them, the sleek chariot whirring and trembling as it slices right to left with the precision of a stitching machine.

It is not the rocks or the turns that undo him. A stag wandering from its field is the mechanism of our destruction. It appears in the road, a hoary brute with thick horns lowered. A gray wall. Why does Dad swerve? I do not know. The chariot would cut the beast down without issue. Nor is it fear that rules him — he has crushed many a foe's glider beneath his own, shorn valiant pilots from their cockpits with a scything sweep of his wing and exulted in the flames and the blood.

Yet, he turns aside. His iron hands are betrayed by a signal, an errant signal that I, with my superior senses, almost apprehend in its passage. I smell guilt and awe. The chariot turns as it is commanded to turn and falls among the sharp rocks. The sky and the ocean grapple, trading positions. I recall that the white stag is Dad's personal standard, the standard of his noble lineage. I should make something of this, yet don't. Not in this moment. Terror masters me as we crash and burn.

Somewhere, dead Aniochles chuckles. Difficult to hear him above the clatter of many shields thrown down at once, my despairing howl…

6.

You are a destroyer, Rex.

It is true, what this ghost voice says. This accusing voice that shivers from wrapping fog. I am now and have ever been a destroyer of men. It is my little niche. Some dogs fetch, some dogs preen. I crunch bones in my teeth and tear down the works of our enemies. Such work is noble. Some things *must* be torn down that more important virtues may thrive. I am needed as a wrecking bar is needed. There is no shame.

Protector of tyrants! The phantom hisses. *Like master, like dog! Lapdog, sycophant!*

The fog lifts and I see my beloved mentor, the Kennel Master Callys, alive in his armor. One of the few men I have ever feared. He is a brick furnace surrounded by soft-mouthed puppies in white tunics. He reeks of blood. The pups shine, eager for his instruction.

Callys teaches us there is nothing complicated about killing a dog or a man. The mechanics are quite straightforward. Some men die easily, other men die hard. Dogs? Dogs are only as good as the hand on the leash. There is no mystery. To reflect upon the destruction of another man is the difficult portion. Instinct has taught us to bow in deference to the sacred pact that has existed since the era of cave dwellers.

First, we must never regard the enemy as men — they are *objectives* given flesh. Next, Callys advises us to wipe their faces from our minds. We must never look back. This applies to humans and dogs alike. It is the deepest secret to success in the Legion. Then he fits me with my first war collar and sends me with my pack-mates to dim Pash to do the Emperor's work.

He is correct, my grizzled Callys. Men are easy to kill.

Common folk tell superstitious tales about the barbarians of Pash. The woodsmen are savages who fight with the vigor of ten centurions. They lay horrible traps and eat the flesh of our poor fighting boys. I find that the barbarian squeal and shit in their death throes much the same as my pack brothers and the hastati who accompany us. It is almost a disappointment.

You are a hound of hell. Your master, your "father," is a traitorous mutt. He is the real cur.

I am positive the barbarians who looked into my grinning face thought me a terror. The Legion is a juggernaut built to destroy the Empire's foes. Nothing else. In the dim jungle my purpose is the juggernaut's terrible purpose, my Dad's purpose. If that makes me a fiend, then yes, I am a fiend. Gladly.

The fog lowers and bells clang, first at distance, now close and all around. War bells, no mistake. My pulse explodes, but the angry bells soon fade. My vision shifts as the fog boils, closing, then receding. The old Emperor awaits my master and I upon the Capitol steps. He is a regal man; a king's king as his title indicates. He loves my master as a son, better than his own sons. My master, my human father, loves him right back. The old Emperor is called tyrant in some quarters. He does not trust in the greatness of Prime. His edicts are harsh. He expects every citizen to weigh his wealth and strength against the welfare of the Empire. The Empire is besieged from without and from within and the old Emperor believes a storm shall someday blow down the towers his ancestors have raised. Yes, the Empire has many enemies. The old Emperor has more. Woe unto him. He hugs Dad to his breast. Dad looks away in shame the way I hang my head after ruining the carpet.

What have you and your master done, hell hound?

I know Dad has come to resent this new, young Emperor. He regrets elevating lofty Trajan, he is disgusted at the debaucheries at court. He broods over the malaise abroad. A storm upon the horizon. The stag regards him with contempt and he turns my chariot toward the ocean.

What has my father done? I do not know. My poor overworked positronic brain is a crude marvel. It can only take me so far.

7.

A spiked collar makes an excellent close-quarters weapon. Drive in with the spikes, rip out with the fangs! *It is among Callys' favorite exhortations.*

The enemy soldier, a barbarian mastiff smeared in red ochre, does both of these things to me. There is a skirmish to end all skirmishes. Chaos and fire. Men squirming in separate pieces; chattering reports of spindles and malspheres. Dogs whining their last. The mastiff whips me with his claws; his spikes tear my neck; his cracked fangs slash the flesh of my belly. I roll away and wheel. My spurting blood forms a circle in the dirt. I charge him through the sudden mud. He sinks his teeth deep into my shoulder and braces for the killing twist. It is too late for him though. My jaws snap shut upon his neck, my diamond-sharp jaws, and there is no escape from them…Then Dad is there with his gladius blazing a nova and he cuts the mastiff in two. Dad is slathered in crimson. His left arm dangles, shattered. His body is full of holes. He laughs.

So I tell you, this small accident by the water is of no consequence.

Reports are we walked away from the wreckage of the chariot. I do not remember anything except darkness and the distant roar of my ancestors on the plain. I remember gauze curtains, leeches hovering in their robes. Mom weeps. She has seen Dad in the yard, gore from toe to crown, clothes rent from his body. Raving of battles long past. He carried me, a bloodied lump of torn fur and exposed bone. Mom thinks me dead while I dream of chasing the horses across endless fields toward the purple sea. The leeches also think me a goner; my injuries are so grave. Ah, they don't know the trouble I've seen. I descend from the supreme canine bloodline. I am augmented with weaponry. I am built to endure.

Only I know that I have seen much worse. I do not say this when I open my eyes and see her nearby, mopping Dad's brow. My vocalizer seems to have been damaged in the crackup. I whine and sleep again.

8.

Dad is a famous man; our accident is reported during numerous newscasts. Sabotage? The broadcasters are titillated. Flowers arrive from all corners of the empire. The Praetorian Guard establishes a cordon around the hospital. Citizens camp in the fields, hoping for a glimpse. It worries me to consider that some of them do not come bearing gifts or fond wishes. Yes, Dad is a famous man, but also a hated one if you ask the right people.

The days roll into weeks.

Faithful Mom keeps vigil, only leaving for the brief visits by Marcello, Iades, and Dad's other confidants. Marcello brings whiskey and cigarettes. The leeches wisely ignore these transactions.

The news from the Capital isn't good. Three more riots in Prime. Food shortages are raising eyebrows among the Senate. However, the senators do not seem concerned that we have lost a garrison near the Pash border. *A few centurions more or less, eh fellows?* These days the state radio does not cover foreign events at all. Football scores, celebrity gossip, music. The masses are surely drugged as our fine

Emperor.

I dream of the wreck. I dream of hunting. In the hunting dreams, the stag emerges from cover. He pauses to regard me, his mortal enemy. My tribe has stalked his kind since time immemorial. That my human father bears the stag as his heraldry seems a paradox, and one I am too weary to sort.

The stag's antlers catch the light and gleam like a crown of blades. His eyes are familiar. He tosses his shaggy head and ambles out onto the plain. The dream is a jumble of life and fantasy — I am injured from the chariot crash, and bleeding heavily, yet I follow my prey. Stubbornness is a virtue among dogs. The stag recedes to a blot and vanishes. I track his prints in the dirt. I snuffle his musk among the blades of the grass. I wander through a copse of trees and piss against one. The stag has escaped. Behind me, the plain is golden gulf edged in darkness.

I begin to retrace my steps back to the house. At first, this isn't difficult since I've left a trail of blood gleaming to light the way. A flake of snow loops around and catches on my tongue. Then a few more, and then many more until a blizzard erases the world and me with it. I awaken, filled with a terrible yearning that I do not understand.

Months burn.

We grow strong, Dad and I, although the leeches suggest Dad's proud visage shall not remind anyone of Adonis. A mild joke assayed by the chief surgeon who is too old to fear execution. Dad was never what you might consider handsome. Now he is a trifle worse. Beauty lines, the legionnaires call such scars. Something has changed in my master. His smell has altered. He smells of sadness and of determination and regret. I know trouble is on the way. He smells of fire and anger and the desperate foolishness of youth.

Mom comforts us. We walk in the hospital garden. She is splendorous in her fear. Her black hair, her carmine lips! Her eyes blaze with mysteries. I am entranced. She and Dad talk of small things and though they are only small things I cannot imagine how I have always overlooked her cleverness. I am sent to guard the front door. They mate there in the garden, beneath an olive tree. I hope he doesn't kill himself in the doing.

Mom has wanted a son. I wonder if now she shall receive her desire. Dad has muttered of it some nights when he'd drunk overmuch and fallen prey to sentiment.

After Mom departs with her handmaidens and bodyguards, Dad mutters to me, "May it please the gods my latest heroics grant her a child as I have failed her as a husband these long years."

In the morning she will find his sick bed empty. She will search while the servants lament. We will not be discovered.

9.

An enclave nestles high in the mountains that shield the Empire from western aggressors. The name of the enclave is unimportant. What is important is that for ages the progeny of various paranoid emperors have been sequestered here among bald monks and bearded goats. Few have heard of this enclave. Fewer know where it stands.

Dad is one of the latter and he lands his glider in a copse of paper birch. The walk is brief — we do not wish to run far if running becomes necessary. Because the air is chill he wraps a cloak about himself. Because he does not care to be recognized he wears a hood. In one hand he carries a lens — it has a nose for human chemicals. In the other hand he carries a rod. I alter my coat to blend with the terrain and lurk near his flank. I am on high alert.

It is late afternoon. The bark and leaves of the trees are changing colors. We pick our way through mossy boulders and across tiny streams. Soon, we spy the ancient stone of a battlement. Left seems a good direction, so we circle that way and mount a low rise screened by more birch and a few pines. A squatty monk in a brown cassock reclines among fallen leaves. Doubtless a lethal guardian. His job appears most boring. Dad whistles to me the whistle of a gyrfalcon. I greet the monk in Praetorian fashion and move on, licking my chops. At the summit there is a rocky clearing with a fine view of distant reaches. The world below is twilight damp.

The sensor blinks and purrs in Dad's hand.

Ahead, a pair of children play at rough and tumble. The children cease their sport and observe our approach with sharp interest. Doubtless, they have been taught to fear strangers. The monks are not fools and know what the Emperor expects of them. Fear, however, is a difficult thing to teach. It is better learned from bitter experience and at unpleasant cost.

Dad is hardly fearsome with those bent shoulders, the exaggerated limp. As for me, I'm huge enough to scare anybody with sense, but I grin a friendly grin and wag my tail. Good dog! Dad lowers the hood and bares an avuncular smile. His scars do not alarm, they attract a natural curiosity, and the boys are his. One strokes my fur, surely wistful for the pets he left in his household. I'm the only domesticated animal around for leagues.

The boys dress simply, yet comport themselves as befits princelings. Neither has met his father, Emperor Trajan. Perhaps unsurprisingly, they are proud little bastards, with hints of requisite cruelty in the crinkle of their eyes. Their teeth are white as young carnivores. I have seen their like in my puppyhood kennels. Brutes in training.

Beyond them, the rearward quarter of the knoll has eroded like a cavity in a molar. Blue light fills the ravine and hides its foot. "A bad place to make sport," Dad says. "The monks would not approve." The boys laugh at his timidity. The elder quips that life in the palace has far deeper pitfalls.

Dad gazes out over the darkening land where the lights of Prime should soon be. And then, casually, he asks which of them shall be master when his illustrious father relinquishes the throne.

They are close enough in age that there is room for doubt, and thus each makes his answer. He nods sagely. And if master of Prime, how would they govern her territories? Again each makes his answer and as they answer I watch their faces and think my own thoughts. They can't smell the iron igniting in Dad's sweat. They cannot smell his smell that is incipient destruction. I hear the creak of his fingers tightening on the weapon at his belt.

Oh, I am certain of what he sees.

In a while he sends the younger boy down to the monastery — the supper bell rings faintly. He keeps the elder at his side — Dad claims he is feeble and will require the lad's muscle. But first, Dad asks him if he knows his brother well. Indeed, the boy does. Does he suppose his brother would truly break the Praetorian Guard? The boy is contemptuous — of course his weakling brother would do such a stupid thing! The younger son lacks the sense to recognize how the powerful must be warded from the madness of their subjects.

Ah, yet don't ceaseless favors to the Praetorian Guard weaken the Legion and therefore the citizens? These are difficult times, are they not?

The boy sneers. If the flock must be sheared to clothe the shepherd, so be it. Dad smiles at his conviction and asks if he has ever seen proud Prime. No? Then come now and look across the chasm where night draws down. Stand here and look and see her lights as they spark and catch…

The boy does this. They stand there, Dad's iron hand loosely upon the boy's fragile shoulder. I whine softly, my tail swishing back and forth in the tough grass. Darkness falls. It is far to the bottom of the ravine.

10.

Dad gets cute and tries to ditch me. He's all sly with the tossing of a treat into the bushes as he makes for the glider. I'm faster and beat him to the vehicle. He grows exasperated. This may be a suicide mission. My growl tells him, no shit, General. I figured that for myself after we murdered that royal brat.

He commands me to lope home to Mom and guard her. The distance is vast. My mighty dog heart and cyborg parts will see me through. I plant my haunches in the copilot seat and snap at his hand when he attempts to drag me out. Eventually he relents, swearing vilely at my disobedience while smiling a secret smile.

"All right, stupid dog. Let's get you metal, at least." I consent to an ancient war harness. The harness is another accessory forged by the old master artificer, Trang, who was peerless in matters of defense. He designed it for the Max Series canines. Such brutes! Such killers! Perhaps less adaptable and handsome than myself, you had to give them credit for ferocity. Scoured with sand and blasted with sonics, I still whiff the taint of gore and death sweat embedded in the harness mesh. My eyes roll back, white, then forward, black. I'm not a lapdog anymore. I am, as the dead philosopher said, a destroyer of worlds. Small worlds, but worlds.

Dad's glider was once a racing machine. It shreds the wind. We beat Rosy Dawn to the Capital. There are a thousand doors into the palace and all one thousand are guarded by his gold-armored Praetorians. We enter by the thousand and first.

Moving within the mazeworks, I speculate as to whether an

alarm has been raised by the monks back on their mountain. Yes. Although it may be delayed while the monks seek a method to extract themselves from an untenable position. Trajan's displeasure is invariably fatal.

This alarm being a given, has the news broadened to include a notice against Dad and me? Yes again. Marcello would add two and two and be first to give the order. Dad trained him well. He is a clockwork, dire Marcello. His loves and hates are suits he folds away as the occasion warrants. His duty shall prevail against all else. There can be no doubt that if he spies us lurking about these halls he will kill us if he can. I drool at the idea of this confrontation

Iades? Iades is loyal to Dad. He is also a Praetorian. He will do as Marcello does. Dad is the most loyal of us all — he could've divided the Legion and loosed his partisans against the Emperor, perhaps even set himself upon the throne. Instead, he's chosen the lonely path of the assassin, the man who will pay to liberate the country from an error in judgment with his own life.

Dad may not desire the death of his men, although I would happily gut them one and all at this point. My ire is stoked. We travel by secret ways and come at last to the inner sanctum of our dear Emperor. The way Dad chooses is arduous — it involves no small measure of slithering through vents and clambering over shelves with precipitous drops yawning at our toes. Dad's wounds pain him; his muscles labor. I worry he will fail. He is tough, my old man. He persists against and my focus narrows to ward him from a sudden fall.

Artificer Lyth nearly has us because of this. He is waiting in the shadowy heights of an arch and descends with horrible alacrity. The pleasure upon his unmasked visage is manifestly unsettling. Artificer Lyth detests us as much as we detest him. He does not summon the Guard. He radiates a craving for homicidal glory. The Artificer thinks us relics easily dispatched by his dreadful craft.

Dad kneels near a vertical drop into a bottomless crevice. His arms shake with the stress of the climb. He snatches for his gladius. Too slowly, alas. Thankfully, my reflexes prevail. I spy the enemy and charge, roaring. Magnetized plasma jets forth and shrouds the enemy in a corona of fire.

To my chagrin, his shielding absorbs the worst I can dish. I suppose I should count myself fortunate he doesn't manage to reflect the sluice back upon me and Dad. That would be embarrassing *and* fatal.

The Artificer bats smoking cinders from his hair, rubbery mouth slack with malice. A drop of blood gathers in his left nostril. The hem of his robe wisps smoke, charred along the panther trim. He flings elongated arms outward and makes claws of his fingers. Around me the air is rent with screeches and flickers of lethal geometry. Cracks race along the ageless granite pillars. Little fires slither, rootless. Most dogs would perish right here — smashed and burned to founding atoms from the grasp of Lyth's telekinetic machinery.

Not me. I am Rex, left paw to the Consulate General, and greatest of my kind. Artificer Lyth isn't the only one who can play this game. Trang embedded a network of kinetic shields and dampers into my war harness to counter precisely this sort of emergency. The harness is a powerful artifact, proof versus any detonation short of a tactical nuke, according to the literature. It's a near thing, regardless. My foe's malevolent gesture shorts the circuit and I bellow in agony as the harness melts and fuses into my hide. Consciousness contracts to a keyhole. Rationality is obliterated. However, I am spared and my foe is screwed.

Artificer Lyth cries in distress when his attack fails. He attempts to scuttle back up to his nesting place, and he is quick, but I am on him and my fangs are at his neck. And that is the end for Artificer Lyth. I hobble back to Dad and drop the Artificer's gaping skull at his feet. Dad nods approvingly and gently scratches my ears like old times. His jovial camaraderie belies a deep concern for my condition. I am brave and try not to signal the graveness of my injuries or how much I suffer. We must hurry, for the commotion will soon draw the attention of the Guard and loose ends yet dangle.

We limp and stagger and redouble our pace through these secret ways.

Emperor Trajan reclines within his vasty solar. Dad has chosen this moment well, for the Emperor is inclined to sleep late after titanic debaucheries. Our leader is alone save for drugged slaves and a handful of Praetorian guards — only select favorites are permitted access to his person at these revelries. Sadly, these dregs are mixed with two or three men who have served honorably. There is nothing for it, however. I lick my wounds as Dad makes his preparations to seal our fates as traitors or liberating heroes.

Dad has brought several terrible weapons, which he activates from the safety of a hidden nook. Soldiers are obliterated where they stand and soon the Emperor has been stripped of his final layer of security. Dad takes a moment to ensure the great obsidiron doors are sealed. It will require technicians with plasma torches many minutes to breach them.

To slay Trajan would be simple. His eyes are glass, he snores. He is unaware of the carnage at his feet; he is oblivious to Dad's looming presence. His slaves suffer from a similar malaise, sprawled about his dais, twitching with visions of erstwhile heroics.

Yes, to slay Trajan would require a mere gesture. Dad must only slide the knife between his ribs. Yet, he stays his hand and Great Trajan snores on. A dull gonging begins against the massive portals. I imagine the chaos beyond, the panic as the Guard is summoned to breach these gates.

So how now? Dad is vexed and bemused. I cannot help him in this matter, notwithstanding my confusion at his hesitation. The will to stand deserts me. I lie on my side and pant heavily, and encourage him with small whines and groans.

"I have destroyed one emperor," Dad says. "How wrong can a man be? This venal creature deserves the mercy of neither bullet nor blade. I will not stain my honor with his thin claret." His gaze wanders the length of the chamber and alights upon the answer to his dilemma. Nine elaborate cages depend above a steaming mud pit in the southwest quadrant. Nearby is a device that controls the pulleys and wires. This device swings the cages to my level and one by one he inspects them. In eight he discovers limp barbarian corpses, but in the ninth, is a healthy specimen who contrives to feign death until I bark a warning and Dad bangs the bars, provoking the prisoner to stir.

Wasted from abuse and neglect, the barbarian remains a formidable mass within his prison. He reeks of righteous malice. Dad smiles at him and burns the lock half through with his gladius. The barbarian observes with hateful stoicism. His tribe plot devilry and vengeance unto their last exhalation. Their clans war in family units. Doubtless it has been his brothers and sisters boiled in these cages. I smell the pungent rage he experiences regarding the fates of his kinsmen.

Dad does not speak the barbarian tongue. Thus, he makes his

intention clear with a casual glance toward the Emperor. Then he drops the gladius and walks away. It would require scant effort for a beast such as this imprisoned warrior to fling his bulk against the lock and be free to raven throughout the peaceful solar. Who knows what havoc he might wreak before the Praetorians gain entrance.

The portals tremble as tremendous efforts begin upon them in earnest. Still faint; there is much time as time goes. Farewell, my Emperor. I think the kid we met in the mountains will do fine in your absence.

Dad makes a travois of his cloak and wraps me in its folds. I protest — he must abandon me to my end and save himself. He doesn't listen. He has spoken, usually when drunk, of the primordial pact between man and dog. The pact has existed since men squatted in caves by their fires. Man and dog have been pack since we were more troglodyte, since we were more wolf.

We depart. Of course, this is a relative term. There is nowhere to go.

11.

Because he was beloved before he earned the title of tyrant, the old Emperor's tomb is a grandiose complex of marble. It is built upon a hill not far from where Dad derailed his train as he escaped from Prime. Wildflowers sprinkle the terraces. The old Emperor's statue rises above the mausoleum dome and its stony eyes do not meet Dad's when he kneels to offer his respects.

I lie nearby, swaddled and if not peaceful, resigned. I press my snout to Mom's white kerchief that Dad took from his pocket to dab the gore draining from me. He whispers that I should go on ahead and clear the way, I am a good dog and he loves me. I breathe Mom's perfume. She is here, her scent stronger than any dim memory of my own canine mother or littermates. She strokes my heaving ribs. Her touch is soft.

Dad's weapons are spread beside me in a fan. Even now my mind ticks with possibilities. Is there any strength left in these bones? Could I summon a last effort to fight at Dad's side when the Legion comes to snuff him for our treason?

Grassy fields curve unto sky notched by clouds. Somewhere the metropolis buzzes and wasps boil from the hive. At last I observe tiny shadow flickers of gliders and kites between the seam of heaven and earth. I imagine Marcello's colors among the van. They search in swooping patterns that will soon intersect our hill.

The sun is warm on my muzzle. I drowse.

A stag appears in the field below. He coughs a challenge and nods his majestic skull. He gives me an insolent flick of his stub tail and eases toward the tall grass. Instinct, oh she truly is a bitch, and I'm on my feet in pursuit.

Pain swells, then recedes. My gait steadies. I breathe deeply of grass and musk. The breeze quickens and the sky dulls. Snow begins to fall. Soon, the stag has vanished. His tracks are swallowed in white drifts. The grass freezes like blades of upright knives.

I don't know how long this goes on. I wander for hours, for days, for ages. Long enough that I forget what drew me here or where I've been. The dark and the cold and the wind and my loneliness are everything. I hear a voice from afar and my ears prick up. The voice of the wind calls my name and draws me to a hill of ice and stone. Ruddy light glimmers from within the mouth of a cave. I smell cooking meat. The two sides of my dog's mind have a skirmish.

In the end, I creep forward. Smells good. I'll go inside and see what's there. Perhaps I'll warm myself by the fire.

III: Tomahawk

Black Dog

While watching the door he found himself humming "Love Will Tear Us Apart" under his breath.

She walked into the restaurant two minutes late. She dusted cigarette ashes off the sleeve of her coat and hugged him and accepted the rose he'd brought. First date and the rose was the nicest of the bunch, wrapped in baby's breath and pink tissue paper. He'd destroyed some other pretty nice flowers to get this sucker out of the refrigerated cabinet at the store. He'd also gotten stabbed by a thorn and it made him wonder if this might be a sign from whatever gods watch over the chariot races of the Hippodrome of Romance.

They sat across from one another for a few moments without speaking. Her eyes were brown. No, her eyes were green. The glow from the lamps changed them moment by moment. Looking into their depths disoriented him as if the building might be rotating upon the crest of a wave. He noticed two things: the top button of her blouse was undone and his collar felt a little tight. Also, the room seemed warm. He gulped some ice water, but the ice had melted and the water went down his throat like blood.

"Your eyes change color," she said.

"I get lizard eye. When I'm tired. Or in a mood."

"In the mood?"

"*A* mood."

She raised her brow and tried her water. Her throat moved and he regarded the patterns in the canopy overhanging the walkway.

Dusk was upon the world again. It was All Hallows Eve. The sky glowed as softly as the belly of a wine bottle. Street lights and lights in shop fronts were flickering to life along the slope of the avenue. The breeze through an open window tasted of wildflowers and moss and dying leaves. Her scent was lilac in his nose.

He'd been drinking. Scotch on the rocks. Probably not enough of it, though. When she removed her coat, he noted that the flesh of her arms was bruised purple. He breathed in the smell of her and observed how her skin shone, how her breast rose and fell, how her lips curved enigmatically, and nope, definitely not enough with the drinking for him.

"Wasn't something there a minute ago?" She pointed to the sidewalk and the sandwich board sign that advertised the restaurant.

"A big fucking black dog," he said. He'd seen the dog all right — huge and shaggy, black as the heart of night. Foam curdled its muzzle. Its tongue had lolled as it grinned at him from where it reclined at the foot of the sign. "Red eyes. Kinda spooky."

"Red eyes like in a photograph, or red eyes like the wolves in a Disney cartoon?"

"Red eyes like a vampire in a motherfucking Hammer flick." Wow; *fucking*, then *motherfucking*, no less, and in under the first twenty seconds. A personal best. He finished his scotch and loosened his collar and stared at the patch of sidewalk where the enormous black dog had lain moments ago. Had there been a leash? A master? He couldn't picture the scene anymore. He remembered the last of the sunlight in its eyes, however. Those eyes were suddenly coals ignited by a breath, and its wide, friendly smile hinted at a sort of knowingness.

"That's not good," she said.

"It's gone now. I've got no problem with dogs. Seemed friendly. Odd, is all."

"No, no, it's bad luck. Or, wait. Not bad luck — a bad omen. To see the black hound means curtains for you or someone close to you."

"Oh. Where do you get that?"

"Britain. A legend from over there. My dad went and lived on the moors when he graduated from school. He photographed mounds and menhirs, pillaged tombs. Et cetera."

"He's an archeologist?"

"Dad?" She laughed. Soft and lovely. "Hell no."

"What does he do?"

"He's dead."

"May I have another?" He quickly raised his empty glass to the passing server. "I'm sorry."

"Makes one of us."

"Ma'am, a double on that scotch, eh?" Yeah, his collar kept cinching in like a noose.

"What about you?" She studied him now. Focused upon him with an intensity that caused his heart to flutter.

"My old man is alive and well and living in Lincoln, Montana. He races huskies. We don't talk."

"Lucky you."

"Trust me, it ain't luck. Years and years of effort."

"Any kids? Wife? Girlfriend?"

"One dog, an ex, my work. Back at you."

"A Cavalier King Charles Spaniel. I've never been married. What kind of dog is yours?"

"A pit bull. I rescued her. She's sweet and gentle."

She nodded. "That's what everybody says right before their darling takes off an arm."

"Don't care for them, eh?"

"I had a bad experience. Where did you grow up?"

"Alaska," he said. "My dad was a hunter."

"Yes…and so the huskies. I think it's cruel to put a harness on an animal."

"How about a saddle?"

"Ha. Screw the Kentucky Derby. Horse racing should be abolished. Don't you agree?"

"Nice weather, isn't it?" He studied his place setting.

"Totally. I spent the day looking at houses for my mom. She's in Florida."

"She's moving back north. How nice for you."

"Nah. She just likes to shop online. Takes one of those video tours and convinces me to see the joint in person and report. She put in a bid on a place last month and then cancelled it. Decided the staircase was too narrow to lug her king sized bed up to the second floor. Jesus Christ. No way she's coming back to New York. She'd freeze."

"Why does she send you around to recon then?"

"She's a sweet old bird. Who the hell knows why she does what she does?"

The server came with another scotch for him and more ice water for her. They ordered dinner. She requested noodles and something else. He chose the fried rice without giving a damn.

"You're divorced, huh? What went wrong?"

"I was a neglectful bastard."

"Really? You seem different."

"I'm working on it."

"Good."

"Are you seeing anyone?" he said because she'd deflected the question earlier. It seemed impossible that she wasn't. For the love of God, look at her. He'd already decided not to involve himself in any triangles, had resolved to get up and walk out depending upon the answer. A brief, early sting was easiest in his estimation.

"Am I seeing anyone…Huh. Two months ago, my boyfriend left me for his ex. That one broke my heart." She glanced at her hands, toying with the rings, then swung back to meet his gaze. "At the moment it's you, only you."

He still wasn't certain whether that was a yes or a no. Another sip, another moment spent lingering upon the lines of her jaw and neck, the sweep of her clavicle, and the strength to move drained from him. He wished like hell that he enjoyed mysteries.

What did he know, then? She was in her thirties. She clerked at the library. She was a karate player at a local school. That's where they'd first met a couple of years back. He'd flown into town to visit friends, a whistle-stop before his book signing at a lit bar in the city. His friends, who also attended the school, dragged him down to the dojo to meet the gang. She arrived on the scene, knotting her second degree black belt and wham, he was smitten. He'd been married at the time, so he shook her hand and smiled and ignored the sparks that shot out of their fingers and into each other.

A lot had changed in three years. But not her.

His pulse thrilled and that worried him. Married forever and a day, then suddenly alone again, and absorbed in his writing, he'd almost forgotten the rush that accompanied the new and the unknown. He felt a curious and unwelcome sense of vulnerability that reminded him of his youth, of plowing headlong into a towering blizzard. Since the divorce he'd spoken to many women. Here was the first one to get his heart beating faster.

So, he tasted his drink and gloomily acknowledged that the tremor in his hand, the faint sickness in his soul, meant she was getting under his skin in a big way. He sighed and smiled at her and vowed, for the umpteenth time so far, not to say anything stupid, or misanthropic, or inane.

The angel on his shoulder laughed and laughed at that one.

* * *

Full darkness arrived. They migrated outdoors.

She took a pack of Camel No. 9s from her coat and lighted one. She smoked and watched him from the corner of her eye. He stood on the sidewalk and breathed heavily. He felt as winded as a prizefighter who'd survived into the later rounds. A cold breeze dried the sweat on his brow. The moon drifted over the black curve of the horizon. Full and radiant as a searchlight, the moon smoldered in the void, frozen as close to them as it would be for another million years.

The couple moved on after a while, stepping through bands of shadow cast by the interlaced branches of lithe potted magnolias and oaks. Many of the shops were locking up. The watchmaker and the baker hunched behind cold display cases, counting tills. A girl in an apron pushed a broom and smiled wistfully. Small groups of college kids drifted between the soft neon oases of bars and restaurants. There were fairy wings, a toga, some glitter and face paint, but few had bothered to get dressed for Halloween. A man played a violin in a second floor window over a darkened bookstore. The musician was a brawny, shirtless lad. Sweat wisped from his glistening shoulders. He nodded gravely and sawed with vigor as they passed.

"Love it," she said. "My brother plays the cello. Damned good. Make you cry." Her shoulder bumped his. "Ah, now check it. This used to be a swell art gallery." She indicated a deserted shop front. The placard promised the impending advent of a chain Irish pub. "Alas, the poor Krams. I knew them, Horatio. Lived here their entire lives, had local artists and poets in all the time. Robert Creeley read here, once. *The* Robert fucking Creeley. Nobody wants art, though. Nobody wants poetry. What they want is another bloody pub the same as every other cookie cutter pub. I hear the Irish mob had a hand in running my friends out."

"Where'd the owners go?" he said, thanking God she'd taken the pressure off him by cursing. He put his hands into his pockets, then took them out again. He wished he'd remembered to bring gum. His bum knee hurt. A panel van rolled by, slow as a shark on the cruise. Its plates were splattered in black mud.

"Yonder." She waved in the direction of the Catskills.

"That reminds me. There are caves nearby."

"Caves everywhere around these parts."

"Something about the mafia or Prohibition I overheard. Maybe the War of Independence. My memory is shot."

"Hm. There's also the Iron Mountain facility. They store all kinds of documents in some limestone caves in Rosendale. Hush-hush stuff."

"Aha." He watched the van's taillights dwindle. "I also heard some murders happened here in town. Gruesome was the word."

"Sure. Those are still going on, though. Have been since the '70s. Cops never bagged anybody. Never will."

"Serial killer?"

She stopped. Her face was luminous as if animated by the prospect of blood. He fell in love a little bit, then and there. "Uh, huh. Creepo snatches hikers and joggers and street people. Leaves them in the woods. Maybe seven, eight years ago, a Boy Scout troop stumbled upon eleven decomposed corpses in a cavern along the Wallkill. What kinda merit badge do you get for that, I wonder?"

"Hold up a sec. The '70s? Forty years, give or take. That seems like a long time for one guy to be about this sort of business."

"I bet it's a family thing," she said. "Pop passes it down to the eldest son the way tradesmen did it during the agrarian era. Some kind of whacked traditionalist."

"Lurid as lurid can be, yet, it never made the national news…"

"It made the news. Twenty-four-hour cycle is the problem. Today it's a mass grave, tomorrow it's back to celebrity meltdowns and the peccadilloes of the rich and the beautiful."

He stared at the moon and thought about her explanation.

"Are you here to research the case?" she said.

"No. My book is about an ornithologist. He dies in a valley in the mountains. Birds eat him."

"Ah, you're researching birds."

"I'm here for you."

Her turn to scrutinize the moon and not say anything.

They kept on. Residential houses now — old, Gothic models that he'd noticed were common here in the Hudson Valley. Iron fences and lush, neglected yards. Televisions flickered blue in certain windows, projecting phantom lovemaking, train wrecks, explosions, murder. Fires flickered inside jack o' lanterns. Lawn gnomes crouched with feral aspects in the long, wet grass.

He loved how she walked. Somewhere between a sway and a shuffle, arms swinging loose, head turning on a swivel in the manner of every professional fighter he'd ever known. She possessed a sort of animal grace that wasn't conscious of itself, but alert to everything occurring within its environment. Heat emanated from her in waves.

He shivered. "Do you go armed, considering the situation?"

"Yeah, sometimes. When I'm not sure of where I'm headed or who I'm meeting. Then I carry a blade."

"Got it on you now?"

"Nope." She kind of smiled and patted his arm. "Didn't figure I needed it. Besides, *I'm* a weapon. You're safe as houses with me."

"I'm sure."

"Ask me where I got the knife."

"The knife you should be packing, but aren't?"

"Ha-ha, I did carry it this afternoon when I met the realtor."

"Okay. Where did you get the knife?"

"From the Sneaky Fucking Russian."

"Let me guess — he's a karate guy."

She grinned. "Right on. Speaking of the mob, this dude's got the swagger. Broken nose and gin blossoms, wears heavy jewelry and a track suit. Thick accent. Eyes like pennies. A scowl mean enough to make a Spetsnaz drop his AK. Kinda skulks around. He asked me out about a hundred times when he arrived at the dojo. He got more and more belligerent about the whole thing. Finally, he exploded and demanded to know what was wrong with me that I wouldn't date him. Shouting and stomping his foot, the whole routine. I told him this was unacceptable behavior and to piss off before he got kicked out onto the street. Very tedious."

"Ah, an old school Eastern gentleman. I like those guys all right."

"Do you?"

"Yeah. They tend to be tough, loyal, no nonsense types. I got a soft spot for that. He'd probably make a great boyfriend after you slap him around a little."

"Sure, it isn't you he's trying to feel up when you're sparring."

"Fair enough. Does he know you call him the Sneaky Fucking Russian?"

She snorted and laughed. "Uh, no. Are you going to listen to the rest of the story? I'm not finished."

"Tell me."

"So, right. A couple of months go by. The Sneaky Fucking Russian keeps training, but he avoids me like the plague. Won't so much as glance in my direction. One night he comes over to me with flowers and a small box wrapped in a bow. I'm thinking, oh shit, here we go again, but he holds up his hand and says, no, no, I was wrong to speak to you in that manner. You are strong American woman and I am the dirt under your shoes. I am not fit to kiss your foot. Then he gives me the box…"

"Thus the knife."

"Yep!"

"What kind is it?"

She shrugged. "What do you mean? It's a knife."

"I mean is it a Randall, a Gerber, a Ka-Bar…?"

"Oh. Well, I don't know. It folds."

"You should get a fixed blade and keep it on you."

"Thanks, Dad. I told you, I'm a weapon." She was quiet for a long moment. "Death doesn't frighten me. I've died plenty of times."

"How does that work?" He squeezed her hand and let it go. "You feel warm enough."

"*Everybody* has died. When I was six I went sledding and hit a concrete retaining wall under the snow. Felt my neck crack and everything faded to white. When the world came back into focus I was right as rain, but…"

"I understand," he said. The booze made him a bit giddy. He remembered a long ago storm on Norton Sound, the rasp of diamond-bright snow scouring the ice, a universe of white; his hands were blurred shadows groping for purchase, and all around him, inside him, a constant dull roar. "And for a few hours after you came to, everything was in too sharp focus. Everything was too real."

"Yes! Too shiny, too present. I felt like a ghost floating through a world that had materialized to accommodate me. By the next day I'd forgotten. Sometimes it comes back when I dream, or at odd moments."

"Like tonight."

"Maybe a little." She gave him a sidelong glance. Her eyes were ringed like a raccoon's and they shone with wary innocence. "The portal opens on All Hallows. Tonight is the night to do a séance or summon a spirit, if that's what floats your boat. All possibilities are viable."

"How many times has it happened? The return from the dead bit?"

"Three. You?"

He considered. "Eleven or twelve."

"Jeez, dude! What the hell were you doing before you started writing?"

"Misspending my youth. Drinking, fighting, whoring around. Tramping across ice packs and climbing mountains. The usual for where I grew up."

"Can't leave it there. Tell me a story."

"Oh, how about I do that on our next date? Give you something to look forward to."

"What makes you think there's going to be another date?" She smiled. "Come along, now."

"I drowned once when I was a kid," he said. "Fell in the creek. Dad had to press the water out of my lungs and get me going again. Another time, very late in the winter, I was training a string of huskies on the Susitna River. The ice gave way under my sled and I went into the black water as deep as my chest before the team somehow dragged me free. There wasn't any bottom to that river. That current is strong and it'll suck you under. Basically a miracle I survived. Got shanked in a bar fight in Dutch Harbor. A deckhand stuck me with a big ass filet knife. Except that's not quite what happened — damned if the point didn't bounce off my chest. Not even a bruise, but I saw my life go pouring out onto the sawdust floor anyhow. There you go. Three stories for the price of one."

She chewed her thumbnail and kept walking, half a stride ahead. She said, "I'm a bitch after you get to know me."

"How many dates in is that, would you say?"

"Usually halfway through the first one. I like my space. Everything tends to be about me, me, me."

"Everything?"

"I'm all I've got."

"You've been fucked over. That's coming through loud and clear."

"With a vengeance," she said.

"Okay," he said.

"Thought it might be useful information. I'd hate to disappoint you down the road."

"That doesn't sound so selfish."

"I like to make people smile, but I hate them too. Ah, the essential dichotomy of me. It might drive you crazy. You'll love me, but you'll be a mad dog."

He chuckled. "The damage was done long before we met. Are you happy?"

"I'm happy and I'm never bored. I've always thought I was meant for great things. But, all that happens is I keep getting older."

"You're in a rut. Press your face to the grindstone and that's all you can see. Same friends, same colleagues, same scenery. The years roll over into one another. Happiness and misery become intertwined."

"I like my rut," she said.

"People always think they do. It's either that or slit your wrists."

Street lights stretched farther and farther apart. The night deepened. They came to a bridge with rusty girders. The water below gleamed in moonlit streaks.

"I've lived in this town for twenty years and never walked across this bridge," she said.

"Tonight is the night?" he said. "For séances and a bridge crossing?"

"Yeah. Watch out for the Hessian." She pulled her collar tight and winked.

* * *

He counted sixty-six steps, measuring each stride with the precision his father, a Marine, had instilled within him. Being slightly drunk concentrated his mind, oddly enough. Seventy-six steps saw them atop a gravel embankment that functioned as a turnout for cars. A heavily trodden path began a yard off the white line of the road and immediately forked. One path descended to the river; the other climbed a hillock toward a copse of gaunt trees and a jumble of rocks. She plucked his sleeve and led the way upward.

The largest, flattest stone shone white. She brushed aside a litter of dead leaves and primly seated herself upon its surface and beckoned him. For a time they sat, shoulder to shoulder; she smoking, he watching the lights of the town and the headlights sparkling along the road. The wind rose in brief gusts and branches moaned in the surrounding woods.

"This is romantic," he said, putting his arm around her. She didn't move one way or another.

"There was a grove here once," she said. "During colonial times those white settlers who followed the Old Gods cultivated this hillside, planted oak and sage and conducted druidic rituals. Naturally, the Christians eventually squashed them. Hanged the 'witches' from the trees, or drowned them in the river. An inquisitor razed the grove to ash and this stone became known as the White Spot."

He raised his head to examine the few scraggly trees that poked from the dense soil, claws raking free of a grave. "Nothing good grows here, I take it."

"Stunted, emaciated shadows of the grand oaks of days gone by. The ground is cursed, but I come here all the same. I feel drawn like a flake of metal hurtling toward a giant magnet. There's a current in the earth, a conduit. It speaks to my blood."

The moon floated across the near pane of sky, visibly traveling like a golden sail on the night sea. She inclined her head toward him and they gazed into each other's eyes. A charge arced from her and into him. His vision doubled. He beheld himself kneeling before her naked form, lips pressed to her sweet hip while the great and deathly blizzard that nearly killed him once raged against the walls of a landlocked cabin. He had the sense of the moon plunging toward the earth, the dissolution of himself within the following shockwave. As he dissolved, the lilac taste of her was the last artifact of his being to go into that good night. A dog or a wolf howled the howl of death.

She touched his neck and her hand was cool. She said, "What's wrong?"

"Must be the Great Conjunction, or too heavy on the booze," he said, shuddering free of the illusion.

"No conjunctions tonight. Plenty of single malt, though." She laughed and kneaded his arm. Her fingers were very strong.

"I like your bruises," he said. "Sexy as hell."

"You are a little nuts, aren't you?" she said and kissed him on the mouth. She was sweet with lip gloss and smoke and spearmint gum.

His toes curled. He thought of the Stevens poem about the wind in the hemlocks and the tails of the peacocks and the dead leaves turning in the fire as the planets aligned and turned outside the window. Fear and exultation turned within him. The wind and the cold in his chest receded, growling.

She separated from him slightly and said, "*And I remembered the cry of the peacocks.*" She licked her lips. "Sometimes I can read minds. Ever since that sledding accident."

He caressed her cheek with the back of his hand. "Precognition. Usually during dreams, but occasionally when I'm walking down the street or chatting on the phone...Zaps me like a bolt from the blue. Too unpredictable or else I'd hop a plane to Vegas and rake it in. Eerie, though."

"That explains your perspicacity."

He kissed her again.

Finally, she said, "All night I've had a feeling of impending doom."

"I'd say everything has turned up aces so far."

"Maybe, maybe. Can't last. Romance with me is fraught with peril. Consider yourself duly warned."

Clouds rolled across the stars and covered the moon.

"Hm, the gods agree," he said noticing the abrupt and precipitous chill that slithered over his flesh and into his bones. He felt her breath against his face, but could barely see the shine of her eyes.

She trembled and tightened her grip on his arms. "All the lights are out. Everywhere."

The chill intensified as he realized that she was indeed correct. While they'd been distracted, a vast, cosmic hand had erased the town with a sweep of darkness. Fog and cloud covered the world. The rock vibrated beneath them and small stones cascaded away toward the water. In the near distance a metallic shriek rent the silence. Its echoes died quickly and the land stilled.

"What the hell?" he said.

"Earthquake," she said. "We get them now and again."

He stood and smiled with faint reassurance. "The witching hour is upon us. Let's start back. I can see pretty well in the dark."

They inched along the path, and gradually were able to discern enough of the landscape to make the road and approach the bridge.

"You've probably already written a story about this while we walked down the hill," she said.

"Of course," he said. "Although, I don't have an ending."

She took his hand and led him onward.

The shadowy lines of the bridge materialized amid the bank of fog that boiled up from the river. As they stepped onto the partitioned walkway, his heart began to drum. He imagined the previous tremor had sheared the bridge in twain and that in a few more paces he'd swing his foot over murky nothingness and fall. There wouldn't be a cold river awaiting his plunge; only the endless void between stars.

Behind them and on a steep grade in the road, a pair of headlights clicked on and pierced the gloom. He understood this was the panel van he'd seen cruising town. He knew with absolute infallibility *who* inhabited the idling vehicle and *what* they intended to do with their ropes and machetes and plastic bags. The dog, or wolf, howled again. Its cry bounced from the fog and could've originated anywhere.

She turned to him and her expression was hidden. "We're not going to die tonight. I promise." Then she released him and stepped backward and vanished. Somewhere in the town ahead, a distant solitary porch light winked into existence.

"What about your sense of impending doom?"

"Melted away by the power of love. Come on."

A pair of red eyes flashed low to the ground and were gone. If they'd ever been.

"*I felt afraid,*" he said, meaning it in every sense of the phrase.

"We're not going to die. Trust me, trust me." Her voice was faint and fading. She laughed a ghostly laugh. "Probably something worse."

He waited for a time, listening to the night and preparing for the inevitable. But nothing happened. In a while he squared his shoulders and began to walk toward the light that flickered and receded with each heartbeat.

Slave Arm

...and begin, again.

Don't begin with a white room, it's not, it's a black room. Hothouse humid, oasis in the subarctic night. A glitter ball strobes, synched with the aurora borealis, the background radiation of the stars. Scandalously clad kids slam dance to a metal band, the bass player wears an executioner's hood, the lead singer has a beard like the front man for Clutch. Smokes a cheroot, swills whiskey, and breathes fire. Benny Three-Trees and Jasper Hostettler were flown in from Anchorage and Fairbanks to make sure this party's got its favors. Blotter, X, Jack Daniels, vodka, tequila, blow, crystal, hash, peyote, smack, Black Bombers, Viagra, California Gold, Matanuska Thunderfuck, nitrous. Window glass quivers like jelly in Dixie cup shooters. It's three A.M. Fuck the police. Your friends are here. Your enemies are here. Everybody you've ever slept with is here. Except Jessica. She's off wandering the earth, righting wrongs. You'll never see her again. That leaves Tom, Margie, Rod, Bill, Thurman, Shelley, Frank, Lisa, Becka, Tomra, Justin, Everett, Kurt, Mina, Tabby, Klein, Regan, Merrit, Luther, Jackson, Morton, Tashondra, Donte, Violet, Simon, Bart, Darcy, Sarah, Clute, Bowie, Pilar, Carol, Eric, Camilla, Brian, Jason, John, Lori, Miller, Parish, Will, Nick, Berrian, Jody, Chandler, Mary, Erin, Clay, Tobias, Judith, Rich, Nelson, Warren, Bob, Sam, Philip, Castor, Steely J, Julie Five, Newhouse, Cole, Esteban, Amy, Tyree, Vernon, Esther, Glenn, Kate, Kathy, Mark, Mark, Jake, Lucy, Ashley, Kyla, River, Arrow, Marsha, Cory, Stephen, Roger, Glory, Grant, Howard, Flynn, Victor, Bubba, Samantha, Custer, Alabama, Truman,

Rupert, June, Ruby, Kirsten, Kevin, Lambert, Robard, Dickie, Ralph, Quinn, Hester, Felix, Dusty, Paul, Byron, Kareem, James, Gunther, Abelard, Queenie, Suri, Rochelle, Theodore, Brunhilde, Molly, Cooper, Wanda, Morris, Michelle, Tammy-Lynn, Starling, Hector, Earl, Kellen, Tiberius, Chance, Dakota, Monson, Spencer, Wayne, Lily, Ramses, Chuck, Portia, Terry, Terri, Trish, Craig, Delaney, Vance, Ed, Carmine, Russo, Penny, Ferris, Noah. The last two are a pair again after a few years apart. Sweet. You don't know the rest, the hangers on, freeloaders, strangers. Moving shadows. The happening is happening at the ancestral home of young rotund Zane Tooms himself, poor rich boy, wannabe Satanist, friend to no one no matter how cool his digs may be, and they are indeed cool. A three-story mansion and an unfinished basement. Basement expands deep into the hillside, ancient bear den, crumbled arches, moldering catacombs, bat roosts, portal to Pluto's Ballroom. Downhill, a lovely hillside, a copse of spruce trees, boulders, a field where fireweed grows; farther on lies the bay, ink-black under a tilted moon, cracked. Moms and Pops jetted to Acapulco for the weekend and the mice will riot. Upstairs in the master suite, you've got your cock halfway into that Ukrainian transfer student, the cheerleader, what's-her-name, and she's throwing her blonde head like a mare, impatient. You're thinking ouch, and man, this is a hell of a fancy bed, are these sheets satin, is the demon-face headboard mahogany, and good God what's with the creepy Gothic architecture anyway, and who's that guy walking into the frame? Is it the cheerleader's boyfriend, what's-his-name, captain of the varsity squad, 'cause that would be very bad, you'd want your steel toe boots for an ape with forearms like he's swinging. No, not the jock. Wait, is that *Russo*? Definitely looks like Russo who runs the forklift on the fresh floor of the cannery. Different though, filling the doorway, cropped hair, pale complexion, eye shadow thick enough for a *Star Trek* cameo, original series, features smoothed and stretched plastic masklike, loose dark shirt and too-tight pants tucked into combat boots. Hefts a club, or a mace, a car axle, something out of a medieval manual of slaughter, two and a half feet of steel wrapped in barbed wire, electric tape on the grip, funny the photographic detail your brain records in moments of stress. The girl kisses your neck, she hasn't seen the freak. It's all wrong. Uncanny resemblance notwithstanding, this isn't the Russo you were blazing with on the loading dock just yesterday, not the Russo who's got a thing for the color grader from Caltech, not the Russo who lost his license drag racing on the Parks Highway and needs a lift everywhere, not the one who's built for a run at the middleweight title but wouldn't hurt a fly, the pacifist, conscientious objector, tofu-munching emo rocker. *This* Russo has taken an ice pick to the brain and become Mr. Flat Affect. He licks his liver lips, and Gene Simmons would shit a brick at the yellow tongue drooped to that pointy chin. Mr. Flat Affect crosses the room in an awkward lunge, the way a toad suddenly decides to jump, and it's so fast your breath stops. You roll off the opposite half of that acre of satin and the club wallops the cheerleader instead of your naked ass. Prior to this moment you've always considered yourself a bit of a tough guy. Lean, mean, scars on your knuckles from a respectable number of barroom brawls; only last fall you socked Tom Gorski in the kisser after one wisecrack too many, dropped him like a bad habit. You're no punk, no wuss, no pantywaist, had your nose busted plenty, lost some teeth in the bargain. You have also come to the realization you aren't Chuck Norris either. The bludgeoning thuds are a message from the universe. You're no shark, you're a feeder fish, aren't you? The interloper whacks her a couple of times, lazy and disinterested. There's blood, a lot of it, all those September hunts when Dad shot the caribou with his .7mm and you slashed the dumb beast's throat and its life gushed out over your Wellies, this is similar. You make your move and fly for the door. You're howling. Demon Russo would catch you, because next to him you're stuck in quicksand, but the club gets snagged in a nest of guts and that second or two is all you need to escape. It's dark and the house is a maze. You've visited twice during daylight when it was just the Tooms family and everybody in polo shirts and golf slacks, sunny dispositions, dinner on the deck with the gob smacking view of Settler's Bay. This is the nightmare version of that scenario, the Bizarro World iteration. Doors are locked and impenetrable. Music rumbles far below and nobody responds to you screaming bloody murder. An accent lamp floats in a golden bubble way down at the end of the hall and you sprint for it, jagged claws of your shadow outstretched in desperation.

* * *

Even all these years after the fact, you recall the cheerleader's expression in a smash close-up. Homegirl doesn't know she's dead, keeps blinking at you, confused as she drowns on herself.

* * *

Your father dies in a tavern parking lot when you are twenty-two. Your mother goes home to Tennessee, sends postcards now and again, the weather's fine. Little brother joins the Marines, like his old man, earns a Bronze Star, opens a gun store in Texas, shoots a couple of kids who try to rob the joint. The jury decides he's justified. You sleep with a lot of women with the light on, lose your erection whenever you stop to think. There are nightmares. One that recurs has you as a child in your old bedroom, you stand near the dresser and a poster of Buck Rogers. A skinny hand and arm slither from beneath your bed, followed by your father. Except his face is angular and cold with alien emotion. He moves the herky-jerky way a marionette does. He wants your blood, projects that desire into your thoughts without opening his mouth. You always awaken before he gets you. Hell of it is, you don't know whether it's really a dream or a suppressed memory. So, you drink. We won't speak of wife one.

* * *

Wife two is Amie. You stole her from Mack the slack, Mack jumped off the bridge into Hurricane Gulch. Oh, Amie, baby, who wouldn't? Brunette, Libra, whip smart, hot as fire. Most importantly, she doesn't give a goddamn how screwed up you are, how wild and strange you are, how damaged, or else she cleverly looks past it to the good points. You have several. Got all your hair, make a decent wage in construction, still cut pretty sharp in a suit. Two of three children tolerate your presence; the dog is also fond. The dog is a German Shepherd you named Chip because of a story that science fiction author Bradley Denton wrote when you were a kid. You and Chip go hunting for ptarmigan every fall, the only good thing you can recall sharing with your dad. Last September you load the guns and drive out to the Little Susitna, follow a game trail away from the Parks Highway, three, maybe four miles where the spruce grows tall and close in, a mossy shadow land. Crack yourself a cool beer, prop against a tree, loyal hound at your feet, the sun a pale reflection against the underside of the canopy. Even sweet wife fades into the ether for a while. Chip looses a stream of piss and whines and then you hear, echoing from not too far away in the arboreal deeps, the most sinister birdcall ever. Laughter of a raven mimicking a man mimicking a hyena. Cackles your name, calls to Chip. *C'mere, doggy!* This lone cry becomes a chorus, converging. Shotgun or not, you and the dog run for your lives. That shrieking laughter pursues you nearly back to the car. You break the speed limit gunning for home, Chip cowers on the floorboard, fangs bared as if some horror rides in the back seat. *We're waiting for you, pal. We know where you live.*

* * *

Zane Tooms got on the Tony Robbins bandwagon and dropped sixty pounds, tried to make something of himself, didn't try all that hard. Heartthrob handsome after the sea change, but fat wasn't truly the root of his problems. Something dark and rotten was going on in that noggin. Capped teeth and a chiseled physique couldn't mitigate the filth beaming from his eyes. He lived alone in that mansion on the hill after Mr. and Mrs. died. Spent his nights at the Bohemian cocktail lounge hitting on the young lasses, became known as the Rohypnol Romeo, bought himself an indictment with a suggested sentencing range of twenty-five to life if it stuck. Blew town and disappeared to the bottom of the FBI most-wanted list. Sends you a letter the day before Christmas, first contact after a decade of silence, arrives in a grimy, blood-spotted envelope, sum of the message a Mexico City phone number, initials *ZT*, smudgy fingerprints all over the stationery. You are wary, but intrigued. There's a twenty-five-thousand-dollar reward, which you don't give a shit about, money isn't a problem for you anymore, you have questions, you have a redaction scribble in the middle of your brain where dreadful memories once clamored for release. You want to talk to fat boy Tooms, want to wring his neck, beg him to put the pieces together. He's living under an assumed name in a fancy hotel on the outskirts, keeps a whole suite to himself. His transformation impresses, dresses in a linen suit, smokes French cigarettes, seems at ease in his own expat skin, but you recognize him, the real him, instantly. You don't talk about what he's done, don't mention the fact FBI and INTERPOL are on the case, could be staking out the joint at that very moment, recording everything for the blockbuster trial. That's a foregone conclusion, written in the stars. You're here for other unfinished business. He pours two glasses of mescal, no lime, no nothing, utters a prayer and downs his, then flashes a revolver and says he asked you here to apologize or to kill you. It depends. Actually, that's a lie, he's already made up his mind, he wants to chat first, so drink your drink, old friend, and you do. Once everything's cozy, you've chuckled over the hijinks of days of yore, his finger relaxes from the trigger and you ask what the hell man? What happened way back when in the bear den beneath the house? He smiles sadly, professes ignorance, but his eyes belong to a snake and though you ask again, nicely, he refuses to answer truly. He was a child then, he dicked about with childish things, any real diabolism that resulted is purely coincidental. The room spins as you go belly up. They don't call the bastard the Rohypnol Romeo for nothing. In the half-dozen beats until the world goes dark you watch a tremor pass through him, crown to toe, and your subconscious wants to make an impossible connection, suggests he's a finger puppet of some primordial malevolence and it's show time. The flesh of his face snaps upward, much as a bank robber pulls on a nylon mask, except from the wrong direction. Hello to Mr. Flat Affect, your old friend.

* * *

Okay, we'll mention wife one, briefly. Her post-coital cigarette didn't package with a *what are you thinking*. Hers was a beady-eyed scowl and a demand to know what your damage was. What had happened to fuck you so thoroughly up, she couldn't begin to fathom. Were you molested as a child? Did Daddy piss in your cornflakes? Did something *awful* transpire to make you so afraid of the dark? You loved her, you desired her happiness with the intensity of a death wish. But you couldn't tell her what was buried in your heart, couldn't articulate the queasy blackness that flooded your mind whenever you tried. If you knew where she'd run off to after your marriage fireballed, you could call her up, tell her about the time you visit Mexico to meet a childhood chum and come to taped hand and foot upon the ledge of a marble tub, IV needle in your femoral artery, half your blood oozing drip by drip through a tube into gallon bags. Classical music plays. There's a muttered conversation that you can't understand, and not because blood pressure drop causes your ears to ring, nor because the voices are muttering in Spanish. It's because whatever language is formed by this combination of glottal stops, clicks and liquid hisses, it isn't human. You manage to peel free of the tape, slick with your fluids as it is, the heat of the room, and slide over the rim of the tub into a heap. You vomit. That's what happens when blood pressure drops to nil. Keep crawling toward the light, all you can do, coherent thought is water through a dribble glass, it makes a mess on your shirt. Three of them stand in the parlor with your host. They wear variations on the face of the grave and very nice suits. There's a naked body curled upon a rubber mat. The body is bound in barbed wire and one of the men, Armani suit and snazzy shoes, sips from a red tube inserted at the victim's neck. Everybody pauses to stare at you, including the dead or dying guy, his glassy eyes are wet as you drag yourself past, hand over hand. His eyes reflect your antlike toil across the killing floor. Maybe he's reenacting Horace Greasley's great escape vicariously through you. Maybe he's already there. The front door swings open and uniformed men burst through screaming *Policía*! Their assault rifles start flashing and the room fills with clouds of dust and smoke. You crawl onward, past threshing jackboots and smoldering shell cases. Explosions and screams continue unabated. It goes on and on. Longest movie you've ever been in. Later at the hospital a tall handsome American sits at your bedside. Tubes everywhere, but at least the fluids are going into you this time. The man introduces himself as Agent Justin Steele. He flashes a badge and declares who he works for, although none of it sticks in your consciousness, you're wrapped in a cocoon of drugs and shock. He lights a Rubios, starts a pocket recorder, and says to tell him everything you know, start at the beginning in Alaska when you were a kid. You comply, half expecting his face to deform at any moment. Takes a while to relate the tale, takes an eon, in fact. Agent Steele doesn't interrupt and when you finish he thanks you for your service to your country, best to never speak of this incident again, Tooms was shot resisting arrest for extradition to the USA, and so forth. You're weak and fading, yet you clutch his sleeve and ask what's it all about, ask what the flat affects are, where they come from, why were you, lowly you, lured to Mexico, and you know what the answer is before it doesn't come. You have so many damned theories burning a hole in your imagination. Could be you babble about space vampires, demonic possession, and Count D his own bad self. Steele smiles as if the cigarette in his hand comes with a blindfold. He leans in close and whispers that he's seen this all before, it's always worse than you think, says it no longer matters. Go home, screw your wife, pet your dog, relive your glory days with a six-pack and a bowl. The end that Eliot spoke of is snuffling at the door.

* * *

Your buddy Felix, an ex-Naval Intelligence officer with connections across the US and Europe, and who also doses himself daily with LSD and vaporized marijuana while listening to talk radio, won't permit dogs into his trailer because *everybody* knows the ID chips implanted at the veterinarian's office are military grade transceivers beaming info to spy satellites. He has a theory about Mr. Flat Affect. It's insane and you also think it has merit. Felix disappears one day, leaves a roach smoldering in the ashtray, a spackle of blood in a tight pattern on the ceiling directly above his easy chair. The police park a van across the street from your apartment for a month. Nobody contacts you.

* * *

The power goes dead after midnight and you lie there, a bundle of twigs, staring out the window, praying for the town lights, any of them, to return. Only stars, the black body of darkness. Chip pads in and sits, muzzle pointed at you. He is a pure black shadow. You begin to cry, terror squeezing tears from your ducts. Amie grips your shoulder, says she has something to tell you, baby. That's when you know the jig is up, the power's never coming back on, you've seen the last of the light, because Amie and Chip died years and years ago. You close your eyes and visualize the faces at Tooms' basement party, the faces in that deathroom at the Mexico City hotel. The images move with the sluggishness of a dream. Your friends and enemies only watch pop-eyed and motionless as you flee the brute and his club. Some observers wear the demented un-mask that drips with earth from the grave. They might've loved or hated you before the rostrum made its pith stroke. Now they grin as you run, your bare feet slapping a treadmill that bores endlessly through a cosmic honeycomb. None of you are going anywhere.

Frontier Death Song

Night descended on Interstate-90 as I crossed over into the Badlands. Real raw weather for October. Snow dusted the asphalt and picnic tables of the deserted rest area. The scene was virginal as death. I parked the Chevy under one of the lamp posts that burned at either end of the lot. A metal building with a canted roof sat low and sleek in the center island, most of its windows dark. Against the black backdrop it reminded me of a crypt or monument to travelers and pioneers lost down through the years. Placards were obscured by shadows and could've pronounced warnings or curses, could've said anything in any language. Reality was pliable tonight.

I loosed Minerva and watched her trot around the perimeter of the sodium glow. She raised her graying snout and growled softly at the void that surrounded us, poured from us. Her tracks and the infrequent firefly sparks on the road were the only signs of life for miles. Snow was falling thick and those small signs wouldn't last long. Periodically a semi chugged along the freeway, its running lights tiny and dim. Other than that, this was the Moon. It was back to the previous ice age for us, the end for us. I kind of, sort of, liked the idea that this might be the end, except for the fact sweet, loyal Minerva hadn't asked for any of it, and my nature, my atavistic shadow, was, as usual, a belligerent sonofabitch. My shadow exhibited the type of primitive stubbornness that causes men to weigh themselves with stones before they jump into the midnight blue, causes them to mix the pills with antifreeze, trade the pistol bullet to the brain for a shotgun barrel in the mouth, to be on the safe side. My shadow didn't give a shit about odds, or eventualities, or pain, or certain death. It wanted to keep shining.

So, Minerva pissed in the snow and I ticked off the seconds until the ultimate showdown.

My ear was killing me tonight, crackling like a busted radio speaker and ringing with good old tinnitus. The sensation was that of an auger boring through membrane and meat. My back and knee ached. I lost the ear to a virus upon contracting pneumonia in Alaska during a long ago Iditarod. The spine and knee got ruined after I fell off a cliff into the Bering Sea and broke almost everything that was breakable. Resilience was my gift and I'd recovered sufficiently to limp through the remainder of a wasted youth, to fake a hale and hearty demeanor. That shit was surely catching up now at the precipice of the miserable slide into middle age. All those forgotten or ignored wounds blooming in a chorus of ghostly pain, reminders of longstanding debts, reminders that a man can't always outrun provenance.

I checked my watch and the numbers blurred. I hadn't slept in way too long, else I never would've pulled over between Bumfuck, Egypt and Timbuktu. Since suicide by passivity was off the table, this was an expression of stubbornness on my part, probably. Grim defiance, or the need to reassert my faith in the logical operations of the universe if but for a moment.

What a joke, faith. What a sham, logic.

A hunting horn sounded far out there in the darkness beyond the humps and swales and treeless drumlin that went on basically forever, past the vast hungry prairies that had swallowed so many wagon trains.

Oh, yes. The horn of the Hunt bugling my death song.

Not simply a horn, but one that could easily be imagined as the hollowed relic from a giant, perverted ram with blood-specked foam lathering its muzzle and hellfire beaming from its eyes. A ram that crunched the bones of Saxons for breakfast and brandished a cock the girth of a wagon axle; the kind of brute that tribes sacrificed babies to when crops were bad and mated unfortunate maidens to when the chief needed some special juju on the eve of a war. Its horn was the sort of artifact that stood on end in a petrified coil and would require a brawny Viking raider to lift. Or a demon.

That wail stood my hair on end, slapped me wide awake. It rolled toward the parking lot, swelling like some medieval air raid klaxon. Snowflakes weren't melting on my cheeks because all the heat, all the blood, went rushing inward. That erstwhile faith in the natural universe, the rational order of reality, wouldn't be troubling me again anytime soon. Nope.

I whistled for Minerva and she leaped into the truck, riding shotgun. Her hackles were bunched. She barked her fury and terror at the night. Sleep, O blessed sleep, how I longed for thee. No time for that. We had to get gone. The Devil would be there soon.

* * *

Years ago when I raced sled dogs for a living, I knew a fellow named Steven Graham, a disgraced lit professor from the University of Colorado. He'd gotten shitcanned for reasons opaque to my blue collar sensibilities — something to do with privileging contemporary zombie stories over the works of the Russian masters. His past was shrouded in mystery and like a lot people, he'd fled to Alaska to reinvent himself.

Nobody on the racing circuit cared much about any of that. Graham was charming and charismatic in spades. He drank and swore with the best of us, but he'd also get three sheets to the wind and recite a bit of *Beowulf* in Olde English and he knew the bloodlines of huskies from Balto onward. Strap a pair of snowshoes to that lanky greenhorn bastard and he'd leave even the most hardened back country trapper in the proverbial dust. All the girlies adored him, and so did the cameras. Like Cummings said, he was a hell of a handsome man.

Too good to be true.

Steven Graham got taken by the Hunt while he was running the '92 Iditarod. That's the big winter event where men and women hook a bunch of huskies to sleds and race twelve hundred miles across Alaska from Anchorage to Nome. There's not much to say about it -- it's long and grueling and lonely. You're always crossing a frozen swamp or mushing up an ice-jammed river or trudging over a mountain. It's dark and cold and mostly devoid of sound or movement but for one's own breath and the muted panting of the huskies, the jingle and clink of their traces.

Official records have it that Graham, young ex professor and dilettante adventurer, took a wrong turn out on Norton Sound between Koyuk and Elim and went through the ice into the sea. *Kasploosh*. No trace of him or the dogs was found. The Lieutenant Governor attended the funeral. CNN covered it live.

The report was bullshit, of course; I saw what really happened. And because I saw what really happened, because I meddled in the Hunt, there would be hell to pay.

* * *

Broad daylight, maybe an hour prior to sunset, mid-March of '92.

All twelve dogs in harness trotted along nicely. The end of the trail in Nome was about two days away. Things hadn't gone particularly well and I was cruising for a middle of the pack finish and a long, destitute summer of begging corporate sponsors not to drop my underachieving ass. But damn, what a gorgeous day in the arctic with the snowpack curving around me to the horizon, the sky frozen between apple-green and steely blue, the orange ball of the sun dipping below the Earth. The effect was something out of *Fantasia*. After days of inadequate sleep, I was lulled by the hiss of the sled runners, the rhythmic scrape and slap of dog paws. I dozed at the handlebars and dreamed of Sharon, the warmth of our home, a cup of real coffee, a hot shower, and the down comforter on our bed.

When my team passed through a gap in a mile-long pressure ridge that had heaved the Bering ice to an eight-foot tall parapet, the Hunt had taken down Graham on the other side, maybe twenty yards off the main drag. This I discovered when one of Graham's huskies loped toward me, free of its traces yet still in harness. The poor critter's head had been lopped at mid-neck and it zig-zagged several strides and then collapsed in the trail. You'd think my own dogs would've spooked. Instead, an atavistic switch was tripped in their doggy brains and they surged forward, yapping and howling.

Several yards to my right so much blood covered the snow I thought I was hallucinating a sunset dripped onto the ice. The scene confused me for a few seconds as my brain locked down and spun in place. The killing ground was a fucking mess like there'd been a mass walrus slaughter committed on the spot. Dead huskies were flung about, intestines looped over berms and piled in loose, steaming coils. Graham himself lay spread-eagle across a blue-white slab of ice repurposed as an impromptu sacrificial altar. He was split wide, eyes blank.

The Huntsman had most of the guy's hide off and was tacking it alongside the carcass as one stretches the skin of a beaver or a bear. Clad in a deerstalker hat surmounted by antlers, a blood-drenched mackinaw coat, canvas breeches, and sealskin boots, the Huntsman stood taller than most men even as he hunched to slice Graham with a large knife of flint or obsidian — I wasn't quite close enough to discern which.

Meanwhile, the Huntsman's wolf pack ranged among the butchered huskies. These wolves were black, and gaunt as cadavers; their narrow eyes glinted, reflecting the snow, the changeable heavens. When several of them reared on hind legs to study me, I decided they weren't wolves at all. Some wore olden leather and caps with splintered nubs of horn; others were garbed in the remnants of military fatigues and camouflage jackets of various styles, gore encrusted and ingrown to the creatures' hides. They grinned at me and their mouths were very, very wide.

Nothing brave in what I did, or at least tried to do. My befuddled intellect was still processing the carnage when I sank the hook and tethered the team, left them baying frantically in the middle of the trail. I wasn't thinking of a damned thing as I walked stiff-legged toward the Hunt and the in-progress evisceration of my comrade. Most mushers carried firearms on the trail. There were moose to contend with and frankly, a gun is pretty much basic equipment in any case. We toted rifles or pistols like folks in the Lower-48 carry cell phones and wallets. Mine was a .357 I stowed inside my anorak to keep the cylinder from freezing into a solid lump. The revolver was in my hand and it jumped twice and I don't recall the booms. No sound, only fire. The closest pair of dog men flipped over and a small part of my mind celebrated that at least the fuckers could be hurt, it wasn't like the legends or the movies; no silver required, lead worked fine.

The Huntsman whirled when I was nearly upon him, and Jesus help me I glimpsed his face. That's probably why my hair went white. I squeezed the trigger three more times, emptied the gun and even as the bullets smacked him, I had the sense of shooting into an abyss — absolute hopeless, soul-draining futility. The Huntsman swayed, humungous knife raised. The blade was flint, by the way.

Worst part was, Graham blinked and looked right at me and I saw his skinned hand twitch. How he could be alive in that condition was no more or less fantastical than anything else, I suppose. Even so, even so. I still get a sick feeling in my stomach when I recall that image.

Apparently, the gods of the north had seen enough. Wind roared around us and everything went white and I was alone. Hurricane force gusts knocked me off my feet and I barely managed to crawl to the team, almost missed them, in fact. Visibility was maybe six feet. Easily, easily could've kept going into the featureless maelstrom until I found the lip at the edge of a bottomless gulf of open water and joined Graham, wherever he'd gone.

That storm pinned the dogs and me to Norton Sound for three days. Gusts of seventy knots. Wind chill in excess of negative one hundred degrees Fahrenheit. You wouldn't understand how cold that is. I can't describe it. It's like trying to explain how far away Alpha Centauri is from Earth in highway miles. The brain isn't equipped. Froze my right hand and foot. Froze my face so that it hardened into a black and blue mask. Froze my dick. Didn't lose anything important, but man, there are few agonies equal to thawing a frostbitten extremity.

I actually managed to cripple across the finish line. Suffering through the aftermath of physical therapy and counseling, the memory of what I'd seen out there was wiped clean from my mind with the efficacy of a kid tipping an Etch A Sketch and giving it a shake. Seven or eight years passed before the horrible event came back to haunt me and by then it was too late to say anything, too late to be certain whether it had happened or if I'd gone around the bend.

*   *   *

Snow drifted both lanes and the wind buffeted the Chevy, and goddamn, but I was reliving that blizzard of '92. The fuel gauge needle fell into the red and I drove another half hour, creeping along in four wheel hi. Radio reception was poor and I'd settled for a static-filled broadcast of '80s rock. Hall & Oates, The Police, a block of Sade and Blue Oyster Cult, all that music our parents hated when we were bopping along in mullets.

"Godzilla" cut in and out during the drum solo and a distorted animal growl that had nothing to do with heavy metal issued from the speakers. My name snarled over and over to the metronome of the wipers.

A truck stop glittered on the horizon of the next off ramp. Exhausted, frazzled, pissed, and afraid, I pulled alongside the pumps and got fuel. Then I hooked Minerva to a leash and brought her inside with me. I patted her head as we went through the door, and wished that I possessed more of her canine equanimity in the face of the unknown.

She curled at my boots while I drank a quart of awful coffee and ate a New York steak with all the trimmings. The waitress didn't say anything about my bringing a pit bull to the table. Maybe the folks in Dakota were hip to that sort of thing. Didn't matter; I'd gotten the little card that proved Minerva was a service dog and of vital importance should I experience an "episode" of depression or mania.

Depression had haunted me since my retirement from mushing, and a friend who worked as counselor at the University of Anchorage suggested that I adopt a shelter puppy and train it as a companion animal. The local police had busted a dog fighting ring and one of the females was pregnant, so Sharon and I eventually picked Minerva from a litter of eleven. A decade later, after my world burned to the ground, career in ashes, wife gone, friends few and far between, Minerva remained steadfast. A man and his dog versus the Outer Dark.

The diner was doing brisk trade. Two burly truckers in company jumpsuits occupied the next booth, but most of the customers were gathered at the counter so they could watch weather reports on TV. Nothing heartening in the reports, either. The storm would definitely delay me by half a day, possibly more. My ardent hope was that I could bull through it and be in the clear by the time I crossed Minnesota tomorrow. I also prayed that the pickup would hang together all the way to Lamprey Isle, New York, my destination at the end of the yellow brick road. My plan was to reach the home of an old friend named Jack Fort, a retired English professor and fellow author. Jack claimed he could help. I had my doubts. The pack and its leader were eternal and relentless. A man could plunk a few, sure. In the end, though, they simply reformed and kept pursuing. The Devil's smoke demons on the hunt.

Be that as it may, I'd decided to go down swinging and that meant a hell-bent for leather ride into the east. Currently, my worries centered on weather and equipment. The drive from Alaska via the AlCan Highway had been rough and I suspected the old engine was fixing to give up the ghost. I could say the same thing about my heart, my sanity, my luck.

Sure enough. Minerva snarled and bolted from her spot under the table. She crouched beside me, shivering. Foam dribbled from her jaw and her eyes bulged.

Graham strolled in, taller and happier than I remembered. Death agreed with some people. He loomed in Technicolor while reality bleached around him. His long black hair was feathered with snowflakes and the lights hit it at the right angle so he appeared angelic, a movie star pausing for his dramatic close-up. He lugged the ivory hunting horn (indeed a ram's horn, albeit much more modest than its report); in his left he carried a faded cowboy hat with a crimson and black patch on the crown. He wore the Huntsman's iceberg-white mackinaw, ceremonial flint knife tucked into his belt so the bone handle jutted in a most phallic statement. He ambled over and slid in across from me. I noticed his sealskin boots left maroon smears on the tiles. I also noticed puffs of steam escaping our mouths as the booth cooled like a meat locker.

I cocked the .357 and braced it across my thigh. "You must not be heralding the great zombie invasion. Lookin' great, Steve. Not chalk white or anything. The rot must be on the inside."

He flipped his hair in a Fabio imitation. His trophy necklace of wedding rings, key fobs, dog tags, driver licenses, and glass eyes clinked and rattled. "Likewise, amigo. You've lost weight? Dyed your hair? What?"

"This and that — diet, exercise. Fleeing in terror has the bonus effect of getting a man in shape. Divorce, too. My wife used to fatten me up pretty good. Since she split... You know. TV dinners and Johnnie Walker. I got it going on, huh?" I gripped Minerva's collar with my free hand. Her growls were deep and ferocious. She strained to lunge over the table, an eighty-pound bowling bowl; rippling muscle and bone crushing jaws and, at the moment, bad intentions.

My arm was tired already. Tempting to let my girl fly, but I loved her.

"I'm yanking your chain. You look like crap. When's the last time you slept? There's a motel a piece up the trail. Why not get room service, watch a porno, drink some booze and fall into peaceful slumber? You won't even notice when I slip in there and slice your fucking throat ear to ear." Graham's smile widened. It was still him, too. Same guy I'd gotten drunk with at Nome saloons. Same perfect teeth, same easy manner, probably sincere. He'd not intimated any malice regarding his intent to skin me alive and eat my beating heart. This was business, mostly. He inclined his head, as if intercepting my thought. "Not so much *business* as tradition. The Hunt is a sacred rite. I gave you the head start as a courtesy."

He was telling the truth as I understood it from my research of the legends. To witness the Hunt, to interfere with the Hunt, was to become prey. I'd wondered why the emissaries of the Horned One waited so long to come after me, especially considering the magnitude of my transgression. "Well, I reckon that was sporting of you. Twenty years. Plenty of time for Odysseus to screw his way home from the front."

"And you're almost there too," Graham said. "Crazy ass scene on the ice, huh? Sergio Leone meets John Landis and they do it up right with razors. Man, you were totally Eastwood, six-gun blazing. Wounded the Huntsman in a serious way. Didn't kill the fucker, though. Don't flatter yourself on that score. Might be able to smoke the hounds with regular bullets. That shit don't work so well on the Huntsman. We're of a higher order. Nah, when that storm hit, some sort of force went through me, electrified me. I tore free of the altar and jumped on the bastard's back, stuck a hunting knife into his kidney. Still wouldn't have worked except the forces of darkness were smiling on me. Grooved on my style. The Boss demoted him, awarded me the mantle and the blade, the hounds, and more bitches in Hell than you can shake a stick at. I've watched you for a while, bro. Watched you lose your woman, your career, your health. You're an old, grizzled bull. No money, no family, no friends, no future. It's culling time, baby."

"Shit, you're doing me a favor! Thanks, pal!"

"Come on, don't be sarcastic. We're still buds. This is going to be super-duper painful, but no reason to make it personal. Your hide will be but one more tossed atop a mountainous pile beside a chthonic lagoon of blood and the Horned One's bone throne. The muster roll of the damned is endless and the next name awaits my attentions."

"Okay, nothing personal. Here's the deal since I'm the one with the hand cannon. You hold still and I'll blow your head off. Take my chances with whomever they send next. No hard feelings." I debated whether to shoot him under the table or risk raising the gun to aim properly.

Graham laughed. "Whoa, chief. This isn't the place. All these hapless customers, the dishwasher, the fry cooks. That sexy waitress. If we turn this into the O-K Corral, the Boss himself will be on the case. The Horned One isn't a kindly soul. He comes around, *everybody* gets it in the neck. Them's the rules, I'm afraid."

A vision splashed across the home cinema of my imagination: every person in the diner strung from the rafters by their living guts, the hounds using the corpses for piñatas and the massive, shadowy bulk of the Horned God flickering fire in the parking lot as he gazed on in infernal joy. Like as not this image was projected by Graham. I glanced out the window and spotted one of the pack, a cadaverous brute in a threadbare parka and snow pants, pissing against the wheel of a semi. In another life he'd been Bukowski or Waits, or a serial killer who rode the rails and shanked fellow hobos, a strangler of coeds, a postman. I knew him for a split second, then not. Other hounds leaped from trailer to trailer, frolicking. Too dark to make out details except that the figures flitted and fluttered with the lithe, rubbery grace of acrobats.

I said, "Tell me, Steve. What would've happened to you if I hadn't interrupted the party? Where would you be tonight?"

He shrugged and his movie star teeth dulled to a shade of rotten ivory. "Ah, those are the sort of questions I try to let lie. The Boss frowns on us worrying about stuff above our pay grade."

"Would you have become a hound?"

"Sometimes a damned soul gets dragged over to join the Hunt. Only the few, the proud. It's a rare honor."

Cold clamped on the back of my neck. "And the rest of the slobs who get taken? Where do they go after you're done with them?"

"Not a clue, amigo. Truly an ineffable mystery." His grin brightened again, so white, so frigid. He put on the cowboy hat. I could see it clear, now — the logo was a red patch with a set of black antlers stitched in the foreground. Sign of the Horned God who was Graham's master on the Other Side.

Minerva's snarls and growls escalated to full-throated barks as she bristled and lunged. She'd had her fill of Mr. Death and his shark smirk. One of the truckers set down his coffee cup, pointed a thick finger at me, and said, "Hey, asshole. Shut that dog up."

Graham's eyes went dark, monitors tuned to deep space. A stain formed on the breast of his lily-white mackinaw. Blood dripped from his sleeve and the stink of carrion wafted from his mouth. He rose and turned and his shoulders seemed to broaden. I caught his profile reflected in the window and something was wrong with it, although I couldn't tell what exactly. He said in a distorted, buzzing voice, *"No, you shut your mouth. Or I'll eat your tongue like a piece of Teriyaki."*

The trucker paled and scrambled from his seat and fled the diner without a word. His buddy followed suit. They didn't grab their coats or pay the tab, or anything. Other folks had twisted in their seats to view the commotion. None of them spoke either. The waitress stood with her ticket book outthrust like a crucifix.

Graham said to them, "Hush, folks. Nothing to see here." And everyone took the hint and went back to his or her business. He nodded and faced me, smile affixed, eyes sort of normal again. "I better get along, li'l doggie. Wanted to say hi. So hi and goodbye. Gonna keep trucking east? Wait, forget I asked. Don't want to spoil the fun. See you soon, wherever that is." Yeah, he grinned, but the wintry night was a heap warmer.

"Wait," I said. "You mentioned rules. Be nice to know what they are."

"Sure, there are lots of rules. However, *you* only need to worry about one of them. Run, motherfucker."

* * *

So, how did I wind up on the road with the hounds of hell on my trail?

I never fully recovered from the incident in '92; not down deep, not in the way that counts. Nightmares plagued me. Oblique, horror-show recreations as seen through the obfuscating mist of a subconscious in denial. Neither I nor the shrink could make sense of them. He put me on pills and that didn't help.

I sold the team to a Japanese millionaire and moved to the suburbs of Anchorage with Sharon, took a series of crummy labor jobs and worked on the Great American horror novel in the evenings. She finished grad school and landed a position teaching elementary grade art. Ever fascinated with pulp classics, when the novel appeared to be a dead end I tried my hand at genre short fiction and immediately landed a few sales. By the early Aughts I was doing well enough to justify quitting the construction gig and staying home to work on stories full-time.

These were supernatural horror stories, fueled by the nightmares I didn't understand until it all came crashing in on me one afternoon during a game of winter golf with some buddies down at the beach. I keeled over on the frozen sand and was momentarily transported back to Norton Sound while my friends stood around wringing their hands. Normal folks don't know what to do around a lunatic writhing on the ground and babbling in tongues.

A week on the couch wrapped in an electric blanket and shaking with terror followed. I didn't level with anyone — not the shrink, not Sharon or my parents, not my friends or writer colleagues. I read a piece on the Wild Hunt in an article concerning world mythology and it was like getting socked in the belly. I finally knew what had happened, if not why. All that was left was to brood.

Life went on. We tried for children without success. I have a hunch Sharon left me because I was shooting blanks. Who the fuck knows, though. Much like the Wild Hunt, the Meaning of Life, and where matching socks vanish to, her motives remain a mystery. Things seemed cozy between us; she'd always been sympathetic of my tics and twitches and I'd tried to be a good and loving husband in return. Obviously, living with a half-crazed author took a greater toll than I'd estimated. Add screams in the night and generally paranoid behavior to the equation...

One day she came home early, packed her bags, and headed for Italy with a music teacher from her school. Not a single tear in her eye when she said adios to me, either. That was the same week my longtime agent, a lewd, crude alcoholic expat Brit editor named Stanley Jones, was indicted on numerous federal charges including embezzlement, wire fraud, and illegal alien residence. He and his lover, the obscure English horror writer Samson Marks, absconded to South America with my life savings, as well as the nest eggs of several other authors. The scandal made all the industry trade rags, but the cops didn't seem overly concerned with chasing the duo.

I depended on those royalty checks as my physical condition was deteriorating. Cold weather made my bones ache. Some mornings my lumbar seized and it took twenty minutes to crawl out of bed. I hung on for a couple of years, but my situation declined. The publishing climate wasn't friendly with the recession and such. Foreclosure notices soon arrived in the mailbox.

Then, last week, while I was out on a nature hike, after all these bloody years, Graham reappeared to put my misery into perspective. We'll get to that in a minute.

You see, prior to this latter event, my colleague, the eminent crime novelist Jack Fort, theorized that Sharon didn't run off to Italy because she was dissatisfied with the way things were going at home. Nor was it a coincidence that Jones robbed me blind and left me in the poorhouse (Jack also employed the crook as an agent and from what I gathered the loss of funds contributed to his own divorce). My friend became convinced dark forces had aligned against me in matters great and small. Figuring he might not dismiss me as a nutcase out of hand, I recounted my brush with the Hunt on the ice in '92, how that particular chicken had come home to roost. He wasn't the least bit surprised. Unflappable Jeffrey Fort; the original drink-boiling-water-and-piss-ice-cubes guy.

The other night when I called him we were both drunk. I spilled the story of how Graham had returned from the grave and wanted to mount my head on a trophy room wall in hell.

Instead of expressing bewilderment or fear for my sanity, Jack said, "Right. I figured it was something like this. From grad school onward, Graham was headed for trouble, pure and simple. He was asshole buddies with exactly the wrong type of people. Occultism is nothing to fuck with. Anyway, you're sure it's the Wild Hunt?"

I gave him the scoop: "Last Wednesday, I was hiking along Hatcher Pass to photograph the mountain for research. Heard a god-awful racket in a nearby canyon. Howling, psycho laughter, screams. Some kind of Viking horn. I knew what was happening before I saw the pack on the summit. Knew it in my bones — the legends vary, of course. Still, the basics are damned clear whether it's the

Norwegians, Germans, or Inuit. The pack wasn't in full chase mode or that would've been curtains. They wanted to scare me; makes the kill sweeter. Anyway, I beat feet. Made it to the truck and burned rubber. Graham showed up at the house later in a greasy puff of smoke, chatted with me through the door. He said I had three days to get my shit in order and then he and his boys would be after me for real. Referred to himself as the Huntsman. So. It happened almost exactly like the legends."

Yeah, I knew all about the legends. I'd done my due diligence; you can bet on that. Granted, there were variations on the theme. Each culture has its peculiarities and each focuses on different aspects. Some versions of the Hunt mythology have Odin calling the tune and the exercise is one of exuberance and feral joy, a celebration of the primal. Odin's pack travels a couple of feet off the ground. Any fool that stands in the way gets mowed like grass. See Odin coming, you grab dirt and pray the spectral procession passes overhead and keeps moving on the trail of its quarry.

The gang from Alaska seemed darker, crueler, dirtier than the storybook versions; Graham and his troops reeked of sadism and madness. That eldritch psychosis leached from them into me, gathered in effluvial dankness in the back of my throat, lay on my tongue as a foul taint. The important details were plenty consistent — slavering hounds, feral Huntsman, a horned deity overseeing the chase, death and damnation to the prey.

Jack remained quiet for a bit, except to cough a horrible phlegmy cough — it sounded wet and entrenched as bronchitis or pneumonia. Finally he said, "Well, head east. I might be able to help you. Graham and I knew each other pretty well once upon a time when he was still teaching and I got some ideas what he was up to after he left Boulder. He was an adventurer, but I doubt he spent all that time in the frozen north for the thrill. Nah, my bet is he was searching for the Hunt and it found him first. Poor silly bastard."

"Thanks, man. Although, I hate to bring this to your doorstep. Interfere in the Hunt and it's you on the skinning board next."

"Shut up, kid. Tend your knitting and I'll see to mine."

Big Jack Fort's nonchalant reaction should've startled me, and under different circumstances I might've pondered how deep the tentacles of this particular conspiracy went. His advice appealed, though. Sure, the Huntsman wanted me to take to my heels; the chase gave him a boner. That said, I'd rather present a moving target than hang around the empty house waiting to get snuffed on the toilet or in my sleep. Graham's flayed body glistening in the arctic twilight was branded into my psyche.

"You better step lively," Jack warned me in that gravelly voice of his that always sounded the same whether sober or stewed. A big dude, built square, the offspring of Raymond Burr and a grand piano. Likely he was sprawled across his couch in a tee shirt and boxers, bottle of Maker's Mark in one paw. "Got complications on my end. Can't talk about them right now. Just haul ass and get here."

I didn't like the sound of that, nor the sound of his coughing. Despite a weakness for booze, Jack was one of the more stable guys in the business. However, he was a bit older than me and playing the role of estranged husband. Then there was the crap with Jones and dwindling book sales in general. I thought maybe he was cracking. I thought maybe we were *both* cracking.

Later that night I loaded the truck with a few essentials, including my wedding album and a handful of paperbacks I'd acquired at various literary conventions, locked the house, and lit out.

In the rearview mirror I saw Graham and three of his hounds as silhouettes on the garage roof, pinprick eyes blazing red as I drove away. It was, as the kids say, game on.

* * *

Rocketing through Indiana, "Slippery People" on the radio, darkness all around, darkness inside. The radio crackled and static erased the Talking Heads and Graham said to me, "Everybody on the lam from the Hunt feels sorry for himself. Thing of it is, amigo, you're dialed to the wrong tune. You should ask yourself, *How did I get here? What have I done?*"

The pack raced alongside the truck. Hounds and master shimmered like starlight against the velvet backdrop, twisted like funnels of smoke. The Huntsman blew me a kiss and I tromped the accelerator and they fell off the pace. One of the hounds leaped the embankment rail and loped after me, snout pressed to the centerline. It darted into the shadows an instant before being overtaken and smooshed by a tractor trailer.

I pushed beyond exhaustion and well into the realm of zombification. The highway was a wormhole between dimensions and Graham occasionally whispered to me through the radio even though I'd hit the kill switch. And what he'd said really worked on me. What *had* I done to come to this pass? Maybe Sharon left me because I was a sonofabitch. Maybe Jones screwing me over was karma. The Wild Hunt might be a case of the universe getting Even-Steven (pardon the pun) with me. Thank the gods I didn't have a bottle of liquor handy or else I'd have spent the remainder of the long night totally blitzed and sobbing like a baby over misdeeds real and imagined. Instead, I popped the blister on a packet of No-Doze and put the hammer down.

* * *

I parked and slept once in a turnout for a couple of hours during the middle of the day when traffic ran thickest. I risked no more than that. The Hunt had its rules regarding the taking of prey in front of too many witnesses, but I didn't have the balls to challenge those traditions.

The Chevy died outside Wilkes-Barre, Pennsylvania. Every gauge went crazy and plumes of steam boiled from the radiator. I got the rig towed to a salvage yard and transferred Minerva and my meager belongings to a compact rental. We were back on the road before breakfast and late afternoon saw us aboard the ferry from Port Sanger, New York, to Lamprey Isle.

What to say about LI West (as Jack Fort referred to it)? Nineteen miles north to south and about half that at its widest, the whole curved into a malformed crescent, the Man in the Moon's visage peeled from Luna and partially submerged in the Atlantic. Its rocky shore was sculpted by the clash of wind and sea; a forest of pine, maple, and oak spanned the interior. Home of hoot owls and red squirrels; good deer hunting along the secret winding trails, I'd heard. Native burial mounds and mysterious megaliths, I'd also heard.

The main population center, Lamprey Township (pop. 999), nestled in a cove on the southwestern tip of the island. Jack had mentioned that the town had been established as a fishing village in the early 19th Century; prior to that, smugglers and slavers made it their refuge from privateers and local authorities. A den of illicit gambling and sodomy, I'd heard. Allegedly, the name arose from a vicious species of eels that infested the local waters. Long as a man's arm, the locals claimed.

Lamprey Township was a fog-shrouded settlement hemmed by the cove and spearhead shoals, a picket of evergreens. A gloomy cathedral fortress reared atop a cliff streaked with seagull shit and pocked by cave entrances. Lovers Leap. In town, everybody wore flannel and rain slickers, boots and sock caps. A folding knife and mackinaw crowd. Everything was covered in salt rime, everything tasted of brine. Piloting the rental down Main Street between boardwalks, compartment of the car flushed with soft blue-red lights reflecting from the ocean, I thought this wouldn't be such a bad place to die. Release my essential salts back into the primordial cradle.

Jack's cabin lay inland at the far end of a dirt spur. Built in the same era as the founding of Lamprey Township, he'd bought it from Katarina Veniti, a paranormal romance author who'd become jaded with all of the tourists and yuppies moving onto "her" island during the last recession. A stone and timber longhouse with ye old-fashioned shingles and moss on the roof surrounded by an acre of sloping yard overgrown with tall, dead grass. An oak had uprooted during a recent windstorm and toppled across the drive.

Minerva and I hoofed it the last quarter of a mile. The faceless moon dripped and shone through scudding clouds and a vault of branches. The house sat in darkness except for a light shining from the kitchen window.

"Welcome to Kat's island," Jack said, and coughed. He reclined in the shadows on a porch swing. Moonlight glinted from the bottle in his hand, the barrel of the pump-action shotgun across his knees. He wore a wool coat, dock-worker's cap snug over his brow, wool pants, and lace-up hiking boots. When he stood to doff his sock hat and shake my hand, I realized his clothes hung loose as sails, that he was frail and shaky.

"Jesus, man," I said, shaken at the sight of him. He appeared more of an apparition than the bona fide spirit pursuing me. I understood why he didn't mind the idea of the Hunt invading his happy home. The man was so emaciated he should've been hanging near the blackboard in science class; a hundred pounds lighter since I'd last seen him, easy. He'd shaved his head and beard to gray stubble; his pallid flesh was dry and hot, his eyes sparkled like bits of quartz. He stank of gun oil, smoke, and rotting fruit.

"Yea. The big C. Doc hit me with the bad news this spring. Deathwatch around the Fort. I sent the pets to live with my sister." He smiled and gestured at the woods. "Just you, me, and the trees. I got nothing better to do than help an old pal in his hour of need." He led the way inside. The kitchen was cheerily lighted and we took residence at the dining table where he poured me a glass of whiskey and listened to my recap of the trip from Alaska.

"I hope you've got a plan," I said.

"Besides blasting them with grandma's twelve gauge?" He patted the stock of his shotgun where it lay on the table. "We're going out like a pair of Vikings."

"I'd be more excited if you had a flamethrower, or some grenades."

"Me too. Me too. I got a few sticks of dynamite for fishing and plenty of ammo."

"Dynamite is good. This is going to be full on Hollywood. Fast cars, shirtless women, explosions…"

"Man, I don't even know if it'll detonate. The shit's been stashed in a leaky box in the cellar for a hundred years. Honestly, my estimation is, we're hosed. Totally up shit creek. Our sole advantage is, prey doesn't usually fight back. Graham's powerful, he's a spirit, or a monster, whatever. But he's new on the job, right? That may be our ray of sunshine. That, and according to the literature, the Pack doesn't fancy crossing large bodies of open water. These haunts prefer ice and snow." Jack coughed into a handkerchief. Belly-ripping, Doc Holliday kind of coughing. He wiped his mouth and had a belt of whiskey. His cheeks were blotched. "Anyway, I brought you here for another reason. This house belonged to a sorcerer once upon a time. Type they used to burn at the stake. An unsavory guy named Ewers Welloc. The Wellocs own most of this island and there's a hell of a story in that. For now, let me say Ewers was blackest in a family of black sheep. The villagers were scared shitless of him, were convinced he practiced necromancy and other dark arts on the property. Considering the stories Kat told me and some of the funky stuff I've found stashed around here, it's hard to dismiss the villagers' claims as superstition."

I could only wonder what he'd unearthed, or Kat before him. Jack bought the place for a dollar and suddenly that factoid assumed an ominous significance. "What were you guys up to? You, Kat, and Graham attended college together. Did you form a club?"

"A witch coven. I kid, I kid. Wasn't college... We met at the Sugar Tree Hill writers' retreat. Five days of sun, fun, booze, and hand jobs. There were quite a few young authors there who went on to become quasi-prominent. Many a friendships and enmities are formed at Sugar Tree Hill. The three of us really clicked. Me and Kat were wild, man, wild. Nothing on Graham's scale, though. He took it way farther. As you can see."

"Yeah." I sipped my drink.

"Me and Graham were pretty tight until he schlepped to Alaska and started in with the sled dogs. Communication tapered off and after a while we fell out of touch. I received a few letters. Guy had the world's shittiest penmanship; would've taken a cryptologist to have deciphered them. I thought he suffered from cabin fever."

"Seemed okay to me," I said. "Gregarious. Popular. Handsome. He was well-regarded."

"Yea, yea...The rot was on the inside," Jack said and I almost spilled my glass. He didn't notice. "As it happens, my hole card is an ace. Lamprey Isle was settled long before the whites landed. Maybe before the Mohawk, Mohican, Seneca. Nobody knows who these people were, but none of the records are flattering. This mystery tribe left megaliths and cairns on islands and along the coast. A few of those megaliths are in the woods around here. Legend has it that the tribe erected them for use in necromantic rituals. Summon, bind, banish. Like Robert Howard hypothesized in his Conan tales — if the demonic manifests on the mortal plane, it becomes subject to the laws of physics, and cold Hyperborean steel. Howard was on to something."

"Fairy rocks, huh?" I said. The whiskey was hitting me.

"Got any problem believing in the Grim Reaper with a hunting knife and a pack of werewolves chasing you from one end of the continent to the other?"

I tried again. "So. Fairy rocks."

"Fuckin' A, boy-o. Fairy rocks. And double aught buckshot."

* * *

We took shifts at watch until dawn. The Hunt didn't arrive and so passed a peaceful evening. I slept for three hours; the most I'd had in a week. Jack fried bacon and eggs for breakfast and we drank a pot of black coffee. Afterward he gave me a tour of the house and the immediate grounds. Much of the house gathered dust, exuding the vibe particular to dwellings of bachelors and widowers. Since his wife flew the coop, Jack's remit had contracted to kitchen, bath, and living room. Too close to a tomb for my liking.

Tromping around the property with our breath streaming slantwise, he showed me a megalith hidden in the underbrush between a pair of sugar maples. Huge and misshapen beneath layers of slime and moss, the stone cast a shadow over us. It radiated the chill of an ice block. One of several in the vicinity, I soon learned.

Jack wasn't eager to hang around it. "There were lots of animal bones piled in the bushes. You'll never catch any animals living here. Wasn't the two decks of Camels I smoked every day since junior high that gave me cancer. It's these damned things. Near as I can figure, they're siphons. Let's pray the effect is magnified upon extra-dimensional beings. Otherwise, Graham will eat our bullets and spit them back at us."

The megalith frightened me. I imagined it as a huge, predatory insect disguised as a stone, its ethereal rostrum stabbing an artery and sucking my life essence. I wondered if the stones were indigenous or if the ancient tribes had fashioned them somehow. I'd never know. "Graham's an occultist. Think he's dumb enough to walk into a trap?"

"Graham ain't Graham anymore. He's the Huntsman." Jack scanned the red-gold horizon and muttered dire predictions of another storm front descending from the west. "Trouble headed this way," he said and hustled me back to the house. We locked and shuttered everything and took positions in the living room; Jack with his shotgun, me with my pistol and dog. Seated on the leather Italian sofa, bolstered by a pitcher of vodka and lemonade, we watched ancient episodes of *The Rockford Files* and *Ironside* and waited.

Several minutes past 2 P.M. the air dimmed to velvety purple and the trees behind the house thrashed and rain spattered the windows. The power died. I whistled a few bars of the *Twilight Zone* theme, shifted the pistol into my shooting hand.

He grinned and went to the window and stood there, a blue silhouette. The booze in my tumbler quivered and the horn bellowed, right on top of us. Glass exploded and I was bleeding from the head and the hand that I'd raised to protect my face. Wood splintered and doors caved in all over the house and the hounds rolled into the living room; long, sinuous figures of pure malevolence with ruby-bright eyes, bodies low to the floor and moving fast, teeth, tongues, appetite. I squinted and fired twice from the hip and a bounding figure jerked short. Minerva pounced, snarling and tearing in frenzy, her doggy mind reverting to the swamps and jungles and caves of her ancestors. Jack's shotgun blazed a stroke of yellow flame and sheared the arm of a fiend who'd scuttled in close. Partially deafened and blinded, I couldn't keep track of much after that. Squeezed the trigger four more times, popped the speed loader with six fresh slugs, kept firing at shadows that leaped and sprang. The Riders of the Apocalypse and Friends galloped through the house; our own private Armageddon. More glass whirled and bits of wood and shreds of drapery; a section of ceiling collapsed in a cascade of sparks and rapidly blooming white carnations of drywall dust. Now the gods could watch.

Thunder of gunshots, Minerva growling, the damned, yodeling cries of the hounds, and crackling bones wound around my brain in a knotted spool. I got knocked down in the melee and watched Minerva swing past, lazily flying, paws limp, guts raveling behind her. I'd owned many dogs, Minerva was my first and only pet, my dearest friend. She was a mewling puppy once more, then inert bone and slack hide, and gone, gone, the last pinprick of my old life snuffed.

Something was on fire. Oily black smoke seethed through a vertical impact crater where the far wall had stood. Clouds and smoke boiled there. A couple of fingers were missing from my left hand and blood pulsed forth; a shiny, crimson bouquet thickening into a lump, a wax sculpture from the house of horrors, an object example of Medieval torture. It didn't hurt. Didn't feel like anything. My jacket had been sliced, and the flesh beneath it so that my innards glistened in the cold air. That didn't hurt either. Instead, I was buoyed by the sense of impending finality. This wouldn't take much longer by the looks of it. I pulled the jacket closed as best I could and began the laborious process of standing. Almost done, almost home.

Jack cursed through a mouthful of dirt. The Huntsman had entered the fray and caught his skull in one splayed hand and sawed through his throat with the jagged dagger hewn from Stone Age crystal. The Huntsman sawed with so much vigor that Jack's limbs flopped crazily, a crash test dummy at the moment of impact. Graham let Jack's carcass thump to the sodden carpet among the savaged bodies of the pack. He pointed at me, him playing the lead man of a rock band shouting out to his audience. Yeah, the gods were with us, and no doubt.

"So, we meet again." He licked his lips and wiped the Satan knife against his gory mackinaw. He approached, shuffling like a seal through the smoldering gloom, lighted by an inner radiance that bathed him in a weird, pale glow as cold and alien as the Aurora Borealis. The death-light of Hades, presumably. His eyes were hidden by the brim of his hat, but his smile curved, joyless and cruel.

I made it to my feet and scrambled backward over the flaming wreckage of coffee tables and easy chairs, the upended couch, and into the hall. All but dead, but still fighting, an animal to the end. Blood came from me in ropes, in sheets. Graham followed, smiling, smiling. Doorframes buckled as his shoulders brushed them. He swiped the knife in a loose and easy diamond pattern. The knife hissed as it rehearsed my evisceration. I wasn't worried about that. I was long past worry. Thoughts of vengeance dominated.

"You killed my dog." Blood bubbles plopped from my lips and that's never good. Another dose of ferocious, joyful melancholy spurred me onward. I pitched the empty revolver at his head, watched the gun glance aside and spin away. My tears froze to salt on my cheeks. Arctic ice groaned beneath my boots as the sea swelled, yearned toward the moon. The sea drained the warmth from me, taking back what it had given in the beginning.

"*You* killed your dog, mon frère. You did for our buddy Jack, too. Bringing me and my boys here like this. Don't beat yourself up. It's a volunteer army, right?"

I turned away, sliding, overbalancing. My legs folded and I slumped before a fallen timber, its charred length licked by small flames. The blood from my ruined hand sizzled and spat. I rubbed my face against the floor, painting myself a war mask of gore and charcoal. By the time he'd crossed the gap between us and seized my hair to flip me onto my back, at the precise moment he sank the blade into my chest, the fuse on the glycerin-wet stick of dynamite was a nub disappearing into its burrow.

Graham's exultant expression changed. "Well, I forgot Jack was a fisherman," he said. That fucking knife kept traveling, the irresistible force, and I embraced it, and him.

The Eternal Footman clapped.

* * *

After an eon of vectoring through infinite night, the door to the tilt-a-whirl opened and I plummeted and hit the earth hard enough to raise dust. Mud instead. An angelic choir serenaded me from stage left, beyond a screen of tall trees and fog. Wagner as interpreted by Homer's sirens. The voices rose and fell, sweetly demanding my blood, the heat of my bones. That sounded fine. I imagined the soft, red lips parted, imagined that they glowed as the Huntsman glowed, but as an expression of erotic passion rather than malice, and I longed to open a vein for them…

I came to, paralyzed. Pieces of me lay scattered across the backyard. For the best that I couldn't turn my neck to properly survey the damage.

Graham sprawled across from me, face-down in the wet leaves. Wisps of smoke curled from him. He shuddered violently and lifted his head. Bones and joints snapped into place again. The left eye shimmered with reflections of fire. The right eye was black. Neither were human.

He said, "Are you dead? Are you dead? Or are you playing possum? I think you're mostly dead. It doesn't matter. Hell is come as you are." He shook himself and began to crawl in my direction, slithering with a horrible serpent-like elasticity.

Mostly dead must've meant 99.9 percent dead, because I couldn't even blink, much less raise a hand to forestall his taking my skull for the mantle, my soul to the bad place. A red haze obscured my vision and the world receded, receded. The sirens in the forest called again, louder yet. Graham hesitated, his glance drawn to the voices that came from many directions now and sang in many languages.

Jack staggered from the smoking ruins of the house. He appeared to have been dunked in a vat of blood. He held his shotgun in a death grip. "The bell tolls for you, Stevie," he said and blew off

Graham's left leg. He racked the slide and blasted Graham's right leg to smithereens below the kneecap. Graham screamed and whipped around and tried to hamstring his tormentor. Not quite fast enough. Jack proved agile for an old guy with a slit throat.

The siren choir screamed in pleasure. *Blam! Blam!* Graham's hands went bye-bye. The next slug severed his spine, judging by the ragdoll effect. His body went limp and he screamed some more and I'm sure he would've happily leaped on Jack and eaten him alive if Jack hadn't already dismembered him with that fancy shotgun work. Jack said something I didn't catch. Might've uttered a curse in a foreign tongue, a Latin epithet. He stuck the barrel under Graham's chin and took his head off with the last round.

I cheered telepathically. Then I finished dying. The score as the curtains closed was so fucking beautiful.

* * *

This time I emerged from eternal night to Minerva kissing my face. I lay on my back in the kitchen. Gray daylight poured through a hole in the ceiling along with steady trickles of water from busted pipes.

Jack slouched at the table, which was stacked with various odds and ends. His shoulders were wide and round as boulders and he'd gained back all the weight cancer had stolen; his old self, only far more so. He clutched a bottle of Old Crow and watched me intently. He said, "Stay away from the light, kid. It's fire and lava."

I spat clotted blood. Finally, I said, "He's dead?"

"Again."

"Singing…" I managed.

"Oh, yeah. Don't listen. That's the vampire stones. They're fat on Graham's energy."

"How'd I get in here?"

"I dragged you by your hair."

The world kept solidifying around me, and my senses along with it. Me, Minerva, and Jack being alive didn't compute. Except, as the cobwebs cleared from my mind, it made a sinister kind of sense. I laid my hand on Minerva's fur and noticed the red sparks in her eyes, how goddamned long and white her teeth were. "Oh, shit," I said.

"Yeah," Jack said. He set aside the bottle and shrugged into the Huntsman's impeccable snow-white mackinaw. Perfect fit. Next came the Huntsman's hat. Different on Jack; broader and of a style I didn't recognize. The red and black crest was gone. Real antlers in its stead. A shadow crossed his expression and the light in the room gathered in his eyes. "Get up," he said. Thunder rumbled.

And I did. Not a mark on me. I felt quite hale and hearty, in fact. Hideous strength coursed through my limbs. I thought of my philandering ex-wife, her music teacher beau, and hideous fantasies coursed through my mind. I must've retained a tiny fragment of humanity because I managed to look away from that vista of terrible and splendorous vengeance. For the moment, at least. I said, "Where now?"

Jack leaned on a long, barbed spear that had replaced his emptied shotgun. "There's this guy in Mexico I'd like to visit," he said. He handed me the flint knife and the herald's horn. "Do the honors, kid."

"Oh, Stanley. It'll be good to see you again." I pressed the horn to my lips and winded it, once. It tasted cold and sweet. The kitchen wall disintegrated and the shockwave traveled swiftly, rippling grass and causing birds to lift in panic from the trees. I imagined Stanley Jones, somewhere far to the south, seated on his veranda, tequila at hand, *The Sun* balanced on his rickety knee, ear cocked, straining to divine the origin of the dim bellow carried by the wind.

Minerva bayed. She gathered her sleek, killing bulk and hurtled across the yard and into the woods. I patted the hilt of the knife and followed. One last glance over my shoulder — Jack laughed and his laugh became the roar of a storm. He loomed above the top of the ruined house and his black horns eclipsed the white sun.

Tomahawk Park Survivors Raffle

1. Anchorage, Alaska. Autumn, 1979. (I'm going to kill you all):

Lucius's orgasm transcended earthquakes and other localized apocalypses — a blue sun on the far side of the universe intoned, HEADS WILL ROLL! The blue sun went supernova and immolated a good chunk of a galaxy and the top of her skull. She gave her legs a minute to quit shaking and went hunting for her clothes.

Her lover, young hapless Esteban, lay spread-eagle across the mattress like he'd gotten flattened by a truck. He didn't even bitch that Lucius was screwing and booking. He groaned and covered his eyes with his left arm.

"Ribbon of Darkness," unspooled mournful and timeless over the cheap AM radio. The Magnificent Seven assembled for a class photo on the wall above a bureau even more hard-bitten than them or the Wild Bunch. Lucius pulled on her stockings, dress, then the knee high go-go boots and leather jacket with Black Flag's four-bar flag hand-stitched between the shoulders. Lucius loved the bad boys as Panic and now they were even better.

She lit a cigarette (*Player No. 6*, no substitutes) and checked her watch. The watch was a high school sophomore graduation present to herself swiped from a tourist-trap gift shop during a summer trip to Washington State a couple years back. A *real* watch with a quartz face, stainless steel butt plate (*water-resistant to 50 meters!*), and a band of interlocking metal links you could wrap around a snow tire. Not the prissy filament-thin chain some girls wore on their delicate widdle wrists. The kind of timepiece construction foremen and steely-nerved execs strapped on the way gladiators did it up with iron bracers and spiked cestuses. Backhand a fool in the chops with this baby and he or she would go down, minus teeth. The glass already had a chip. She couldn't remember how it happened.

Save your life one day, Dad said when he examined the watch. Dad: King of foreshadowing. His wedding ring had kept his finger attached after a piebald stallion chomped it in his horse-breaking days of yore. Keen on serendipity and Jim Beam, was Dad.

Gods help her if she needed more saving in this short life. She'd almost bought the farm during that WA State vacation. The disaster at Tomahawk Park killed how many kids? Seven? Nine? An explosion? A collapsed structure? Poison gas? It slipped her mind now as the psychic wounds healed. The school counselor had spoken of survivor's guilt and compartmentalization. Have some pills of forgetting, the woman said. Move on, kid.

Lucius finished the cigarette. She slid on five rings — three costume gemstones on her right hand; a mood ring and a silver death's head on the left. She scooped her clutch (black vinyl with a small bronze clasp of a bald eagle descending, talons out) and strode through the doorway without saying goodbye. *I don't say goodbye, ever*, she'd told Esteban when they first knocked boots (which occurred during that fateful trip to Tomahawk Park). *Especially to you.*

She stashed a switchblade in her purse alongside the compact and black cherry lipstick. The switchblade recently belonged to a gangster wannabe, ass-slapping hick, of which all too many bred in fetid Alaskan backwaters. The hick didn't come around town much since prom. The gemstone dents and death's head tattoos on his greasy face were possibly permanent.

"Hi, Mrs. Mace," she said to Esteban's mom as they passed on the stairs.

"Hello, dear." The older woman wore a kimono with a red heron stitched on the breast. Her hair was bound in green curlers at half past ten PM. "I miss anything?"

"Not a damned thing."

"His father's son. How's your mother?"

"A-Okay, ma'am." Lucius didn't speak to her parents anymore. They didn't appear to notice.

Meanwhile:

Finally dark enough.

Butch Tooms slumped low in the backseat of the stolen Pontiac. Nobody ever looks in the backseat until it's too late. He wore his mother's thigh-high silk stocking over his face. He twisted its mate into a garrote. Motown drained the car battery. *Friday Night Countdown.*

Across the way, Lucius Lochinvar exited the Mace house and walked into the gloom toward Northern Lights Boulevard. She tromped along, mouth set, stern as hell, arms swinging like she was on her weekend job as roller derby enforcer Scara Fawcett at the *Hippodrome North.* Tough little broad. He evaluated her the way a cobra assesses a mongoose. Kill now, kill later, or avoid entirely? He decided to kill her next week at the party. Easier to keep the bodies in one pile, right?

Those undulating hips stirred his ambition. If the death gods were with him he'd get his freak on, too. *After* he'd let the air out of her tires, for safety's sake.

The Jackson 5 came on the radio to agree. *XYZ, baby! OneTwoThree, baby!*

Somewhere, Sometime (WA State, many years after the events of '77 &'79):

It was a fifteen-minute drive from Odd Fellows cemetery into the foothills on the fringe of Capitol National Park. Fifteen minutes with the pedal to the floor and no traffic.

Dr. Erika Bakker Shunn beat Jimmy Flank to his cabin by a nose. He wished he could say the visit was a surprise, except it was far too late for that. Self-delusion was out of his market. Self-preservation looked shaky too.

After a third go-round with the grieving widow, Jimmy was an enervated wreck, ready to cry uncle, to call it a day. Thank everything unholy, now the formalities were complete, Mrs. Shunn was briskly business.

"So, you'll help me." Her tone suggested she expected Jimmy to kill someone. The arch-conspirator's whisper. Her nails drew Aztec dimples on his graying chest. He felt relief that since her husband was dead, whatever she wanted couldn't be *that* bad. Right?

She'd brought him a list of names on a dirty piece of memo paper. Five of them were familiar to varying degrees — *Toshi Ryoko, Howard Campbell, Louis Plimpton, Lucius Mace, and Harrison J*. Ryoko and Campbell were famous zoologists; Louis Plimpton was another dead rich scientist who treated his profession like the world's most vital hobby — he'd been a rival of Linwood's in the bug field. Plimpton smoked himself in 1980. Lucius Mace (formerly Lochinvar) dated his best friend in high school. Lucius popped out three kids and ran for the hills, abandoning them and her husband. Last, but not least, Jimmy had also known Harrison J during their teen years in Alaska. Weird kid. Nobody called him Harrison or Harry; ever Smiling J. Worked for NASA in some deep earth research site studying cosmic rays.

Why were these names collected by an antisocial scientist whose best friend was a jar of formaldehyde? *If I help her it won't be from guilt. I won't do it because I owed Linwood a damned thing.* Linwood Shunn, being a rich kid from Olympia, of course he married a rich girl from the hometown. Dr. Erika Bakker-Shunn, psychiatrist of renown, her claim to fame owed to the fact she'd had three quarters of the Hollywood A-list on her couch — one way or another. A sly one, the missus. An Amherst product (Ph.D. in clinical psychiatry) with the fangs to match.

"You brought the tapes?" Sweat burned his eyes. *You bet she did.* No chance she'd risk holding his interest for the trip to town, the ubiquitous distractions of his trade. She'd have brought the hook with her. Her kind didn't miss a trick.

"Oh, yes! They're in the car." That was all she needed. She gilded her decaying splendor in Jimmy's robe and flounced from the cabin. The door banged in her wake, let in a chilly draft. Marty Robbins was crooning about devil women on the transistor radio and that was damned apropos.

A filthy canvas sea bag leaned in the corner, opposite the sliding glass door of the shoebox terrace. Woods and more woods out there. The cabin was otherwise barren except for a toothbrush and an electric razor in the bathroom, some food items in the cupboards. Dirty dishes, bottles. Mice.

Jimmy blinked at watermarks in the rafters. "Goddamn it, Linwood. Why'd you do this to me?" He wanted a cigarette, a drink, preferably in the tropics. The cabin was an icebox. He pulled the army blanket to his neck and groaned.

Linwood Shunn's mortal remains lined the bottom of a ceramic urn in the trunk of his loving wife's '69 Mustang. Dead, but not out of the picture. Not out of Jimmy's hair from the size of it. As a part-time private eye, a man met his share of cranks and eccentrics. Linwood Shunn had taken the cake, a first class head-job with a trophy case full of degrees and a ritzy pedigree he seldom admitted because it embarrassed him to no end. He'd also been, as recently as last week, one of North America's preeminent entomologists, whatever use that was in the grand scheme.

In Jimmy's opinion, entomologist was a creepy vocation. Why would a man born to old money waste so much precious time pulling wings off flies? The Bug Man, is what everyone called the late Dr. Shunn. Cockroach Lover. A radical professor with Evergreen College, until they axed him for eccentric behavior, alcoholism, and derogatory comments regarding the dean. Eccentric kook or not, his work ethic and ambition put the rest of the faculty to shame. Nothing short of the eventual coronary conclusion could've derailed Shunn's gusto for research — a dozen companies courted his services. As a trust fund hippie, money was never a real consideration. He always had an iron in the fire, always came up roses.

Jimmy and the doctor first met when Linwood was looking for a rough and tumble character to perpetrate some deeds on the shady side of the law. He hired Jimmy to follow his sweet, younger wife around, see if she was cheating on him — it was damned hard to track her movements, what with her Beverly Hills practice and their homes in Mexico, California, Long Island, and Tumwater.

Had she cheated on her crazy, dry as bones, ant-loving husband? Dumb question — Erika had been taking ski lessons in July, for God's sake, buzzing about the strapping person of a super Swedish beefcake, an ex-Olympic slalom champion named Hans Zwick. Hans had the goods — blond as a Norse god, steely-eyed and a codpiece to rival a blue-ribbon zucchini. *Hell, doc, I'd bang him myself if I had a shot!*

Jimmy and his trusty roll of incriminating film — pictures that captured Hans glorying in the company of a brutal-looking transvestite on Seattle's Aurora Avenue — convinced Hans to fly home early lest he lose his corporate sponsorship from a chopstick manufacturer. All was well with the world once more. The Shunn marriage skidded a bit, but didn't quite crash through the guardrail. At least she hadn't seemed to take it personally. Not that a man could ever be certain what was going on upstairs with a woman like Erika Shunn. Linwood's reaction proved more alarming because Jimmy earned himself a friend for life — for better or worse. The good professor called him two or three times a week, begged to ride along on stakeouts, and showed up in biker bars tossing around Jimmy's name. He behaved as if the detective's cachet at the Brotherhood Tavern was equal to a country club membership.

Erika returned with a cardboard box. She shoved a mass of Jimmy's papers and empty beer cans aside to make a home on the table for her exhibit. "Jesus, it's freezing in here! Can't you get the heat going?"

"Propane's out. My truck has a great heater, if you want to sit in there a spell."

"You're kidding."

"Keys are in my pants. Have a ball."

She gave him a look and began rummaging; unpacked an antiquated tape recorder approximately the size of a car battery, and a stack of number ten envelopes. The envelopes were slathered with Linwood's cryptic handwriting. They bulged with cassettes, photographs, and press clippings. She quickly segregated the envelopes into jagged piles.

"He gave me this stuff a couple months ago. Tried to be casual about it an' all — but, hell, not many people were more obvious than poor Linwood. He knew this was coming."

"Told me the bum ticker ran in the family."

"No — that's —" She grimaced and resumed sorting with a kind of manic intensity. "I don't think it's that simple."

"No?" He needed a drink, all right.

Her eyes gleamed perilously. "Linwood wasn't too organized. This is kind of a bitch."

"Sorry." Jimmy shrugged on a shirt and glanced around for his pants. Pants on, feet turning alabaster against the grimy floorboards, he found his least filthy glass amongst its brethren in the wasteland kitchenette, dumped in a lethal dose of vodka and muttered, "Cheers."

"God. He wanted me to keep this crap under my bed. After he left, I put it in my fire safe. But I didn't think...I had no idea at the time. He told me if anything ever happened to him, anything suspicious, I was to hand everything over to you, that you'd figure it out and do whatever needed to be done. Linwood was such an eccentric I never thought it really meant anything." She spilled a batch of cassettes. She closed her eyes and hummed a faint, disjointed tune.

Jimmy pressed a fresh drink into her hand. He collected the fallen articles while she downed the liquor and swayed in place. "What's on the tapes?" he said, to make conversation. Her closed eyes and dreamy expression were getting to him.

"Um, bugs. Bug noises. Put one in — try the, not that one, the other one. Yeah. Wait, don't play it yet. Gimme a minute to collect myself."

"Bugs," he said. "Shocker there. I thought maybe some rambling about government plots, an extortion racket. A confession to embezzling from the Evergreen College marijuana party fund. Good stuff."

"Listen to me, Jimmy. People are watching my house. A couple suits followed me around one day." Erika looked at him and held out her glass until he filled it again. "Maybe cops. Maybe Feds. Maybe some kind of Nobel Mafia. They're spooky, whoever they are."

Jimmy parted the drapes over the sink, checked the environs. Shadows crept from the undeveloped wilderness beyond the rude cul-de-sac. There was the Mustang and his modest Toyota pickup. The lake lurked somewhere farther on. "When was this?"

"Uh — last week. The day after Linwood dropped dead."

"The FBI agents, or whomever. Did you get their names or see badges?"

"No. Cold-blooded is what they were. Black suits, black hats, sunglasses. Stood around like they had curtain rods up the ass. I felt compelled to speak to them. It was weird."

He clicked on a reading lamp, began peering at the newspaper clippings and photos. Mostly stories about scientific conferences, ant swarms, and planet-killing comets. "So…what was the conversational gambit?"

She sipped her drink and winced as the vodka hit bottom. "The suits wanted to know the last time I'd seen Lucius Lochinvar or Harrison J. I'm unaware who the hell Lochinvar or J are supposed to be. Friends of Linwood? Enemies? We've got terrorists blowing apart skyscrapers and they're investigating my husband for suspicion of…I dunno quite what. Okay, ready?" She laughed shrilly and forced down the *play* button on the recorder.

After about fifteen seconds of listening to bug noises, Jimmy said, "What in the hell am I hearing?"

"Beetles. A whole bunch of beetles. Linwood told me insects are acting strange — ant supercolonies, bee die-offs…said it has something to do with a solar alignment affecting electromagnetic fields. Planet X…"

"I don't like that. At all." He disliked it because it didn't sound like cicadas. Hissing, warbling, and alien trilling mixed with female screams. The orchestra pit at the Devil's concert. Jimmy's teeth were on edge. A memory partially surfaced. Waterslides, a bonfire, shadows cavorting beneath the stars, and those screams…He blinked rapidly and glimpsed a man in a black hat and blacker shades, and another man, younger and heavier, covered in blood. *Whatever happened to Butch Tooms, anyway? I haven't thought of that bastard since 1979…*

"Creepy, huh? They're harmless, though."

"Sure they are." He cut the tape in mid screech. "I've got a headache and that shit isn't helping."

"Well?"

"I dunno. If the government is involved I don't think I want to be. No offense. Hell, Linwood's gone. My opinion? Cover your ass; be a patriot — hand this stuff over. It's no use to you."

"It's not your opinion I'm buying, Jimmy."

"Well, it's the only offer on the table."

"All I'm asking—"

"I know what you're asking."

"And it isn't really about me, sweetie. He wanted it to be you. I dunno why. Silly bastard worshipped you, called you the real deal. A man's man."

"Yeah? Well, he didn't know much."

"What — too much trouble for you to nose around and ask a few questions? I can understand, really. It must be difficult to tear yourself away from your little palace." Her cheeks were flushed. She stared at him for a long moment, mouth set at a hard angle. "I can provide an incentive."

"I'm retired." Half true. His license recently lapsed and he hadn't taken a job in nine months. He was also forty-two years old. Practically good enough for senior citizen rates at the movies.

Erika nodded and retrieved a checkbook from her leather purse. She filled in an immodest sum, signed it with a spiky flourish. "C'mon, Jimmy. Talk to Linwood's colleagues."

Jimmy tried not to stare at the check, its obscene number, but it grabbed him by the face and refused to let go. *What were you up to, Linwood, old chap? Were you always more than what you seemed?* The possibility gained weight even as he turned it over in his mind. "I knew J — we called him Smiling J."

"It truly is a small world. Linwood probably took that into consideration. Why else would he want me to hire you?"

"You haven't hired me…"

Five days later, Jimmy lay in a shallow grave in the hills north of Olympia. He stared sightlessly as Smiling J shoveled dirt over his face. The evening sun pulsed crimson and cold and blue around the edges.

Smiling J said, "You had two chances, Jim. None of us gets a third."

2. Rally, Washington. Spring, 1977. (Planet X)

Nineteen youth players for the Chugiak Wolverines Roller Derby and the Timberwolf Hockey teams (mostly incoming Onager High juniors and a handful of outgoing seniors who weren't invited on the graduate trip to D.C.) flew from Anchorage to Spokane, Washington courtesy of Butch Tooms, whose father bankrolled both clubs. They hopped a bus to Rally, Outpost of the Atomic Frontier! Rally was a twenty-minute commute to the fence line of the Hanford Nuclear Reservation on the Columbia River. They'd refined the plutonium for Fat Man and Little Boy on the reservation. Fancy as that might be, the real attraction for this crowd of young tourists lay a few miles upriver in neighboring Tomahawk, home of Tomahawk

Park; by its own admission, the most dangerous waterpark and motor entertainment arena in North America. Merchants sold ball caps and tee shirts that read, TOMAHAWK PARK SURVIVOR! in bloody letters. The shirts came in green, white, and black.

The kids doubled up in rooms at the Rocket Inn. Mr. Hyjak, Mr. Three Trees, and Mrs. Buntline had drawn the short straws when it came time to sacrifice parents as chaperones. Upon arrival, the trio immediately repaired to the lounge and told the kids not to bother them unless a nuclear reactor went China Syndrome.

Esteban Mace and Jimmy Flank sat on a retaining wall in front of the motel. A juniper hedge dug into their backs. Mosquitoes were biting hard, which made the Alaskans feel right at home. Most of the gang milled self-consciously in the middle of the courtyard, either heckling or studiously ignoring one another depending on the factions involved.

Rich boy (moderately well-off, at any rate) Butch Tooms, tall and sleek and softly athletic in a charcoal turtleneck, leaned against the trunk of Mr. Hyjak's rented sedan and flirted with Threnody Rudnick, Molly Vile, and Sarah Peters. Threnody favored a midriff tee (Chewbacca from the epic new flick, *Star Wars*), short-shorts, and roller-skates. She hadn't made the derby team and her getup raised eyebrows among the other girls. Tooms obviously liked it, though. He had the come-hither lean and not-so subtle pelvic thrust combo going. His henchman, Smiling J, lurked nearby. Smiling J dressed like he'd stumbled away from a marathon shift in a NASA control room — thick glasses, rumpled white shirt and dark tie, corduroy slacks, and scuffed dress shoes. He seldom smiled, of course, and his servitude to Butch Tooms mystified those who'd grappled with the muscularity of his intellect on the debate team or chess club. "Weird dude" was the consensus.

"Cheesy bastard." Esteban spat between his sneakers. He played backup center on the hockey team. A lean, wiry boy who knew how to duck the worst shots. Papa Mace had taught him that much. You can slip your old man's drunken haymakers, you can handle pimple-faced goons in pads all the livelong day.

"Who?" Jimmy concentrated on rolling a bomber. Jimmy wrestled at 152 for Onager High. He showed up to skate for the Timberwolves Hockey Club whenever he pleased. The coaches hated the arrangement, but he paid his fee and it was hard to deny a left forward who led with his helmet.

"BT. Clown prince and heir-apparent of the Tooms Estate."

"Butch paid for everything, man. My traveling expenses now amount to beer and ganja. I like that about him." Jimmy lit the joint and dragged hard.

"*Daddy* paid for everything." It sounded harsher than Esteban intended. He had radiation sickness from mooning over Lucius Lochinvar and twiddling his thumbs wasn't doing much to smooth the edges. *You hate Butch because he's smooth and blond and the girls love his sense of humor. He dropped out of school his junior year and he'll always have more money than you and get farther. Maybe get farther with Lucius...*

"Relax. Lochinvar doesn't give him the time of day."

"Did I say that out loud?"

"No, man. Your face kinda scrunches when you got angst. Your angst is attached to your blue balls. You're also staring death rays at our patron over there innocently chatting up the hoochies. He's going to be a senator; you're going to be a Marine. It rubs ya raw."

"I'm all right with joining the Corps."

"You ain't all right. You need to chill. Chicks dig chill. Tooms is chill as a goddamned winter's day." Jimmy waved the joint under Esteban's nose. "Take it. Have a hit off the northern lights, my brother."

"Twist my arm, will ya?" Esteban accepted the joint, inhaled and felt a small fire begin in his chest. Easier that way when it came to dealing with his friend. He and Jimmy hunted ptarmigan in Hatcher Pass and caribou in Copper River Valley with Keith Norse and Bruce Three-Trees. Bruce's dad or Keith's uncle usually drove them and stayed at camp and drank while the boys hiked into the hills. Keith was one of six black kids at Onager, including senior fullback heartthrob Clyde Zant. Bruce was Aleut. He and Sarah Peters (Athabascan; her extended family lived in Ruby on the mighty Yukon) endured an inordinate amount of crap for being the only natives at a school of eighteen hundred students.

When they first met in junior high, Bruce and Keith razzed Esteban about being the whitest Mexican in Alaska. *We're Scotch Irish,* he'd explained about a hundred times. Keith said "Scotch Irish" didn't exist. Nobody, including Esteban, could figure out why his Mom and Dad had chosen his name, except that maybe it had something to do with Mom's crush on Ricardo Montelban. Jimmy said, *Yo, mystery solved. Who don't wanna ball Montelban?* Jimmy's sister, Lynne, said, *Like totally!* Afterward, Esteban's closest friends called him Ricardo as often as not.

Raised voices snapped his attention around. Jackie Brock and Lucius Lochinvar were in the middle of a shoving match. Jackie Brock's mascara streamed rivulets and rendered her a particularly ineffective Boadicea. Quick JB background: She dressed in all black and droned Fleetwood Mac non-fucking stop on her portable eight track player. As if that wasn't enough, she declared herself a witch — actually she claimed to be a Wiccan. *Witch* stuck.

"Uh, oh," Jimmy said. "Catfight at nine o' clock. Your girlfriend's got her rings on. Here comes the dentist."

Jackie made the fatal mistake of socking Lucius in the eye. There wasn't any mustard on it; Jackie preferred clawing and hair-pulling and she tucked her thumb under. Esteban leaped into action as Lucius grinned and got a fistful of Jackie's brand new do and reared back to deliver the hammer of the gods with a Coke bottle. He caught Lucius from behind in a bear hug and spun her 180. Under the Blue Oyster Cult T-shirt, her body rippled with animal muscle, suppressed for the moment, thankfully. Lucius could've rearranged his nose or smashed in his teeth. She'd gotten to be hell on wheels for the derby team (so, so many punch-ups) and had developed a lethal right cross to go with her forearm shiver. Plus, the rings, those bone crunching rings.

She allowed him to set her down. "My tits got magnets, or what?"

He realized where his hands lingered and jumped back as if he'd touched a hotplate. "Oh, shit. Sorry."

Jimmy said, "Where's your badge? Cause you were coppin' a feel, son."

Meanwhile, Lucius' older brother Pierce and his pal Jeff Vellum gently took custody of hysterical Jackie and led her away. Same old scene, a little less bloodletting than usual. So far, Lucius had thrashed everybody in the Brock household except for Mr. and Mrs. Brock.

"You got some color there." Lucius brushed her knuckle, softly-roughly, against Esteban's cheek. "Virgin."

"Naw, that's frostbite," he said. "My cheeks are always kinda rosy."

"This is more like the hood of a fire truck."

"Jesus H Christian." Cassidy Sloan strolled over and whacked Lucius on the arm. "You can't kill Jackie yet. We had a deal. No sacrifices before the full moon."

"When's the next one?" Lucius said.

"After we get our day at the park."

"*After* the bonfire party," Esteban said.

"There's a bonfire party? It's been decided?"

"The word has been given."

Lucius adjusted her left-hand rings. "Fine. I won't murder her until the party."

"You're a pal." Sloan also skated for the Wolverines derby girls. Her handle was Slugger Sloan. She wore the team shirt and warmup jacket for every occasion. All the boys wanted her, especially the adventuresome jocks. She didn't have much use for any of them.

Later:

Smiling J paid for drinks at the Fat Boy Lounge. A neon sign over the door blinked:

Proud of the Cloud! Nuke em til they glow!

Eighteen years old as of May, bartenders bounced right off his receding hairline and stern gauntness and poured the booze without a second glance.

The cowboy in the rear booth accepted a scotch and soda. Rally was one of those towns where a man could get away with dressing like a shitkicker or a laboratory tech and be lost in the forest for the trees. Mr. Speck did not belong in Rally. He blended with the laborer set of the local scene in a scuffed Stetson hat, Levi jacket, and plaid shirt. On other occasions in other towns he wore a dyed-in-the-wool G-man black suit and shades. He'd gotten some rays since last Smiling J had seen him.

"Where's Mr. Hyjak?" Mr. Speck said.

"Hanging with the parents. Got to make it look legit."

"Our friend will be ready tomorrow night?"

"Without a doubt. Told me to tell you to be cool."

"It's sad." Mr. Speck didn't appear sad. He sipped his scotch and nodded in bland satisfaction. Doodles covered his napkin and the reverse of his coaster. Equations and mathematical gibberish. Moon skulls baring sharp teeth. A cross-sectioned mastiff revealing circuitry and gears. Guns.

"What is sad?" Smiling J glanced at the door, wary of a classmate or chaperone wandering in. He saw only a crowd of strangers. Eyes and hair gleamed strangely in the reddish, negative glare of panel lamps. A DJ in Kit Carson-era buckskins spun disco and up-tempo jazz.

"None of your friends miss you. The adults in charge don't even realize you've jumped the fence. You have a big brain. Could be Oppenheimer or Sagan and yet…"

"Mr. Hyjak—"

"Considers you a disposable asset. Pot, meet Kettle, let me tell you. It's hard to believe Hyjak is the best the Central Intelligence Apparatus could offer—"

"Agency. Butch realizes. He's a true friend."

"Mr. Tooms does not count. He is evolving beyond human sensibility."

"His *dad* is Mr. Tooms. Butch is plain old Butch."

"Mr. Butch Tooms is less than that. He'll be more, soon. He'll be full."

"What's so special about Butch? Or me? You could select anyone…"

"Our relationship with the Tooms and J families is longstanding. There are rules. Protocols. Don't kid yourself, though. Mr. Tooms is merely the first of a horde."

Smiling J pictured Butch Tooms in their shared motel room, lying on a double bed, arms folded, gaze fixed on the ceiling while Threnody Rudnick and Molly Vile took turns polishing his knob. The girls enjoyed poppers — the expensive, exotic varieties. Butch had a steady connection. Butch could have afforded a suite in a better hotel with real pro call girls, but preferred to chum with hoi polloi.

"You're not hoi polloi," Mr. Speck said. "From our perspective you are an important performer in the flea circus. We've named you, groomed you, told our friends, made plans for your future."

"Huh? Am I talking to myself again?" The J men were infamous for externalizing interior monologues.

"Did you enjoy *Star Wars?* The kids are absolutely crazy about it."

"Meh. Wasn't bad." The boy wouldn't admit he'd sat through eleven showings of the film and memorized half the lines. Princess Leia in virginal white, at odds with her name, inflamed his imagination, so to speak. "The plot is sort of ridiculous—"

"Drink your drink. Put some hair on your chest. You're off to Caltech this autumn. Pussy doesn't exactly form a queuefor the pocket protector set. Remember — alcohol is the best friend an ugly person will ever have."

Smiling J didn't retort despite the heat in his cheeks. During a previous meeting he'd witnessed a display of the man's capabilities. Terror and exultation were indeed bedfellows. Could he simultaneously love and dread Mr. Speck? His wiser angels said he only loved what Mr. Speck could do for him and feared what Mr. Speck might do *to* him.

"J, consider this — the tasks I perform are not tasks, but choices in service of a cause. I live for the moment, and you should too. Car accident, heart attack, gunshot, alien abduction, extinction event; the end is always nigh."

Smiling J pushed his glasses up. He waited without speaking because he knew from experience there'd be more.

"Allow me to give you an example. There is a doomsday theory among your physicists." Mr. Speck touched his scribbled napkin. "Those who speak of it, speak quietly, because it is forbidden. Planet X...Oh, you are familiar with this theory?"

"Uh, I'm not sure whether..."

"I won't take offense. This is your education."

"I've heard of it. I mean, Planet X isn't a secret. You said it yourself, though. Nobody thinks there's a killer planet out there. Fun to noodle around, like UFO theory and crop circles."

Smiling J's Uncle Willard worked at a high security installation in Gakona. Since 1970, the military spent a pile of tax dollars building a mystery project in the hills. Uncle Willard refused to speak of his assignment. However, he gave his nephew a telescope and an astronomical catalogue with the covers and title pages snipped.

"You'd be surprised," Mr. Speck said. "Certain individuals behind the scenes are true believers regarding the existence of Planet X. The worst case scenario is a repeat of what happened in the Yucatan."

"The Yucatan, sir?"

"Ah, I leap ahead of myself. Short version: Next summer a gravity anomaly map made in the 1960s will fall into the hands of a geophysicist employed by a foreign energy corporation. His research will reveal evidence of a massive crater in the Yucatan obscured by jungle and bodies of water. The Chicxulub Crater's existence will in turn generate a theory that dinosaurs were wiped from the face of the Earth sixty-six million years ago by the deep impact of a celestial body."

"Makes sense," Smiling J said, completely uncertain whether it truly did. "Are you saying Earth is going get smacked by a meteor?"

Mr. Speck nodded and his face tipped into the light, then darkness. "In the relative near future, Planet X, with a mass thirteen times that of Earth, will heave in its long orbit beyond Pluto and disrupt the delicate stream of the Kuiper Belt. The gravity well is immense. Planet X drags a tidal wave of debris in its wake. Imagine this tidal wave of space debris directed toward your solar system." He traced a line from the edge of the napkin toward its center and circled back. "Pack an umbrella because it will rain shit down like you've never seen."

"Humankind would go the way of the dino."

"Should this scenario come to pass, *every* living organism will be made extinct except for cockroaches and bacteria."

"Oh, man. What we're doing tomorrow…Jeez, Mr. Speck. If this exercise can help avert Doomsday, then I'm in for sure."

Mr. Speck leaned back until his features sank into shadow. "Averting global annihilation is hardly the goal of our operation." He sounded amused. "Planet X might destroy your species this summer or it might wait another twenty-seven million years and pulverize an Earth devoid of sapient creatures. Possibly it will disrupt certain fields and play havoc with human evolution. I have no idea. What I know is this: Tomorrow, you will facilitate a culling of brainless, oversexed youth. One thing has nothing to do with the other."

"Okay. I'm sorry. I thought the purpose—"

"What we do, we do to satisfy intellectual curiosity and for the fun. It's important to love what you do, kid."

Somewhere, Sometime II:

Deep night gathered around the cabin. A candle shone through the window into a lonely gulf that descended past Alpha Centauri and into the outer dark.

He said, "Baby, pumpkin pie, honeybunch, whatever is the matter?"

She sat at the foot of the bed, facing away from him. "Someone else's dream isn't the most compelling item. But, good God, last night."

He clasped his hands behind his head and regarded the exposed beams in the ceiling of the cabin. "Tell me, sugar-booger."

"Ugh. C'mon."

"Sorry. Sugar plum. Go ahead, lay it on me."

"Really?"

"Yep! Ready and raring—"

"I dreamed the world was grinding to a stop, dark side-light side and all was being revealed. My body fell to the dead grass, paralyzed, and my mind's eye zipped in and out of the heads of several persons. I was staring from the eyes of a woman in the passenger seat of a luxury car. The driver, a corn-fed fellow in a suit, looked at her and *his* eyes went black and his mouth was a hole reversing over his body to reveal something, but my astral self flitted into the ether. The man in the disintegrating suit came after me, saying there was no escape. Then I was inside a raven that swooped over a great brooding mansion where a cheerleader had been impaled upon the weather vane. The mansion sat on an island of dry, dead grass and a sea of darkness rushed in from the horizon. Another raven swooped past me and cawed, 'Nevermore! Nevermore!' as if, perhaps, I hadn't gotten the hint. The man in the suit, far below, pointed at me and I fell out of the sky like a stone."

He stroked her back through the flimsy nightgown. "Sexual repression."

"Seriously?"

"That's what it's always about. Or death. Got to admit, the death vibe is strong."

"No, it frightened me. Frightened me in a way I can't—"

"Most of us find death a scary prospect. Death comes to everyone; no use worrying." He was an English major with a minor in psychology. A pain in the ass.

"Death isn't the worst. There's dementia. Mental anguish. Physical debilitation. Torture. Death is sleep."

He thought sleep sounded terrific. His eyes were heavy. "Baby, come over here."

"Come over where?"

He patted her pillow. The case had several large hearts sewn in. A fresh drop of blood formed at the heart of a heart, grew fat, and stained the cotton. A flute shrilled from the shadows where the ceiling sloped down to meet the wall.

She twisted to look at him. Her eyes belonged to an impressionist painting. Eyes Picasso might have given a woman were he in a savage mood. Her smile extended to her ears. She climbed atop the bed and began to dance. Every gyration swung her jackknifing upper torso closer to him. Her hair grazed his lips. Her lips grazed his lips.

He longed to protest. His muscles were paralyzed.

Somewhere, Sometime III (phone recording; probably Alaska, probably 1979):

Esteban: "…I don't…remember. A fire? Why don't I have scars? Kids screaming…it's like a dream. Not even real though it scares me shitless."

Concerned Friend: "You have nightmares?"

Esteban: "Nightmares, daymares. Flashbacks. It's driving me nuts and all I get are jags of images and sounds. Like a bad trip."

Concerned Friend: "My brother's platoon got hit with a mortar round in 'Nam. Killed thirty-eight of his buddies. He took shrapnel in the leg. Doesn't remember anything. Doctor had to tell him the story when he came to."

Esteban: "Paper says the park exploded. Gas pipes weren't up to code. Whole damned place was sketchy as hell. Duct tape on the rides. Half the staff had prison tats and smelled like liquor. Makes sense there'd be an industrial accident. Makes a plausible story."

Concerned Friend: "Makes sense because that's exactly how it went down. Don't go wrapping that fat head of yours in tinfoil."

Esteban: "I'm not sure. Story they fed the parents, the press, the entire world, is that somebody spiked the refreshments with acid and when the accident happened, we panicked. Bullshit. A couple of the kids were tripping, sure. And we were all boozing, yeah. Acid in the water? No way."

Concerned Friend: "Ain't gonna argue."

Esteban: "Nine kids died. Molly Vile disappeared. None of us talk about it. We try to pretend it didn't happen. Except Butch. Butch thinks it's amusing."

Concerned Friend: "People cope in different ways."

Esteban (after a long pause): "I think Lucius is cheating on me."

Concerned Friend: "She loves you, man."

Esteban: "Maybe. Her mom sleeps around. Everybody knows it except for Mr. Lochinvar. Like mother, like daughter."

Concerned Friend: "How much you have to drink? Are you crying? You're done and you're full of shit. Lucius ain't fucking around. Sleep it off."

Esteban: "She digs older guys…"

Somewhere, Sometime IV (Probably Alaska, probably the latter 1980s):

From the mind of Esteban Mace:

We'd been an item since junior high, but we moved in together during a false Alaska spring in 1980, several months after we realized baby Jessica was on the way. Come real spring I'd ship out for Camp Pendleton and my stint with the United States Marine Corps. My parents were none too pleased and I guess hers weren't either.

One night we lay in bed as flurries of snow piled against the window. The local oldies station said it wasn't quite a blizzard but stay indoors with your main squeeze to be on the safe side. As we neared the bottom of a bottle of red wine, she started talking about dead dogs she'd known.

"When I was eleven, my folks went to Florida for a week and I stayed behind with Sasha, the family dog. My dog, really. She was a mix; retriever and something else. Her fur was so soft and it gleamed. I didn't even brush her that often. She was the mooch queen. Whenever my family would swing over, my parents' friends were like, 'Hey, I'm grilling a steak, maybe Sasha would like one'…had to be those big brown eyes, the pleading look. She was a pro, my old gal. You'd a loved her. Everybody did. She slipped out the door one night and got hit by a car on Spenard Road. Vet tried every trick in the book. Six grand later we finally gave her the needle. Shitty way to go."

I'd seen plenty of pictures of Sasha. A sleek red dog who'd hammed for the camera. A lot of other dog pics too; my girl apparently had a thing, but mostly Sasha. I realized, and for the first time, that she didn't keep any shots of her current pet, Lily, even though she'd kept the Cavalier Spaniel for seventeen years having inherited full ownership from her mom and dad junior year of high school. Neither of us really spoke of the dog either. Wheezing and coughing, eternally moribund, Lily had become another piece of furniture, albeit one that had to be moved several times a day. Maybe that was weird.

"Mine committed suicide," I said.

She lit a cigarette, then rolled onto her side and gazed at me. Her eyes shone in the gloom, as if she'd been crying. "I didn't know that was possible. Animals opting out."

"It's possible. Once in a blue moon kind a deal. We had a black lab when I was a kid. Inherited from my granddad who'd named him Buster after that actor Buster Crabbe. Guy who played Tarzan in the dark ages before network TV."

"Handsome fella that BC," she said with languid appreciation.

"Oh, yeah? You ever watch him? Talk about way before our time."

"Grandmother was a fan. Had a steamer trunk with a shitload of memorabilia. She chased autographs when she was a girl. Gable, Hepburn, Kirk Douglas, Douglas Fairbanks, Vivien Leigh; you call it, she had a postcard or photo with the star's John Hancock on there. Crabbe gave her a signed photo of him in his swim trunks, gold medal around his neck. She swooned every time we took it out of the box. Me too, I guess. First erotic dream I ever had was about Buster Crabbe."

I shook the empty wine bottle. "That's a new one on me, honey. Anyway. My black lab didn't give a tinker's damn about Gramps. However, the mutt made friends with one of the horses. They were real tight. Bumped muzzles whenever we visited the corral. After the horse died, poor Buster became despondent and one day he ended it all."

"How did the horse die?"

"Dad shot her."

Lucius exhaled smoke. "Your dad had a good reason?"

"He was a little trigger happy."

"Okay, on with the ballad of Buster."

"Thank you. Buster moped around for weeks. Wouldn't eat, got really skinny. I tried to cheer him up. You know how kids are. He was my pal. But nothing doing. He sat by the corral gate, head down, mourning. Slept there, rain or shine. Dad had to lug him inside at night because he wouldn't come on his own. One morning I looked out the window as Buster climbed under the fence and walked into the duck pond. Trudged straight in and sank. Didn't doggie paddle or anything. Glub, glub, glub. Bunch a bubbles, then zilch. Nobody was around, so I jumped in. Couldn't find him, though. Dad came home and called a couple of his work buddies to help drag the pond. Found Buster in the silt."

"That's it?"

"All she wrote."

"Might've been an accident," she said.

"No way. I hollered at him right before he went into the drink. He glanced back at me. Never saw an expression like that on a dog. Same look you see on a war widow's face as she's weeping in a bombed-out village. Despair. Pure despair."

We fell asleep on that happy note.

The radio alarm blared "I love the Night" by Blue Oyster Cult at three in the A.M. Time to walk Lily again. Every four hours it had to be done; like feeding and changing an infant, only in this case a dog who'd regressed to puppyhood forever. Lucius snored on her side, belly bulging the coverlet, reminding me that one soul enters as another leaves.

The truth of it was, while I liked dogs, and probably would've gotten attached to dearly-departed Sasha too, I didn't harbor much affection for Lily. She wasn't particularly friendly, a fact I'd attributed to my status as a Johnny-come-lately, and to her ancientness. She preferred to be left in peace under the table, a vague lump, eyes glistening with inscrutable philosophies; Queen of the Dark upon her satin pillow.

Something is wrong with the baby. You won't ever know what, you won't even be alive by the time her curse manifests in full. Neither will Lucius. Lily yawned and her ancient, corroded fangs were larger and brighter than any dog had a right to own.

I snapped awake from the dream-within-a-dream to BOC playing my wakeup serenade, Lucius and the dog snoring and a cold dread in my heart.

Thirty-odd years have rolled by since that dream and the phantom dog had it right — Lucius is vanished, likely dead; my boy Elwood, he's gone too, blown to smithereens in Afghanistan; this ship is taking on water and the black sea will soon drag me down the way it dragged down my would-be son-in-law (see you soon, Jackson Bane!) ... Small mercy, Jessica is alive and well and living in Eagle Talon.

Right before I head to the bottom, Lily's ghost says, *Every one of you had your mind wiped that night in Rally. Saps. Behold the terrible truth.*

The secrets of the universe unfold then implode and suck me into an obliterating chamber. I remember everything and know everything, potentially, to come. I'd cry if the pressure and the currents hadn't reduced me to motes of motes.

3. Anchorage, Alaska. Autumn, 1979. (Rabbit Creek)

Rabbit Creek occupied a few neighborhoods and industrial zones between Potter's Marsh and the Chugach National Forest. Basically the ass-end of Anchorage, built atop a thin permafrost crust over primordial muck. Several state geologists had opined the whole area might well sink straight to hell in one of the region's frequent earthquakes. Lucius Lochinvar thought such a cataclysm couldn't happen soon enough.

Cassidy Sloan, helming an Oldsmobile she'd borrowed from her dad, dropped Lucius at Mr. Hyjak's place. It was a few minutes before dark. A light burned on the porch of the split-level house.

Sloan popped a bubble with her pink gum and glared. Her right eye was blacked from a flying elbow at a recent roller derby match.

"Is that a pudge? You don't button your coat anymore. You preggo? Aw shit, you're preggo."

"I am not," Lucius reflexively crossed her fingers.

"Maybe I should hang around. Want me to stay? I can sit here and listen to the radio. In case…"

"In case?"

"I dunno — in case the scene goes sour."

"He's nice. He isn't going to turn into Mr. Goodbar. Besides." Lucius slapped her purse and its arsenal of knife, hatpin, and mace.

"Nice?" Pop went the gum.

"Like I said, nice. Too nice. He's a wuss. I scare him."

"Nice guys ain't fuckin' teen girls half their age on the sly."

"He's not married."

"Yeah, that's weird too. Anyway — forgetting about the Boy Scout?"

"Esteban and I aren't married either."

"Same diff."

"Meet you at the diner. I can book it from here in twenty."

"Yeah?"

"Yeah, I do it whenever I come over here for a screw." Lucius climbed out.

Sloan clutched at her sleeve and missed. "The bastard doesn't even give you a lift after you ball him?"

"Nunya, Sloan. See you in an hour. Pancakes on me."

"Hell with pancakes. Ronnie Diamond has some people over tonight."

"I'm saving myself for the bash over at Tooms' place tomorrow."

"It's a pre-party. I dunno. Who cares? We're goin' over and getting' shitfaced to the max. If we screw it up, tomorrow night is do-over."

"Okay. Meet me at the diner in an hour."

Alan Hyjak worked as an engineer in Prudhoe Bay which meant he split the year between Barrow and Anchorage. He rented the house and kept a side door unlocked on the nights Lucius stopped over. She went in and felt around in the murk until she reached the living room. It glowed with firelight like the wizard's lab in *Fantasia*. Peculiar music (perhaps a monumental long-lost Jethro Tull flute solo) floated from a set of speakers as wide as suitcases. Hyjak reposed naked on a bearskin rug before the hearth. Not a shabby bod for an older guy, if a bit pallid.

"Hey, cutie." He sipped from a tumbler. "Do yourself a drink."

Lucius sighed and perched on stool by the wet bar. "I won't be long. We need to talk."

"Huh. Talk. Talk is never good. Let's skip it and say we did. Let's screw."

She shook her head.

Hyjak sighed. "Don't tell me. Plans with the boyfriend? As you can see, I got dressed for the occasion. Be a shame to spoil all my efforts."

"You look cozy." She studied the room, squinting to discern the mounted wolf head, an oil painting of a Roman coliseum, and the odd, plastic furniture that belonged to a science fiction movie set. "Are you comfortable here? Just you, alone every night?"

"Not every night. I live plenty of my life in a modular with four other guys. Certainly don't get to lounge around in the buff."

"Sure you don't."

He stroked his chest and winked. "I suppose the joint could stand a woman's touch...me too!" When she didn't smile, he rose and stood directly before the fire so the red light made him a silhouette. "It was bound to come to this. The girl has melted and the woman rises in her stead. Reforged and lethal."

"Alan, Alan. I was never much of a girl. That's why you're obsessed with me."

"Fair enough. I am obsessed. Although it's not what you think."

"My friends say it's weird you don't have a wife or a girlfriend."

"What you mean is, your girlfriend, Sloan, says it's weird."

"Dude. You live alone in a big house. No pals, no family. You don't even own a goldfish. Something's funky."

"I like to get funky. I like to get down. Why the third degree?"

"Two years. Two years and I haven't learned anything real except your CV. My hunch? There's nothing to learn."

"Because I choose not to share that part of my life with you doesn't mean it isn't there."

"Ouch. Guess you told me." She spoke quietly, body tensed. The interminable fluting devolved into a single piercing bleep similar to the emergency broadcast signal, then ceased. Flames crackled. Her heart beat. She hadn't realized how much the music had gotten on her nerves.

"Do my words hurt?" Hyjak said.

She glanced toward a hallway that led deeper into the house. "A pinprick on the Dol Scale." She paid attention in class. "Emphasis on prick. No need to agonize in guilt."

"Guilt isn't my bag. We both got what we wanted and now it's over. Going to miss your precociousness, and them perky tits."

"Precociousness is code for bitchiness."

"Not usually. However, Ambrose Bierce said that politeness is an acceptable form of hypocrisy. I'm curious — is this going how you rehearsed?"

"So far so good, said the man who jumped off the Empire State Building after every floor." Again she glanced toward the hallway. "You have company?"

"Company? According to you, nobody visits me in my hermitage." Hyjak spread his shadowy arms. He undulated to a phantom rhythm. His shadow crawled across the floor, four-armed. "It's only me and thee." He finished his drink and tossed the glass over his shoulder into the fire; kept on swaying. "Since this won't matter much longer, I'll let you in on a secret."

"Ooh, a secret." She reached into her purse and got a cigarette and lit up. The action disguised her true intention as she slipped the mace canister into her left hand. "Okay, I'm ready. Lay it on me." She watched Hyjak's undulating silhouette and considered that Sloan's cynicism might have been warranted. Her man on the side had slipped a gear. Rejection summoned the beast from certain wrecked egos.

"I'm not an engineer; I don't work in Prudhoe Bay; and I don't feel a thing for you, you arrogant little twat." He snapped his fingers. "Damn, that's nice."

"Truly fascinating. Yes, well. Bye." Lucius stood and moved away at an angle. She didn't think the guy would rush her, although she didn't turn her back on him.

"Wait...You're jetting?"

"I am."

"Ask me what I really do for a job. Ask me who pays the freight. Lucius!"

"Piss up a rope!" she called cheerfully on her way through the door.

"I lie for a living, baby! I lie and I touch myself! My letter sweater spells CIA!"

The door slammed.

Then:

The girl left in a huff.

Mr. Hyjak turned so the heat from the flames warmed his testicles. He shimmied and capered, miming a folk dance. Mr. Speck and Butch Tooms emerged from the passage that led to the bedroom. Both men were also naked. Mr. Speck wore a black baseball cap and black shades. His paunch drooped.

Mr. Hyjak had previously asked Mr. Speck why he always wore a hat. Mr. Speck said his exposed brain matter needed protection from Earth atmosphere.

"Lucky I don't hurt you," Butch Tooms said to Mr. Hyjak. "Hurt you bad."

"Say what? Why would you want to hurt me?"

"Our friend is jealous," Mr. Speck said.

"Butch, baby — what are you jealous about? Have a drink. Have two."

"Mr. Tooms is jealous because you've copulated with the female he desires."

"Lochinvar? Yeah? You didn't...I guess we kept it on the down low. Well, we're splitsville now. Surely you heard that bad scene?"

"Her departure seemed abrupt," Mr. Speck said. "The females are deadly and unpredictable. Or the tachyon bombardment of her cells precipitated a hostile mood."

"Chick dropped me hard. Hey, Butch, go on, fix a drink."

"Lucky I don't smash your teeth in." Butch Tooms spoke in a monotone. His hand tightened into a fist against his hip. "Real lucky, man. Smash your teeth."

"Should I—?" Mr. Hyjak gestured to Mr. Speck for assistance.

"Should you *what*, Mr. Hyjak?" Mr. Speck took down a bottle of vodka and sniffed, unimpressed.

"Should I kill the music? It's agitating Butch. Butch, you aren't chill. You're uptight."

Mr. Speck stoppered the bottle. "Kill the music?"

"Yeah. I mean, if it's all right."

"The signal isn't playing at a decibel you are capable of registering. Listen carefully. Yes? The music, as you perceive it, ceased minutes ago. It's in your head. Your neurons are chasing phantoms."

"Beautiful," Butch Tooms said. His fist relaxed. He stared into the gloom and smiled.

"Oh yeah?" Mr. Hyjak said. "Then what's he listening to?"

"Nothing," Mr. Speck said. "Echoes of dust falling in a mausoleum in ancient Greece. Your mother climaxing at the moment of your conception. A rabbit decomposing in a bog."

"Oh, crap," Mr. Hyjak said. "You aren't kidding. I can't hear it anymore."

"Rubbing your ear won't help."

"Oh, crap. Crap!"

"The signal can be damaging. Especially when it transcends the spectrum of physics that operate here."

"Look, wait. He's — Butch isn't on a full dose, right? There are levels of progression to the action threshold. That's what I was told. We control his escalation with incremental micro-doses. Safe as houses as long as the doses are small. Right? Right? Damn it, you told me to play the recording!"

"Are you British?" Mr. Speck said. "My survey suggested milk-bland USA."

"No, I'm — you see, my dad—"

"Calm yourself. Death will be among us tomorrow, the next day…soon. Horrors piled upon horrors. Such is the way of the universe."

"Horrors!" Butch Tooms said.

"Everything's okay?" Mr. Hyjak said. "I'm bleeding." He wiped his nose on the back of his hand. "I've got a nosebleed. Bad one."

"A real gusher," Mr. Speck said.

"Am I dying?"

"No, your brain is softening. The signal is squeezing your frontal lobe the way clay is compressed when the earth shifts. Water oozes from its pores. Perfectly normal. The gray matter must become malleable for our purposes. Malleable, Mr. Hyjak. Be brave."

Butch Tooms also bled. It dripped from his chin and spattered his toes. He continued to gaze serenely into the grave-cold heart of the cosmos, or wherever. Shadows near the far wall thickened and changed and glimmered purple. Purple-black. Voluptuous, unctuous rings of mute, irradiated darkness. The men's faces dimmed.

Mr. Hyjak spilled blood from his cupped palm. He glanced around. "Oh. Oh! The music. It's back! Radical!" He swiveled his hips and arms in a counter rhythm to a low hiss emanating from the speakers.

Mr. Speck inclined his head. His glasses cracked and reflected the purple dark.

Meanwhile (small get-together at Ronnie Diamond's pad):

"Like, we were all sitting around a campfire in the mountains and Abraham Vile started in with ghost stories. Drinkin' cocoa and making s'mores and here he comes with the spooky stuff. Ghost stories. I hate em, man..."

"Why you hate ghost stories...?"

"My mom died when I was little..."

"How she die — oh, right. Big C..."

"Man, I told you before, she die of the cancer...!"

"What I said. She got cancer..."

"After she did that, she used to come into my room all late at night and shit, and hang upside down in my closet. The door would swing open and she'd be in there between my sweatshirts and snow jackets, grinnin' at me, pasty-faced as fuck. That's why..."

"Your mom ain't no ghost. She a vampire..."

"See this pistol...?"

"That's a pellet gun..."

"Yeah, that's right. I blow a hole through your head. Dump you in Rabbit Creek..."

"I'd come back as a ghost and fuck you up..."

"Man, you're outta beer," Jeff Vellum said, staring disconsolately into the fridge. The pale light rendered his broad features vaguely moon-like. "This is our last fling before we part ways for college and you're dry." He wandered away in defeat.

"Oops," Jimmy said. "Jackie's gonna nut him for returning empty-handed."

"College, my ass," Esteban said, trying not to slur. Jimmy, Jackie, Jeff, and J — the four J's. He'd downed a man's portion of a sixer of Bud. "Some of us whose names don't begin with J are headed for vocational school after a pit stop in the military and glad for it. This isn't the last fandango, man. Tooms' shindig, tomorrow night.

Tomahawk Park Survivors bash." The prospect didn't thrill him — he'd toned down the old drinking game and his current heroics were sure to exact a stiff price.

"Make a beer run?" Jimmy said. "Anybody got any cash? I don't."

"I'll just put it on my Diner's Card," Ronnie Diamond said. "No worries." He'd played offensive tackle, all state. His hair hung long as his daddy's (doing fifteen to life in Spring Creek). He owned a hand-me-down Harley (dead uncle) and an El Camino (jailed uncle).

"Diner's Card?" Esteban said.

"Yeah. I got a Diner's Card. Check it, dude."

Esteban and Jimmy looked at each other.

"Ronnie, I thought you were broke," Jimmy said. "You owe me twenty bucks."

"Right, but I got plastic."

"Wait, what are you talking about?" Esteban said.

"What are YOU talking about, man?" Ronnie said with sudden panic in his eyes.

"But when you have to pay the balance—"

"The balance?"

Jimmy cracked up. "Yeah, pay it down at the end of the month. What did you think, dumbass?"

"Like, it's money in a bank, only negative."

"Ronnie, that's not—"

"Y'know, you spend a hundred bucks and you can't spend it again until you put some money back."

"No, dude, no. It's a short term loan. The company charges interest."

"Oh, dear God." Ronnie's color drained to match his dingy white tee.

"Thanks for the beer!" Timbi Showalter yelled from the sofa.

"Hurrah!" Abraham Vile yelled from the opposite end of the sofa. He had a can in each hand. The stereo blared "I'm Not in Love." Some of the kids were pretending to dance. Mainly they were content to grind against one another.

The doorbell rang. Cassidy Sloan and Lucius Lochinvar waltzed into the kitchen. Sloan shoved past the boys. She rummaged through the fridge, her habitual frown deepening.

"Where's the damned beer?" She slammed the fridge and rummaged through the cabinets.

"Hey." Esteban kissed Lucius' cheek. She gripped his hand, hard. He didn't like the dark-bright glare in her eyes. "What's the matter?"

"Absolutely nothing. Ronnie, where's your mom?"

"Beatrice got called in to the hospital," Ronnie said. "Sloan! No way, dude, that's Bea's secret, double secret, stash. Don't fucking touch that shit; she measures it with a dipstick."

"I would too, with you around, you fucking lush." Sloan unscrewed the top and had a jolt of Mrs. Diamond's private stock of Johnnie Walker Black.

"Let's go," Lucius seized Esteban's arm.

"Uh, baby, I'm not quite done—"

"You're done."

"She got all the testosterone in your relationship," Jimmy said.

"Not all... a bunch," Esteban said.

Lucius dragged him through the house to Ronnie's room where everybody had piled their jackets on Ronnie's bed. She pushed him down and unbuckled his belt one-handed. Her eyes grew shinier by the heartbeat.

"Sweetie," he said as she shucked his jeans. "I'm not complaining, but why?"

"Dunno. It feels important."

"I don't—"

She squeezed his throat. One squeeze and done. She raised her skirt and mounted him and he lost his train of thought.

Somewhere, Sometime V (Probably New England, the early Aughts):

From the mind of Lucius Lochinvar Mace

Esteban and the kids think I ran away from home. Wish I could tell them the truth that every night after Tomahawk Park and every night after the post high school bash at the Toomses has taught me cheating death isn't necessarily the way to go.

Here I am at the end of the road and no brakes.

Doctors C & R put me through a battery of tests. Psychological, physical, chemical. They strap me into a machine called the Black

Kaleidoscope and send my consciousness into astral projection mode. A sort of regression therapy.

Some tech gives me a horse needle of happiness and then the drip goes in smooth, trickles down my throat and into my heart. The tech slips red headphones over my ears and right off the bat I recollect all kinds of neat shit like…

…how my brothers and I exchanged jewelry for Christmas and weapons on birthdays and that sweet moment when I punched Jackie Brock in the kisser in middle school. I slashed my knuckles on her braces and stood over her, her limbs like matchsticks at odd angles to one another, and uttered a curse *May you come back as a chandelier — hang by day, burn by night!* Two and a half decades of water under the bridge and I still savor that moment, hold it in my mouth like the sweetest liquor…The day Jessica came into the world, my firstborn, lovely angry doomed daughter. I'm sorry, kid, for what will come…

Problem is, I can't stop, can't even slow down and memory unravels around me at 16X speed. A phantom wind tears me to ribbons with razor shards of my past misdeeds. Dr. Campbell had cautioned that whatever resides within a traveler gets writ large inside the Kaleidoscope and I'd stifled a giggle thinking of Yoda dispatching Luke to that cave in *The Empire Strikes Back.* Laughing out the other side of my face now.

Oh, the misery of an eventful life. The things you discover when blood is oozing from your nose and the silver screen of your mind's eye collapses inward and reveals an ice sheet and a red nail bed of horizon. A figure in an anorak with the hood up approaches.

My dead uncle, Bradley, says, *Your daughter is born of evil, your sons will be sacrificed as I was sacrificed. I loved your mother.* True confessions of the dearly-departed. His blackened hand sears my cheek with cold. Doesn't seem to matter he'd gotten obliterated in Vietnam, he's put himself together again. I convince myself that the blast had hurled him into a parallel universe. That's what ghosts are — souls who've reconstituted a frequency up or down the radio dial. Death as we know it is simply a process of osmosis, a trickle charge into a cosmic battery. Hard to tell whether that's a pleasant thought or a preview of Hell.

Three non-human intelligences interfere with the course of life on Earth the way little kids play with ant farms. Your doctor friends are in the know

and they are only aware of two of the players. You're at the end of your rope,
sweetheart. We'll be together real soon.

Uncle Brad hums a strange melody; a Saturday kid's show actor
summoning cardboard flying saucers from the interstellar divide. It
gives me the mother of all ear worms. Ice buckles and groans and
stars rush toward me.

I crash back into the here and now, fling the headphones aside
and draw down with Beasley's (the unhandsome, but spectacularly
virile bodyguard/valet to the scientists) spare Saturday Night Special
that I've taped against the small of my back, uncomfortable to say the
least, and aim it at Dr. C. I'm no Annie Oakley. Still, I feel better
holding the gun, feel more in control, illusory as that might be.
Somebody had neglected to tick the box next to *Propensity for Violence*
on my chart. Goes to show that psych evaluations aren't all created
equal.

"Mr. Beasley and his unsecured firearms," Dr. C says,
disappointed. He's survived cannibals, cultists, intestinal parasites,
kidnapping and torture in the Far East, and decades as second-fiddle
to his senior partner, the infamous Dr. R. A girl with a gun doesn't
scare him unduly. "Do you mind?" He strikes a match from the case
he keeps in his coat pocket and lights his pipe. "I didn't foresee this
variable. My calculations need a double-check. Is that weapon
loaded, Mrs. Mace? Does your family know where you've run off to?
Does your husband?"

"Don't worry about them. The fam is used to my comings and
goings."

"Yes. They assume you've run away with one of your many
flings. Excellent cover. Do you maintain the façade for their
protection or your convenience?"

"A little of column A, a little of column B."

I divide my attention between him and the rear wall of the
interview room. A fractal three-dee print adorns the otherwise bare
wall. Psychotropic dope still swims through my consciousness. It
puffs in tiny cotton detonations and clouds my blood with lead
sinkers. The whine of a drill bit scratches at my brain, high and thin.
Muzak of dead stars.

"Who the fuck is behind that wall?" I say.

"You are under the influence of a powerful hallucinogen. It has rendered you more volatile than usual. There is nothing behind the wall."

"Try again."

"A friend of some friends."

"Not helpful, doc."

"I could tell you, but then you'd have to kill yourself." He smirks and inhales from his pipe. A cold, contemptuous gesture from a wizened child who fried ants with a magnifying glass. Also, possibly, a dare.

I take his dare and cock the hammer. I swing the barrel until it points where the red and gold panels intersect behind the print. "*What*. What is behind the wall?"

"I am sure you remember your old friend, Mr. Speck. His interference helped transform you, mutate you."

"He's gone." My mouth tastes sour. Suppressed memories of slaughter and mayhem yammer and boil behind a psychic dam I've built with drugs and raw willpower.

"Speck is gone, yes. Amanda Bole yet lurks; we know not where. Those two had enemies, or rivals, if you will. Competing interests for the hearts and minds of Terra. Some of them are here with us, recording this conversation. These...neighbors have emerged from the deep places to observe and advise. Ostensibly our friends mean well. However, their temperament is hazardous to the health of obstreperous primates."

"Show me the man behind the curtain."

"You'll regret it instantly."

"Will I?"

He breathes out a cloud. "It is worse than you can imagine."

"Bullshit. I've seen the worst."

"Wrong, my dear. Look, if you're going to be a prig, put the gun into your mouth and do us both a favor. Or shoot me first, if you please."

"Fine, Mr. Wizard. I call." I squeeze off the entire magazine into the fractal print and whatever alleged monstrosity lurks behind the thin paneling. Bull's eye.

Fuck me running, the doctor knew whereof he spoke. It is worse.

4. Rally, Washington. Spring, 1977 (Sample from Massacre)

The gang from Alaska ran amok an entire day at Tomahawk Park with only one major casualty (Jude Kowalski busted his arm on a concrete water slide) and a few bumps and bruises (the aforementioned slide and a go-cart duel between Keith Norse and Jimmy Flank that concluded in a six cart pileup and a tire fire). The park had operated since 1957 and garnered a reputation for shoddy construction, incompetent employees, and third world safety standards. Everyone agreed (as bandages and casts were applied) that it had exceeded expectations.

After showering away (most of) the chlorine, everybody chowed on burgers. Small groups formed and slipped away for a secluded beach on the river. Ronnie Diamond and Esteban recruited a half-dozen warm bodies to secure driftwood for the epic bonfire. Jeff Vellum ignited the sucker with a splash of unleaded gasoline. The resulting fireball could've been sighted from space and singed his eyebrows off. Somebody with a fake ID had secured a keg of the good stuff and plenty of cases of PBR and Colt 45 for backup. Mr. Three Trees and Mr. Hyjak got Mrs. Buntline crocked on margaritas at the Fat Boy so the kids could have their fun unimpeded. Esteban heard Butch Tooms (courtesy Daddy Tooms' bankroll) slipped the so-called chaperones a C-note to make it happen.

Meanwhile:

Threnody Rudnick and Molly Vile stayed behind in room 119, an end unit on the wing that lay in gloom beneath a stand of Douglas firs. The light over the door also *happened* to be broken, ensuring a multitude of shadows to cloak young ne'er-do-wells, Bobby Flank and Vern Oglesby. The boys (hockey players both) peeped through the window and a narrow divide in the drapes, watching as the girls laughed drunkenly and undressed one another. Led Zeppelin played "Black Dog" as Molly Vile leaned in and laid a kiss on Rudnick.

"See, told ya," Vern said.

"I hope Butch don't catch us," Bobby said. His head was on a swivel for Butch Tooms.

"Be totally worth it."

"Getting maimed isn't a fun way to end a vacation."

"He wouldn't maim us, he'd murder us."

"Goddamnit, they aren't taking off their bras," Bobby said after a while.

"Give it a minute." Vern hesitated. "Dude…You hear that?"

"Hear what?"

"Sounded like…sounds like…"

"Aw, I think you're right — they're just going to neck. What a gyp!"

"…a whistle. You don't hear it?"

"Man, this is PG bullshit," Bobby said. "I vote we haul ass to the beach and get lit." He realized Vern wasn't crouched beside him anymore. "Vern?"

To Bobby's right, a door slammed and a car engine fired. Lights twinkled across the parking lot. To his left, the great black mass of trees inhaled the light and gave back scents of sap, fir needles, and deathly must.

A night bird screamed. Chimes jangled. Wind chimes? He strained to determine the direction and proximity. The sound changed. Whistling? Pipes? The melody floated from the woods, near then far. His muscles went rigid and he gripped the window sill. His nails dug in and split. The sinews in his neck spasmed and he bit through his tongue.

A shape rose from where it had lain in a bed of dead leaves. Its eyes collected sparks of sodium fire. The shape seized Bobby. It pried his jaws apart and formed a seal with its own mouth, and drank. Bobby remained a statue. A vein in his temple pulsed, pulsed…

Meanwhile (Inside 119):

Molly Vile broke off her kiss. "Whoa, weird."

"That you want to parlay roller-skating into a profession?" Threnody Rudnick said. "Sounds golden."

"Thanks. I heard something…"

"Make with the smooching already." Lost in euphoria, Threnody Rudnick didn't open her eyes. She'd nearly forgotten they were simply warming up for the main event, if lover boy Butch (and the promised eight-ball) could be troubled to make an appearance.

"Swear to gods somebody whispered my name." Molly crossed her arms defensively. "I think one of those perv hockey guys is spying on us."

"Which one?"

"Take your pick. Could be the whole team."

"We should charge a buck a peek."

Molly sighed. She went to the window and stood for a few moments. "Ugh, can't see a damned thing. The light's not on. Bulb burned out, or I don't know."

"Squash your tits on the glass and wait a few seconds for a reaction."

"Threnody, be serious."

"Deadly serious." Threnody undid her bra and gave it a twirl while jiggling her boobs directly at the window and the theoretical peeping jackasses. "Hey, chickie, I double dog dare ya! Off with your top!"

Molly's scandalized expression dissolved and she laughed. A moment later both girls faced the window and shook their assets with the gusto, if not the finesse, of seasoned burlesque dancers. The lamp on the dresser dimmed and brightened as its bulb filled with blood and emitted purple light. Led Zeppelin vanished into softly buzzing static. Patterns of purple light spun on the ceiling.

"Satan's watching," Molly said. Her bra dangled in her left hand. She turned from the window and tilted her head back to study the weird lightshow.

Threnody's sense of pleasurable sloth dissolved. Her thighs cramped the way they occasionally did after a marathon skating session. The radio static hummed and drilled into her brain, pulsing in synchronicity with the lamp. Instinctively, and with tremendous effort, she extended her leaden arm and slapped the radio power button to OFF.

"Satan's watching. Satan's watching!" Molly raised her voice to counter the abrupt stillness. She laughed with great gulping inhalations. She clasped her hands and raised them and danced in place. The front door flew open and slammed closed. The window shattered inward. A severed head rebounded from the far wall and rolled under the table. Threnody's fuzzed brain required several moments to process this development, to evaluate the array of implications. A second severed head struck a fake Vermeer still life and left a bloody splotch.

"That's fucking it!" Naked except for panties and go-go boots, she grabbed the edge of the mattress and flipped it against the window. Fighting wasn't her gig (thus she hadn't made the roller derby squad despite above average skating chops; the fact practically killed her inside), and she didn't know what to do next. She locked the door and shoved a chair under the knob like she'd seen it done in the movies. Now, to find a weapon...

Molly fell to her knees and screamed a singsong prayer. "O Horned God, haunter of the Black Forest of Night, forgive our weakness! Ravish me, Devil! Devour my unworthy soul! Bear my disemboweled corpse aloft to the Nemesis Star—"

"Shut up!" Threnody yanked her friend's hair and as the girl recoiled, claws bared like a pissed cat.

Molly curled into a ball, mewling Latin. Had she secretly taken wannabe goth lessons from Jackie Brock? The door swung wide and the chair shattered. Butch Tooms lurched across the threshold. He wore a white paper suit similar to the work clothes of a janitor or hazardous materials laborer. Blood spackled his shiny white arms. His dead white welder's mitts glittered with embedded glass shards and roofing nails and hanks of hair.

"Why are you doing this?" Threnody tried not to whine. Terror inflated her body and lifted her to tiptoes. She'd suspected Butch had a screw or two loose — although nothing this dramatic. Her more cynical angels whispered, *Told ya so!*

Butch Tooms showed his teeth. "Teenagers experimenting with sex, drugs, and devil music. A cursed theme park and a toxic waste site. The summoning ritual is complete."

"Satan? We've summoned the Dark Lord!" Molly Vile gazed up at him with rapt adoration.

"No, sweet thing. You summoned me." He slapped her face off, lazily as a grizzly taking a swipe at immobilized prey. Bits splattered the lamp and stuck to the wall. A coarse, jagged pipe note warbled from outside. His eyes rolled and his nose streamed blood. "Oh, the strident caller beckons. Come with me, girl."

Threnody snatched the lamp and slung it by the cord at Butch Tooms' head. Porcelain and glass exploded. She dove past her nemesis and through the open door—

Somewhere, Sometime VI (Probably Alaska, probably the 21st Century):

From the Mind of Julie Brock Vellum:

I came home from a West Coast appearance a few nights ago, and as I sat on a bench in the terminal, the late August light moved like a glacial sheet across the stained carpet and the pants legs of businessmen and stockings of businesswomen and caught in momentary flares in the buckles and clasps and bits of jewelry. Their hair spray shone like glints from helmets. A Boeing 747 rolled into its dock and cut off the sunrays. Dinosaurs died beneath a meteor's shadow; oceans scummed over with ice and farther out, a rime of salt. Elsewhere, a star exploded and cooked a solar system where, fortunately, no organism more complex than a microbe existed. We're next one day.

I went back to the moleskin notebook, dutifully recording the names of the several new enemies I'd made at the conference. My boyfriend hates that I do this. He says, *Julie, you're borrowing trouble.* I'm like, *Rent to own!*

He's a new boyfriend. Seven months and ticking. I haven't bothered to memorize his name. He's Brian the fourth (fifth?). Brian the first was killed three years ago. I hid in a wicker laundry hamper while a shadowy figure disemboweled him with a carving knife. Man, it seemed to go on forever. The killer took his sweet time, pulling out the intestines and making a neat pile. He did it slow to keep Brian awake, I guess. Stuffed some of the guts into his mouth to muffle the screams. Most of it has gotten fuzzy in my mind. I vomited once and orgasmed twice. So, I totally won.

My shrink says you have to do what it takes to survive. He says a lot of people look down on survivors. He says I could be a rich wife. I always smile slyly and think it's better to be a rich girl with a secret life. My head hurts all the time.

Mom…Jackie…kicked the bucket last month. Aneurism. Figures…

(after a significant time lapse)

…it has been nice to stay here at my buddy Roland's ranch in Montana for a few weeks. Up late working on the project. Roland and his family went into town this afternoon, so it's me, the house, and the animals. Huge thunderstorm rolled through a few hours ago. Now the moon is a blur through those torpedo clouds you see in horror flicks, and the wind is roaring. The property takes on a completely different character when the family is absent. There's that sense of the wilderness waiting to reclaim its territory, that those goodbyes and slamming car doors, then the long silence after, is the first sign. The Only light is the kitchen light. The other You stands out there in the dark, watching me do dishes. She slurps from a badly-patched wineglass and works on the problem of getting in...

Mom and I didn't always get along when she was alive. It's better now.

5. *Anchorage, Alaska. Autumn 1979 (Tomahawk Park Survivors Party):*

The Tooms family home sat atop a hill with views of everywhere. Three stories plus the unfinished basement — the Bear Den; Pluto's Ballroom. Lucius wondered if anybody else found the basement creepy — dripping pipes, chest-high cinderblock walls and exposed soil, and cracks that reminded her of animal burrows. The other kids seemed oblivious to the Edgar Allan Poe décor as they boozed and danced with pagan abandon.

Butch Tooms had the run of the place for several days (his parents, two younger brothers, and sister flew the coop for somewhere sandy and tropical) and what with the gang scattering to the four winds, it seemed apropos to throw a wild farewell party. The Tomahawk Park Survivors Party and Raffle, according to Butch Tooms. Every guest received an engraved invitation (a cheapo flyer) and a ticket for the drawing. Timbi Showalter asked what the prizes were. Butch Tooms said, sanity, prosperity, a good fuck, and a clean death. Timbi Showalter laughed because her host laughed.

This hoedown had it all: catered munchies; liquor galore; kegs of beer (cheap and imported, depending on one's preference); plenty of Maryjane; a pair of college guys to man the turntables; and a big fat glitter ball hoisted to a place of resplendent honor in the basement ceiling.

A quarter past nine and Jimmy Flank had already gotten sloppy drunk on boilermakers. Lucius watched him perform the "lean" on Cassidy Sloan, who rolled her eyes and smiled with thin-lipped patience as the kid explained how he planned to ditch Alaska and become a private eye. Jimmy didn't confine his drinking to parties; he got going around breakfast time and never throttled back. Esteban worried this portended a sign of misery to come; tonight and for all the nights of Jimmy's life.

Jimmy said, "I stopped being afraid of bigger guys 'cause they ain't tougher. Nicked my throat shaving with Dad's straight razor and the blood oozed and for a split second, it wasn't my face in the mirror, it was a Roman centurion getting his throat cut. I was a bad, bad man in a past life. Fuckers had to sneak up to take me out. Nah, what scares me are these dreams I have of getting buried alive."

Lucius winked at Sloan and cast around for Esteban without luck. It alarmed her to realize that she'd become more than a little possessive of the boy. She frowned and twisted her rings until they abraded flesh. This weak sister bullshit wouldn't do. The room, the music, the drunk and stoned teens grinding against one another on a patch of dizzily illuminated floor made her queasy. An odd, butterfly sensation in her stomach had come and gone all day. Keyboard notes and synthesizers combined for a strident melody that excited the dancers. The light dimmed to infrared and their faces slackened and tightened and altered. The light brightened and all was vapid and normal. Her stomach settled.

She headed upstairs contemplating a nice quiet smoke break on the front porch. Such is the inevitably of certain patterns in the narrative of the universe that she poked around the main floor instead. Compared to the sweaty, bass-thumping confines of the cellar, the central living areas stretched cool and dim and tomblike.

"You should've stayed home tonight..." Mr. Hyjak stood in the light of an accent lamp, his arms crossed. Unshaven, pale, and fox-sharp in the eyes, as if he'd recently returned from a tour of the wilds. "We might lose control. Butch has plans for your sweet ass. Be interesting to see who prevails — Speck or Speck's toy."

Lucius strode past him, insolence disguising her surprise and discomfort. She didn't speak; his words neither invited nor required an answer. She wore her leather jacket over a blouse and skirt and fancy hiking shoes. Sensible clothes for partying or fighting. The switchblade lay heavy in her jacket pocket. She'd punched her share of foes; smacked one or two around with a club, and given others a sound kicking. Could she actually stab someone? Mr. Hyjak's dull, covetous expression convinced her, yes, definitely, if her safety depended on it.

Mr. Hyjak said, "Speck says there's two kinds of human female — prey and predator. There's but one kind of man. Smoke that, Lochinvar."

Smiling J bolted out of a doorway at the end of the hall. He moaned a litany that she couldn't quite understand. He grimaced at her and fled up the stairs. A metallic pinging emanated from the room he'd vacated. Lucius recalled a nightmare that went similar to this. Was she in a dream? The sensations of helplessness and inevitability suggested a waking dream, and yet the sights and sounds, the copper fear on her tongue, made a case for awful, violent reality. She went to the doorway and beheld a tableau in the Tooms kitchen.

Butch Tooms leaned over the center island, shirtless and clad in a stocking mask, black linen pants, and combat boots. The stocking squashed his features. She shouldn't have recognized him, except it occurred to her she'd seen him with the mask once before under similar circumstances.

He plunged his fists into a pair of mixing bowls. Crunch, crunch, crunch! The bowls were full of broken glass and sharp bits of metal. A man in a black ball cap and sunglasses rubbed Butch Tooms's shoulders the way a corner man prepares his boxer in the minutes before a fight.

The man in the shades said, "Hi, Lucius Lochinvar. Have you heard the golden tone?"

"You!" she said. A dim nightmare memory bobbed to the surface — Butch Tooms in his stocking mask pursued her through a maze of silent waterslides while Hyjak, Smiling J, and the man in glasses, Mr. Speck, watched through binoculars from atop a building, and laughed. "I got away…How did I get away?" She'd backhanded Butch Tooms with her fancy new watch and chipped the faceplate. He'd accepted the blow the way a telephone pole might be expected to absorb a punch.

"We permitted you to escape. Your future and the future of your progeny represent a matrix of fascinating variables." He whistled softly and the sound sent a chill into her heart. "The signal can be modulated to achieve a variety of effects. Homicidal mania, punctuated equilibrium, and cellular mutation. I am interested to discover how it interacts with human embryos. Half the female subjects present are impregnated. You people are fecund as rabbits. My two-year experiment is expanding into a multigenerational project..."

Butch Tooms raised his arms. Glass, razorblades, and nails studded the gray, wasted flesh and embedded in tendon and bone. "I'm ready. I'm..." He gobbled and gargled as Mr. Speck gently shucked the stocking. Instead of his features relaxing, the opposite occurred. Butch Tooms' mouth wrapped around his cheeks. His eyes elongated and thinned back toward his ears.

Lucius split. She sprinted to the front entrance and flung open the door and nearly took a fateful plunge into a purple-black void shot through with the occasional dying star. "Are you shitting me?"

"The maze is closed until we determine the outcome of this phase." Mr. Speck's voice traveled to her from the length of the abruptly lightless hallway. "Tell us, have you noted any sensory enhancements today? Acute sight or hearing? Increased strength?"

Butch Tooms shambled forth. He'd seized Mr. Hyjak's neck and now dragged the man's body as he came at her, free hand extended and shiny and sharp. She acted on impulse — she took two steps away from the portal and the sucking void and latched onto a granite slab coffee table that rather nicely pulled the room together. She flung it like a discus and the slab decapitated Butch Tooms and shattered against a wall somewhere in the darkness. Butch Tooms keeled over and lay on his side, pumping blood. His limbs twitched.

"I'm gonna go with heightened strength," Lucius said.

"It won't be enough," Mr. Speck said right beside her. He easily caught her right hook and sent her flying across the room with a dismissive flick. "Crawl, girl. Hey, I said crawl!"

She scrambled to her feet and limped for her life.

Meanwhile (The Donald Pleasence Effect):

"There's the Donald Pleasence Effect to consider," Abraham Vile said, wiping a stray tear from the tip of his nose. Melancholy consumed him since his sister Molly disappeared at Tomahawk Park. He'd cornered Esteban (who'd gone in quest of an unoccupied toilet) on the second floor of the Tooms manse and dove into an analysis of his latest film of the century, John Carpenter's *Halloween*. Esteban tried not to panic. He was half in the bag and armed with a semi-full can of Rainier. He sighed and slumped at the foot of Mr. and Mrs. Tooms' king-sized bed and waited for it to end.

Abraham wiped beer foam from his lips. "Gonna do my dissertation on the relationship between Loomis, Laurie Strode, and Michael Myers. I mean, it's a low-budget flick and you can't trust the editing. Still, Carpenter's no fool. The Shape isn't a little boy psycho grown into a hulking adult psycho. No, sir. The Shape is a receptacle of evil. Evil wears Michael like a suit, it manipulates him. Sure, violent injury can temporarily slow The Shape — he, or it, is limited by mortal frailty. Yet, three quarters of the film and Myers mows through sanitarium employees, German Shepherds, teens great and small, and then boom! Jaime Lee Curtis eludes him at every turn and Loomis takes him down with a .38 revolver. Before Myers gets blasted through the window, it's clear he's afraid of the doctor. The doctor is Yang to the babysitter's Ying; masculine maturity and female fertility conjoined. The Shape can't handle it and bails. Takes the bullets and hoofs it when nobody's looking."

"Yeah," Esteban said in a feeble attempt to participate. "I didn't understand how Loomis and his popgun were a threat to Myers. He's a killing-machine."

"The Loomis figure represents the priesthood, the Judeo-Christian alliance against Satan. That gun isn't a gun, it's a crucifix. Satan wilts when the power of Christ compels him."

"Wow, dude. Going to be a bitchin' thesis."

"I know!"

Smiling J entered the master bedroom. His face was blotched and puffy. He groaned and turned on his heel and ran away.

"Jeez, that guy," Abraham said with solemn pity. "Not a film lover, either."

Something crashed downstairs hard enough to shake the bed.

"I better go see who's wrecking the joint." Esteban rejoiced at the opportunity to gracefully make his exit. He descended to the main hall and discovered a chunk of stone tabletop wedged in the wall and the overhead lights sparking and fizzing. In his confusion, he tripped over some jackass sleeping in the middle of the floor and went sprawling. His head rebounded from the tiles and as consciousness ebbed, he could've sworn he was lying in a pool of blood, that blood was oozing into his mouth…

Meanwhile II:

Lucius returned to the basement, seeking the safety of numbers. She tried, at any rate. The narrow stairwell twisted at a strange angle and she stumbled into a chamber made of brass plates and a concrete floor. Double doors slammed shut and sealed her fate.

Mr. Speck waited patiently. "To think, a mere flute solo could induce such dramatic metabolic changes. Were you to live another thirty years, I'm confident you'd exhibit an array of phenomenal adaptive responses. You'd transcend the bonds of your waterlogged skin and become superhuman by any local objective measure. The tiny mass of cells incubating within your womb represents even greater potential. A girl, by the way. That's why, upon due consideration, I've decided to cut to the chase and dig it out of you and take my leave." He flexed his fingers like a pianist limbering up.

To her credit, she didn't dwell upon the unreality of the situation; she didn't assume someone had dosed her with LSD and everything was a hallucination. She didn't bother with who, what, or why. Mr. Speck was insane, or something far worse, or she'd fallen headfirst into a nightmare of the likes Alice never conceived. Lucius simply bared her teeth and girded herself for whatever fresh hell came next.

"I *have* felt strange today. Feels like a high voltage current in my guts." She clenched her right hand. "I'm a mother, you say?"

"Yes, for a moment longer."

"Mothers are dangerous animals, Mr. Speck. Don't underestimate us."

"Dangerous animals are still animals."

"When I kill you will it all be over?"

"We control everything you see and hear. One experiment ends and another begins. So, yes, and no."

She tried to answer, but the electric sensation spread from her middle and blocked her throat. Power filled her lungs. Power clogged her veins. Lucius stared at her fist. Bubbles formed in the metal of her rings. Crimson radiation leaked between her fingers and boiled down her arm. Her reflection warped in the brass double doors — her eyes were violet magma against the silhouette of her skull. Her jacket flapped gently, like a cape. The concrete walls flexed in, then out, with the rhythm of her breath.

The angel on her left shoulder, the teenaged spirit who delighted in cruelty and schadenfreude, murmured that perhaps Mr. Speck's experiment with punctuated equilibrium had surpassed his estimation.

"Now, now, Lucius—" Mr. Speck said.

She laughed and swung.

Somewhere, Sometime VII (The Purgatory of Slasher Victims, 1977):

...Molly Vile dove through the motel doorway and plummeted into a well of darkness. The fall knocked the breath from her lungs. After a flash of sickening pain, her legs went dead. She dragged herself forward, digging her nails into soft earth. The night sky glazed and coagulated until it scraped her shoulders and spine. She crawled through a dirt tunnel lit by the soft purple light. Rivulets of blood glistened between her fingers and trickled over patches of bare rock. Butch Tooms could be gaining. She imagined him at her heels, expressionlessly burrowing with his arms at his sides like an earthworm. The visual elicited a gibbering moan and spurred her onward.

She forced her way through an opening, born again. A steep downslope caught her by surprise and she began to slide across a stone rim scored with ancient grooves that channeled the streams of blood toward a lip and a vertical drop. She wedged her forearms into the groove and arrested her momentum, albeit only for an instant or two. Long enough she took in the Plutonian vault, its upper limits shrouded in pinkish miasma.

The stone rim encircled a colossal pit sloshing full with a lake of blood and gore and partially-submerged bodies. Hundreds of tunnel exits, like the one she'd crawled through, drooled crimson above the pit. Each of the tunnels periodically emitted a battered and bloodied figure. Some alive, some dead; girls and boys alike, each wounded, each fleeing a mortal doom only to land someplace worse. The living corpses came skidding down the sluices and plopped into the frothy stew.

Molly tried to reverse direction and climb toward the mundane awfulness of her own past. She shrieked prayers to her God.

Unfortunately, her God didn't seem to be present and there was no going home.

Epilogue (Anchorage, winter 1979/1980):

Esteban didn't remember the party. He'd gotten crocked and smacked his skull. Lucky to be alive, the docs said.

"We're pregnant," Lucius said with menacing cheer as she snuggled into the hospital bed next to him.

"Oh, sweetheart, that's wonderful!" Esteban's own smile concealed his horror.

Laird Barron spent his early years in Alaska, where he raced the Iditarod three times during the early 1990s and worked in the fishing and construction industries. He is the author of several books, including *The Croning, The Imago Sequence, Occultation, The Light Is the Darkness,* and *The Beautiful Thing That Awaits Us All.* His work has also appeared in many magazines and anthologies. An expatriate Alaskan, Barron currently resides in upstate New York.

Photo taken by: Henry Stampfel

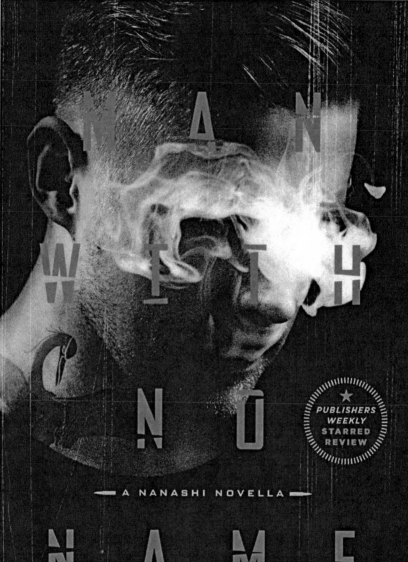

MAN WITH NO NAME

A NANASHI NOVELLA

PUBLISHERS
WEEKLY
STARRED
REVIEW

NAME

LAIRD BARRON

CPSIA information can be obtained
at www.ICGtesting.com
Printed in the USA
FSOW02n0236111016
25874FS